Dancing in the Grass

Book One

Misty River Series

Published by Lori DiAnni 2021

First Edition Published 2021

Cover Art by: Jade Webb—MeetCuteCreative

This book is Dedicated to my Family:

To my husband, Michael, who encouraged every night to sit at the computer and write. Thank you for helping me in so many ways to see my dream come true.
I love you!

To Valerie, who nudged me out of my shell by posting on Facebook that I was writing a book and asked everyone to encourage me to keep going. It worked!
I love you!

And to Jackie, who supported me with her own encouragement and didn't mind losing out on some shopping trips because I had to stay home and finish the story.
I love you!

Ballet Terms:

Arabesque: A pose in which the dancer stands on one leg—either straight or demi-plié, and either flat-footed or en pointe—while extending the other leg straight behind at a right angle. The shoulders are square with the arms held to create a long line from fingertips to toes.

Ballon: "To bounce." A light jump. Used to indicate the delicacy of the movement or jump.

First position: The heels stay together, and the feet turn outward in a straight line.

Fouetté: "Whipped." A whipping movement. It can refer to one foot whipping in front of or behind the other foot, or when the body whips around from one direction to another.

Grand jeté: "Large throw." A high jump in which the legs are extended to 90 degrees. It is preceded by a preliminary movement, like a glissade (a gliding step).

Pirouette: A complete turn of the body on one foot, either turning inward or outward, with the body centered over the supporting leg, the arms propelling the turn but remaining stationary during the turn, and the eyes "spotting" a fixed point while the head quickly turns.

Plié: Bending the knees in either a grand plié (full bending of the knees) or a demi-plié (half bending of the knees), with the legs turned out from the hips and the knees open and over the toes.

Author Note:

I apologize if there are any mistakes in which I portray how a ballet dancer performs. I did a lot of research and believe I got most of it correct. If I misconstrued anything in regard to the world of ballet, I regret the mistake.

One

Bree Thompson leaned against the granite counter, clasping her mug of coffee. She closed her eyes and inhaled it's rich, earthy scent. She took a sip and sighed. It didn't get any better than this, except for a good night's sleep. She headed for the table when her aunt strode in, grinning.

"Good morning, Bree!" Aunt Merry sang out as she headed toward the coffee maker. "It's a beautiful day, isn't it?

"You're much too cheerful in the morning, Aunt Merry." She took a seat and slumped forward, closing her eyes and resting her head on her folded arms.

"Another bad night?"

"Hmm-mm." She couldn't continue like this. She felt like the walking dead.

"Well, I have a remedy for that."

"More coffee?"

"You don't need more coffee, young lady." Aunt Merry came over to the table and sat next to her. "You need to get dressed and go out." Her aunt took a sip from the bright yellow owl-shaped mug. "You've been like this for a week, ever since you came in from California."

"Jet lag."

Her aunt shook her head. "Jet lag, my foot. You've travelled all over the world, and I'm sure jet lag never affected you for a week."

Busted. She had travelled to many major cities in several countries in her decade of dancing first with the Boston Ballet and then the Bay City Ballet Company, and, although she might have had some jet lag, it had only lingered for a day. She knew what it was. She just didn't want to have to deal with it.

"I think it would do you a world of good to get out, visit

some friends or go shopping," Aunt Merry suggested, patting her hand.

She picked up her mug and took a sip. Her aunt meant well, but she wasn't in the mood to see people or even socialize. "I need at least two more cups before I go anywhere."

"Honey, I know what you're going through. I've been there."

"You lost a contract due to an injury?"

"Well, I've lost a contract to another dancer, but I've never been injured. I'm sorry it happened to you."

"I swear Wyatt did it on purpose so his new girlfriend could get the part."

"What makes you say that?"

"Aunt Merry, I've danced with Wyatt more times than I can count. We could anticipate each other's moves, every nuance of every move. We were that good together. And then, during rehearsal, I felt his hand turn the wrong way on my waist and I landed in a painful heap on the floor."

"It doesn't mean he intentionally dropped you." Aunt Merry always gave the benefit of the doubt, regardless.

"Yeah, it does." She set her mug down and turned to face her aunt. "You know what it's like to dance with the same partner, don't you?"

Aunt Merry nodded.

"Well, didn't you trust your partner with every part of your being?"

"I did. And I was never dropped." Aunt Merry sat back. "You could be right, Bree."

"I know I'm right. I'll never forgive him for what he did. Never." Wyatt had betrayed her trust, in more ways than one.

"Are you sure you're one hundred percent back to normal?"

Bree smiled. "Yes, Aunt Merry, I am."

"Well, I'm not so sure. You've been home a week, and I haven't seen you do anything that remotely resembles dancing." Her aunt released her hand. "I'm worried about you. You're not eating. You're not sleeping. You're a shadow of yourself, Bree, and I'm worried."

She glanced down at the table. She hated to admit it, but her aunt was right. If she was fortunate enough to get a call to audition, she wouldn't be ready. She hadn't danced in several months. Actually, the last time she danced had been the day of her injury.

"Maybe you should make an appointment to see. . .someone?"

Exasperated, she smoothed back the fly-aways from her face and blew out a breath. "Aunt Merry. I know you mean well, but I don't want to talk to a psychiatrist, and I don't want meds, either. I just want to dance." She hugged her aunt who had been a mother to her, Brett and Anna since their mother had passed away when she was ten. "Dancing is my therapy."

"You're right. I should know that. Ever since you were a little girl, whenever you were stressed or unhappy, you would dance. And then you were as right as rain. Look, it won't do you any good to sit around this old farmhouse and think about what could have been. I have errands to do. I want you to get dressed and come with me. I'm sure you'll feel better after you get out for a while." She stood and headed to the sink.

"Alright, but I can't promise I'll feel any better.

Within a half hour she was showered and dressed, her long hair pulled back into a ponytail. She decided against the makeup. It was a reminder of her time with Wyatt when he preferred, she wear it every day, even during rehearsals. Since their break-up, she rarely wore it. She headed back down to the kitchen where her aunt was waiting.

"Don't you look like a breath of fresh air." Her aunt beamed. "That color looks great on you."

"Thank you." She glanced down at the robins-egg blue blouse and shrugged. She didn't think she looked like a breath of sunshine, nor did she feel like one, but at least she was dressed which was the most productive thing she'd done in the last few days.

Ten minutes later, they were driving down Main Street of Misty River, Maine, the hometown she had left ten years ago to pursue her dream of ballet and dancing on some of the biggest stages in the world. She had only been back twice before—the marriage of her sister and the birth of her niece. She had only stayed for a couple of nights and then flown back. At that time in her life, dance meant more than family. How foolish she had been.

"Remind me to stop at the bakery before we head home," Aunt Merry said.

"Sure." She hadn't seen Chloe in five years. Her friend was the current owner of Sweet Cheeks Bakery, which was across the street from her aunt's old dance studio. They texted one another as often as they could, and kept in touch through Facebook, but it wasn't the same as seeing someone face to face. And, as they passed the diner, she thought of her closest friend, Jamie, who managed Jamie's Jukebox Diner. She felt awful for neglecting her friends. Once she had left this rinky-dink town, ten years ago, she had pretty much pushed everyone out. What would they think of her now? What would she say when she had to face them?

"First things first, I need to stop at the studio." Her aunt made a right turn and drove into the small parking lot on the side of the old building. A dark blue pickup truck was parked in the lot as well. She cut off the ignition. "I have to check in on the contractor."

"Wait. Contractor? You're rebuilding?" She couldn't believe it. Why hadn't her aunt shared this information with her? She'd been a home a week and not a word had been said about it.

"I'm not rebuilding, Bree. I'm renovating." Aunt Merry looked back at her. "I thought I told you."

"No, you didn't tell me."

"Could be that you've spent the last week sulking and didn't care what was happening in my life, or your father's."

The comment stung. She wanted to defend her actions, but her aunt was right. She had been depressed and in her own world of self-doubt. She hadn't been paying any attention to what was going on around her. Perhaps her aunt and father had discussed it in her presence, but she had ignored it. As her aunt got out of the car, she did the same. She closed the door. "Why are you renovating? Are you selling?"

Aunt Merry shrugged. "I don't know what I'm going to do yet. All I know is that it's old and needs updates. Even if I decide to sell, I can't in its current condition."

"Why not?" She turned and swept her gaze over the one-story building. "You'll still make a profit. Let the new owners renovate."

Aunt Merry walked to her side. She looked at her aunt, who peered at the building with a look akin to sadness. "It's been good to me all these years. It holds a lot of memories. I can't let it go just yet, at least not to strangers." She huffed out a breath. "Come on, let's go inside."

They headed for the side door as her aunt fished out her keys. Once the door was unlocked, they stepped inside where they were greeted with darkness and a lingering odor of paint fumes. They passed the restrooms on their right and changing rooms on the left. Nothing had changed since she was a little girl. They came to the reception area at the end of the hall, and she stopped dead in her tracks.

"Whoa!"

"Oh, it's beautiful!" Aunt Merry grinned from ear to ear. "It came out better than I imagined."

Bree glanced around the reception area. It was no longer the old, dreary room she remembered from her childhood days. The contractor, whoever he might be, had done an extraordinary job renovating the area to accommodate more people and to bring the place up to current standards. Bright sunshine bounced off the newly painted light teal walls creating spots of color on the vibrant carpet in shades of teal, raspberry and white. A couple of small tables separated the black and teal cushioned chairs. If she walked in from the street, she would immediately feel happy here. And that should be the intent of the business. The only things missing were the personal touches. It didn't look or feel like Aunt Merry's studio anymore. "It's gorgeous, Aunt Merry, and so. . .unlike you."

"It is." Her aunt turned in a circle, grinning. "To be honest, it's better than the pictures I showed him."

"Who's the contractor, Aunt Merry?" She moved from the dove gray club chair to the window where two sofas, in a teal and dark gray swirl design, sat in an L shape beneath it.

Her aunt swung her gaze back to her. "Oh, just a local guy. You'll meet him soon enough." Aunt Merry answered, but there was something in her words that made Bree wonder what her aunt had up her sleeve.

"What aren't you telling me, Aunt Merry?"

"Nothing, Bree. By the way, I'd love your opinions on what I want to do in the other rooms. I can't decide between two shades of paint."

"You need me to pick out paint?"

Aunt Merry nodded. "Is that a problem?"

"No." She shook her head, "Of course not."

"Good. Follow me."

They left the reception area and walked down a short hallway. They came to the smaller of the two dance rooms. She stepped inside, behind her aunt, and noticed the mirrors had been taken down and the old flooring had been taken out as well.

"When did the contractor start renovations?" she asked, glancing down at the sub-flooring.

"A couple of weeks ago."

"Are you renovating both rooms?"

Aunt Merry nodded. "The floors need to be replaced with

Marley flooring and the mirrors are old. Might as well gut the rooms and start fresh."

"I'm still wondering why you're putting so much money into this."

"Well, I do have an ulterior motive."

"I bet."

Her aunt sighed, again. "Do you remember when you and Anna used to scramble in here, excited to dance with your friends?"

She remembered all too well how her dream had been born. She had been five years old when she walked into this very room wearing her leotard and ballet slippers and twirled around, pretending she was dancing in front of a huge audience. That pretend dream had become reality. And she had her Aunt Merry to thank.

"And the ballet bug bit you," her aunt said. "Your mother was afraid of that, you know. She saw in you, what she had seen in me. The fever. The determination. The desire to dance."

It had been her aunt's idea to have her start dance lessons. Her mother had been against it. But, once she started, she didn't want to stop, and her mother didn't really have much of a choice after that.

Aunt Merry twisted away. "Since you've been home, I've been thinking. . .about how this studio could be a new adventure for you."

"What?" Had she just heard her aunt correctly? A new adventure? What was she talking about?

"Since you're not working—"

"Yet," Bree interrupted. She couldn't let Aunt Merry talk her into this. Opening the dance studio? What was her aunt thinking?

Aunt Merry's smiled slipped, replaced with a slight frown. "But it'll keep you busy, and it'll make the kids so happy, Bree."

Her aunt had been teaching the kids in town basic ballet

for twenty years. Dancing had been in her blood, too. She had danced with the Boston Ballet for several years before retiring at the ripe old dance age of thirty-five. Bree groaned and gave her aunt a hug. "I know you want me to do this, but I. . . What if I get the opportunity to audition and get accepted at another company? What happens then?" She twisted her ponytail. "Did you ask Anna?"

"I did, and she doesn't want to commit to running a business. She has a young daughter to raise and, well, she said you should do it. In her words, you 'have the talent'." Her aunt made quote marks in the air. "And she's right."

She smiled at the compliment but still wasn't going to waver in her decision. "And when did you and Anna decide I should run the studio?"

"A few days ago."

"Why didn't you ask me then?"

"Because you weren't in the right frame of mind."

"I'm still not!" Bree bit her lip. It wouldn't do to lose her temper.

"So, what do you think?" Aunt Merry asked. Her aunt's gaze held hope.

"I don't think I can make a commitment, Aunt Merry." She was in Misty River for a short time. Once she got accepted for a position, preferably as principal dancer, she'd be leaving the little town quicker than she could pirouette. Dancing was her dream, her life's blood. She couldn't give it up. Her aunt and sister would have to understand.

"It'll be good for you," Aunt Merry said.

She supposed she could think about it.

"Look at this way, it'll keep you busy, physically and mentally. And when the time comes for you to audition, then I'll give my blessing." Aunt Merry caressed the side of her face and she leaned into the warmth of her aunt's palm. "I've always wanted the best for you, Bree. I'm glad you're home and I want you to stay, but if you have the chance to do what you were born to do, then I won't stop you."

"I can't believe I'm even thinking about doing this." They stood in silence for a moment, then she asked, "By the way, Aunt Merry, who's the contractor?"

* * * *

Lucas Tanner sat back against the red leather seat in the vintage 50's-style diner, surrounded by the lively sounds of laughter, chatter, and the clink of silverware against china. Jamie's Jukebox Diner was the epitome of home-cooked meals against a backdrop of an eclectic world of old records, vintage signage, poodle skirts, and jukebox machines.

The sun streamed in through the wide windows creating a glare against the white tabletop with chrome edging. A small replica jukebox sat at the end of the table beneath the window. He knew the machine didn't work. It was there for show only, but a five-foot-tall jukebox sat in the far corner of the diner if patrons wanted to insert some coins and listen to one of the oldies.

"What's the plan for today?" Devon asked as he leaned back and folded his arms across his chest.

He looked at his cousin, co-owner of their business, Tanner Construction. "I think we'll work on the smaller of the two dance rooms. We'll take down the mirrors and prep the walls for paint."

"The crew will be there to help. They finished the kitchen at the Markham Farm yesterday." Devon said, glancing up from his cell phone.

He smiled. "I bet Mrs. Markham is happy to have the kitchen of her dreams now. She's been waiting a long time."

Devon chuckled. "She has this huge kitchen now with only her and her husband. Their kids are grown and moved out."

"All except Grace," he added. "Besides, once grandchildren come along, she'll be happy she has such a large kitchen."

"Here are your eggs, Lucas," the waitress said, setting down his plate. "And the super deluxe breakfast for you, Devon." She tilted her head towards their mugs. "Do you need a refill?"

"Sure." Lucas slid his mug over. Devon did the same.

"How's the house coming along?" Amy inquired, as she tilted the carafe toward the mug.

"Almost done," he answered. "I'll finish it up between jobs. Hopefully by early summer."

Amy nodded and smiled as she poured coffee into Devon's mug. She pulled the carafe closer to her body, cradling it with her left hand. "How's Danica doing? She's so sweet."

"She's doing well. There are days, though, where she gives me a run for my money."

Amy blurted out a quick laugh. "I know how that is. I've got three of my own. I come here to get a break!"

"You have three kids?" Devon looked her up and down. "You look really good, Amy."

Amy swatted Devon playfully on the shoulder. "You're a flirt, Devon, but I'm taken."

"Lucky man," Devon said, then plunged his fork into a pancake.

"There's a woman out there for you, Devon. She just hasn't come along yet." Amy twisted her gaze back to him. "And you too, Lucas. She's out there, waiting for the right guy."

"If you say so." He peered down at his plate, lifting his fork.

"Don't let those eggs get cold. I'll see you around,"

"Thanks."

Amy turned to head to the next table.

"Too bad she's married. I'd ask her out," Devon said, his gaze following Amy as she strode into the kitchen.

"She's not your type."

"Really? And what's my type?"

"Someone who doesn't want a lot of children. Someone who likes to go out and have a good time. Someone—"

"Wait," Devon started. "Who said I didn't want a family?" He pointed his fork at him. "I may seem like the kind of guy who likes to go to the tavern and hang out with my buddies and drink, but that's because, well, at the moment, I don't have a woman in my life to settle down with."

"Huh. Learn something new about a guy every day." Lucas picked up his mug. "Never thought of you as the marrying kind, Dev."

"If I find the right woman, I will be." Devon took a gulp of his coffee then set the mug down. "What about you? Ever think of remarrying?"

Remarry? He shrugged. "Someday, maybe. She'd have to be the right person to help raise Dani. Other women from my past took one look at my daughter and, well, you can guess the rest."

"Too bad. Dani's a sweet kid. Any woman would be lucky to have her as their little girl."

"You're right."

They fell into a companionable silence, eating their breakfast.

"Hey, Devon!" Kris Galloway, a short and slender woman with shoulder length dark hair, bounded over to their table. "I thought it was you sitting here." She looked at him. "Hi, Lucas."

"Hi, Kris." Devon lifted his fork in greeting.

"Hi, Kris," Lucas said, giving a nod.

Kris looked down at Devon. "We're heading to the tavern tonight around seven. You going?"

"Of course," Devon answered. "Lucas, why don't you hang out with us tonight? You haven't been out in a while."

"It'll be good for you," Kris added.

He wasn't sure. He hated to ask his parents to babysit after his mother had stayed with Dani every afternoon after school.

Grace headed to their table. "Hi, Lucas. Devon." She

grinned moving her gaze between the two of them. "Ready, Kris?"

"Catch you later, Devon. Maybe we'll see you tonight, Lucas," Kris waved and stepped away from the table.

"Maybe," he responded.

"Later, Kris," Devon said.

He swallowed the last bite of his eggs followed by a gulp of coffee. He glanced at his watch. "We need to head out. We have a long day ahead of us."

He finished off his coffee then stood, dropping some bills on the table. As they stepped out of the diner, Devon turned to him. "Let's head to the bakery. I'm in the mood for some donuts."

"Do you ever stop eating?"

"Nope."

They walked down the street toward Sweet Cheeks Bakery. A minute later, Lucas opened the door and the bell jingled above their heads, announcing their arrival. The sweet scent of sugar and caramel wafted in the air. He had to admit the bakery had a tantalizing smell along with whimsical decor which would make anyone want to buy a dozen or more confections.

"Hey guys!" Chloe called out from behind the pink and white counter. "The usual, Dev?"

Devon chuckled. "Everything in here is my usual, Chloe."

She laughed as she bent down to grab a box. She stood and opened the pink cover with a glassine window. "What'll it be, Lucas?"

"Nothing for me, Chloe," he answered, as he watched Devon lick his lips while glancing at the assortment of decadent cupcakes on the cake stand and in the display case.

While Devon rattled off what he wanted, he ogled a cupcake, heavily frosted in a swirl of chocolate fudge and mini chocolate bars that oozed richness and calories. His mouth watered just looking at the sweet mound of deliciousness sitting on top of the cake stand. He was tempted.

"I see you eyeing my latest creation, Lucas," Chloe said, winking at him. "As long as Devon doesn't buy it, it's yours."

"Don't even think about it," he said to Devon, nudging his cousin's shoulder. "It's mine."

"Wouldn't think of stealing your chocolate. I'd have to hear you whine about it all day. No thanks. It's yours."

Chloe closed the box and taped it shut. She then reached for the cupcake he had been eyeing and was about to put it in a bag when he stopped her. "No need, Chloe. I may eat it on the way over to the studio."

After Chloe handed him the cupcake, she asked, "How's Dani doing, Lucas? Sophie asks about her all the time."

"She's doing great." He smiled at her. "Tell Sophie we'll try to have a playdate." He heard the jingle of the bell, announcing another customer. "Thanks for the cupcake, Chloe, I'll let you know how good it is." He turned and smacked into silky softness. "What the—!" Something metallic clattered to the floor.

For a moment, he stared at the squashed cupcake in his hand to the dark chocolate frosting smeared on a light blue silk blouse. He lifted his gaze and inhaled sharply. Bree! Bree was back! Her cinnamon-brown eyes widened. Her mouth formed a quick smile, then it disappeared as quickly as it had come. Her face and neck flushed pink.

"Lucas?" She instinctively wiped the chocolate frosting and only managed to smear it further down the length of her blouse.

Flustered, he reached out to wipe the frosting off her blouse at the same time she attempted to do so. She pushed his hand away and a jolt of awareness tingled his fingers. He stepped back, feeling like a total idiot. "I'm sorry, Bree. I didn't see you--"

"Obviously not." She looked down at the blouse, frowning.

"Bree, I believe you remember Lucas Tanner, from high

school?" Merry Thompson quipped. Miss Thompson grinned and didn't appear to be shaken by the fact he had just smashed a cupcake into her niece's blouse.

"I remember Lucas." Her gaze pierced him. "The bad boy, I recall."

His heart thudded. Devon coughed from a few feet away. Bree was back?

Chloe scrambled out from behind the counter. "Bree, I have an extra shirt in the back."

"Thanks, Chloe." She moved past him, shaking her head.

"Well, bro, I'll say you have an unusual way of introducing yourself to a lady," Devon said, his grin splitting his face in two. "Did I mention Bree was back in town?"

He glared at his cousin, then looked at the woman who had hired him to renovate the studio. "I'm sorry, Miss Thompson. It wasn't intentional." He bent down to retrieve Bree's cell phone.

Merry Thompson laughed. "Oh, I know that. If Bree hadn't been texting, maybe she would've been able to dodge you and the menacing cupcake."

He grimaced. "She hasn't changed. Bree's still a whirlwind wherever she goes." He handed the phone to Bree's aunt.

"True."

"When did Bree get back in town?" he asked, glancing around for a trash receptacle and a napkin to wipe off his hands.

"Last week."

A week ago! Hurt stabbed him in the chest. She hadn't even tried to contact him. He was about to ask Miss Thompson another question, when Bree's voice rang out.

"Aunt Merry hired you?"

He snapped his gaze between Bree, who now wore a white tee shirt with the Sweet Cheeks Bakery logo emblazoned on the front, to her aunt. "Yeah, is that a problem?"

"It might be." Bree's look could've turned him to stone. "Let's go, Aunt Merry. I've had my cupcake."

He didn't know what to say, but he certainly knew what he wanted to do. He wanted to rush over to her, crush her against him and kiss her. He hadn't realized how much he had missed her until now, despite the awkward situation.

"Wait for me in the car, then. I still have to get my cupcakes," Merry Thompson said, as Bree shoved open the door, the overhead bell jingling loud. Merry winked at him as she turned away and headed for the counter where Chloe stood, opening a box.

"Well, that was one helluva hello," he said. "I was wondering when I'd bump into her." He watched from the window as Bree marched across the street, obviously angry with him. He was about to turn away and head to the door himself, when Bree turned around. Their eyes met and to his disbelief, she smiled.

Two

Bree stepped out of the shower, thinking about Lucas. Actually, she had been thinking about him the entire afternoon, ever since he had slammed into her, smearing his chocolate cupcake onto her new blouse. She couldn't tamp down the old feelings she once had for Lucas, the guy she had a crush on in high school. The same guy who pretty much ignored her when he was hanging out with her brother, Brett. As much as she wanted to be angry with him, she couldn't. The shock of his hard body slamming against hers stirred her senses into overdrive. Her best defense was to lash out at him, but what she wanted to do was hug him closer. It had been an accident and she had treated him horribly.

As she dressed into a pair of slim black jeans and a red shirt, she couldn't believe how he had grown from a lanky good-looking teen to a handsome broad-shouldered man with a close-cropped beard and mustache to boot. She had to admit he was definitely eye candy.

She wondered what Lucas was doing at this moment. She felt awful she hadn't kept in touch as often as she should have. She tried to keep up with the goings on in town through Facebook and talking to her family, but they had never brought up Lucas's name, and she had never asked. When she had left town to make a name for herself as a dancer, she had decided to leave him behind to. She couldn't focus on her career if her heart was focused on an old crush.

And now, her career could be over. She'd been out of work since December without a single phone call or email. Granted, she had been in physical therapy for eight weeks and hadn't been cleared to go back to dancing. But it was now April, and she had yet to hear from any of the companies she had sent resume's too a month ago, maybe five weeks, once she had been cleared by her physical therapist. She was sure she would've heard from a company by now.

She was a great dancer, or so she thought. She had put in the time, hours of time! She had always showed for practice. Always showed for rehearsals. She never complained about the choreography, although there were times she wanted to. Maybe she wasn't as good anymore. She was still young, but in the ballet world, she was nearing retirement at the ripe old age of twenty-eight. Nine years she had danced professionally, without injury.

The mirror blurred before her eyes, and she swiped at the tears. She wasn't going to give up dancing. Not yet. She had plenty of years left before she had to hang up her pointe shoes. After all, her aunt retired at thirty-five. She inhaled deeply, gave herself one last look then dashed down the stairs.

Her father dozed in his easy chair in front of the TV. She walked over to his chair and kissed the top of his bald head. She hadn't realized how much she had missed her family until recently. But, if she had the opportunity to join another company, she would say her good-byes again, but would make a promise to call and visit more often.

"You going out?" Aunt Merry asked, as she came into the living room carrying her yellow owl mug.

"Yeah. I'm meeting the girls at the tavern." She walked over to her aunt and kissed her cheek. "I won't be late."

"Have fun!"

"I'll try."

Fifteen minutes later, Bree entered The Riverside Tavern, keeping an eye out for of her friends. The plan was that whoever got there first would save a table. The tavern was filled to capacity. She didn't remember it ever being this busy before. The last time she had been in here, about five years ago when Heather was born, the tavern hadn't been this big or this crowded. Obviously, business was thriving.

"Over here, Bree," she heard someone shout. She turned

and saw Jamie waving frantically. As she moved toward the table, the girls stood and rushed to her, each one vying for a hug.

"I've missed you so much!" Jamie said, as she squeezed her in a bear hug. "Don't ever leave again!" She flinched on that comment.

"Ditto." Grace hugged her. "We've missed you."

Chloe flung her arms around her, although she had seen Chloe earlier in the day, if only briefly, and had received an overwhelming hug from her. Kris was the last one to embrace her. She sat and glanced at the faces around her. All of them classmates since grade school. They had tried to keep in touch through the years, but as with anyone who grows to adulthood, life takes over and sometimes friendships get put on the back burner.

"I can't believe this," she huffed out. "What happened to this place in five years?"

"Tom decided to expand and add another bar, a bigger dining room and banquet area. He also has a game room. People love this place! They come from the outlying towns too."

She nodded and glanced around. "Is it always this busy?"

Chloe shook her head. "Only the locals come in during the winter. It'll get even busier once the tourists get here."

She couldn't imagine it. The din of the place increased as more people came in.

"In the summer," Jamie started, "the line goes to the end of the parking lot. There can be a one hour wait, sometimes longer."

"Wow."

"It's busy tonight because of the band. They're fantastic. Everyone from all around comes to hear them play," Grace added, picking up her beer.

"Who are they?" She asked, turning her gaze around the room to see if she could flag down a waitress.

"The Blue Horse Country Boys."

She laughed. "What kind of a name is that? And they're good?"

Grace beamed. "They're great!"

"If you say so." She shrugged, lifting her arm to get the waitress's attention. The young woman came over, smiling.

"Can I get you anything?"

"A wine spritzer."

"Anything else for you ladies?"

"No, we're all set," Jamie said.

"Be back in a jiff."

"So, Bree, this must be so different than the city life." Jamie lifted her beer and took a swig.

"Yeah. It's definitely. . .different." She peered around the room. Every resident of Misty River had to be here, plus some. Yet, the tavern was small and rustic compared to the places she frequented in the city. It was like night and day.

"You must be bored," Grace added. "I don't mean that in a bad way."

She tilted her head. "I wouldn't say bored. I'm in limbo, I guess." And depressed. And lonely. "But I'm pretty sure I'll get a call soon, asking me to come back to the Bay City Company."

Everyone's gaze snapped to her.

"You're not staying?" Grace sounded shocked.

"I came back to Misty River temporarily. I thought everyone knew."

They shook their heads.

"We thought you were back for good," Kris spoke up. "We figured since you posted your injury on Facebook, you were here to stay."

She sighed. "I didn't have anywhere else to go after my ACL injury. And, well, I don't have a job because my contract was up. Great timing, right?"

"Why didn't you stay to renew your contract?" Grace asked, lifting her glass of wine.

Ahhh, how was she going to answer that question. Tell

them her boyfriend cheated on her? Tell them, she wasn't good enough and her prima role went to his girlfriend? She swiped her fingers through her hair, closing her eyes.

"You don't need to tell us, Bree." Jamie said, twirling her bottle of beer. "If it's too difficult, just say so."

She glanced at her closest friend. "Thanks, Jamie. It's okay. Really." She sighed. "Because my injury happened so close to my renewal date, the company decided not to renew. They gave my position as principal dancer to another."

"What?!"

"Yeah." She shrugged, pulling a thick strand of hair behind her ear. "Wyatt never came to the hospital the entire time I was in there." She leaned on her elbow. "And he never visited me at home while I was recuperating."

"Oh, Bree, we're so sorry," Kris reached over and clasped her hand. "He's a jerk and doesn't deserve you."

"Here, here," Jamie and Grace added, lifting their drinks. Another sigh spilled from her mouth. Her throat tightened as tears filled her eyes. "He had the audacity to give my prima role to his. . ."

"New girlfriend." Grace finished for her. "Why didn't you tell us this before? We could've supported you through it all."

The waitress came to their table and set down a napkin in front of her then placed the chilled wine glass on it. She walked away, heading to another table.

She inhaled and squeezed her eyes shut, hoping it would stop the tears from falling. She took a sip of wine to soothe the burn in her throat. "Because, it was my problem, and I didn't want to bother you with the details of my sad love-life, or lack of."

"Seriously, Bree?" Kris looked at the other girls. "We're here for you."

She wanted to cry. She never expected them to support her or even want to continue the friendship, but here they were, supporting her.

"I always thought he was a jerk." Jamie took a swig of her

beer. “No offense, Bree.”

“None taken.” She swept her hair back. "Two years I gave him. Two years down the drain." How had her life ended up like this? She was back in her hometown, surrounded by friends, but it still didn’t feel like home. She didn’t belong here anymore than her friends belonged in San Francisco.

“I talked to your aunt earlier today,” Kris spoke up.

"You did? About what?” she asked.

“I saw her at the market, and we started talking about you being home and. . .”

“And?” She took a sip of her wine. There was something in Kris’s gaze.

“She brought up how the studio is getting a makeover. . ."

"Ahhh," she said with a nod. "She told you she wants me to open the studio, right?"

Kris picked up her glass. "She's hoping you will.”

“Oh, that’d be great!” Grace squealed a little bit louder than she intended. She slapped a hand over her mouth, grinning.

“I think so too.” Jamie said.

“I agree.” Kris said as well.

“So, are you?” This came from Grace.

She didn’t know how to answer. She hadn’t decided yet. She was still waiting for a call. And yet, she had to realize the chances of getting her job back were slim to none. The Bay City Ballet Company wasn't going to call her back. And why would she want to go back only to see Wyatt and Pam together every day? Was she foolish? Besides, too much time had gone by. “I. . .I’m not sure.”

“I bet the studio will get a ton of applicants if you reopen it, Bree.”

“I know you mean well, but I’m not staying.” She leaned forward and tucked a strand of hair behind her ear. “I’ve sent out several resume's and I'm waiting to hear back, soon."

Her friends stared; their faces frozen in shock.

“I’m sorry." She grabbed her wine glass and took a healthy

gulp. “What happens if I open the studio, start teaching classes, and I get a call to audition? What do I do then?"

"Deal with it when the time comes, but for now, why don't you take the chance, Bree. You don’t have a job now.” Kris looked at her, her gaze begging for an answer.

“Just what Aunt Merry said.” Another sigh. She’d been doing a lot of that lately. She didn’t have any place to go right now. Her life was stagnant, boring, dull. She missed dancing. Missed the camaraderie with her cast mates. She even missed the criticism from Wyatt. But, she couldn't hide in her bedroom. Her friends had been kind enough to invite her out. They wanted to spend time with her. Maybe she needed to get to know Misty River again. Maybe she should take the chance.

“You know what?” she started, not expecting to get any sort of an answer. “I’m going to do it. I’m going to reopen the studio.”

“Seriously?” Chloe said then beamed.

The other girls grinned as well.

"Best news I've heard in a long time," Jamie said, lifting her beer. "Let's make a toast." They lifted their drinks. "To new beginnings and old friendships."

"Here, here." They clinked their glasses and laughed.

"We have some celebrating to do!" Grace added.

She laughed. She suddenly felt a sense of relief and purpose.

* * * *

Lucas sat back in the chair, rubbing his belly. “That was delicious, Mom.”

“Thanks, Lucas.” His mother stood, picking up her plate and reaching over to grab his. “What time are you heading out?”

He ruffled Danica’s curly dark hair. She smiled up at him with adoring eyes. “I thought I’d get Danica ready for bed first and head out afterwards.”

His mother picked up Danica's plate and set the utensils on top. "Why don't you help Grandma in the kitchen, Dani."

His daughter scrambled off the chair, her right arm angled and unmoving. He thought he'd be used to the sight by now, but there were times it hurt to see his daughter, so full of energy and laughter, have to struggle with the simplest of movements most people did without thinking. His little girl followed his mother into the kitchen.

"What are your plans for tonight, son. You don't normally go out."

Leaning forward, he reached for his glass of water. "Thought I'd head out to the tavern. I haven't seen the guys in a while and, since Mom offered to babysit, I thought it'd be an opportunity to do something other than looking over blueprints."

His father nodded. "It'll be good for you. A guy needs to get out once in a while and be, well, a guy." He chuckled and lifted his cup of coffee.

"You got that right, Dad." He took a sip of his water. "You don't mind babysitting?"

His father's thick brows furrowed. "What? Of course not! She's our granddaughter. Your mother's thrilled. She loves every minute she gets to spend with Dani.""

"Well, I appreciate it. It isn't easy sometimes." Guilt infused him. He loved Dani more than life, but there were times he felt it was his fault.

"I know. But Dani's disability isn't your fault, son. She doesn't let it hinder her. Why should you?"

His father made a good point. He was too over-protective of Dani but, he couldn't help it. She was the world to him, and if anything happened to her, he would never forgive himself.

"Go out, have fun and don't worry."

"Alright then." He moved away from the table and headed to the kitchen while his father walked off toward the living room. He knew how much his father loved the Red Sox and didn't want to miss a game.

As he walked into the kitchen, he brightened. Danica stood on a stool, next to his mother, helping her wash dishes. Dani held the dish against her with her bad hand and used her left hand to scrub the plate. A few soap suds splashed from the sponge onto her face, and she giggled. He laughed. Dani turned and gave him a grin.

"Daddy!" The plate dropped into the water, splashing up more suds.

"Hey, Pumpkin? You having fun?" He grabbed a towel then wiped the suds from her face.

"Yup. Gramma showed me how to wash dishes."

Leave it to his mother to look beyond Dani's disability and show her how to wash dishes. "And you're doing a great job!" He helped her down from the stool. "Let's get you ready for bed."

"Okay. Can I stay up late, Daddy?"

"Well—"

"It'll be fine, Lucas," his mother said, twisting around and wiping her hands with the dishtowel. "We'll watch a movie, have some popcorn and watch Grandpa snore in his favorite chair."

Danica giggled then made a snoring sound while closing her eyes and tilting her head. "Grandpa sounds funny when he snores."

"He sure does," he stated. "Thanks, Mom." He put a hand to Dani's shoulder. "C'mon Pumpkin, let's get your pj's on and grab your favorite blanket."

"Why don't you take a shower and head on out. I can help Dani get changed."

"You sure, Mom?"

"Of course! Go out and have some fun. You deserve it."

"You don't have to tell me twice." Smiling, he left the kitchen. He ran up the stairs and into the bathroom.

While showering, he wondered if he'd see Bree. He knew Jamie and her friends would be there, but he didn't know if

Bree would show up. What would he say when he saw her? Better yet, what would she do when she saw him? She had left the bakery in a huff after finding out he was the contractor her aunt hired. And, it didn't help he had ruined a beautiful blouse. He definitely had to apologize. He didn't know if she'd accept it, though.

He stepped out of the shower, wrapped a towel around his waist and reached for the shaving cream. He lathered his face then started shaving. Whatever you do, don't cut yourself. That's all you need. He took his time and several minutes later, he had a smooth face and no cuts. He combed his hair then headed to his old bedroom.

The room still looked as it had when he moved out seven years ago. He never thought he'd be back, sleeping in the old twin bed. Dani had the guest room across the hall. It would only be for a few more months then they'd move into the cabin. He pulled open the drawer of his childhood dresser and grabbed a pair of jeans and a tee shirt. He dressed quickly then headed back downstairs.

He heard Danica's giggle when he stopped at the bottom, his hand on the newel post. He watched the interaction between his daughter and father. Dani was in her favorite princess pajamas and sat in the crook of his father's arm, her head leaning against his shoulder, as he read her a story.

"The end," his father said as he closed the book and hugged Dani.

"Read it again, Grampa."

He headed toward the sofa. "I think it's time to watch the movie." He tickled her tummy and laughed when she squirmed and blurted out a belly laugh. Not wanting her to possibly hurt his father, he lifted his daughter up and swung her around like an airplane. "Whoosh!"

"I'm flying, Daddy," she squealed, throwing her arms out. Her right arm couldn't straighten out and resembled what he could only describe as a chicken wing. He dipped her low then up high and the more she laughed, the more he laughed.

Maybe he'd stay home and play with his little girl.

"Okay, kids," his mother said when she walked in carrying a big bowl of popcorn. "It's time to watch Dani's favorite movie." She set the bowl on the coffee table. "Frozen. We've watched it so many times, I think I have every line memorized."

"I bet," he said, hugging Dani close.

"Let it go. Let it goooo," Danica sang as he set her down on the couch next to his mother. "When I grow up, Daddy, I'm gonna be a singer and a dancer."

"I know you will, Pumpkin." He gave her a kiss on the cheek then smoothed his hand down the side of her face. "Be good for Gramma and Grandpa. Love you."

"Love you, Daddy. You be good, too."

His heart stopped. She was so innocent of life's trials. She didn't have a clue as to how the world could treat those who didn't appear 'normal'. He never wanted to shatter his daughter's dreams, but he needed to be realistic. Dani would never dance.

Three

Lucas opened the door of the tavern where raucous laughter and rowdiness followed him as friends shook his hand or clapped his back.

"Usual?" the bartender asked as Lucas moved toward the bar.

"Yeah." He glanced around the room but didn't see Bree. Maybe she hadn't come. His heart tumbled. C'mon, man. You're acting like a love-sick teen.

"Here ya' go, Lucas."

"Thanks." He paid the bartender then grabbed his beer, opened it and took a swig. He leaned on the bar counter, looking sideways toward the dance floor. The band, with the crazy name of 'Blue Horse Country Boys', got on stage to the explosive applause of the patrons.

"How ya' all doin' out there tonight?" the lead singer bellowed into his mic. "We've got a great show for you, so come out to the dance floor with your gal or beau and enjoy the music."

Several people swarmed to the dance floor, making it nearly impossible to move around, but where there was a will, there was a way.

"I love this band!" a petite young woman yelled, leaning into him. "Wanna dance?"

He shook his head. "I prefer to listen."

"Suit yourself," and she strode off to another guy just a few feet away.

He frowned. The woman was half-way to being drunk and he didn't need anyone making the moves on him. He stood there, watching, and listening until someone yelled out his name. Turning, he grinned. "Hey, Blake!"

"Hey, man!" Blake gave him a one-arm hug and a slap on the back. "How's it goin?"

"Not too bad." He took a swallow of his beer. Blake did the same. "How's business?"

"Great! Can't complain. More business coming in from out of town by word of mouth."

"That's great."

'How 'bout you? Keeping busy?" Blake lifted a hand for the bartender's attention.

He nodded. "Business is picking up, little by little. I'm working on my cabin and making plans for a glamping resort on my off-time."

Blake laughed, his blue eyes crinkling. "What the hell is glamping anyway?"

Lucas twisted around and leaned back, propping his elbows on the counter. His beer dangled from his right hand. "Glamping is short for 'glamourous camping'."

"Ahh, a girl thing."

Laughing, he shook his head. "It sounds like it, but it's a more comfortable way of camping with the amenities of being in a tent with the luxuries of being at a hotel or at home."

"Sounds weird to me. Like I said, a girl thing." Blake took a long swallow. "I mean, if you have to go somewhere that's as comfortable as your house, why leave your house?"

"Good point. But it really is a growing market. And I plan on getting in on it."

Blake shrugged. "If you say so. When will it be open for business?"

"Late summer, early Fall, if everything goes as planned."

"I wish you luck, buddy." Blake lifted his beer and gave a toast in the air.

He straightened and scanned the room. He still didn't see Bree.

"Looking for someone?" Blake asked, following his gaze.

The question took him by surprise. Did he have to make it that obvious? "No. Not really."

Blake turned back to face him. "Sure. If you say so."

He tapped his foot to the beat of the music and took another swallow of his beer. While Blake watched the band, he took a moment to scan the room without his friend questioning him. Then he saw her. She walked down the hall from the ladies room. She angled herself through a crowd as she attempted to get to her table. He watched as she sat with four other women. He recognized the others--Jamie, Kris, Grace and Chloe. He couldn't help but stare. Bree looked gorgeous in her bright red blouse and her black slender jeans which fit her dancer body to perfection. Her dark hair glistened like onyx in the dim lights. He started toward her table but was stopped by Blake.

"Hey, c'mon over and play a game of pool with the guys."

"Ah. No. Thanks anyway."

"Suit yourself." Blake walked in the opposite direction as he strode toward Bree's table.

As he neared, he heard them laughing. He stopped, wondering if he was doing the right thing. She had come here to spend time with her friends. He needed to apologize whether or not she ever spoke to him again.

Bree turned and looked at him. His heart nearly jumped out of his chest. Turn around. Pretend you didn't see her. He expelled a breath and hoped she wouldn't turn away and ignore him. Her brow furrowed as he stepped closer. She grinned. She was even more beautiful when she smiled. His heart thundered, drowning out the band, and suddenly, he felt like an awkward teen all over again. His breath caught as Bree stood. She walked closer until she was standing in front of him.

"Hi."

"Hi." He gripped the beer bottle. God, had she always been this beautiful? What had happened to the skinny nerdy girl he once knew? She looked stunning. Her eyes, the color of cinnamon, he thought, seemed darker, perhaps due to the lighting or the smoky makeup. He cleared his throat. "I want to—" Did his voice just crack? C'mon, man. You're not fifteen years old! "I—"

"Look, Lucas, I—"

"Me first, please." he said.

"Alright."

"I want to apologize for this morning. I wasn't looking and—"

"It was as much my fault as yours," she interrupted. "I was texting, didn't see you and well, we both know what happened next. I owe you a cupcake."

He chuckled. "And I owe you a new blouse."

She shooed his comment away. "No need."

"Really, I want to." He didn't know what to say next. He had done what he came to do. He noticed the band had switched to a slow song. "Hey, ah, would you like to dance?"

She tilted her head, reminding him of how she looked at the age of sixteen when he first met her. He had gone over to her house to pick up her brother. Bree had been standing in the kitchen, her head tilted the same way, her hands folded in front and staring at him with a dreamy smile. This time, though, she smiled broadly. A good sign.

"Sure. Why not?"

"Why not," he echoed. She turned and headed for the dance floor. Jamie winked at them as they walked past. He smiled down at Jamie. He could feel the eyes of her friends watching him closely. Bree turned to face him, and he stepped closer, putting a hand to her waist as she set her hand on his shoulder. She stood about three inches shorter than his six-foot, two-inch frame in her heels. He reached for her hand. She expelled a tiny gasp and a jolt of awareness shot down his spine. He settled his hand to her lower back, and she took another step closer to him. He smiled. She was warming up to him. Good. She didn't hate him.

"This is a first," he said, as they moved across the dance

floor. Never did he think he'd be dancing with Bree in his arms. He could admit it now, but not when he was a teen. He had always liked Bree. Hell, he'd been lovesick. He had always thought she was the prettiest girl in school, but he never asked her out. He had promised her brother, Brett—his best friend, that he wouldn't touch his sister. Of course, her father was the one who convinced him. He grinned. What would Brett, and her father, think now, knowing he was dancing with Bree?

"What are you smiling about?" Bree asked, looking at him with her bright, dark brown eyes.

"Memories."

"Of what?"

"You'll laugh."

"Maybe." She giggled. "You don't need to tell me."

He shrugged. "Maybe I'll share some other time."

"That'd be nice," she responded. "Wait. Are we going to see each other again?"

"Probably."

She grinned again and his heart soared. She pressed her hand against his shoulder. "I'd like that."

Now he was the one grinning as he turned, pulling her with him. "How's the ballet dancing going?"

Bree's grin faded. "It's. . .going."

"Are you in Misty River long?"

She shrugged. "Maybe."

"If you don't mind me asking, what brought you back to town?" He remembered how Bree couldn't wait to leave their little town ten years ago and pursue her dreams of dancing on the stage.

She glanced toward the wall, then back to him. He felt her hand tighten on his shoulder. "I don't think you really want to know."

"Of course I do, but only if you want to tell me. I don't want to pry."

She tilted her head back. "You're different Lucas. You've

changed."

He swung her in a circle and brought her up close to his body. She gasped. "Oh? How so?"

"I don't know. You're just different than what I remember."

"A person can change a lot in ten years, Bree."

"I suppose." Her hand slid down his back. He wanted to pull her closer, but he kept himself in check. Both of them looked at each other, neither one speaking. What amazed him most was how well they danced together. They had never danced, never held each other and yet, it seemed perfect as though it was meant to be. The song ended. She stepped back and he reluctantly let her go.

"Thanks for the dance," she said, then turned with a smile.

"You're welcome," he answered, as he stood alone, in the middle of the dance floor. He was soon swallowed up by the crowd moving around him.

The band started up another song, this one a line dance as a crowd of people lined up in rows on the dance floor. He scooted away and headed for the pool tables. The room exploded with the sound of boot stomping and hand clapping.

Blake, along with a couple of other guys, played a game of 8-ball.

"Great timing, Lucas," Blake said, as he leaned over and struck the ball with the cue stick. "We're one man down. Wanna play?"

"Sure. Why not." He grabbed a cue stick and leaned against the wall. A pretty waitress came by and winked at him then asked him if he wanted anything. He ordered another beer, not knowing where his other one ended up. Ah, on Bree's table. He could go back and get it, but he had a feeling he should wait. Give Bree a moment with her friends.

"You're up," Blake said, coming over to stand beside him.

He positioned himself at the table then aimed the cue stick to the bottom of the cue ball. He gave it a gentle nudge, just enough to move the ball forward to knock the nine ball in the corner pocket. He moved to the other side and thought he'd try a more difficult shot. They weren't playing for money, so it didn't matter. But it would be nice to see if he could manage the difficult shot. As he took aim, he saw a flash of red from the corner of his eye. He turned his gaze sideways and saw that it was Bree. She moved to the dance floor. The cue stick twisted in his hand, sending the cue ball straight toward his intended target but, the angle in which it hit the ball, turned it to knock the opponent's ball into the side pocket. Lucas groaned and slumped forward.

"Oh man!" Blake said.

He stood and reached for his beer. He took a swallow then set his beer down while watching Bree. Moving away from the pool table, he peered at the dancers. Bree sashayed, foot-stomped and clapped her hands. She turned in a circle, laughing. Her laughter touched his heart. He continued to watch as she moved fluidly with the other line dancers. It was as if she had always done this. He set the cue stick down and moved toward the dance floor.

"Hey, Tanner!"

He twisted around to face Blake.

"Where you going? Thought we were playing a game?"

"You do. I have other plans." And he walked to the dance floor, squeezing in next to Bree He fell into step without missing a beat.

She looked surprised, then she smiled. This beat playing pool, by a long shot.

* * * *

Bree felt more positive and energized than she had in a long time. Last night had been more fun than she could've imagined. Who knew listening and dancing to The Blue Horse Country Boys would be so much fun? She scrambled out of bed. It was going to be a great day!

She slipped on a robe then headed for the bathroom.

Afterwards, she went downstairs. The smell of fresh coffee brewing, mingled with bacon, made her stomach growl. As she passed by the living room, she saw her father sitting on the couch watching an old John Wayne movie. Buster was laying on the couch beside him, snoozing.

"Morning Dad," she said, giving him a smile and quick wave.

"Mornin', Honey," he answered, his gaze never leaving the television.

He hadn't changed a bit. She walked into the kitchen where Aunt Merry stood at the stove cooking bacon. "It smells good in here. I hope you made extra coffee and bacon for me."

"Of course I did. Plenty of eggs too. I go all out on Sundays. Been doing it for years now. I never know if Anna and Heather will stop in." Aunt Merry stirred the scrambled eggs.

She glanced at the wall clock. Eight o'clock. "Are you going to church?" She took down a mug and turned to the coffeemaker. She poured the coffee into the mug then added a small amount sugar and a dash of creamer.

"Yeah." Aunt Merry spooned fluffy scrambled eggs onto three plates. "I'll leave around nine-thirty for the ten o'clock service. She placed bacon on each plate. "Why don't you go with me? Anna and Heather are going."

"I might." She had always gone to church throughout her childhood but, when she started with the company, her days of going to church were minimal. Not that she didn't like to go, but she usually had rehearsals, or she was exhausted from the shows they had performed during the week. She usually kept Sundays for sleeping in late and relaxing. And, oftentimes, Wyatt discouraged her from going. He didn't seem to understand the reason for attending church.

"Come to the table, Dad. Breakfast is ready," she called out, bringing a full plate to the big oak table and setting it down in front of his usual chair.

He ambled in, groaned, then sat. Buster walked in behind him, whining, most likely because he smelled the bacon. The kitchen door opened, and Heather came in, twirling around.

"Hi, Grampa!" She kissed her grandfather on the cheek. "Guess what?"

"What?" her father said, looking at Heather.

"I'm gonna be a princess who loves to dance, just like Aunt Bree."

Anna strolled in. "She's been dancing all morning. She can't wait to start classes and be a famous ballerina someday."

Her father glanced from Heather to her and frowned. What was that about?

"You know, Heather, when I went on stage, I always felt like a princess. I hope your dream comes true."

"I hope she does something that doesn't keep her away from her family for months, or years, at a time," her father grumbled, stabbing his scrambled eggs with the fork. Obviously, he was upset.

"Dad, I. . .I'm sorry I didn't visit more often."

Anna took the plates Aunt Merry offered and set them down. "Dad, Bree hasn't done anything wrong. It's in her blood, just like it was with Aunt Merry."

"And he scolded me many times too." Aunt Merry said, as she sat across from her with her own plate of food.

"I know I should've visited more often, and called too," She huffed out a breath. "I —"

"She's home now, Dad," Anna spoke up. "Let's enjoy the time she's here."

She smiled at Anna. Her sister always had her back. The room was quiet except for the sounds of the silverware against their plates and the thumping of Heather's foot against the chair leg.

"So, how was last night, Bree?" Anna asked, helping Heather with her eggs. "Have a good time?"

She swallowed her mouthful of food and picked up her mug. "Yeah, I did." She sipped her coffee. "I hadn't expected to have so much fun, but it was a really good time."

"I bet." Anna smirked. "What band was playing?"

She laughed, setting her mug down. "The Blue Horse Country Boys."

"They're a great band," Aunt Merry piped in.

"You've heard of them?" she and Anna said at the same time. Their father glanced between them and shook his head. She couldn't believe her aunt would know a country band.

"I go out once in a while," Aunt Merry answered.

She and Anna laughed, and she noticed her father smirking, although he pretended he wasn't listening.

"But, Blue Horse? It's a silly name," she added.

"I know, but, funny name aside, they play some great songs," Anna said.

"True." She scooped up a mouthful of eggs. "They certainly know how to draw in a crowd. I never thought line-dancing was so popular."

"It is around here. Did you dance?" Aunt Merry asked.

She grinned, thinking of Lucas. She hadn't expected him to be there and hadn't expected him to ask her to dance. But she was glad she had accepted. She felt heat rise along her neck and creep into her face.

"You're blushing, Bree." Anna stated. "You met someone and danced with him, didn't you? Did you kiss him?"

"Aunt Bree kissed a man?" Heather interrupted, laughing.

"Tell me you didn't kiss a man you met at a bar," her father said. "Why would you kiss a man you had just met?"

"Dad, I didn't kiss anyone."

"Did you dance with him?" Anna asked, taking a bite of her bacon.

Heat rose further up her neck. Heck, her whole body warmed just thinking about her dance with Lucas.

"So, who is this guy?" Aunt Merry asked, darting her gaze between her and Anna.

"Who did you kiss, Aunt Bree?" Heather piped in.

She laughed. "I didn't kiss anyone, munchkin." She

glanced at her sister. "But I did dance with him."

"Who?"

"Lucas. Tanner."

Anna nearly spit out her coffee. Her father jerked up. Aunt Merry beamed and set a hand on her father's arm.

"Lucas Tanner?" He shot her a glance, his brows furrowed. Now he'd ask a million questions. Perhaps that's why her aunt had her hand settled on his arm. To calm him. Or warn him. "Is this the guy you liked back in high school?"

"You knew I liked him?" She couldn't believe her father had noticed. She stuffed a mouthful of eggs in her mouth. Maybe if she continued eating, she wouldn't have to answer any more questions. She knew her father. He'd want answers. She shouldn't have said anything.

"It was pretty obvious with his name scribbled all over your notebooks," her father said. "It was hard not to notice."

"Well, from what I observed," Anna started, "Back in the day, he didn't like you. He always ignored you."

She lowered her gaze to her plate, staring at the bacon. Anna was right. Lucas had ignored her throughout high school. She had had such a crush on him, but he only saw her as his best friend's sister—the nerdy, toothy girl who only liked to dance. Oh, she had heard the remarks. Some of them were hurtful.

"I didn't like that boy," her father said. "But—,"

"He wasn't trouble," Aunt Merry scoffed. "Henry, she's a grown woman. She can date whoever she wants without your permission." She patted his arm. "Besides, I'm pretty sure she'll be seeing more of him."

She watched the exchange between her father and aunt. She was waiting for her father to question her.

"Out with it, Merry."

"I hired him. He's my contractor, renovating the studio."

"You hired Lucas Tanner?"

"I did. He's a fine man and a great contractor." She lifted her fork and wagged it at him. "You don't get to tell me who

I can hire for my business."

"I wouldn't think of it. I happen to agree with you, Merry. He's a nice guy. I like him."

"You do?" She and Anna said at the same time. She couldn't believe it. She had always thought her father despised Lucas.

"I do."

"Wow." She shook her head. Ten years away from home did change things. Then she realized what her Aunt Merry had said a moment ago. "By the way, I'm not dating Lucas. We only danced."

"Was it a slow dance?" Anna asked. She grinned.

"Yes, it was." She heaved a sigh. "And it was. . .nice. He was a gentleman."

"I'm sure he was. Lucas isn't the 'bad boy' he portrayed when he was hanging out with our brother," Anna quipped. "And you only danced once with him?"

She thought back to the line dance when he had scooted in next to her after playing a game of pool. His friends hadn't looked too happy he was leaving them, but she had been thrilled when he joined her. She had been even more amazed that he had known the steps to the dance. She hadn't imagined him being the kind of guy who danced, let alone line danced. He had surprised her. After that, they had danced again before she called it a night. By the time ten o'clock rolled around, she was exhausted. Her normal bedtime was nine o'clock on most nights due to having to wake up so early in the morning to get to the studio by eight.

"Earth to Bree," Anna sang out.

"Oh. Yeah." She looked around the table. "We danced a couple of times before I left. He's a great dancer."

Aunt Merry laughed. "I knew you two would hit it off."

Anna winked, giving her one of her trademark smirks. Aunt Merry grinned and gave her a thumbs up. Her father shook his head. "Bree, you better watch out. They're a matchmaking duo."

Anna and Aunt Merry tossed conspiratorial glances her way. She ignored it. "The girls and I were talking about the studio."

"Oh-oh." Aunt Merry set her mug down.

Anna just stared at her. "And you told them you weren't staying. You were going back to San Francisco, right?"

She sat back and smiled and, to keep Anna and her aunt curious, she deliberately took her time and picked up her mug, sipping her coffee.

"And?"

"And. . .I've decided, after much thought and consideration, I'm going to—" she took another sip of her coffee.

"C'mon Bree. Out with it," Anna coaxed.

"I'm going to take over the studio."

Aunt Merry's mouth opened. Her eyes widened. Then she smiled which broadened to a grin in a half-second. "Oh, Bree!" Her aunt stood quickly, the chair scraping across the floor. The next thing she knew, she was enveloped in a hug from her aunt and sister that nearly took her breath away.

"This is great news! What made you decide?" Anna asked, sitting back down.

"I need something to do. I don't have a company to go back to right now, so I decided to open the studio."

"This is so exciting!" Aunt Merry squealed, as though she had won the lottery. She sat back down. "I think you made the right decision, Bree. Seriously."

"I do, too." It was a good decision. She had to believe that.

Four

"C'mon, slowpoke," Lucas called out to Dani who ran behind him. He walked past the gazebo and found a grassy spot overlooking the river. It was another beautiful, sunny day with temps in the seventies. It was warmer than usual for early spring in April, but he wouldn't complain. Several other families and couples took advantage of the beautiful weather and set up blankets and chairs as well. Some kids fished off the small pier while a few people paddled their kayaks, enjoying the scenery of the river and the marshlands.

"Daddy, I'm hungry." Dani plunked herself down in the middle of the blanket. "Can I have my sandwich now?"

Lucas moved the picnic basket over and settled it next to him as he sat next to his daughter. It was still too early for the trees to have leaves so the sun shone brightly, spilling a puddle of warmth over them. "Okay, let's see what Gramma made for us."

"She made peanut butter and jelly for me, Daddy."

"And how do you know that?" he teased.

"Because I helped her make it!" Danica giggled, tilting her head back as though it was the funniest thing she had ever said. "And I made you one, too!"

"You did? Well, I can't wait to eat it!" Lucas leaned forward and kissed her on the nose. He pulled the sandwiches out of the basket along with a carton of juice for Dani and bottled water for him. He unwrapped the sandwich and set a paper plate in front of her with the sandwich cut in four pieces. Dani loved her sandwiches cut in squares probably because her mother had cut them that way since she was a toddler. Once she picked up a piece, he unwrapped his, brought it to his mouth, knowing Dani watched him, and took a bite. He rolled his eyes and groaned. "This is the *best* sandwich I have ever eaten!"

His daughter giggled. "You always say that."

"And it's always true." He tapped her on the nose. "You and Gramma make the best sandwiches—"

"In the whole wide world!" Dani said spreading her left arm out wide while her right arm lifted up slightly.

He laughed. He had taught her that when she had been a little over two and, whenever she liked something, she would always say it was the best 'in the whole wide world.' He took another bite of his peanut butter and jelly sandwich and looked out to the river. Dani sat silent, concentrating on her lunch and occasionally taking a sip of her drink.

One boy on the dock jumped excitedly as he looked at the fish he had just caught. An older man stood next to him, unhooking the fish from the line and helping the boy hold it so the young woman, whom he assumed was the mother, took a picture. Off to his right, he watched a couple of young men tossing a Frisbee back and forth. Several families lingered in various parts of the park enjoying the weather and each other's company. A loud bark sounded behind him. It sounded as though the animal was right behind him. He twisted around and scrambled in front of Dani as the large dog ran toward their blanket, with a leggy brunette running behind the animal.

"Buster! Stop!"

Was that Bree?

A shrill whistle sounded, and Buster stopped, his tongue hanging out, the tail wagging. "Sit."

"Daddy, a doggie!"

"Yes, honey. It's a. . .big dog." He liked dogs, from a distance. The bigger the dog, the longer the distance is how he liked them.

"I am so, so sorry—Lucas?" Bree started, flicking her gaze between him and his daughter. "What are you doing here?"

"Uh, having a picnic?" He shifted, moving away from the

beast who stood only a few feet from him. Danica moved around him, but he placed a hand on her. "Don't move, Dani."

"Oh. You don't need to worry about Buster." She waved a hand toward the dog. "He's totally harmless. He's just an overgrown puppy, aren't you, boy?"

"Can I pet him?" Dani asked, as she stood.

He stood as well, placing a hand on Dani's shoulder, urging her to stay next to him. Bree looked at Dani, wincing slightly as her gaze took in Dani's limp arm.

"I don't think so, Dani. Some dogs are—"

"Please Daddy?"

"Lucas, I promise Buster won't hurt her. He loves children."

"Well, alright then." Dani squealed in delight. He would take Bree's word, but anxiety still swirled in his stomach.

Buster sat on his haunches as Dani stepped closer and petted the animal on top of his head. The dog remained still, panting, his tongue lolling out. Dani then stroked the dog's back up and down repeatedly. He noticed the dog's front paws moving up and down. Would the dog get up and start running? Would he jump on Dani? Feeling apprehensive, he stepped closer and placed his arm around Dani's shoulders.

"You don't need to be nervous. Buster really is good around kids."

"Is he yours?"

Bree shook her head. "No. He belongs to my dad."

"Oh. I'm surprised he follows your commands."

"He's gotten used to me in the last couple of weeks, I guess. I haven't had any problems."

"Well, let's hope he obeys you."

"Are you afraid he'll hurt Dani?"

He felt like she had punched him in the gut, but, if he was being honest, he had to admit he was nervous having a dog around Dani. She wasn't always steady on her feet and Buster was a good-sized dog. One wrong move and Dani would fall flat on her back or on her face.

"Lucas?"

"Ah, well, he is kind of big."

"Daddy, I wanna play with Buster."

He scrunched down beside Dani and slid a hand down her back. "I don't know—"

"Please Daddy. He won't hurt me."

"Lucas, Buster will be fine with her."

"He won't hurt me." Dani turned and grinned at the golden retriever. "Right, Buster?"

The dog barked and whined, thumping his tail on the ground.

As much as he wanted to say no, he couldn't. "Okay. But, be careful."

Bree removed the leash and Buster ran around in circles. Dani followed suit, laughing. Maybe this was a good thing. He hadn't seen Dani this happy in a long time.

"See? I told you he won't hurt her." Bree turned to him. "Relax, Lucas,"

He watched Danica and Buster chasing each other. He had to trust Bree knew the dog well enough not to hurt his daughter. "You want to sit?" He indicated the blanket.

"Sure." Bree stepped to the edge then sat. "Did I interrupt your lunch?"

He peered down at the remnants of their sandwiches. "No. Want an apple?" He picked one up and held it out. Bree shook her head. She watched him as he sat a few feet away from her. He glanced back at Dani who ran around with Buster following her. Grinning, he leaned back on his forearms, stretching his legs out. "Dani sure is having fun."

"She is. Buster's good around kids. He won't let anything happen to her."

He had to trust she was right. "You left early last night." He watched her reaction from the corner of his eye. Her eyes widened for a split second then it was gone.

"Yeah. I'm not used to staying up late."

"How late is late?"

She bent her knees and rested her arms on them. "Nine, nine-thirty. I'm usually up at six so by nine, I'm exhausted. I used to dance from eight to five, some days longer the closer we got to the performance date."

He shook his head. "Kudos to you. I don't think I could do it."

She glanced at him. "If it's something you love, you don't mind the craziness."

"True." He loved being a contractor and didn't mind the hours he had to put into his job, other than the fact it sometimes pulled him away from quality time with his daughter.

"Buster and your daughter are having a great time," Bree said, as her gaze followed them.

He watched as well and smiled. He wished he could grant Dani's wish of having a dog, but he couldn't.

"Why don't you like dogs?"

"What?" He twisted his gaze to her. He was surprised by her sudden question. "What makes you think that?"

She snickered. "Because of the way you protected Dani from a *ferocious* dog, and how you were so nervous around Buster."

"It's not that I don't like dogs. It's. . .more personal."

"Oh." Bree straightened up, pulling her arms behind her and resting against her hands. "I'm sorry."

"No need to be. Maybe I'll share the story with you someday." He looked at her at the same time she glanced at him. She smiled and his heart thudded. Why hadn't he asked her out all those years ago? Because she would've said no. And he didn't like rejection.

* * * *

"Daddy!"

Bree spun her gaze toward Dani, her heart leaping to her

throat. She slapped a hand to her chest. Lucas jumped up.

"Watch this." Danica twirled in a circle and Buster twisted in a circle as well. The dog barked happily while Dani giggled.

She and Lucas laughed as he sat back down. She was happy to see Dani and Buster getting along so well. She didn't know what she would've done if Dani had been hurt and it had been the result of playing with Buster. Lucas would have a reason not to see her and the thought bothered her. She enjoyed Lucas's company and wanted to see more of him.

"I haven't seen Dani this happy in a long time."

"I'm glad I brought Buster then. He's getting a lot of attention, for sure." She picked at a piece of grass. "I don't mean to pry, but why would you say that?"

Lucas scowled. "Ah, Dani's mother passed away two years ago. And, since then, it's been a little tough."

"Oh, Lucas, I'm so sorry."

He continued watching Dani play and dance with Buster. "Dani misses her, but she's adjusted well."

"She looks happy and well adjusted," she acknowledged and moved her position to sit cross-legged on the blanket. She watched Dani dance around despite her disability. And Buster seemed to be extra careful around her. "Can I ask a personal question?" Lucas looked at her as she plucked a piece of grass and fingered it.

"You can ask, but I may not answer."

"Sounds fair." She cleared her throat. "What happened to Dani's arm?"

He sighed. "It's something I don't talk about. It happened when her mother died."

"Oh." That surprised her. Obviously, something tragic had happened and she wasn't privy to it. "I'm so sorry, Lucas."

"Thank you."

She tossed the piece of grass on the ground. "She does really well, considering her disability."

"She does. She needs help with dressing, but she pretty much does everything else on her own. She just uses her left arm and hand more."

"That's good. It must be hard being a single father."

Lucas leaned back on his elbows; his long legs stretched out in front. "It can be at times. But my parents help out a lot. I couldn't do it without them."

"You're very fortunate. You're obviously doing everything right."

"Thanks." He turned his gaze from watching his daughter to her. "So. . .?"

"Soooo," she echoed, smiling at him. She knew what he wanted to ask. She was pretending she didn't know.

"Last night. At the tavern," Lucas started. He tapped his fingers on the blanket. "Did you have a good time?"

She grinned. "Yes, I did. It was great hanging out with friends, enjoying a few glasses of wine, listening to the band with the crazy-sounding name."

"It is a crazy name for a band. And they played some great music."

His warm, dark gaze seemed to reach into her soul.

"Slow music," Lucas murmured.

Her tummy fluttered, remembering the dance, the feel of him holding her. "Oh, yes, I forgot about the dancing."

"You did?"

She laughed. The sensuous gaze had disappeared, replaced with a serious frown. Had he really thought she'd forget about the slow dance they had shared and the line dancing? "I'm kidding, Lucas." She lowered her gaze, looking at his hand. He wasn't tapping anymore. "I. . .I really enjoyed the dance. The slow dance." Heat rose to her neck, and it wasn't the sun warming her skin.

He clasped her hand and squeezed it lightly. "I'm glad. I enjoyed it too."

She squirmed as his gaze warmed her insides. Flutters exploded low in her abdomen. "I didn't realize how good you were at line dancing, Lucas. You've got some serious talent."

"I might not be light on my feet like the guys you dance

with, but I can keep up with the best of them when it comes to line dancing." He chuckled. "I actually took lessons."

"You did?" That surprised her. She couldn't imagine Lucas in a dance studio taking lessons.

"Yeah. My wife loved it and convinced me to take lessons so we could dance together." His look sobered. "I wasn't into it too much. I would've rather been playing pool, then dancing in a line, hootin' and hollerin' and clapping." He clasped her hand tighter. "But, you know, I'm really glad I took those lessons. If I hadn't, I certainly wouldn't have been on the dance floor with you."

"Well, I'm glad you did." She grinned. Should she tell him? "I made a decision yesterday."

"Oh?" His brows furrowed, creating deep creases. "You're leaving town?"

She shook her head. "I'm reopening the studio." The more she said it, the happier she was in her decision.

"You are?" He grinned and the butterflies swirled again.

"Yeah. I decided last night."

"That's great news!" He sat straighter. "So, you're staying?" "For a while." Even to her own ears she sounded doubtful. Lucas's grin faded.

"You don't sound too happy about the prospect."

"It's not that. I. . ." She pulled at her ponytail and huffed out a breath. "I'm not sure if I can run a business and teach classes. I'm used to dancing and being told what to do, not managing people."

"Do you know of anybody who can be an assistant manager while you focus on teaching?"

She grinned. "Huh. I never thought of that. To be honest, I haven't put a lot of thought into the business at all. I only decided last night."

"Well, give it more thought. Write your ideas down, what you're looking for in an employee, that sort of thing."

"Yeah, I will. Thanks. So, when did you become a contractor?"

"Since I graduated high school. Actually, Dad encouraged me to take the vocational classes in high school, and then I worked full time for him after graduation. He occasionally works with me, now that he's retired, but my cousin, Devon, and I pretty much run the business." He shifted. "Because I'm working on the studio, we should exchange numbers. . .in case there's a problem."

"Definitely. Text me first and I'll text you back."

Lucas sat up straighter and pulled his cell phone from his back pocket. Smiling, he typed then grinned. She couldn't figure out what he was writing. Her phone dinged. She had expected his number but hadn't expected the smiley face and heart emojis. She tossed him a smile then started typing on her phone. She hit Send and glanced back at him.

He laughed. "Thanks." He looked back at Dani and Buster while chewing on a thin blade of grass.

Dani came running back, panting and grinning. "Buster's so much fun!" She plunked down on the blanket and reached for her juice box. Buster followed behind Dani and sat next to her, panting loud. She ruffled Buster's ear then stroked his back. "Can I have a dog, Daddy?"

Lucas seemed taken aback. "I.. . I'm not sure."

"Please, Daddy?" Dani pleaded. "I'll take good care of a dog. I promise."

Lucas looked to her for help. She got his silent message. "Well, Danica," she started, "having a dog is a lot of work. It takes dedication."

"What's ded…cation?"

"It means you have to feed them and walk them every day. And, you have to give them baths," she explained.

Lucas nodded in agreement. Danica bounced on her bottom.

"Yay! I can give my doggie a bath, Daddy!"

Lucas shook his head and pinched the bridge of his nose. "Tell you what, Dani. Let's talk about having a dog after we move into the house, okay? We shouldn't have a dog right now when Daddy still has a lot of work to do."

Dani's laughter faded and she pouted. "Okay."

"Hey," he started, leaning forward and stroking her hair. "I didn't say no, did I?"

Dani shook her head.

"We just need to wait a little while, okay?"

"Okay," Danica mumbled then sipped from her juice box. She brightened suddenly. "Can we visit Buster at his house?"

She shot Lucas a glance. "Ahh, well. . ."

"Please?"

"Dani, I think you've done enough begging for one day," Lucas stated. "Let's not ruin a good time." He glanced at her and shrugged.

"Tell you what," she said. "Let me talk to my father first. Buster's really his dog but, because I live there too, it's like he's mine sometimes. I help take care of him when he's busy." She looked from Lucas to Dani. "If it's okay with my father, I'll call your Daddy so you can come and visit."

"That'd be great!"

"Well then," She stood, and Lucas did the same. "I think I better get back."

Lucas nodded, tucking his hands into his pockets.

"Um, Thanks for the dance last night." She wanted him to know she enjoyed his company.

"You're welcome. Anytime."

Again, the pesky butterflies swirled, and heat rose to her face. Would she always blush when he looked at her or said something nice? Smiling, she moved toward Buster. She attached the leash to his collar. As she moved past Lucas and Dani, she said, "I'll call you."

"Sounds good."

She looked at him and held his gaze for a long moment. "Well, gotta go. C'mon Buster."

He smiled. "See ya'."

"See ya'."

"Bye, Buster!" Dani called out as she and Buster walked

away. Buster turned around, barked, and then whined.

"C'mon, boy. We'll see them again. Soon." She waved at Lucas and her insides warmed when he grinned back.

Five

Lucas tapped his fingers on the steering wheel to the lively toon playing on the radio. As he drove, he thought about Saturday night and dancing with Bree. She had fit so perfect in his arms. He hadn't wanted the music to end as they held onto each other, moving to the flow of the music. It had been a dream come true for him. He had always imagined what it would be like to dance with her, to hold her close, perhaps to kiss her, although that hadn't happened. Holding her in his arms made him realize what an idiot he had been in high school. Why hadn't he asked her out? Because her brother was his best friend at the time and there was no way in hell Brett would allow him to date Bree. Instead, he had watched her from a distance, always admiring her dancing skills and her discipline to train harder. She wanted to be the best of the best. When he had been at their house, he pretended he didn't really like her. But, in reality, he adored her.

And when she showed up at the park yesterday, she filled his heart with more longing. He couldn't wait to see her again. He didn't know when it would be though. He was sure she wouldn't be at the studio while they worked. He may have to find a reason to call her. Seeing her again, after all this time, felt as though he had been sucker-punched. He couldn't believe how beautiful she had become. He probably looked like an overgrown teen ogling a pretty girl. And he had been.

The loud honk of a car startled him. He twisted the steering wheel to the right to get back in his lane. Damn! He had been so lost in thoughts of Bree that he had driven over the white line. Thank God Dani wasn't in the car. She would've panicked and would be screaming right now. Her PTSD would've kicked in, causing her to remember the heart-wrenching car accident she had been in two years ago. His heart thundered. He rolled down the window and inhaled deeply, letting the cool spring air calm his racing heart.

He was relieved when the studio came into view and wondered if he'd see Bree. Maybe she was already there, dancing her heart out as she had the other day. When he pulled into the lot, he saw her car and grinned. He parked the truck and stepped out. As he entered the studio, he called out.

"I'm in here," she called out. "In the office."

He heard shuffling and the scrape of furniture being pulled across a bare floor.

"Hey," he said, as he peeked inside the small office space. Bree was bent over, facing away from him, her tight butt encased in black leggings. Her long, shapely legs made him think of things he shouldn't. Not at the moment anyway. She stood up quickly and turned to face him.

"Oh, hi." She straightened the long shirt, or short dress, whatever woman called those outfits they wore with leggings. "I lost track of time." Her face was flushed. Was it from exertion or seeing him? He hoped it was due to the sight of him.

"What were you doing?"

"Oh. . ." She turned her gaze to the desk. "I didn't like where the desk was sitting, so I thought I'd move it."

He cleared his throat. "Here, I'll help you move it." He walked to the narrow side of the desk away from her. "Where do you want it?"

"By the window," she answered, tilting her chin toward the wall behind her as she put her hands to the edge of the desk. "That way I'll get more light shining on the desk."

"Okay. On the count of three." He gripped the edge. "One. Two. Three." Together, they lifted the desk and moved it to the opposite side of the room. After straightening the desk and getting it to where she liked it, they both backed away. She blew out a breath and fanned herself with her hand. "I need to get back to dancing before I lose any strength I have left. I haven't worked out in a while, and I'm starting to feel it. Moving the desk made me realize if I don't exercise and start dancing more, I won't be in any shape to teach the kids or. . ."

"Or?" He watched her. Her mouth opened, then closed. She must've thought better of it.

"Nothing." She turned away.

"Well, if you're interested in a dance partner, I'm more than happy to help."

She laughed, and the sound wrapped around his heart, sending pleasure through him. He had missed her laughter. He had missed her.

"No doubt." She moved closer to him and smoothed a hand through her ponytail. "I'll keep that in mind."

"I had a great time Saturday night, and Sunday." He looked down at the desk when their hands touched. She sucked in a breath as her eyes rounded. Awareness shot up his arm. He yanked his hand away, although what he really wanted to do was wrap his arms around her, pull her close and hold her tight against him.

"I did too."

"Maybe we can do it again. . .soon."

"I'd like that." She smiled and pleasure skittered up his spine. He could drown in those deep pools of tawny-gold.

"Lucas?"

"Hmm?"

"I'm glad Aunt Merry hired you."

"Me too." He swept a hand up and captured her jaw, smoothing his thumb along its edge. She sighed and tilted her head into his palm. She smiled at him. Not a playful smile, but a tender one which spoke to his heart. Her cinnamon-brown eyes shone bright, making them appear to be deep pools of rich coffee. She wet her lips. He shifted his stance to face her, and she did the same. Her eyes flitted back and forth, watching his reaction to her. The tip of her tongue came out, wetting her lips. He couldn't help himself. Her scent floated around him. He wanted to pull her close and kiss her senseless, but instead, he stepped back. She frowned, her forehead crinkling.

"Well," his voice sounded raspy. "I should check out what needs to be done and.. ."

"Yeah." She stepped sideways.

He cleared his throat. "I was wondering if you'd like to have dinner soon, so we can go over some more details of the renovations." He watched her. Her smile faded. She bit her lip and looked down at the floor. His heart thundered and skittered, and he remembered what it felt like to be a gawky teen asking a girl out for the first time.

"I'd love to."

He grinned. "Great!" He suddenly didn't have any words. His brain seemed foggy, and he lost the ability to speak.

"What day, or do you want to call me?"

"Oh, I'll call you. I need to see when my mom can babysit."

"Or, we can hang out at your parents. It doesn't matter to me."

"That would work too. I'll call you and we'll set up a date." Bree was remarkable. He didn't think she'd offer to do such a thing. The few women he had dated in the past had wanted to go out, not hang around with his parents and especially not with Dani.

"Alright then, it's a date!" She laughed and it was music to his ears.

Maybe he could make it work this time.

* * * *

"You seem really happy today," Aunt Merry said from the kitchen table.

"I am happy." Bree couldn't help it. She smiled from ear to ear. She had a date with Lucas!

"Ahh. Does it have anything to do with a particular contractor?"

"It might," she sang out. As she went about pouring water into the kettle, she thought about Lucas. It was a feeling of excitable energy before going on stage and she hadn't been this excited in a long time. Her nerves sang, like a girl going to the dance with her high school crush. And, he had been her crush, although Lucas hadn't known it at the time.

"When did this happen?" Aunt Merry asked.

"At the studio, early this morning." She noticed a twinkle in her aunt's eyes and wondered if her aunt knew more than she was letting on. She set the kettle on the stove and turned on the burner. She pulled two mugs from the cabinet and two teabags from the canister. After setting the teabags in the mugs, she leaned against the counter and folded her arms, waiting for the kettle to whistle.

"You definitely have that dreamy look in your eyes."

"What? I do not." But, maybe she did. Whenever she was around Lucas, or thought about him, her insides would stir into a frenzy, like the fluttering of a thousand butterflies trying to escape. She knew she was always blushing around him and wondered if he noticed. She was sure he had. Although she thought she had loved Wyatt, it didn't compare to how she felt around Lucas. Come to think of it, she had never felt this way for Wyatt.

"So, when is this big date?"

"I don't know. He said he'd call and let me know." The kettle shrieked and she pulled it off the burner. "He has to see when his mother can babysit." She poured the hot water into the two mugs. When her aunt made an eye roll, she shook her head. "Lucas will call, Aunt Merry." She held a mug in each hand and walked to the table. "Here you go." She set one mug down in front of her aunt and then sat, her hand clasped around her own mug. "We'll probably go to the tavern."

"Well, I think he should take you out of town. Go to Portland, to a nicer restaurant than what we have around here."

She shrugged. "I like the tavern. And I'm not sure how far

he wants to drive away from Dani."

"Hmm." Aunt Merry nodded and smiled. "He dotes on that little girl. He's such a nice man." She set her mug down. "I always liked Lucas, although your father had his doubts about the boy back when you were in high school."

"But Dad obviously feels differently about him now."

"Lucas has helped us out here and there." Aunt Merry sighed. "The place is getting old and needs a lot of upkeep. Some things your father can't do anymore. When Lucas offered, your Dad wouldn't accept his help, until I asked Lucas. His mother and I are good friends."

"I didn't know that!"

"Theresa and I have known each other for a long time."

She thought of how close Lucas was to his family and a sudden wave of guilt spilled over her. Maybe if she had been on social media more often, she would've known what was happening in Misty River. And with Lucas. Even more important, she would've been more in tune with her family and perhaps wouldn't feel like an outsider at times. Her family had been Wyatt and the other dancers. They had spent hours a day together, so it went without saying they would grow close and be a dance family when most had families living hundreds, even thousands of miles away. She should've called more often. Should've been on FaceTime or on Zoom. There were a dozen ways she could've kept in touch. She had turned away from them all.

"You're quiet all of a sudden, Bree. What's wrong?"

"Oh, just thinking about what an idiot I am."

"Why would you think that?"

"Because who leaves town and rarely visits? Or calls?"

"Well. . .you were busy." Aunt Merry picked up her mug of tea and took a sip, looking at her over the rim. "Remember, I've been where you are. I understand. What made you think that?"

She slid her hand through her hair. "Lucas is so close to his family. I had that, and I threw it away when I left town."

"Hey, don't beat yourself up over it." Her aunt lowered her mug. "I did the same thing. I lived my own life and forgot I had a family back home. It happens, Bree." She smiled. "We still love you, you know."

"Thank you. I needed to hear that." She fingered the edge of the placemat. "It's no excuse, though, for not staying in touch. I have a cell, and a laptop, and I could've taken some time during the week and called. No wonder Dad doesn't talk to me. He's still angry."

Aunt Merry waved a hand in the air. "Oh, he is not. That's just him. He's sullen and moody. If he says two words to you, then you know he's not mad."

She couldn't help it, she laughed. And it felt good. "Well, I'm here now and I'm going to make up for it. I love you, Aunt Merry."

"And I love you."

"Anyway, I'm excited to work on the studio. I didn't think I would be, but I am." Again, guilt flooded her. She wouldn't give in to it. She was back, at least for now, and she would make amends where she could. She thought of the studio and how much work Lucas and Devon and the crew had already done. Had it only been a couple of days since Aunt Merry had asked her to take over the studio? Originally, she hadn't wanted to do this, but now that she had committed herself, she was actually excited to have something to look forward to each day. And it helped that Lucas would be there as well.

"I am beyond excited you're going to teach classes. The kids will love you. And, I'll still help out of course." Aunt Merry beamed. "I'm glad you're back, Bree. I hope you stay, but—"

Her phone rang, jolting both of them. She picked up her cell and clicked on the green button. "Hi Lucas!" She glanced at her aunt, who was nodding and smiling. Aunt Merry gave her a thumbs up.

"Hey, Bree. I didn't get you at a bad time, did I?"

"No, not at all. I'm sitting here with Aunt Merry, having

tea."

"Sounds like fun."

There was a pause. She could hear Dani in the background and Lucas's muffled voice. "How does Wednesday sound?"

"Wednesday sounds perfect." Her voice sounded breathy. His husky voice sent a flush of heat through her body. She swore if he kept talking, she'd melt in a pool of lust on the floor.

"Good. I'll pick you up around five."

"I can't wait." She was breathy!

"I can't wait, either," Lucas responded. "See you soon."

"Okay. See you soon." She clicked off and grinned. She wanted to dance around the room. Suddenly, the thought of hanging around in Misty River wasn't so bad after all.

Six

"Daddy, why are you dressed up?"

Lucas looked down at his daughter. "Because I'm meeting a very special lady."

"Who?" She sat on the edge of his bed, kicking her legs back and forth.

"Remember Bree? The lady we saw at the park?"

"The one who brought Buster?"

"Yes. I'm taking her out to dinner."

"Can I go with you?"

He chuckled. "Not this time, Munchkin. Maybe next time."

"Are you gonna be back to tuck me in?"

"Sure thing." He chucked her under the chin. "Why don't you see what Gramma's up to and I'll be right down."

"Okay, Daddy." She skipped out of his bedroom and started down the stairs. "Gramma!"

He shook his head then combed his hair. He debated on whether he should shave as he ran a hand down his cheek and across his chin. He liked his close-cropped beard and mustache. And he didn't think Bree had an issue with it either. Excitement filled him, reminding him of his days back in high school when he knew he'd be seeing Bree.

For the first time in years, he wasn't sure how he should dress. Should he go all casual or put on a dress shirt and tie? He rummaged through the closet and pulled out a mint green IZOD button-down shirt. He slipped his arms through the sleeves and buttoned up the shirt. He then rolled the sleeves up to his elbows. There. He took a quick look in the mirror.

No need for a tie.

He headed out of the bedroom and hurried down the stairs. As he turned at the bottom, he was greeted with a whistle from his father.

"Got a date, son?"

"Business meeting," he answered. He knew if he said it was a date, he'd be teased. Then again, maybe his father would cheer. It had been a while since he had dated anyone.

"Never saw you dress like that for a business meeting before." His father winked.

He shook his head, smiling and headed into the kitchen. "Hi Mom."

His mother turned from where she stood at the counter, peeling potatoes and nodded her approval. "You look very handsome, Lucas." She set the potato down and wiped her hands on her apron. "And who's the lucky young lady?"

"Like I said to Dad, it's not a date."

"Okay. If you say so." She came over to him. "It's alright if you do have a date." She smiled as she fixed his collar. "We aren't judging you."

"I know, Mom." He kissed her forehead. "I love you for caring."

She smiled up at him and smoothed her hands down his arms. "You're too young to let your life go to waste. Go out. Have fun."

"Is that an order?"

She laughed and swatted him playfully on his upper arm. "Have fun. Danica will be fine."

"I know."

"Daddy's gonna read me a story when he gets home, right Daddy?"

He walked over to where she sat at the kitchen table, coloring. "I sure am. Be good for Gramma and Grampa." He kissed the top of her head.

"I will, Daddy. Love you."

"Love you too, Peanut."

He waved to his mother who had gone back to peeling potatoes. As he headed for the back door, he heard his father call out. "Don't do anything I wouldn't do, Son." He shook his head and laughed as he closed the door behind him. He skipped down the steps and headed to his car.

As he drove toward the farmhouse, he felt like a high school kid picking up his girl. He tapped his fingers on the steering wheel while listening to the radio. Several minutes later, he pulled into the driveway of the big, white New Englander-style farmhouse. A small garden lined the front of the porch and already, small sprigs of flowers pierced the earth. Most likely crocuses. Several hostas already sprouted long spikes A giant lilac bush stood on the corner, not yet in bloom. The last time he had been here, it had been February and most everything had been covered in snow.

He got out of the car and headed up the walkway toward the front of the house. The gravel crunched beneath his feet, alerting Buster to his arrival. The dog barked and a moment later, Merry Thompson opened the screen door. He hurried up the steps. He remembered building them back in February when the previous steps had to be taken down due to rot.

"Hi, Lucas!" she greeted him. "Come on in." She held the door open while a dish towel hung from her hand. "Bree's just about ready."

He strode in and nearly jumped back and into Miss Thompson as Buster rushed to him, his tail wagging furiously. His heart jumped to his mouth, and he caught himself on the doorframe.

"Buster!" Merry Thompson scolded the dog as she stepped around him. The dog immediately sat, his tail thumping on the hardwood floor. "He won't hurt you, Lucas. He's a bit on the hyper side."

"I can see that." He pushed off from the door and followed Bree's aunt into the living room. Buster followed behind but kept his distance. He mentally prepared himself for seeing her father. Henry Thompson had been pleasant while he worked on the property, but it was a different scenario now. He was her to pick up Mr. Thompson's daughter which put a whole new spin on things.

"Oh, Henry's out in the barn. I can get him if you want to say hello," Miss Thompson said.

"No need to bother him if he's busy." He sat in the chair by the window while Bree's aunt sat on the sofa across from him.

"Any idea where you're going to dinner?" she asked.

"I was planning on going into Port—" Bree stood in the entrance of the living room. "Wow!" he stood, staring at her. His breath caught. She wore a turquoise wrap dress and it clung to her in all the right places. Matching earrings sparkled in the sunlight streaming in from the side window. If he had thought her beautiful without makeup, she was even more so with makeup. Her hair hung long and curling down her back. He ached to pull his hands through the silky strands. "Bree, you look. . .beautiful."

"Thank you. You look great as well."

"Look at you two kids." Miss Thompson nudged him toward Bree, and he obliged. "Now, you two have fun and," she grinned as she looked from Bree to him. "Remember, don't do anything I wouldn't do." She blurted out a laugh.

"Aunt Merry!" Bree admonished, although she didn't seem upset. He did notice her cheeks redden though.

"My father said the same thing as I walked out of the house."

"I like your father. We think alike," Miss Thompson said, as she led them to the door.

"No need to worry, Miss Thompson. She's in good hands."

"Oh, I'm sure she is." Merry winked, and he couldn't help but laugh.

"Aunt Merry, seriously? You're embarrassing Lucas, and me." Bree's face turned crimson.

He held the door open, and Bree walked onto the porch.

He closed it behind him as Miss Thompson stood in the entry, waving to them. They walked down the wide wooden steps then down the gravel walkway toward his car. He held the door open for her and after she was settled, he closed the door and headed for the other side of the car.

"Hey there, Lucas!"

He turned. Mr. Thompson waved to him. He waved back. "How you doing?"

"Fine." Her father nodded. "Have a good time."

Bree rolled down the window. "Bye, Dad."

"Bye, hon. Have fun." He waved again then strode up the steps onto the porch. He turned and watched them.

There was a sad look in his eyes, Lucas noticed. But, then again, every time he saw Mr. Thompson, he appeared that way. He turned around in the driveway and headed back down the long drive to the main road. Bree was quiet. "Anything wrong?"

"No. I'm wondering why my father looks so sad."

"Huh. I thought it was me. I noticed it too." He shrugged, not knowing what else to say. He turned on the radio. "This station okay for you?"

Bree nodded. "It's fine."

Suddenly, he felt awkward and unsure of himself. It had been six months since he had gone on a date. And it failed, miserably. It had felt as though he were cheating on his wife. She had passed away a little over two years ago, but no one had turned his head accept Bree. He had never taken the chance back in high school and he didn't want to miss the opportunity now. He'd take it one step at a time. He glanced at Bree, who looked out the side window.

"Any place in particular you want to go?" he asked. "I wasn't sure if you had a favorite place in Portland."

She shook her head. "You choose. To be honest, I don't know of any place in Portland. I haven't been there since I was in high school."

"Well, I know of a great place. We'll go there."

She nodded. "Can I ask you a question?"

"Sure."

"Can you tell me about Danica?"

He hadn't expected Bree to ask about Dani's injury. "Ah, yeah, I guess." He looked back at her. She smiled. "What did you want to know?"

"Well, I'm curious. Since you couldn't finish the story on Sunday, I was wondering how Danica became paralyzed on her right side."

He had said he would tell her the rest of the story, but he had hoped it wouldn't be tonight. The memory depressed him, and he didn't want to deal with the pain tonight when he wanted to have a nice time with Bree, having a wonderful dinner and enjoying each other's company. "I did say I'd tell you, didn't I?" He blew out a breath. "It's not easy to share."

"I'm sorry, Lucas. I don't mean to pry, and I don't want you to be uncomfortable." She waved a hand at him, dismissing the question. "We can talk about it another time. I'm sorry."

He brought a hand down from the steering wheel and touched her forearm. "It's okay." She didn't move her arm, which was a good sign. "But let's talk about it when I'm not driving."

She chewed her bottom lip. "Danica's a wonderful little girl. Very happy."

"Yes, she is. She doesn't let anything get in the way of her disability."

"I've always admired people who can overcome their disabilities to create lives for themselves and their families. They're stronger than I could ever be."

"I doubt that. You seem strong to me."

"Physically, maybe. But, after my injury, and the weeks of therapy, knowing I couldn't dance, I felt as though my world had ended. I didn't do a thing except sulk and feel sorry for myself. I spiraled into depression. My life was over, so I thought. If I couldn't dance, I couldn't live." She looked down at her lap.

He looked sideways. "Don't let it get to you, Bree. Of course you're going to feel depressed, and angry. It had to have been tough on you, considering dancing is your passion, your life."

She glanced at him. "Although I'm not working for the Bay City Ballet anymore, at least I can dance. Some never dance again if the injury is severe enough." She swept her hair back. "Maybe my career is over."

He patted her hand and smiled when she took his hand in hers and looked at him. As much as he wanted to stare into her beautiful eyes, he had to keep his own on the road. But, he could enjoy the feel of her hand in his. Soft fingers brushed his calloused ones. He squeezed her hand. Was she having second thoughts? Did she want to go back to San Francisco? Why would she do all this work on the studio if she was going to just pack up and leave? Then again, it wasn't Bree who was having the studio renovated. It was her aunt. Bree could up and leave if she wanted to. She had no commitment to Misty River.

"I'm sorry, Lucas. You don't want to hear about my problems."

"Hey, if it helps, I don't mind listening."

"You're a good guy, Lucas." She pulled her hand from his and he felt a sudden loss. He curled his fingers and brought his hand back to the steering wheel. They sat silent for the rest of the ride, each of them lost in their own thoughts.

* * * *

They finally arrived at Captain Jack's in Portland. Lucas got out of the car and walked to her side as she opened the door. She looked up at him, startled.

"Oh. I'm not used to a guy wanting to open the door for me."

"No? Well, my father instilled in me that I should always

open and close the door for a woman. Women were to be treated with respect."

"Smart guy, your father."

"He is." They walked side by side to the entrance and again, he held the door open for her.

"I could get used to this." She gave Lucas a bright smile and glanced around. "This is a nice place," she added as they came to the podium.

"It is. I haven't been here in a while though."

The waitress picked up two menus. "Will you be eating in the lounge or in the dining room."

"Dining room," they said in unison, then Lucas laughed. She loved the sound. It warmed her to her soul.

The waitress led them to a table by the window looking out to the water. The view of the ocean was beautiful. Several wooden docks reached out like fingers into the bay while expensive yachts sat between the docks.

"What can I get you to drink?" the waitress asked.

"I'll have a Goat Island Light," Lucas started, "and. . ."

"I'll have the same." She grinned when Lucas's brows arched. The waitress nodded, then turned and walked away. "I do drink beer once in a while."

Lucas shook his head.

"What?" She asked. "You don't believe me?"

"No. I mean, yes, I believe you." He smiled and reached for her hand. "I'm surprised you ordered a beer. You don't seem like the type."

"I've been dying for one. I usually drink wine or plain water, but a beer sounds so good right now."

Lucas grinned at her. "There's so much I want to learn about you, Bree."

"Well, I'm sure there'll be plenty of time while I'm in Misty River."

"I hope so." He lifted his menu and opened it, scanning the laminated pages.

She followed his lead and looked at the menu, trying to

decide if she wanted fish or another type of seafood. She liked just about everything they offered.

"I know what I'm getting," Lucas said, setting the menu down and clasping his hands together.

"Wow, that didn't take long." She glanced at him from over the menu.

He grinned. "I have a secret."

"Ohhhh. Do tell."

"No matter where I go, I always get the same thing."

"And what would that be?"

"Steak. Medium rare. Mashed potatoes and whatever veggie they have."

She nodded. "Sounds delicious. I pegged you for a meat and potatoes kind of guy."

"I am definitely a meat and potatoes kind of guy."

"But, don't you ever want to try something different?"

"I never thought about it. Maybe I will. . .but not tonight." He chuckled.

She laughed and scanned the options. "Hmm, I'm still not sure what I want."

The waitress came back with their drinks. "Here you go." She set the beers down in front of them, then pulled out her order pad. "Have you decided yet?"

"Can we have another couple of minutes?" he said, looking over at her.

She smiled at the waitress, embarrassed, and quickly glanced down at the menu. When the waitress left, she looked back at him. "Thanks. I hate asking her to come back but, everything looks and sounds so delicious. I can't decide."

"Take your time."

Maybe she would go for the steak. Then again, the fish looked good, too. She tilted her head back and forth as though the motion would help her decide. Finally, she set the menu down. "I know what I want. Baked haddock and rice pilaf."

He twisted his gaze back to her. "Sounds good. I've never

had it."

"I love fish, or any kind of seafood."

"I can take it or leave it."

"Right. Because you're a meat and potatoes kind of guy."

"Exactly."

They laughed, which was a positive sign. It meant she could be herself around him. If they were going to work together, they would have to get along, for the most part.

The waitress returned. "All set?"

"Yes," she stated. "I'll have the baked haddock with rice pilaf. And a salad."

The waitress nodded then glanced down at him. "I'll have the rib-eye steak, medium rare, mashed potatoes and whatever house veggie you have."

"Sure thing." She scooped up the menus. "Any appetizers?"

He looked at Bree.

"Not for me, but if you want anything, Lucas, go ahead."

"No, I'm fine."

The waitress tucked her pad in her apron and turned around.

"Are you sure you didn't want an appetizer? I feel guilty you're not ordering one because I won't have one."

"Don't worry about it."

"Oh, I want to show you," she turned sideways and reached into her purse. She pulled out a piece of paper then opened it. "I printed off pictures from Pinterest—"

"Pinterest?"

"You've never heard of Pinterest?"

He shook his head. "Can't say I have. What is it?"

"It's an app where you create boards of things you like." She looked down at the table for a quick second then glanced back at Lucas. "Think of it as a virtual bulletin board. You find pictures you like and pin them on your boards."

"Ahh. I get it, but it's not for me."

"You never know, Lucas. It could be a great resource for

your business."

He fingered his glass of beer. "I'll check it out." He smirked. "Maybe I'll check out your boards and see what you like."

Again, her neck and cheeks warmed. Thank goodness for the dim lighting or he'd see her blushing. "Anyway, I thought these would give you an idea of what I'd like for colors and the overall concept of what I want the office to look like."

"You've really been thinking about this. Can I see what you have in mind?"

"Sure." She slid the paper toward him then leaned back against the cushion of the bench seat. She hoped he could see her vision.

He looked at the pictures and seemed to be studying them. Then he looked back up at her. "I like your ideas." He pointed to one picture. "Is this the kind of desk you want?"

"Yah. Why?" He was going to talk her out of it.

"Well, it's. . .big."

"Yes it is." She wanted lots of room to spread out.

"Okay. If that's what you want." Lucas huffed. "Devon and I will start on your office probably in a day or two." He handed the paper back to her. "You want to help?"

"Sure. You tell me when, and I'll be there." She grinned. She took a sip of her beer, peering at Lucas. He smiled back at her. A twinge of want curled inside her. Did he know what an affect he had on her? She hadn't felt this way in a long time. She didn't think she'd want to work on the studio or even like the idea, but it was growing on her, and she was excited about the prospect of seeing the finished product. Who was she kidding? She was looking forward to seeing Lucas at the studio. She knew he would do everything in his power to make the studio into the place she dreamed it could be.

The meals came and, although her haddock looked delicious, she glanced at Lucas's steak and wished she had ordered it instead.

"You're salivating over my steak," he said, and grinned. "Want a bite?"

"No, but thank you." She did, but she wasn't going to admit it. She dug into her haddock and took a bite. The fish practically melted in her mouth. "God, this is good!"

Lucas grinned as he lifted a piece of steak to his mouth. "Glad you like it. Although, I think you still need to try my steak." He took a bite.

She watched as he made a grand gesture of rolling his eyes and licking his lips.

"You've got to try this steak, Bree. It's fantastic."

"If you insist." She pushed her plate closer to his so he could put a piece on it. Once he did, she pulled her plate back and stabbed it with her fork. She popped it in her mouth and groaned. She chewed, enjoying the mouthful of flavor then swallowed. "Wow! This is the best steak I've ever tasted."

"Isn't it?"

"I'm ordering the rib-eye the next time we come here." She went back to her own dinner and realized Lucas was watching her. His gaze held longing and hope. "What?"

"I'm happy to hear you want to come here again, because I plan on asking you out again."

"I'd like that." She was glad she had accepted his invitation. It gave her a chance to get to know him outside of the studio. She was seeing a side of him she hadn't seen as a teen, but then again, they had matured in ten years. She wasn't the same girl she used to be either.

Soft music played over the intercom while low chatter from the other diners spilled around them. It was relaxing. She lifted her beer to take a sip and watched Lucas as he cut into his steak. His head was lowered, and he couldn't see her watching him. His thick and wavy dark hair gleamed in the muted light. She wanted to run her fingers through it. Lucas looked at her. A warmth crept up her neck, again, and infused her cheeks. She knew he noticed it. He winked. Immediately, more heat swept through her. Did he know what kind of an affect he had on her?

"So, how's your construction business going?" she asked. She was curious to know more about him, and his life, from the past ten years.

He took a swig of his beer then set the glass down. "It's going well. Devon and I took over after our Dads retired. Devon's father, and my dad, were partners since they started the business right out of high school."

"You and Devon are cousins, right?"

Lucas nodded. After taking a bite of his potato, he continued. "Dev and I worked as apprentices for a few years until we learned everything we needed to know about the business. It's not as easy as people think."

"I'm sure."

"As I gained experienced, Dad would give me more responsibility." He smiled. "I remember thinking it was because he didn't want me on site to do the manual labor, but it was his way of helping me gain confidence with meeting people, giving them estimates and bringing in more business. He knew he'd be retiring and needed to know I could run the business. Devon's father did the same to him."

"You two make a good team."

He nodded. "We do at that. Although there are times when we're sick and tired of seeing each other."

"I can imagine. It was like that with me and Wy--" She stopped. She shouldn't have mentioned her ex. They were having a wonderful meal, and she didn't need to ruin it by mentioning Wyatt. She shook her head. "I'm sorry. I don't know why I had to mention his name."

Lucas shook his head. "No need to apologize, Bree. You had a life before you came back. It's to be expected his name will come up at times, as well as Daniella's."

"True." She took another swallow of her beer and Lucas did the same. "I went to your website and checked you out, you know."

"You checked me out, huh?" His grin couldn't get any

bigger. It practically split his handsome face in two. His eyes crinkled and shone bright in the dim lighting. "And what do you think?"

She swallowed hard. Did he know what he was doing? She wanted his arms wrapped around her, holding her tight against his broad chest. She--

"Bree?"

"Hmm?"

"What did you think?"

"Oh." She closed her eyes for a second and inhaled. Get your thoughts in check, girl. She found Lucas too distracting at the moment. She couldn't even focus on a simple question. How was she going to see him nearly every day without melting at his feet? "I thought you looked amazing." The heat of embarrassment rushed to her face.

He laughed, a deep, sensual sound and again, her insides warmed. "That's not what I meant, Lucas." She wanted to crawl under the table. "What I want to say is, you're doing an amazing job with the business. Customers have given you great reviews."

He smiled. "Devon and I are proud of what we've done with the business. Dad, and my uncle, were losing money. They wanted to be nice to their neighbors and friends and often did work for free." He sighed. "And, unfortunately, there are still some in town who expect me and Devon to do the same."

"I'm sure there are." She took another sip of her beer. "My aunt wasn't--"

"No, she wasn't, Bree." He reached out and clasped her hand. "She's a wonderful lady and even though she's your aunt, and a good friend of my mother's, I still have to charge her."

"I understand."

"Although I did give her a substantial discount."

She laughed and squeezed his hand. "You're a good man, Lucas." Almost too good.

Seven

"So, what do you do in your spare time besides playing pool and line-dancing?" Bree asked after the waitress cleared the plates away.

"I'm building a house, a cabin to be more precise."

"Really? That's great! Where?"

"About two miles down river." He leaned forward. "It's a beautiful cabin, Bree. I've been pecking away at it between jobs." He lifted his beer bottle. "Maybe I'll bring you by sometime."

She grinned. "I'd love that. What made you decide to build a cabin?"

He set the bottle down. "I've always wanted to live in a cabin, since I was a little boy." He smiled. "I think it stems from the times I went away with my dad to a hunting lodge, and we'd spend an entire week fishing, or hunting, in New Hampshire."

She tucked a strand of hair behind her ear. "I assumed you and Dani were living in the house you shared with your wife, until you told me you were living with your parents."

He sobered. "We couldn't live there after the accident. It was too much for Dani. Too many memories."

"I'm sorry, Lucas."

"Don't be. Dani remembers some things about her mother, but not a lot. She was only three when her mother passed, so she wouldn't have a lot of memories, but I do. Most of which, I don't want to remember."

She leaned forward and reached for his hand. He allowed her to clasp it in her own. It was strong and warm and calloused. "I lost my mother when I was ten. It was hard. Really hard." Lucas squeezed her hand in support and nodded.

"I acted out and wanted to die myself. My father closed himself off. Finally, Aunt Merry came to live with us." She sighed. "She gave up her career to be a mom to me, Anna and Brett. I didn't understand, at the time, how much it had cost her."

"I'm sure she doesn't have any regrets." He smoothed a thumb across the top of her hand. They looked at each other, trying to understand the other's pain.

"I often asked her if she wished she hadn't given up her career to take care of us, but she would always smile and tell us that it was time to retire anyway and it wasn't a hardship for her." She looked down at their hands. "Aunt Merry was a wonderful mother. Almost better than my own."

"Well, she did a fantastic job helping to raise you, Brett and Anna. She should be very proud."

She squeezed his hand. "I'll tell her you said so." Reluctantly, she let go when the waitress set the receipt on the table. She realized she had found out more about Lucas than she ever thought she would. Lucas pulled out his credit card and signed the receipt. "Thanks for the dinner, Lucas."

"You're welcome." He tucked his wallet in his back pocket. "I hope we can do this again, soon."

She grinned. "We will."

The drive home seemed shorter than the drive to the restaurant. Too suddenly, her time with Lucas had come to an end.

"I'm glad we had the chance to go out for dinner, Bree."

She spun her gaze to him. "Me too." She couldn't turn away. Lucas's eyes, so deep and dark, pulled her in to see what secrets he held there. It was like gazing into a pool of dark, decadent chocolate. His hand cupped her jaw, his thumb smoothing the hollow of her cheek. She tilted into his hand.

"Bree," he whispered, and he leaned toward her. She sighed, feeling like she could drown in his gaze. His hand left her jaw and curled itself at the base of her neck, pulling her toward him. His breath, warm and smelling of cinnamon, brushed her lips. Then his mouth pressed against hers and she whimpered. His mustache skimmed the top of her lip as his tongue caressed the seam of her mouth and she opened for him, letting out another sigh.

She reached out and wrapped her arms around him, clasping her hands around his neck. They kissed as he smoothed a hand down her back, drawing her even closer. She tilted her head as the kiss grew deeper. They both sighed.

"Lucas," she breathed against his mouth. She needed air but needed his kiss more. With a groan, she tugged him closer, angled her head and kissed him back with all the longing she had held for him for ten years.

"Bree," he started, his chest heaving. "We need to stop." He pulled back and smiled. "We're fogging up the windows and I don't need your father coming out here with a bat."

She giggled at the image it brought to her. "Okay. Will I see you tomorrow?"

"Definitely." He got out of the car and came to her side, opening the door.

As much as she didn't want to, she got out of the car, then leaned into him. "Goodnight, Lucas." She kissed him, then sighed, drawing a hand through her hair. "Sweet dreams." She side-stepped him as he groaned.

"Oh, they'll be more than sweet, my love."

She turned as she walked up the gravel path to the steps. She waved and watched as he got back into the car. She opened the door, hoping Aunt Merry and her father wouldn't ask her a bunch of questions. She wanted to go to bed and think about the kiss. For a few moments, she had been in heaven.

"So, how'd the date go?"

She squealed and turned to see Aunt Merry standing in the hallway, smiling. She had a cup of tea in her hand. "It was nice."

"Just. . .nice?" Aunt Merry winked at her and headed for

the living room to her left. She realized her aunt knew she had kissed Lucas. "Are you sure it wasn't fantastic?"

"It was great, Aunt Merry." She followed her aunt into the living room and sat in the easy chair. "Hey, Dad."

"Hi," her father greeted her as he stepped into the living room from the kitchen. "How'd your date go with Lucas?"

She couldn't help it. She grinned. "It was great. We went to Captain Jack's in Portland. The food was fantastic."

"I've heard it is. Never been there though. Too expensive for my taste," her father answered. "But, I'm glad you had a good time."

"Do you mean it, Dad?"

He looked at her over the rim of his cup. "Of course I do. Lucas is a nice guy, Bree."

She let out an audible sigh. "Dad, you don't know how much that means to me." She looked from her aunt, who sat down and picked up her knitting, then back to her father. "How come you looked so sad when I left with Lucas earlier?"

"I did?"

She nodded. "I've seen it quite a few times, Dad, and it worries me."

He shrugged and set his cup on the table next to his chair. "I guess I keep thinking it's the last time I'll see you until you decide to come home again."

"Oh, Dad!" She stood and walked over to his chair. She knelt down then leaned in to hug him close to her. "I am so sorry. I didn't realize how much my leaving had hurt you." Her father gripped her in a bear hug, and she sighed, remembering the times in her childhood when he had held her like this. She leaned back. "I can't promise that I won't be leaving again, but," she looked over at her aunt, who smiled at her, then back to her father. "If I do join another company, I promise I'll call more often and definitely visit more."

He nodded and smiled softly at her. "Unless, by some miracle, a certain someone has the ability to keep you home."

She stood, surprised by his statement. Was her father implying he hoped Lucas would make a commitment to her so she'd stay? She kind of hoped he would, too.

"By the way, Bree," her aunt started, "If that kiss is any indication of your feelings, I think you just might stay."

"What are you talking about, Aunt Merry?" She heard her father laugh behind her.

"I was young once. You can't fool me."

"Me too," her father stated. "I still remember."

She brushed her fingers over her lips, still feeling the sensation of his mouth on hers. She smiled. "Well, I'm heading to bed. Good night."

"Sweet dreams, Bree." Aunt Merry called out as she left the living room and headed up the stairs. Those were the same words she had said to Lucas.

After brushing her teeth and putting on a t-shirt and shorts, she settled herself into bed. It wasn't late, but she wanted to fall asleep and dream of Lucas. She grinned, thinking of their kiss. Again, she touched her lips, the memory still lingering. She never expected him to kiss her. Heck, she hadn't expected she'd kiss him before walking to the door! She closed her eyes. "They'll be more than sweet, my love,"

My love. She sighed. She was sure he wasn't in love with her, but it was such a sweet endearment. She didn't want to second guess a slip of the tongue. She giggled at the pun. Had he really spoken his feelings out loud?

* * * *

Bree didn't have the ambition or motivation to work on business cards and pamphlets. Feeling thirsty, she headed to the kitchen and pulled a water bottle from the fridge. She heard giggling from the backyard. Aunt Merry and Anna were digging in the garden. Heather was kneeling beside her mother, doing the same with a plastic garden shovel. She started for the door when she heard her phone. Twisting around, she grabbed the cell phone off the counter. Grinning, she pressed the green button.

"Hi Lucas!"

"Hi. You sound happy."

"Very."

"You in the mood for coffee?"

"Sure! Where and when?"

He chuckled. "Excited are we?"

Oh, if he only knew. His voice could make her turn into a puddle on the floor. "Well, of course I am!"

"How about we meet at the bakery in a half-hour?"

"Okay. Meet you then."

"See you then, Bree."

She hung up and grinned.

After changing into something more appealing, she dabbed on mascara and some lipstick. She didn't want to wear too much. She had a feeling Lucas didn't like to see her in a lot of makeup. She stepped outside and walked to the garden. "I'm heading out. I'm meeting Lucas at the bakery for coffee."

Anna looked up, shielding her eyes from the afternoon sun. "Have fun."

Aunt Merry waved. "Bring back some goodies."

"I will. See you later." She turned to leave.

Fifteen minutes later, she pulled in front of Sweet Cheeks Bakery and walked in. The aroma of fresh brewed coffee, mixed with the lingering scent of chocolate, assailed her. She headed to the counter when she heard Lucas call her name.

"Hey!" she called back. He looked wonderful, although he was in his work clothes. He could be in a bear suit and he'd still look gorgeous.

"Have you ordered yet?" he asked, standing beside her. He put his hand to the small of her back. Heat radiated through her blouse and those darn butterflies took flight.

"Hey, I thought I heard familiar voices," Chloe said, as she came out from the kitchen.

"Good morning, Chloe," she said. "We're here for coffee,

and I need a batch of your cookies for Aunt Merry and Dad."

Chloe grinned. "The usual?"

She nodded.

"And what about you, Lucas? Anything you want to bring home to the family?"

"It's very tempting, but I think I'll hold off."

"Suit yourself, but you're missing out on my newest creation."

His brow lifted. "Really? What did you make this time?"

"A Cherry-Coke cupcake."

"Oh, man, that sounds delicious," Lucas said. "I'll take half a dozen."

Chloe laughed. "It doesn't take much to please you, does it Lucas?"

"No, it doesn't." He twisted his gaze to Chloe and grinned.

"What do you want for coffees?" Chloe asked as she put the cupcakes in a pink box.

"I'll take a regular," Lucas said.

"And I'll have French Vanilla, skim milk."

Lucas peered at her and screwed up his face. "And it actually tastes good?"

"It's delicious. I'll let you take a sip of mine."

He waved a hand at her. "No thanks." He took out his wallet and pulled out some bills, handing them to Chloe as she passed a coffee to her. She handed Lucas his coffee. "Keep the change, Chloe."

"Thanks."

"Do you want to sit here or go for a walk?" Lucas asked, stuffing his wallet in his back pocket.

"It's so nice out. Let's take a walk."

He nodded and they walked out the door. They crossed the street and headed for the park, but then she decided she wanted to take a quick glance at the studio.

"Can I see what you've done since I was here last?" she asked. She was curious to see how far Lucas and Devon had come with the renovations.

"Sure. C'mon."

Lucas gently tucked the box of cupcakes under his arm, while holding his coffee. He unlocked the front door with the other. He held the door open for her, and she swept past him. She smiled at her new reception area. This is what people would see when they entered. It felt right. Aunt Merry had done a great job choosing the colors. There was still a smell of lingering paint, but it would dissipate soon. Maybe she'd bring in a fan.

Lucas set his box of cupcakes on one of the chairs and turned to her. "When do you want to do the office?"

"Whenever you want. We can wait until the other rooms are complete." She took a sip from the cup. "How long will it take for the office?"

"A couple of days, probably." He started for the dance rooms toward the back. "Since you were here last, with your aunt, we tore up the flooring in the bigger of the two rooms and took down the mirrors. Your aunt wants everything gutted and redone."

"Yeah. She mentioned that to me. The first day I came here, I tried to convince her to sell the place as is. I told her to let the new owners do the remodeling."

"And, if she had listened to you, we wouldn't be standing here, would we?"

She looked at him, smiling. "No. And we wouldn't have had dinner." Immediately, her thoughts went to Wednesday night and how his mouth felt on hers. Warm, firm, and coaxing.

"Or shared that kiss," Lucas finished.

He had read her mind.

He touched the side of her face, smiled, then kissed her forehead. He grinned, lifting his cup to his lips. "I don't want to spoil you." He chuckled and walked into the larger of the two dance rooms.

She laughed. "I can't wait to brighten up this place. The

minute I walk in here with its dark colors, I feel depressed. Dancers should feel happy and energized when they arrive for class." She turned in a circle until she faced Lucas. He smiled and she smiled back and suddenly felt awkward. It was just the two of them. What was he thinking?

His chest expanded, she noticed, as he inhaled deeply and purveyed the room. He wore a gray t-shirt, and the short sleeves hugged his biceps. When he lifted an arm and bent it, his bicep bulged, and she wondered what it would be like to have him hug her—tight. She could become lost in his embrace, and she wouldn't mind one darn bit.

He pointed out all the changes she had wanted. She decided it was time to tell him of her new plan.

"Ah, Lucas, I've made a change."

His brows rose and a crinkle formed between his eyes. "Oh-Oh."

"I hope it doesn't screw things up, but," she looked at him. "I want to make the studio handicap accessible. Isn't it a law that all businesses need to have handicap access anyway?"

"There are laws, yes, but your business is fine. A wheelchair is able to get through the front door without an issue and the doorways are wide enough for a wheelchair to pass through." His brow furrowed. "Why do you ask? Do you have handicapped students?"

She squirmed. "Well, I might. I want to. It may get to that point." She inhaled and glanced at Lucas. "Which brings me to my next question." She took a fortifying sip of her coffee, watching his reaction. She had to ask. "Is Danica still interested in dancing?"

He shot a glance at her as deep creases formed in his forehead, marring his handsome features. "Dani only thinks she wants to dance. She really doesn't have any desire."

She continued to watch the emotions flit across his face. He seemed to go from unsure to confusion to anger. "Did she tell you that?"

"Look, Bree, I know you mean well, but Dani isn't going

to dance. She. . ." He turned away from her and walked to the mirrored wall. "Dani's disability prevents her from doing the normal things a lot of other kids can do. But Dani. . ." Another sigh escaped and he closed his eyes. He massaged the bridge of his nose. "She doesn't understand."

"I guess that makes two of us." She wanted to set his mind at ease. "Dani can dance, Lucas, if she wants to."

"She can't!"

The words were flung at her with such vehemence, she stepped back, startled. She slapped a hand over her mouth.

"Dani can't be exposed to kids who will make fun of her. She'll think they're laughing with her but they're really laughing at her." He swung around, his eyes skewing hers. She was seeing a side of him she didn't think she'd ever see. Lucas pulled his hands from his pockets. "Why would I put my daughter through that kind of humiliation? Why?"

"I—I'm sorry. I didn't realize—"

"That's the point, Bree. You didn't realize. You don't know what it's like to have a child with disabilities. A child who wants to be normal, but is restricted by her. . ." He shook his head. "I don't want to talk about it." He thrust a hand through his hair. "We'll finish this another day. I can't do this right now."

She was afraid to say a single word. She wanted to console him, but knew it was the last thing Lucas wanted or needed from her. Lucas grumbled then strode to the door in a rush.

"I need to leave."

"Lucas, wait. Let's talk this out." She followed him to the reception area. Why did she have to ruin a good time by mentioning something that would obviously make Lucas angry? She didn't know him as well as she thought. His hand was on the knob of the front door. She rushed to him. "Lucas."

He spun around. "I know you mean well, Bree, but, I don't want to talk about it." He opened the door and stepped out. She followed him, desperate to make amends and spend time together. He shook his head and put up a hand, letting her know he didn't want her following him. He ran across the street to his truck, which was parked in front of the bakery. She watched him with tears in her eyes.

Eight

Lucas glanced in his rearview mirror and cringed. Bree stood on the sidewalk looking at him with despair and hurt. He wanted to hop out and apologize for his attitude, but he stayed in his truck, turned the key, and when it was clear, he pulled out onto Main Street, leaving Bree behind.

Why did she have to mention Dani wanting to dance? He knew his daughter had a dream of dancing. But, like all little girls, most of the dreams they had as kids were nothing more than that—dreams. She was too young to understand human nature and how people can be cruel. Most didn't understand those who had disabilities, and how difficult it could be on the families. Sometimes, it tore families apart. Marriages broke up. Although Dani's disability was minor compared to some other children, he still couldn't bear to see other kids tease her, belittle her, humiliate her. It would tear his heart out. And he didn't know if he could handle his temper if he ever witnessed Dani being bullied. That would send him over the edge for sure and he'd most likely end up in jail. No, he had to protect Dani. He slammed his hand against the steering wheel.

Maybe he'd go out to the tavern tonight and hang out with the guys. Blow off some steam. Dance with anyone but Bree. And, if Bree happened to show up there, he'd have to ignore her. Yeah, right! What the hell had he gotten himself into? He couldn't ignore the woman who was running the studio. But, she didn't call the shots. Her aunt did.

Deciding he needed some music to calm his anger, he switched on the radio. A groan slipped out. It was the song they had danced to last week. *Perfect.* He had never expected to see Bree back in town. Had never expected her to be at the tavern that night, and he had never thought he would've been dancing with her. And a slow song too.

He replayed the dance in his mind. He held her close, feeling her heart thundering against his chest. He had felt her nervousness as he pulled her closer to him, but as they danced, swaying in time to the ballad, it was as if they had danced this way many times before, always in step, always heart to heart. He never wanted the music to end, but like all good things, it did come to an end.

It was odd he never felt that way towards Daniella. Something about Bree held him, no matter how angry she had made him. He knew he wouldn't stay angry at her for long. And then he realized, he wasn't really mad at her. He was mad at himself, because whenever he saw her, he wanted to kiss her senseless, wanted to hold her and never let her go. And that made him feel guilty. And the guilt made him angry. None of it had been Bree's fault.

He pulled into the drive of his parents' home and got out of the car. He debated on whether he should call Bree and apologize but instead, he got out of the truck and headed toward the house. The moment he entered, Dani ran toward him, her arm outstretched, her injured arm lifting up and out at the elbow. Dani didn't realize she was disabled. She didn't know she had limitations. What five year old would?

"Daddy!" She flung herself into his arms and he hugged her close, breathing in her sweetness.

"Hi Pumpkin. Did you have a good day?"

Her head bobbed and she grinned. "Yup. Gramma and I had lots of fun. We went to the park and got an ice cream too!"

He stood and smoothed his hand down her curly brown hair. She was a miniature version of Daniella. "I guess you did have a fun day. Did Gramma behave herself?"

Dani tilted her head back and laughed. "You're silly, Daddy."

"I know." He playfully swatted her bottom. "Go wash

your hands. It's almost time to eat."

"Okay, Daddy." She skipped away, heading to the bathroom.

He shrugged off his jacket then opened the closet door and hung his coat up. A whiff of his mother's homemade spaghetti sauce floated toward him, and he inhaled. No one could make sauce like his mother. Like a bloodhound, he followed the scent to the kitchen where he found his mother cutting up veggies for a salad.

"Hi Mom."

"Hi Lucas."

"Sure smells good in here." He grabbed a glass from the cabinet. "You know, I may never leave. Who's going to feed me when I move out?"

His mother laughed, not taking her gaze off the tomato she sliced. "Your next wife will cook for you."

He filled the glass with water from the tap and turned, leaning against the counter. "And where am I going to find another woman who can cook like you?"

She shrugged. "I'm sure she's out there. You just have to find her."

He had found the woman he wanted but wasn't sure if marriage would ever be in the cards for him again. He was tired of being hurt and tired of people hurting Dani.

"You weren't out long. I thought you were going for coffee with a friend?"

"I did, but she—"

"She? The same woman you had dinner with the other night?"

He nodded. "Yeah. I met with Bree Thompson, the new owner of the studio."

"Ohhh," his mother sang out. "Merry tells me a lot about her. She sounds like a nice person."

"She is."

"So, what's the problem?" His mother added the tomatoes to the salad.

"She's decided to make some changes to the studio."

"What kind of changes?"

"She wants to have handicap access, which is fine, but, she also . . ."

His mother looked at him, a crease forming between her eyes. "Also. . .what?" She prodded, as she started to slice a cucumber.

"She asked if Dani was interested in dancing."

Just as he thought, his mother smiled broadly. "Really?"

He snatched a piece of cucumber. "I told her I wasn't interested in Dani taking lessons."

"You did? Why?"

"You know why, Mom." Was his mother going to beg him to let Dani dance as well? Wasn't there anybody on his side who understood how he felt?

"Lucas," she said, wiping her hands on the kitchen towel. She turned to face him. "What are you afraid of?"

"I think you know the answer to that one, Mom." He grabbed a piece of tomato.

"Tell me. I want to hear the words, Lucas."

"I don't want her to be bullied." There, he said it. The words soured his stomach.

His mother gave him one of her half-smiles. The one which told him she knew more than him. She knew what was best for him. "Dani wants to dance." She sighed and looked away.

"But what if the other kids laugh at her because she can't do the right steps. What if they mimic her movements, making her look like a chicken dancing." An image of Dani dancing with one arm flapping up and down made him cringe. Now he knew what the problem was. The kids would laugh, point at her and make her cry. His heart ached at the thought.

"You can't protect her all the time. We all love her, Lucas, but we have to let her go someday."

"I know that, Mom, but I don't have to let her go now, do I? She's only five and it's my duty to protect her. I need to protect her!" His words came out harsh, angry. He looked at his mother who stared at him, her mouth open, her eyes wide.

"Daddy?"

"What!" He spun around. She let out a cry and ran from the kitchen.

"Lucas!" His mother slapped the knife on the counter and started after Dani.

"No, Mom." He thrust a hand through his hair, spiking it up. "I'll go to her." His voice softened, to reassure his mother he wouldn't yell at Dani.

"Apologize to her."

He pressed the bridge of his nose and inhaled deeply. He couldn't believe he had just snapped like a crazy man to his daughter. He walked into her room and found her lying on her side on the bed, crying into her favorite stuffed animal, Bubbles. It had been the last gift Daniella had bought her.

He scooted next to her and rubbed her back. "Dani, I'm sorry."

"You scared me, Daddy." She stroked the fluffy pink elephant and whimpered. "I don't like it when you yell at me."

"I know, honey. I'm sorry." Her heart beat like hummingbird's wings, through the palm of his hand. His heart ached.

"Why'd you get mad at me?" She turned to face him, and his hand dropped to the mattress. He smoothed the sheet, thinking of how to explain it to her.

"I'm not mad at you, Pumpkin." He blew out a breath. "I'm mad at me."

"How can you be mad at you? That's silly." Her crying had subsided to a sniffle, and she wiped her good arm across her nose.

"Because adults sometimes act silly and do stupid things." He put a hand to her shoulder and nudged her toward him. "Come sit in my lap."

She wiped her eyes with the palm of her hand and

scrambled into his lap. He leaned his chin on the top of her head and rocked her. She closed her eyes.

"Daddy?"

"Yeah?"

"Are you mad at the lady who's your friend?"

He smiled. "No, I'm not mad at Bree." He stroked her hair and continued to rock her. It reminded him of when she had been a baby before the tragedy, when everything was right with the world.

"Daddy?"

"Yeah?"

"I heard you talkin' to Gramma."

"You did?"

She nodded, bumping his chin lightly. "I was done washin' my hands and I wanted to help Gramma."

"And what did you hear?"

"That you don't want me to dance." She looked up at him, her dark eyes swimming with unshed tears. Her mouth quivered. She looked so vulnerable right now. He had to protect her. If anything happened to her, he'd never forgive himself.

"I wanna dance, Daddy. Please?"

He closed his eyes and hugged her close. How could he fight this? He'd talk to Bree and get her opinion. After all, she was the pro. "Let me talk to Bree first and if she's okay with it, then. . .okay, I'll let you dance."

"Yay!"

He hugged her again and grinned when she wrapped her arms around him and kissed him on the cheek. How he loved her little girl kisses. Now, he had to talk to Bree and have her reassure him he was doing the right thing.

* * * *

Bree stood by the big kitchen table after cleaning up from supper and looked down at the pink box which held the cupcakes Lucas had bought that afternoon. She had waited most of the afternoon to see if he'd call or stop by. She didn't want to toss them out and went back and forth wondering if she should text him and find out what he wanted to to. She hoped he'd want to swing by and pick them up. She wanted a chance to talk to him. She grabbed her phone, clicked on his name and started a text.

Hey, it's me. I've got your cupcakes. Should I bring them by?

She waited for the three dots to jump around, but no response. After a few minutes, she gave up and decided if he really wanted to talk to her, he'd text her, or call. She wondered what her friends were up to. She hadn't seen them in a week, and she really wanted to get together. She glanced at her phone, hoping Lucas would text her back, but he was obviously still upset with her. She set the phone on the table and walked to the fridge. Her phone rang. Lucas! She headed back to the table and glanced at the phone. She smiled and answered. "Hey, Chloe!"

"Hi. You busy?"

"No. Just sitting around. What's up?"

"Jamie texted me and wants to get together. She's depressed. She thought it'd be fun to hang out, have some wine, and complain about the men in our lives. I'm all for it. My mom offered to babysit, so I'm free."

"Great. What time?"

"Now. Bring yourself. No need to bring anything else."

"Sounds good. See you soon."

"See you soon," Chloe acknowledged.

She ended the call and smiled, feeling like a part of the crowd now. Her friends hadn't forgotten about her or ignored her. If anything, she had ignored them. She had allowed her career to stand in the way of her friendships and her family. She would never allow that to happen again.

She decided to text Lucas one more time. She flung her phone in her purse a minute later when he still hadn't responded. Aunt Merry and her father came into the kitchen from the back door, laughing. It was good to see her Dad laughing again. “Hey guys. You’re happy.”

“Your father shared one of his ridiculous jokes with me.”

She grinned. “I’m sure it was very funny.”

Her aunt rolled her eyes, heading for the sink.

“It was,” her father called out as he headed toward the living room, most likely to settle down and watch the Red Sox game.

“I’m heading out.” She grabbed her purse and the box of cupcakes from the table.

“Ohhh, a date with Lucas?” her aunt sang out as she washed her hands.

She wished. “No, I’m meeting up with the girls. We’re having a girl's night. Wine, movies and talking about men.”

“Sounds like fun,” Aunt Merry said, swinging her gaze back to her. “Everything okay? Something else bothering you?”

She shrugged. She really didn’t want to talk about it. “No, everything’s fine.” She kissed her aunt on the cheek. “Don’t worry.”

“Alright then. Have fun.”

“I will,” she said, as she headed down the short hallway to the back door. She walked to her car, slid into the driver’s seat and set the cupcake box on the passenger seat. Should she swing by Lucas’s? She shook her head. He’d probably throw the box at her. His attitude still bothered her. Hanging out with her friends would help her get over her depression. And, the girls would love Chloe’s cupcakes.

An hour later, she was sitting on the sofa in Jamie's living room, drinking a glass of wine and laughing at Grace's lame jokes.

"I think we should turn on Hallmark and have ourselves a binge-watching session. We can compare our love lives with those on TV," Grace said, reaching for a chip. "I mean, isn't that why we're here?"

"Hey, I love Hallmark!" Kris remarked. "I'm game."

"I have all day and night. We can binge watch Hallmark into the wee hours of the morning and get thoroughly depressed," Jamie said then took a swig of her wine.

"Don't you have to work?" She asked Jamie, glancing at her from the opposite side of the couch.

"No. Day off. I take Mondays off now."

"To recuperate from her Saturday nights and lack of sleep on Sundays," Chloe added, smirking and smacking Jamie on the arm.

"Hey, I can't help it if I enjoy my weekends, although getting up on Sunday mornings is tough. Going to bed at midnight and getting up at four in the morning doesn't work for me."

The girls giggled and Jamie picked up the remote, clicking it to the Hallmark channel. For a little while they were quiet. The only sounds were the munching of chips and popcorn and the clink of wine glasses.

"I wish my love life was like that," Kris said with a sigh.

"You don't have a love life," Grace said, tossing a popcorn kernel at her.

"You're right, but if I did, I'd want it to be like that."

"We're all pretty pathetic, you know that? Not one of us is in a relationship." Jamie said then glanced at her. "Except for you, Bree."

She blinked. "What? Me?"

"Yeah, you. Don't act so innocent. I've seen you with Lucas. You're dating him, aren't you?"

She laughed, or rather barked out a sarcastic laugh. "No. Lucas and I are not dating." She bit into a chip and chewed slowly to avoid answering questions.

"But you two looked like you were interested in one another when you were in the diner last week," Jamie said, twirling the stem of her wine glass in her hand. "I saw the look in Lucas's eyes."

"And, you two looked like you were on a date when you came into the bakery this morning," Chloe added. "By the way, why is that box of Lucas's cupcakes sitting on Jamie's table?"

She inhaled. "Well, Lucas and I stopped at the studio, and we had a . . .disagreement." She took a swallow of her wine. The girls said nothing and looked at her. "He left in a hurry, leaving the cupcakes behind."

"Did you text him? You could've met up with him and made up." Kris smirked, lifting her wine glass.

"I did text him. A couple of times. He's ignoring me. As far as I'm concerned, he's acting like a jerk right now." She took a hefty swallow of her wine.

"What did he do?" Jamie asked. "He had to have been pretty angry to ignore your texts."

"We were talking about the changes I want to make to the studio, and then I mentioned how Dani wants to dance." She needed more wine. She pushed her hair back. "He got angry. Told me I didn't have a clue what it was like to raise a child with a disability and that Dani was *not* going to dance." She sighed and and emptied the glass.

"Ouch," Chloe said.

"So, what was his reasoning?" Kris grabbed a chip from the bowl.

"He thinks the kids will make fun of her and, obviously, he doesn't want that."

"He is overly protective of his daughter," Jamie added, leaning toward the coffee table to grab some chips as well. "Although I'm not a parent, I can understand his way of thinking." She bit the chip in half. "But, I think he's too over-protective. He needs to let Dani be a kid."

She felt the anger bubbling up. "I can't believe he'd think I would allow the other students to bully her. That hurt. It stung."

"I can see why." Chloe said. "But I wouldn't worry about it. He'll come around."

She admired Chloe's positive outlook. "I hope you're right."

"I agree with Chloe," Jamie added. "I can tell by the way he looks at you. He's not going to give up. He's just being stubborn."

"You have quite the imagination, Jamie," she said. But, if she were honest, she'd have to agree with her friend. There had been something between her and Lucas, but she wasn't so sure now.

"By the way, Bree, how's that handsome brother of yours doing?" Jamie asked, tossing her a conspiratorial look.

She knew Jamie had always had a thing for her brother, Brett. Jamie had always made comments to her through their childhood years and especially during high school how cute Brett was. She remembered Jamie asking her if he liked her and to get him to ask her out on a date. Bree couldn't do it. She knew her brother would scoff and had no plans on dating any of *her friends.* He told her outright that if he dated any of her friends, they'd be telling her all about it and he didn't need his sister knowing about his 'love life.'

"He's doing fine. I haven't talked to him since I came back to town."

"Well, I'm sure he's busy fighting fires and rescuing cute little kittens out of trees."

"Or, maybe he's performing CPR on some gorgeous woman who faked a choking episode!" This came from Grace. She also thought Brett was cute, but she didn't want to date him. She always thought of Brett as a brother.

They laughed, ignoring the movie for a little while.

"Bree," Jamie started. "If you talk to him, let him know I still think about him."

"Sure, Jamie," she said. "I'll make sure it's the first thing I mention when I text him." She needed to talk to her brother soon though. She missed him. He was a year older than her, actually only eleven months. They were 'Irish twins' her mother had said. Maybe he could give her some advice on how to handle her situation. And she didn't mean Lucas either. Her brother always had a way of showing her the brighter and more logical side of things. Would he convince her to try out for the dance company in New Hampshire or convince her to stay in Misty River?

"How's the studio coming along?" Kris asked, pouring more wine into her glass.

“It’s coming along nice. Should be done in a couple of weeks, I think.” She reached out for the bottle and Kris handed it to her. She poured the last of it into her glass. "We need more."

"No worries, Bree. I have plenty," Jamie said and stood. She headed to the kitchen. "Watch the movie. No talking. I don't want to miss anything," she called out from the kitchen.

“And how is Devon? Is he working or slacking off?” Kris asked. She noticed the flush edging Kris’s face.

“Devon’s a wonderful worker. No need to remind him to keep his nose to the grindstone.”

“Good. That’s what I like about him. He gives one hundred percent to anything he pursues.”

“Does that include women?” Jamie teased.

Kris gave a half-hearted laugh. “You’re just jealous, Jamie. And I believe Devon would give his all in a relationship.”

She had to agree with Kris. Devon seemed the type to fight for the woman he loved and stand by her side.

The girls sat silent, doing as Jamie suggested. The couple on screen vowed their love for one another and kissed. They smiled, oohed and ahhed as Jamie came back into the room, bearing another bottle of wine.

"Did I miss anything?" she asked as she set the bottle on the coffee table then sat back in her corner of the couch.

"Nope," Grace answered. "Just a couple deeply in love, vowing to stay together forever and sealed their promise with a kiss. Ahh, sweet love." She splayed her hands over her heart and pretended to swoon. "If only that happened in real life."

"I think it can," she said. "I believe people can have that kind of love." She glanced at each of her friends who looked at her as though she was crazy. She lifted the bottle and poured the deep red wine into her glass. She set the bottle down and glanced at Kris who shook her head.

"We'd all like that kind of love." Kris said. "I still haven't found the man of my dreams, but I'm hoping." She crossed her fingers.

"Me too," Grace said with a sigh. "Isn't it every girl's dream to find a man like that?" She tilted her head to the TV where, at that moment, the couple strolled among cherry trees holding hands. "My parents fell in love at first sight and will be celebrating their thirty-fourth wedding anniversary next spring. Can you imagine being married to someone that long?"

She shrugged. "I think my parents would still be married if Mom hadn't passed away. Dad never dated. He said my mother was the only woman for him and he'd never get remarried."

"See? That's true love," Grace said. "I think my parents have been married close to forty years."

"My parents have been married for a long time, too," Jamie added. "Thirty-two years, I think. Dad ran the diner with my grandfather, and Mom stayed home with us. I think she helped with the accounts for the diner."

"There are three of us with parents who have been married for over thirty years. See? It can happen! We just have to find our soul-mates," Grace said.

Jamie winked at her. "I found mine. He just doesn't know it, yet."

She smirked while her friends laughed. "How awkward would it be for you to date my brother? I can't have any of my friends dating my brother. Ewww!"

"You never know," Kris said. "When love finds you, you can't stop it. Even if it happens to be one of your friends."

"Well, I'm warning my brother to stay away from all of you," she stated, her eyes narrowing as she looked at each friend.

"I propose a toast," Grace said, lifting her wine glass.

"Kris, fill your glass. We can't have a toast with an empty glass."

Kris filled her wine glass, then lifted it.

"Here's hoping we all find wonderful men to fall in love with," Grace said as all the girls touched their glasses to one another. "Here. Here."

While the girls laughed and talked about their future, she let her mind drift to a man whom she thought could be her soulmate. But didn't you know your soulmate the moment your eyes met? Weren't you supposed to get that 'I'm going to marry that girl or guy' feeling the moment you meet each other? She had felt that way. Back in high school when she had first met Lucas. She had known then he was the one she would marry. But she had been more interested in dancing than marriage. Still was, to a degree. But the more she thought about it, she wondered if she could hang up her ballet shoes and settle down.

Nine

Sunday morning found Bree stumbling to the kitchen, bleary-eyed and in need of coffee, bad. She had a horrible headache, thanks to drinking too much red wine. And it didn't help that thoughts of Lucas's angry face swirling around in her head over and over with him leaving her in a wake of dust had caused her to have too little sleep. She groaned and slumped in the chair. Coffee would have to wait a minute.

"How'd you sleep?" Aunt Merry asked from her seat at the table. "You look terrible."

"Geez, thanks. Remind me to give you the same compliment when you feel like crap."

"And we're cranky too," her father added from the opposite end of the table. "Too much to drink?"

She nodded and stood. "When will I ever learn that red wine gives me a migraine." She yawned then moved to the Keurig machine tucked in the corner of the counter. She leaned in and checked the level of water. It was half-way, so she grabbed a cup from the cupboard, stuck it on the stand and then added a cup of Columbian coffee. She needed something stronger than her usual hazelnut or french vanilla. Once the machine gurgled and the rich, dark coffee poured into her mug, she heaved a sigh and leaned back against the counter. "God, I slept terrible."

"I can tell." Her aunt said as she took a sip of her coffee, peering at her over the rim.

"Men," Bree answered back.

"Oh-Oh. Fight with Lucas?" her father asked, setting his fork down and lifting his mug.

"Yeah. Kind of. We had a misunderstanding, that's all."

She turned to get her mug off the machine. She set it aside then walked to the fridge to get the creamer. She went through the motions of making her coffee. "I don't even know what happened."

"Tell me. Maybe I can figure it out," Aunt Merry encouraged, patting the chair next to her.

She walked to the table and plunked herself into the chair, resting her elbows on the table. "I met Lucas at the bakery, and then we took a walk. We ended up at the studio. She took a sip of the coffee and groaned. "God, this is just what I need." She took another. Aunt Merry waited patiently for her to continue while she sipped her own coffee.

"And I mentioned that Dani wants to dance." She leaned on an elbow. "That's all I said."

"You must've hit a nerve. Some men are very protective of their daughters." Aunt Merry glanced at her father and winked. He pretended he wasn't listening, but his mouth tilted up in the corner.

"He said Dani only thinks she wants to dance but can't." Another sigh spilled forth. "He's afraid the kids will make fun of her. I tried to reassure him that I wouldn't let that happen, but he was insistent Dani wasn't going to dance."

"That was it?"

"Pretty much." She didn't want to admit it to herself that the little bit of feelings developing between them had probably disappeared in that moment. "God, why can't I keep my mouth shut?"

"You didn't say anything wrong, Bree. Don't let it eat you up inside."

"Your aunt's right," her father added. "If he's going to be that thick-headed then he's not worth hanging around for."

"You're right." She smoothed a finger around the edge of her mug. "Dani wants to dance though. She has the same spark I had at that age."

"But doesn't she have a disability?" Aunt Merry questioned, wrapping her hands around her mug.

"Yeah, but she can still dance, with limitations, of course. Lucas should at least give her a chance. If he doesn't' let her try, how will she know what she's capable of?"

"Sounds to me, like you need to be saying this to Lucas," her father added.

She shot a glance at her father. "You're right." She slapped her hand on the table. "I will. As soon as he feels like talking to me."

Aunt Merry laughed. "He'll talk to you. Probably sooner than you realize." She winked. "So, what are your plans for the day?"

She shrugged. "Now that the studio is half-way to being done, and I've already ordered business cards, I think it's time I created a website or a blog. I was hoping Anna could help me."

"I'm sure she will. Didn't she say she'd help you with the business side of things?" Aunt Merry asked.

"Yeah, she did." She sat up straighter. "I'll call her and see what her ideas are." She picked up her coffee mug. "Right now, I need caffeine. Lots of it."

Several minutes later, she was settled at the desk, with a fresh cup of coffee, looking through her emails. As she read through them, one in particular stood out. It was from an up and coming company in Philadelphia. She had sent them her resume' three months ago, when she had been recuperating and knew she wasn't going back to the San Francisco Ballet Company. She clicked on the email and started reading.

We have reviewed your resume' and find you to be a wonderful and talented individual for whom we are interested in talking to. We'd like to do a phone interview at your convenience, the sooner the better due to a busy upcoming season. If the interview goes well, we'll notify you of a time where you can come to our studio and audition for us. Please email us with any questions you may have and a time we can do the interview. As always, thank you for your interest our company. Sincerely, Margo Delacroix

Yes! Finally, a response to the handful of resume's she had

sent out eight weeks ago. Her day just got better. She emailed Margo, stating she could talk any day and any time, at their convenience. She reiterated how much she would love to dance for their company and for the opportunity for an interview. She then hit *Send* and crossed her fingers.

With a dance in her heart, she read through her other emails. Nothing of importance and most were spam. But at least she had heard from one company. So far. The only thing that could make this day even better would be to get a text or a call from Lucas.

A half-hour later, she was showered and dressed. She grabbed her phone and started to call Anna to see when they could meet and talk about creating a web site, when her heart thudded. What was she doing? The studio would be done in a couple of weeks or so and she may have an interview soon as well. She couldn't do both. Since reading the email, she now had second thoughts about the studio. Why was she doing all this if she was planning on interviewing and perhaps auditioning for another company? She couldn't run a business here and perform elsewhere.

When she had sent out her resume's, she had been living in San Francisco, but knew she'd be heading home. The little studio in her small hometown of Misty River hadn't been on her mind. God, what had she gotten herself into? Her moment of happiness vanished in an instant, replaced with worry and frustration.

Aunt Merry stepped into the room. One glance at her and her aunt frowned. "Oh-oh, what's wrong?"

She looked at Aunt Merry, wondering how to explain it all. "I got an email from a company in Philadelphia."

"A dance company?"

"Yeah. They want to do a phone interview as soon as possible and, if they like me, they want me to audition."

Aunt Merry's face fell. "What?" She sat on the edge of the bed.

"I had sent out resume's weeks ago and I honestly didn't

think I'd hear from anyone after being here for a month. I figured I was a 'has-been."

"So, what are you going to do now?"

She shrugged again, confused and overwhelmed. "I.. .I don't know, Aunt Merry. I really don't know." Maybe she'd flip a coin. Didn't that work in resolving problems?

"Well," her aunt started, reaching for her hand. "I think you need to do some soul-searching but, if I were you, I'd stay in town. You've got friends and family here, the studio is getting renovated, so it'll be a better place to teach kids and adults, and you've met a great guy. What's there to decide?" Aunt Merry patted her hand, the same way she had done when she had been a young child and was anxious about a test or meeting someone new. "I think you know the answer."

She squeezed her aunt's hand. "I need to think about this." She stood and walked away from her aunt. "Right now, I'm going to the studio to work off some stress. I need to move my body and dance. I've been lazy since I haven't had to practice every day."

"I hope it helps." Her aunt stood and headed for the door. "See you later, then."

"See ya."

A half-hour later, she stood at the barre, stretching and prepping for a routine she had imagined on her way over. After warming up, she set up her cell phone to the blue-tooth speakers. She scrolled through her long list of music titles and clicked on one of her favorites. As the music started, she strode to the center of the floor and struck the fifth position. As the music drifted around her, she danced. She spun in pirouettes. She leaped and twirled and did everything she had done in the show *Swan Lake* before getting injured. When the routine was finished, which was just a warm up for her, she clicked on the music she wanted for the dance she had created in her mind.

As she moved around the dance floor, she felt freer than

she had in a long time. The stress flowed away. She emptied her mind of anything negative and focused on the music. Dancing always took her to another plateau where negativity and stress didn't exist. She ended with a pas de chat. She found herself stopping in front of the mirror. She was out of breath, more than she should be, but did it feel good! Her body vibrated with energy now and her spirits lifted. She beamed in the mirror, then shrieked when loud clapping resounded. Her heart slammed into her throat.

* * * *

Lucas clapped and Bree jumped.

Her hand slapped against her chest. "Lucas! My God, you scared me half to death!"

"I'm sorry, Bree." He started toward her, but she moved away. "I didn't mean to scare you. I knocked, but you didn't hear me."

"It's not your fault." She walked over to the speakers and turned it off. She then walked to a small bag and reached in, removing a bottle of water and a small towel. She opened the water bottle and took a long drink, then she wiped her neck and her brow. He wondered if she was still upset with him. She was stand-offish. "What are you doing here?" She blew out a breath, swirling some straggling tendrils of hair on her forehead and ears. "I figured you wouldn't want to speak to me for a while." She took another swallow of water, then set it down by the towel. She turned to face him.

He squirmed inside. She didn't act angry, but she was treating him as an employee. She wasn't as outgoing as she had been the other day. What did he expect anyway? For her to run into this arms? No, although that would've been nice. "I actually want to apologize for yesterday. I shouldn't have said what I did."

She padded across the floor and lifted a leg to the barre. "I was only trying to help." She leaned forward, stretching her arms toward her ankles.

He walked to the barre and stopped a few feet away from her. "I know you were. I. . ." He swept a hand across the back of his neck and looked sideways at her. What should he say? He was suddenly at a loss for words. "I talked to Dani, after getting some sound advice from my mother, and told her that I would consider signing her up for classes after I got your opinion."

"My opinion?" She stopped stretching and moved her leg from the barre.

"Yeah. I want to know," he huffed out a breath. "I want to make sure you won't allow the other children to bully her. I can't—I won't allow the other kids to humiliate her."

"Lucas, I would never allow any child to bully Dani or any other child in class. It cannot and will not be tolerated. You have my word."

He should've known Bree would have Dani's best interests at heart. Why had he been an idiot and thought otherwise? "Dani wants so much to dance, but I just want to keep her safe at home. I'm afraid to let her into the world and experience the danger it holds." He gave a short laugh. "I was thinking of hiring a tutor when she starts school next year, because I'm so afraid of what the students will do."

"Keeping her home isn't going to help her, Lucas. You must know that."

He inhaled as she stepped closer to him. Her forehead glistened and her dark hair shone bright under the lights. "I know, but it's hard to let go." He twisted away from her. "I lost Daniella; I can't lose Dani. It's my fault, you know."

She took a step closer and touched his shoulder. He turned around, his fingers pressed against his eyes.

"Hey, it's going to be alright, Lucas. I promise." She wrapped her arms around him, holding him close. She nestled her head against his shoulder. He felt her heart fluttering like a hummingbird's wings against his chest. She lifted her head from his shoulder and looked up at him. His heart stuttered. The coppery-brown depths darkened as he cupped her jaw.

She sucked in a breath as he lowered his face to hers. He pressed his lips against hers. Her hands came up and curled in his hair. He groaned and pulled her closer. He should stop, but he couldn't. They kissed until the need for air pulled them apart. Lucas pressed his forehead against hers and smiled. She entwined her fingers behind his head and returned his smile. "Wanna dance?"

"I'd love to."

He didn't let go of her. Instead, he swayed his hips to and fro urging her to follow his lead. He still had his forehead pressed against hers. Her dark eyes crinkled up at him. He straightened an arm out and tugged one of hers from the back of his neck. He entwined his fingers in hers. His other arm clasped her around her tiny waist. She relaxed against him, and he heard her sigh. He danced with her to invisible music, and she followed his lead as though they had always danced together. He did a few spins and she laughed, tilting her head back. He ended the dance with a low dip. She leaned back, her head mere inches above the floor, her leg sticking out. She grinned as he brought her back up against his chest.

"Wow. I'm impressed, Lucas! I didn't think you could dance. . .like that."

"I'm no slouch on the dance floor."

"You didn't dance like that at the tavern."

"No. I didn't. There wasn't enough room and besides, I didn't want the other guys to be jealous."

"Or have all the women swooning at your feet," she added.

"That too." He leaned down, hoping for another kiss, but she pulled back and he let her go. He didn't want to push it. Maybe he should leave before he did something he'd regret.

"I was wondering if you'd want to have dinner sometime soon. At my parents."

She smiled again, tilting her head. "Is that why you danced with me? To butter me up so I'd say yes?"

"Did it work?"

She laughed and he grinned in return. This is how he wanted to be with her. All the time.

"Well, it worked. Yes, I'll have dinner with you."

"Great! Dani will be so excited." He stepped closer to her. It was so hard to walk away. "It's pasta night on Wednesday and my mother makes one hell of a sauce."

"Alright then. Wednesday it is."

"Okay. I'll see you then."

"See you then."

He couldn't help it. He pulled her close and planted another firm kiss on her mouth. He didn't linger but wanted her to know it wouldn't be the last one. As he walked away, he could see her touching her mouth. He smiled.

Ten

Lucas arrived early with Devon on Tuesday morning excited to start work on Bree's office. He really wanted to make this perfect for her. After leaving her yesterday, he couldn't get the kiss off his mind. Slowly, but surely, he was falling for her, and he believed Bree felt the same. He was hoping she'd stop by sometime today to see him, but he also hoped she wouldn't. He was afraid if he took one look at her, he'd make up some kind of excuse not to finish the job and take off with her for the rest of the day. No, he had to focus on work and not on Bree.

He and Devon had just finished taping the walls as well as around the windows which had taken them a couple of hours to complete. Now, it was time to paint the office and transform it into Bree's personal space.

"When did you tell her we'd be done with the renovations?" Devon asked as he brought in cans of paint.

"I didn't give her an exact date. Just told her we were hoping to have the studio finished in a couple of weeks."

Devon nodded. "Should work. We're more than half-way done. As long as we don't find any other problems."

"I checked out the basement yesterday before we carried the boxes down there. I didn't see anything wrong. Considering it hasn't been used for a few years, the place isn't that bad."

"No, it's not. Thank God for small miracles," Devon said, as he set a can of paint on a worktable.

He grabbed a roller as Devon poured the teal-colored paint in the pan. He and Devon had a routine when they worked together. They knew what the other wanted before it was even asked. They could anticipate each other's moves like two well-trained dancers—flowing and moving with the rhythm of the music, but in their case, it was the 'music' of the skill-saw.

"Some of the guys are getting together to play cards tomorrow. You interested?" Devon asked as he applied paint to the roller.

"Bree's coming over for dinner. I'll have to pass."

"Whoa. Where did this come from? I thought we were working for her. I didn't think you were dating our client."

He hadn't realized it, but he guessed they were dating. Did Bree think the same? "I guess we are. And, we're not technically working for Bree. We're working for her aunt."

"Okay then. Whatever makes it work for you," Devon replied, applying the paint to the wall. "Hm. I remember how much you'd talk about Bree back in high school. I think you only hung out with her brother to have an excuse to see her." He chuckled. "You thought you were such a bad boy and Bree would fall for you." Devon said making quote marks in the air.

"Hey, I was cool, man."

"Sure. Keep believing that, cuz."

Lucas thought back to the days of high school, remembering how he wanted to be the 'bad boy' to impress the ladies. He heard, through friends, that the pretty girls really liked a bad boy. So, when he started going to Bree's house a few times a week with her brother, he couldn't help but notice the cute brunette who was a little too skinny for him. He would watch her from the corner of his eye when no one thought he had been looking and he'd catch glimpses of her in her home studio doing stretches, leg lifts and twirls. There was a French name for it, but he couldn't remember.

When he had caught her checking him out, he had quickly looked away or he would give her a look as though to tell her to back off. He had wanted to ask her out so many times, yet he hadn't wanted to offend his best friend. Eventually, he and Bree pretended neither one cared or even like the other one and they went their own ways after high school. He had graduated a year before her and immediately had gone to work for his father. He didn't visit as often as he had during school and then one day, Bree was gone. She had been accepted at an elite ballet school. Her dream had come true. He had only known of her dream to be a ballerina through her brother. He had always thought she danced because she liked it. Well, she not only liked it, she loved it and had always planned on being a star on the stage and traveling all over the world.

"Hey, you gonna work or daydream the shift away," Devon said, nudging him on the backside as he passed Lucas.

"I'm thinking."

"And I bet it's about a pretty brunette who happens to be our boss, sort of, and may get upset if she knows you're slacking off."

"Nah. Bree isn't like that."

"So, you are getting to know her better," Devon said, smirking over his shoulder toward him. "Maybe I should let her know you're not doing your part."

"Sure, you do that, Dev." He grinned and turned away, sticking the roller back in the pan. "I think we should bring in the crew."

Devon glanced at him. "They should be done in a few days. We could have them start on Monday. I'll call Joe and have them start next week. They should be done with the current job by Friday, if not sooner."

"Well, the sooner, the better. They're good men. Good workers."

Lucas and Devon worked steadily through the morning then headed to the tavern for lunch. When they got back to the studio, Lucas was surprised to find Bree standing in the office.

"I don't recognize the room anymore," Bree said, as she moved around the office. "And I can't believe how much you've done since this morning." She glanced at the newly painted walls. "I love the color. It looks a lot brighter, and bigger, already." She looked at him. "Do you guys need more help?"

"We have a crew who'll be here next week. They're finishing up another job which will be done in a couple of days," Lucas explained.

"You guys should be done with the studio fairly soon, I would think."

"Should be. I don't expect any problems to come up."

"Well, I wanted to see what the room looked like and, I was curious to see what you guys had already done." She started for the door. "We still on for tomorrow?"

"Sure are."

"I'm looking forward to it." Bree gave him a small wave. "See ya'"

"Bye." He waved back.

Devon chuckled behind him. "Bye."

After Bree left, Devon whistled. "Don't you two look cute, giving each other the sweet looks, as if you two were the only ones in the room. I saw how you two were looking at each other."

"We're friends, Dev. Just friends."

"Sure, Lucas. Keep saying that and you might convince yourself of it. But, I see more than that. A lot more."

He ignored his cousin and went about putting paint on the roller.

"She is one beautiful lady. What the heck does she see in you?" The room echoed with Devon's laughter.

* * * *

Bree wanted to make sure she looked her best when she met Lucas's parents. She decided on a pair of skinny jeans with black ankle boots and a lightweight copper jersey. The color brought out the flecks of gold in her eyes. She took her time putting on her makeup and doing her hair which she had curled in waves down to the middle of her back. Normally she would've had it shoulder length due to having to have it put up in a bun during her performances. The longer the hair, the bigger the knot and it made it too heavy for the head and most of the time, it caused headaches. She did a turn in front of the full-length mirror then headed downstairs.

She had talked to Lucas earlier and said he would pick her up at 4:30. She insisted she could drive to his place, but he insisted he had to be a gentleman. His parents would never forgive him if they found out he had allowed her to drive herself to their house. She waited patiently by the door and a moment later saw a car pull into the driveway. She had never seen it before and wondered who it could be. Someone for Aunt Merry? The door opened and a man stepped out. It was Lucas. She smiled. She had expected him to come in his truck. She opened the door as he came up the steps.

"Hi."

"Hi," she said in return. "Want to come in for a minute?"

"Sure." He stepped in and then darted his gaze around.

"Ah, you looking for something?"

"Yeah. The dog. Where is he?"

She laughed.

"Go ahead and laugh. He's big and nearly knocked me on my butt the last time I was here."

"Buster's in the kitchen, probably sleeping under my Dad's chair." She walked ahead of him into the kitchen where Aunt Merry was working at the stove and her father was reading the paper at the table.

"Hello, Mr. Thompson, Miss Thompson."

"Hi, Lucas." Aunt Merry sang out as she stirred something in a big pot.

"Hi, Lucas. Nice to see you." Her father stood and shook Lucas's hand which made Lucas smile and made her feel more relaxed. If she hadn't seen it with her own eyes, she never would've believed it. Her memories from the past still had her believing her father despised Lucas. Obviously, that had changed.

Buster scrambled up and lumbered over to Lucas who stepped back, his eyes round. She wanted to laugh but bit her lip instead. "Sit, Buster." The dog obeyed her and sat on his haunches, still looking up at Lucas. "Buster, you're scaring Lucas. Go lie down."

The dog whined, tossed his gaze between her and Lucas then settled down at Lucas's feet.

"He won't hurt you, Lucas," her father stated. "He's a big old teddy bear, aren't you, boy?"

Buster gave a quick bark, then nudged Lucas's hand. Again, she wanted to laugh when Lucas stiffened and lifted his hands to his pockets.

"He wants you to pet him," she said, leaning over and ruffling the top of the dog's head. "Go ahead. If you don't, he'll continue to stare you down and nudge your hand."

"Oh." Lucas slowly took his hand from his pocket and held it palm down over the top of Buster's head. "You sure he—?"

"I'm sure."

"Trust me when I say that Henry here will bite you before the dog ever does." Aunt Merry said as she covered the pot and wiped her hands. "The worse Buster will do is lick your hand off."

Her father tilted his head to her aunt. "She's right."

Lucas lowered his hand. She grinned when he actually petted Buster's head and the dog sat there, his tongue lolling out of his mouth.

"See? He's just a big puppy who wouldn't hurt a fly." She hugged the dog close and kissed him. The dog licked her face and the quick movement caused Lucas to inhale sharply and snap his hand back. Maybe after a few more visits with the dog, he'd relax around him. "You did good, Lucas." She stood and gave him a peck on the cheek. Her lips tingled when they made contact with his cropped beard.

"Well, we'd better get going. Mom's got supper waiting,"

Lucas said, bringing his arm around her waist.

She looked at her father to see his response. He smiled back and sat down. He slapped his knee and Buster ambled over then hunkered down under the chair. And all was back to normal. "I won't be out late."

"Have a good time," her father said, then picked up his paper.

"Tell your mom I said hello," Aunt Merry said as she reached into a cabinet.

"I will. Nice to see you two again," Lucas said as they turned and headed down the hall.

A moment later, they were at the car. He held the door open for her and she slid in, looking up at him with a smile. She buckled up as he got in the car, closed the door, and started it up. She thought she'd be more relaxed after seeing the interaction between her father and Lucas, but her nerves were on fire. She was meeting his parents for the first time, and she wondered what they would think of her. If this wasn't a sign of a date, nothing was. Didn't guys bring their dates to meet their parents when they were getting serious? Her heart did a few extra beats. Was Lucas getting serious about her?

Lucas expelled a sigh. "That went better than I expected."

She laughed. "Why?"

"First of all, I wasn't sure how your father would react to me and second, your dog is. . .big."

"But not ferocious and scary."

He grinned. "No. Not at all." He backed out of the drive and headed down the road. "I think I handled that quite well."

She patted his knee. "Wait until Buster really gets to know you." She was about to laugh out loud when he snapped his gaze to her, his eyes as round as saucers. She tended to laugh more when she was anxious.

"Nervous?"

"No."

"The tapping of your feet tells me a different story, and I don't have the radio on."

He was observant, she'd give him that. "Okay. A little." She brushed her hair back, another nervous habit.

"Don't be. They're good, down-to-earth people. Just like your father and aunt. They won't interrogate you, I promise, but I can't speak for Dani though. She's a chatterbox and will probably talk your ear off, if you let her."

She laughed, again. "I don't mind."

"Well, if she gets to be too much, I'll send her off to the den to watch a movie or to her room to chat with her dolls."

"Oh, you don't have to make her do that, Lucas. She's a part of the family and shouldn't be relegated to another room."

He shot her a glance and something in his eyes made her insides warm and turn to mush.

"You know, you're not like most women I've met, or even like Daniella." He glanced at her and smiled, then looked back to the road. "That was actually a compliment, although it came out wrong."

She smiled back. "Thanks."

"Daniella was a nervous wreck the first time she met my parents. But, after a while, she realized they had made her a part of the family."

"And the other women?"

"Oh. Yeah." He cleared his throat. "Well, I haven't really dated since Daniella passed. I've invited them over for dinner to meet Dani more than meeting my parents, but, because of Dani's disability, they were uncomfortable, I guess. The few I dated, couldn't connect with my daughter, and because of that, I didn't want to connect with them. As simple as that. Dani and I are a package deal. If you accept one, you have to accept the other." He peered over at her, his face solemn, serious.

"Dani's a wonderful girl. I can't imagine anyone not liking her or wanting to be around her."

"She's a great kid. And, she really likes you."

"Are you telling me that I'm a potential date?"

Again, he chuckled and her toes curled. God, she loved his laugh.

"Ahh, yeah. We can call this a date." He shot her a glance, and she wanted to laugh. He looked worried as though she was about to reject the idea.

"Okay then. We'll call this our first date."

He visibly relaxed, and while he steered the car with his left hand, he reached for hers with the other and entwined their fingers. His hand was big and warm and calloused. Definitely not a male dancer's hands which were strong, yet soft. "Our first date. Wow." He looked at her. "Unless you—"

"No. I'm glad we finally made it official." She squeezed his hand to reassure him, and he squeezed back. They fell into momentary silence, each in their own thoughts.

He turned into a driveway where a simple white Cape Cod home stood, similar to Anna's.

"Here we are."

After getting out of the car, he walked to her side and opened the door for her. She could get used to this, but most of the time she forgot and would already have the door opened before he got to it. They walked to the door and with each step, her nerves grew more taut. What if his parents didn't like her? What if they thought she was too good for him? Huh. Was she? After all, she was a star performer in the ballet world and, maybe they would think she was a celebrity of sorts and, maybe they would be uncomfortable around her. And, maybe she needed to calm her racing thoughts. Lucas opened the door. Breathe, Bree. Just breathe. She inhaled then smiled up at Lucas. He held her hand as they walked to the front steps. He opened the door and held out a hand, indicating for her to step inside.

The house smelled like an Italian restaurant and her mouth watered. If it smelled this good, the meal had to taste great.

"Hi Mom. Dad. We're here."

A squeal of delight cut through the air, and she suddenly saw a whirlwind of pink streak into the room and run into Lucas's arms. Dani. Lucas picked her up and hugged her then kissed her cheek.

"Hey, Pumpkin. Thanks for the welcome, but I haven't been gone that long."

Dani giggled then twisted around in Lucas's arms to look at her. "Hi Bree." She waved. "Did you bring Buster?"

"No, not today. He's home playing with my dad."

Dani squirmed and Lucas set her down on the floor. Dani stepped over to her and reached out her hand. "C'mon, I want to show you my dollies."

She shot her gaze to Lucas. She knew how to handle a little girl because of her niece, but she wasn't sure about Dani. Is this how she had acted towards his other dates when he had brought them home? If that was the case, then she could understand how they would be nervous. Especially if they never had the experience of being around small children. Dani was an excitable girl for sure.

"Dani," Lucas started. "You can show Bree your dolls later, but right now, I'm going to introduce her to Gramma and Grandpa, okay?"

"Okay," Dani grumbled. "Will you come to my room later, Bree?"

"Sure."

"Is this Bree, Lucas?" his mother asked, as she came to the living room from the kitchen. "Hi. I'm Theresa. I'm so glad to finally meet you."

"Nice to meet you, too," she said, holding out her hand, but his mom took her into her arms and gave her a hug. A really tight hug, which eased her nerves.

"Ah, I forgot to mention that Mom, and Dad, are huggers." Lucas mouthed an apology.

His father came up to her after his mother stepped aside and gave her a hug as well. He was a broad chested man and strong. It was like being enveloped by a bear. Which, to her, was fine. "So good to finally meet you, Bree. And I hope my son has been a gentleman."

"Oh, he has. He told me how upset you'd be if you found out he hadn't been a gentleman."

His father glanced at Lucas. "All the Tanner men are gentlemen."

"Well, dinner is ready. Come into the dining room."

"Dani, did you wash your hands?"

"Yes, Daddy," she answered, as she hurried off in her bright pink tutu and sparkly top to sit in her chair. "This one's for you," Dani pointed out, stepping into the room in front of Lucas. "Right next to me."

"It's okay if you want to sit somewhere else," Lucas whispered close to her and the vibrations of his words tickled her ear. His warm breath caressed her cheek.

"No, this is fine," she answered and sat down next to Dani. Lucas sat across from her at the moderately-sized dining room table. She looked to her right where his father sat at the head of the table. There was an empty seat next to Lucas and she assumed his mom would sit on the opposite end.

Theresa came into the room, a moment later, carrying a huge bowl of spaghetti along with a bowl of sauce. The aroma of the homemade sauce was mouth-watering, and Bree couldn't wait to dive in. Steam arose from the hot dishes.

"I'll be right back." Theresa said. She left the room, hurrying to the kitchen and returned carrying a loaf of warm garlic bread. Her stomach grumbled. Seriously? God, she hoped no one had heard it. She'd die of embarrassment if anyone had.

"Okay, let's say grace." Theresa bowed her head.

She wasn't used to saying grace before a meal and for an instant, she didn't know what to do, so she followed Theresa's lead.

"God in Heaven, we ask that you bless this food before us and bless our family. And thank you for bringing a nice woman into Lucas's life. Amen."

"Amen," they responded in unison. Lucas shot a glance at his mother, then at her. She shrugged and smiled.

Theresa offered her the bowl of spaghetti first, then pushed the sauce bowl over. "Normally, Dad serves himself first, but because we have a guest tonight, you'll be first," Lucas explained. She didn't quite know how to respond. She hadn't participated in these types of family gatherings before, so this felt strange, yet nice. She could get used to this. Her family filled their plates from the pots and pans on the stove or from the counter. Cafeteria style, they called it. She spooned spaghetti onto her plate then passed it to Lucas's father. Next came the sauce with meatballs. The bowl was passed around until everyone had food on their plates.

They ate while chatting about the work on her studio. They also talked about how long she'd been dancing and how many performances she had done in her career. She explained her routine and how some routines were different than others depending on the show they were doing.

"That's why I wore my pink outfit," Dani said, looking down at her bright pink sparkly outfit. "I wanted to look like a ballerina for you."

"And you're a very pretty ballerina, too," she said, reaching over and touching Dani's left hand. "Do you know pink is one of my favorite colors?"

"It is!" Dani grinned.

"Hmm-mm. Some of the rooms are decorated in pink."

"Yay!" she said. "Can I look at it when it's done?"

"Sure. I don't see why not." Then she realized she had made a decision without Lucas's say-so.

"And I'm gonna dance there too!"

"Well, I think that's something you and your daddy need to talk about."

"We did. Right, Daddy?" Dani was so excited, her legs were scissoring back and forth as though she were dancing on air.

"Yes, we did." Lucas looked at Dani, who was still grinning, then to his mother and father. "I've decided Dani can take dancing lessons."

"That's great, honey!" Theresa said. "Oh, I can't wait to see you dance in your beautiful tutu."

"I think it's wonderful, too," Mr. Tanner said, smiling at his granddaughter.

Dani grinned so wide it looked as though her face would split in two. "So, can I start dancing tomorrow?"

Everyone laughed. "No, not tomorrow. Daddy has to finish a few more things first," she explained, patting the girl's hand. "Maybe in a couple of weeks."

"Aww, that's like. . .forever!" Dani responded, her smile turning to a pout.

"No, not really. It'll go by fast, I promise," she said. "I'll make sure your Daddy and Uncle Devon work really hard and, maybe I'll help too." She turned to Lucas and winked.

Eleven

After dropping Bree of at her house, he drove back home as he had promised Dani he would be back in time to put her to bed. Devon had texted him to see if he wanted to get a beer at the tavern, but he'd said no, another time. He smiled, thinking about Bree and the time he had spent with her at the house had been the most enjoyable he'd had in a long time.

Bree had helped his mother load the dishwasher and when she was about to help dry the pots and pans, his mom said she'd done enough and to spend time with Lucas. So, Bree left the kitchen and found him and Dani in the den. He had been discovered holding onto two of Dani's dolls, singing a lullaby and when she had stepped into the room, smiling and sat down next to him, his heart had swelled. Immediately, his mind had conjured up a fantasy of him and Bree and Dani in their own home, going through the motions of putting Dani to bed. When he heard Bree sing the lullaby with him, he wanted to kiss her right then and there, and would've proposed to her, if Dani hadn't told him the babies were asleep and that they had to be quiet.

Lucas had opened the door for her as he'd always done and when Bree had stepped out, he offered her his hand. She took it and smiled. He had walked her to the door and leaned in to kiss when Bree's hands had suddenly cupped his jaw, bringing his face to hers and she kissed him. He hadn't expected her to make the first move, but once her soft lips danced on his, he was gone. He had responded with a low groan and delved into her mouth, bringing her tight against him. His hands brushed her back then came up to thread into her hair, cupping the nape of her neck. He couldn't get enough of her. Bree sighed softly as they broke away.

After saying goodbye and wanting one more kiss, Bree had gone into the house, waving back at him. He grinned as he backed out of the driveway. He hadn't felt this good in a long, long time. Unfortunately, he had to admit, he had never felt this way when he had been with Daniella. Their relationship had been short and sweet. Although he had felt love for his wife, it wasn't the all consuming love he knew he was feeling for Bree. He never thought he'd be falling in love in such a short time, but when he thought about it, he had always loved Bree since he had first met her back in high school. Seeing her again, only made the flame grow stronger and brighter. Heck, the flame had ignited into a full-fledged fire.

Twenty minutes later, he walked into the house to find his parents and Dani sitting on the couch, all smiles. He knew they wanted answers. He shrugged out of his jacket. As he started to hang it up in the front hall closet, he heard his mother clear her throat. Now the questions and comments would start. Man, this brought back memories.

"Son, she's a wonderful girl. You should bring her here more often," his father said.

He moved to one of the empty chairs kitty-corner to the sofa. "Yes, she is, Dad."

"She's beautiful, Lucas!" his mother exclaimed. "Nothing like how I had imagined."

"She is pretty, Daddy," Dani chimed in. "I like her a lot. She loves playing with my dollies and she sings nice, too!"

"She does, honey," he said to Dani. Her opinion, of course, was the most important. If Bree was going to be in their lives, he had to know how Dani and Bree would get along or even better, if they could love one another.

"How long have you two been dating?" his mother questioned, peering at him.

"We haven't." He laughed. "We actually decided tonight was our first date."

"Really?" his parents said in unison.

"Yeah. We were talking on the way over here, before

dinner, and, because it felt like a date, we thought we should count it as one."

His mother clasped her hands together. "This is wonderful, Lucas. I'm so happy you found a nice, decent girl. And," she looked down at Dani. "She seems to really like Dani, too. That's important, you know."

"Yes, Mom. I know." He lifted his leg and crossed it over the other knee at the ankle. "Bree said she really enjoyed dinner and that you're a wonderful cook, Mom. She says nothing but nice things about you, too, Dani."

"She likes me?"

"Yes, she does. A lot."

"Yay!" Dani said.

"And she complimented you, Dad, on raising such a smart, responsible, good-looking guy who knows how to treat a woman right."

His father let out a bark of laughter. "I doubt she used all those words to describe you, Son."

"Well, no. She did say I was smart and responsible." He grinned. "Dani, why don't you pick out a book and I'll read it to you right here."

"Okay, Daddy." She hopped off the couch and ran to the den.

"You didn't make up any of that, did you?" his mother asked, concern creasing her brows. "I'd hate think she didn't like us."

"No, Mom, not at all! Bree really likes you. I thought I'd ask her over again next week."

"Oh, that would be great! Let's see, I'll have to go through some of my recipes to make a special dish." She stood. "I'm going to need all this time to figure out the recipe so it's perfect for Wednesday." She turned to look back at him. "You said Wednesday, right?"

"No, but Wednesday will work, I'm sure. I'll ask her and let you know."

"Okay." His mom nodded. "I need to get my cookbook."

She headed back to the kitchen.

"You know how your mother is," his father stated. "If she doesn't have someone to cook for, she'd be bored to tears."

Dani came running back to the room, clasping a book almost as big as her.

"Whoa! I'm not sure there'll be room on my lap for you if I have to hold the book too. You'll have to help me, okay?"

"Okay, Daddy."

He lifted Dani onto his lap, settling her against him, her head leaning on his chest as he opened the book. He started reading. His father headed out back, probably to tinker around in the garage while he heard his mother puttering around in the kitchen. They were the easy, comfortable sounds of the house, sounds of a family content with living with one another. Home.

Once the story was over, he had Dani get ready for bed, promising her he'd be in soon. After putting the book away, he went into her room where she was snuggled under her Disney Princesses comforter.

"Did you have fun with Bree?"

"Yeah! Can she come over tomorrow night, Daddy?"

He sat on the edge of her bed, smoothing her curly hair. "No, not tomorrow night, honey. But, I'm going to invite her over for supper again, next week, okay?"

"Okay," she answered brightly, her eyes shining with excitement. "Daddy?"

"Yeah?"

"Do you think Mommy's happy?"

He hadn't expected that remark. "I'm sure she's very happy. She's up there with all the angels."

"I miss Mommy, a lot."

He hated to see the gleam in her eyes disappear, replaced with glittering tears. "I'm sure Mommy is looking down on us right now, and she's smiling. Close your eyes and think about Mommy." Dani's lids closed. "Now, do you see Mommy?" She nodded. "Is she smiling?" Another nod. "She's giving you a kiss goodnight. Can you feel it?" And he leaned down, placing a soft, feathery kiss on her cheek, then he sat up.

"Good night Mommy. I love you," Dani whispered.

"Mommy loves you too, Pumpkin. Now, go to sleep. Have sweet dreams."

"Goodnight, Daddy. I love you."

"Love you too, sweetheart." He kissed her again then rubbed her back in a slow, rhythmic motion until her breathing slowed and he knew she was sound asleep. As he stepped out of her room, closing the door behind him, he had imagined Bree leaning over Dani and giving her a kiss good night, not his wife.

* * * *

Bree sat on her bed with her laptop opened to her emails. She was curious to know if any companies had contacted her for any auditions since getting a response from the company in Philadelphia. Two had responded. One from Chicago and another in Orlando, Florida. Both explained that, while they found her to be an exemplary performer and would love to have her as a member of their team, they currently were not in need of a principal dancer, or even a soloist. They will keep her resume' on file and contact her next year when they audition for the following season.

Yet, while she read about how much they would love for her to audition for them, the excitement wasn't there. Normally, she would've felt joy and been leaping off the bed right now and doing a happy dance. But it wasn't the case for her. And she knew why. Lucas and Dani. They had become a part of her heart now, and she wasn't sure she could leave them. How had they insinuated themselves in her heart in such a short time?

Maybe because she always had the hots for Lucas and had never really forgotten him. And, somewhere, deep down, she had loved him all these years, even though she had been dating someone else. And Dani. Who could not love that little girl? She was a reminder of how she had been at that age--full of energy and spunk and the desire to dance. Although surprised by Dani's disability, when they first met, she found herself looking beyond it and seeing what Dani could do, not focusing on what she couldn't do.

She read through the two emails again. Now that she was back in her small town, Chicago and Orlando seemed so far away even though she had spent the last five years in San Francisco. She surprised herself again. Misty River was becoming home again after all the years spent away. Never would she have thought any place was too far away if it meant dancing with a well-known ballet company. In a heartbeat, she would've been packing her bags and flying out to the city, her heart soaring in the clouds.

Sighing, she closed the laptop and fell back against the bed. She wanted to dance. It was in her blood, but she didn't want to leave her little town. Well, not go too far away, at least. Maybe if she found something in Portland or maybe she would hear from the Philadelphia company? If she danced for Portland, she could commute. And, she had sent a resume' out to them. She hadn't heard back. . .yet. Maybe she should call and see if they had even looked at her resume'. Sitting back up, she opened the laptop and scanned through all her emails again to make sure she hadn't missed any. Then she checked her Spam folder. Nothing.

She had a sudden urge to research some of these companies on YouTube, if they even had a channel. This could give her a better idea of their performances. In the process, she discovered several videos of her dancing, which felt really strange. She clicked on the one of her dancing in The Nutcracker a year ago. It seemed like a lifetime. As she listened to the music, and watched herself on the stage, she wanted to get up and do the performance right there in the bedroom. She smiled as the memories came back, flooding her with happiness. She had to admit, she was good. Heck, better than good. So why wasn't anyone contacting her for a job?

She glanced to the left side of the screen and noticed several video thumbnails of small children dancing. Curious, she clicked on one. The children were adorable in their outfits prancing on the stage, twirling around, swaying side to side and doing plie's. The instructor was off camera, but she could hear the woman's voice encouraging them through the routine. How cute were these kids! She could see herself doing this. Perhaps this was her new calling. It excited her to start a new chapter in her life, yet at the same time, it saddened her.

She clicked on another thumbnail. Then the idea hit her. She could do a recital. Why not? It didn't have to be something fancy or very long. She'd be starting classes in a few weeks, hopefully, and they could do a recital at the end of May. Excited now to have a new plan, she watched several videos of children's recitals. She'd have to write down some ideas.

Deciding to get a tall glass of iced tea, she headed downstairs to the kitchen. She grabbed a glass, filled it with ice then added the homemade iced tea mixture Aunt Merry was fond of making. Then she headed into the den and grabbed a pen and a pad of paper from the desk to write down her ideas. Because it was a beautiful, warm sunny day, she thought she'd sit outside by the garden and list her thoughts for a recital.

She stepped outside with glass in hand and found her aunt puttering away in her garden. She waved when Aunt Merry looked up at her. Aunt Merry nodded, then stood.

"Can you grab me one, too?" she yelled over, pointing to Bree's glass of iced tea.

"Sure." She set her pen and pad of paper on the table and headed back inside. She went through the motions, again, of making a glass of iced tea, then headed back outside. Aunt Merry was wiping off her jeans.

"Whew, it's getting hot," she said, stripping off her hat and removing her dirty gloves. She tossed them on the grass by the chair before sitting down. "This looks so good. Thanks." Her aunt lifted the glass and drank. "I needed that," she said as she leaned back.

"Do you have much more to do?" Bree asked, sitting down in the Adirondack chair next to her aunt.

"No. I just planted the last bulb. Perfect timing," Aunt Merry said, as she picked up the glass again and took another swallow. Her aunt's face was flushed with exertion and a dirt streak marred her right cheek. "What have you been up to?"

"I just looked through my emails to see if any dance companies had contacted me." She blew out a breath. "Two. And, they both rejected me."

"Maybe it's not meant to be, Bree. I'm not being rude, but maybe this happened for a reason. Like staying here. Being with Lucas and Danica. Teaching at the studio."

She nodded. "You could be right. It's frustrating, though. I'm good. Really good, Aunt Merry."

"You don't have to tell me twice," Aunt Merry said, bringing the cold glass to her face.

"As a matter of fact, I was watching some YouTube videos of some of my performances, and my blood sang with the movements. I wanted to get up and dance in the bedroom." She laughed. "I didn't, in case you were wondering, but I miss it, Aunt Merry."

"I know you do."

"But, I did discover something. . .fun,"

"Oh? And what would that be?" Aunt Merry asked.

"I watched some videos of little kids performing in their dance recitals. Oh my goodness, they were so cute!" She took a swallow of her drink. "I think I want to do a recital."

Aunt Merry's eyes rounded then slanted in a grin. "That's wonderful! And, I know the perfect weekend."

"You do?"

"Do you remember when you were little and we attended

the Founder's Day festivities? They had a parade and a carnival at the park?"

"Oh my gosh, yes! That was so long ago." She had loved standing on Main Street watching the floats go by, each one decorated in a scene from Misty River's past. And the school bands would play. It had been a small parade, but none the less exciting. From the parade, her father and aunt would take her, Anna and Brett to the park to go on the carnival rides and fill their bellies with cotton candy and fried dough. "I looked forward to that event every year. Do they still do the parade and the rides?"

"They do!" Aunt Merry set her glass on a small table next to their chairs. "I have an idea."

Oh-oh. Aunt Merry's ideas often involved her, against her wishes most of the time. The studio being one of them.

"I can't believe I didn't think of this earlier."

"What's brewing in that conniving mind of yours, Aunt Merry?"

Her aunt's eyes twinkled, and she gave a lop-sided grin. "I think you should sign up to participate."

"What?" She knew her aunt had something up her sleeve. "I barely have any students. I haven't even started classes yet." She exhaled.

"Oh, you'll have plenty of time. Besides, the people in town don't care how good or bad your students dance. They just want to see them participate and have fun."

She heaved another sigh and shrugged. "What weekend is it?"

"The same as it's always been. Mother's Day weekend." Aunt Merry twisted around to face her. "Bree, the kids will love it. You'll love it! Just call the town hall and sign up."

"But, what if the students don't want to be in the parade?"

Her aunt waved her away as though swatting a fly. "Seriously? What kid doesn't want to be in a parade? I'll have your father and his friends build a float. Lucas can help. Oh, Bree, it's going to be so much fun!"

How could she say no to her aunt's exuberance? Besides, it did sound like fun. "Okay. I'll call the town hall and sign up my students. You've convinced me."

"That's wonderful, Bree." Her aunt beamed. "I can't wait to see the kids dance at the festival."

"Oh! Ahh, where will they dance, Aunt Merry? Is this something new?" She needed to get all the info before committing herself and the students to the Founder's Day Festival and Parade.

"That's right. You haven't been to the event in years." Aunt Merry looked back at her garden then faced her. "Over the years, the committee has changed things up a bit to include a barbecue, which is catered by the local VFW, and added a talent show with local performers, ranging from magicians to comedians. And dancers. We have quite a few talented people in this town. People you would never guess."

Now she was curious. "Tell me."

Aunt Merry shook her head. "Nope. You have to attend to find out." She laughed. "Oh, and there's a pie contest."

"Of course, you signed up for that, right?"

"Of course!" She grinned again. "And Lucas's mom, Theresa, is also signed up. She beats me every year. This year, I'm going to win."

"I hope so, Aunt Merry. You've got some tough competition."

"I do. And thank you."

They sat silent for a few minutes, enjoying the quiet and sipping their iced teas. A warm breeze rustled through the trees, carrying the scent of pine. Her first class was coming up and she'd have one room to practice in.

"Aunt Merry, where do the people perform?"

"Oh, they'll be in a tent. There's a stage set up, too."

"And if it rains?"

Then the festival will be held the following weekend, Memorial Day weekend." She lifted her iced tea. "We've never had rain on Founder's Day." She took a swallow. "How are the sign ups coming along?"

"Not too bad. I've got Heather, of course, and Dani, as well as Chloe's daughter, Sophie." She went down the list of names, mentally. "I think I have about ten kids, so far. I think that's a good start."

"I agree," Aunt Merry said. "Start small for now. That way you won't get discouraged or stressed."

"I'm planning on having a student do a solo part in the recital and I have the perfect person in mind."

Aunt Merry grinned, then winked. "I bet I know who."

"I think Dani will do great."

"Oh." Her aunt's face fell, then she smiled. "Are you trying to impress Lucas?"

"No, not at all. I actually want to do this to prove to Lucas that Dani can dance."

"Well, I think it's a great idea."

"You're not upset I didn't choose Heather?"

"Of course not! I think Dani's the right choice. And besides," Her aunt winked at her. "I know you'll use Heather in a lead role in another recital."

She laughed. "Yes. For sure."

"Well, I'm going to putter around some more." Aunt Merry stood and headed back to the garden.

She picked up the pen and pad of paper and started writing down her ideas for a recital. She also wrote down her To Do list. First things first, call the town hall and sign up for the parade and performance. Secondly, she needed to come up with a solid dance routine. They didn't have much time to practice. They had four weeks, that's all. As she jotted down notes, she realized she should write down her ideas for the float. She'd ask Lucas for help too. She wrote down the title: *Misty River Dance Company presents "Dancing in the Grass" performed by:*

Smiling, she wrote down all the names of the students, then added: *Solo performance by Danica Tanner.* She put down a question mark next to her name. What if Dani didn't want to do a solo? Yeah, right. Dani would be thrilled with the idea.

Realizing the time, she decided she'd surprise Lucas and Devon with lunch from the diner. She called out to her aunt, telling her she'd be gone for a little while. She couldn't wait to see Lucas and tell him of her plans.

Twelve

Lucas was surprised when Bree showed up with two meals from the diner for him and Devon. Even more to his surprise it was his favorite--meatloaf. She had remembered. Knowing that made him realized how much she cared. Bree handed Devon his box.

"Thanks, Bree, for doing this," Devon said, as he took his boxed lunch and sat on the floor of the second dance room, also known as Studio Room 2.

He walked over to Bree and kissed her on the cheek. She flushed.

"No need to feel embarrassed around me, Bree. Lucas told me you two were dating. So, there's no need to hold back on my account." Devon dove into his meal.

She smiled up at him. They sat side by side, across from Devon. "Jamie added extra, she said. I'm not exactly sure what she meant by that."

"That means she had the cook give me and Dev double the amount, at no extra cost."

"Oh. Well, that was nice of her. As a matter of fact, the bag was a bit heavy. I didn't know meatloaf and mashed potatoes could be so heavy."

"Jamie's cook makes the best." He opened his boxed lunch. "I'll marry the woman who can make meatloaf this good." He glanced at Bree and winked.

"You better get the recipe quick," Devon suggested. "Or else he'll have to marry Harry, Jamie's cook."

Bree blurted out a belly laugh.

He scooped up more meatloaf and held the fork out to her. "Bree, you have to try this."

She shook her head. "I'm not really--"

"I know. You're not into red meat. But try one bite." He lifted the fork closer to her. "Please? C'mon, you know you want to try it. Doesn't it smell delicious." He wiggled the fork in front of her nose.

She smiled. "Okay. One bite." She opened her mouth and drew the food off the fork while watching his face. His heart nearly stopped, and his breath hitched. Was she doing that on purpose? If so, she good at teasing. She chewed slowly, closing her eyes.

"Good, huh?"

She snapped open her eyes and grinned. "Hmm-mmm."

"You'll be a red meat eater in no time."

She licked her bottom lip, getting the last of the gravy into her mouth. He sucked in a breath, and she smiled. She had to know she was getting to him.

"Get a room you two," Devon grumbled from across the way. "The way you two make eyes at each other makes me—"

"Want a woman of your own?" He asked, teasing his cousin.

"Don't need one in my life right now."

"Sure, Dev. You keep believing that."

Devon rolled his eyes and snickered then continued eating his lunch. "Don't go playing matchmaker with me either." He waved his fork in the air. "I'll find her when I'm ready."

He laughed, nudging Bree's arm.

"So," Bree started, darting her eyes between him and Devon. "Do you guys have any idea when the renovations will be done? I'm only asking in order to get a timeline for when I can start classes."

He glanced at Devon. "Two weeks maybe. We have a crew of four other guys starting in a few days, so it should only be a couple of weeks, if I had to make a rough guess. I know you want to open the studio up as soon as possible." He took a swallow of his water.

"Well, don't rush it. Take whatever time is necessary."

He wiped his hands with a napkin. "The guys are great,

Bree. They won't slack off or do sloppy work, if that's what's worrying you. Devon and I have our reputations on the line and we definitely won't let the crew take short cuts."

Devon nodded. "Damn right."

“I’m not worried. I trust you guys to do the job right."

He noticed her fidgeting with her pant leg.

“Was there a reason you need us to be done sooner?”

“Well, I'm getting calls asking when I'm starting my classes and I've been telling them I think it’ll be soon.” Her brow creased, and he wondered what was worrying her. “Plus, I’m signing my students up for the Founder’s Day Talent Show.”

“That's a great idea,” he said. “Isn’t that Mother’s Day weekend?”

Bree nodded. “But I can have the kids practice in Studio One while you’re working on the other room. It’s no big deal. Oh!” Bree glanced at him quickly. “I have something to ask you.”

“Sure, what is it?”

“I was wondering. . .”

He waited a beat, but she didn’t continue. “Wondering?”

“If Dani would like to do one of the solos?”

“Could you, and Devon, build a float?”

“A float?”

“Yeah, for the parade.”

“Oh. Well. . .” he looked over at Devon. “What’d you think?”

“I think we can do it. Sure, why not?”

“Alright. We’ll build you a float.” He didn’t know when he’d find the time, but he would get it done, regardless.

“Oh, Lucas, thank you!” Bree turned sideways and hugged him, nearly knocking over his box of meatloaf.

He chuckled. “You’re welcome.”

“Well, I’ll leave you two alone,” Devon said, as he stood. He walked to the door and tossed his empty box into the trash bin then smiled at them as he passed and headed to Studio 2.

"God, I didn't think he'd ever finish and leave," he said, as he wrapped his arms around Bree. "Thanks again, for lunch. It was very thoughtful of you."

"Well, I couldn't let you go hungry."

"I'm always hungry," he said as he kissed the tip of her nose. "For you." He kissed her cheeks.

Bree gripped him harder, pulling him towards her.

"And now I think I'll have dessert," he whispered as he pressed his mouth against hers. He angled his head as she opened her mouth to him. They kissed as though they'd never see one another again. A moment later, they pulled apart, breathing heavy.

"And how was your dessert?" she asked, cupping her hands along the back of his neck.

"Dessert was delicious," he answered. "But I want seconds." He gave her a quick kiss.

She laughed. He gave her a quick kiss. "But I'll wait until tonight."

"Okay," she said. Heat flushed her cheeks once again. "Until tonight." As she stepped away from him, he swatted her bottom and she giggled. "Have a great afternoon."

"Will do. See you at five."

"I'll be ready."

* * * *

Bree cradled the pink Sweet Cheeks Bakery box in her lap. She knew Lucas would try to open the box and take one of the cupcakes.

"Did you happen to buy some cupcakes?" He reached out to lift the lid.

"I did." She swatted his hand away. "And you can't have any. They're for dessert."

"Are you sure I can't try just one cupcake?"

"No. Besides, I want your parents to have first choice of the selection."

He backed out of the driveway and headed down the street.

"Trust me, you'll like whatever cupcake you get."

"I agree. I don't think Chloe has ever made a cupcake I haven't liked."

"She makes the best, that's for sure." She looked out the window, thinking about her friend. She wished Chloe could find a man who would care for her and Sophie. But she still held the torch for her high school sweetheart, Tyler Anderson. She turned away from the window.

"By the way, whatever happened to my cupcakes from last week?" Lucas asked, turning off Main Street.

"I texted you and you never answered. So. . ."

"So?" Lucas turned his gaze to her. His eyes crinkled.

"So, we ate them. Me and the girls. At Jamie's."

"Were they good?" He kept his eyes on the road.

"Delicious."

"That's what I get for storming out on you."

"Tell you what." She patted his thigh. "I'll let you have an extra."

"Maybe I'll take the box when you're not looking, and hide them, so I'll have them all to myself." He chuckled.

"Won't happen." She loved how they could banter and tease back and forth. It was new and fun for her. Lucas brought out a side of her she didn't know existed.

"So, what are your plans for the rest of the week?" Lucas asked.

"I still have to work on my website and create a few blog posts," she let out a breath. "And get ready for my first class. The list goes on." She looked over at him. "And you?"

He grinned. "I think you know the answer to that. I'll be at the studio, working all day. You know, the owner can be quite the task master and has a very threatening look if I don't keep up with the demands of the job."

She swatted him playful on his arm and laughed. "I am not!"

"Okay, we'll leave out the 'threatening look'."

"You're too kind."

"Seriously, Devon and I will get the second room done by the end of the week, once the rest of the crew joins us."

She nodded. "That's great. I can't wait to see it when everything is done."

"You're going to love it, Bree. I promise."

A moment later they pulled into the driveway of his parents' house. They walked in and were greeted with hugs and Dani's squeals of happiness. His mother's eyes lit up when she accepted the box of cupcakes from Bree. They headed to the living room to talk to his father. Dani followed them while his mother finished up in the kitchen.

"Hey Dad."

"Hey, Son." His father looked comfortable sitting back in his easy chair, with his feet up, watching the news. "Hi Bree. Glad you could come by tonight."

She nodded and sat next to Lucas on the sofa. "Thank you for inviting me."

"We love having you here, Bree," Mr. Tanner said, and it warmed her insides. She sat back against the sofa.

"Do you want anything to drink? Coffee, tea, water. . .hard liquor?" Lucas teased.

She laughed, tossing a quick glance to his father to see if the man disapproved. Instead, Mr. Tanner grinned. "I'll wait until we eat. I'll have water."

Dani came into the room, smiling and full of energy. "Bree, can you show me a few dance moves?"

She looked from Dani to Lucas. He smiled back at her and nodded. "No leaps in the living room though."

She and Dani laughed. She stood and moved to stand beside Danica. "Okay, first things first. Before you can even dance, you have to learn the positions."

Dani scrunched her face, looking up at her. "Positions? What're those?"

"Well, it's how we hold our body in order to do a certain dance step. That's what dancing really is. Just different positions moving around to the music."

"Ohhh, I get it," Dani said, but shrugged her shoulders and shook her head. She, along with Lucas and his father laughed. "Can you show me?"

"Sure." She got into the first position which was putting her right foot and her left foot together at the heels with the feet pointing outward.

Dani looked down at her feet, trying to copy Bree's stance. She grimaced. "This is hard."

"Yes, it is, but the more you do it, the easier it becomes." She then showed Dani how to place her arms. "It's like holding a bouquet of flowers."

Dani nodded and held her arms down and out, her hands curling as though she was holding a bouquet. "Like this?" She beamed.

"Yes! Exactly!" She smoothed Dani's hair and smiled at her. "Okay, now onto the second position. Stay just the way you are, but watch me, okay?"

Dani nodded and smiled up at her. She quickly got back into first position then moved her feet apart about a foot then lifted her arms out and to the sides. "Do you think you can do that?" Then she winced. She looked over at Lucas who had been watching them intently, but all of a sudden, he frowned. "If you can't, it's okay, we--"

"I can do it!" Dani said, then slid her feet apart and spread her arms out. Granted, the right arm didn't go as high as her left, but it was enough to know she had reached the second position.

Lucas clapped and smiled. He really did seem pleased by what his daughter had just done. His father grinned.

"I think you've got some talent there, young lady," Mr. Tanner said.

"And I agree," Lucas said.

"Thank you, Grampa. It's gonna be fun to dance!" She lowered her arm and rushed over to her father. "Thank you Daddy."

"You're welcome, honey," he said and hugged her.

"Okay, folks, time to eat," Mrs. Tanner announced, coming into the living room. "I watched from the kitchen, Dani. You did a wonderful job. I'm proud of you."

"Thank you, Gramma." Dani headed into the dining room with the rest of them following.

After seating themselves, they held hands and said grace. A platter of roasted chicken was passed around along with mashed potatoes, carrots and broccoli. When Lucas set some broccoli on Dani's plate, she scoffed.

"Dani, try one piece. Remember what I've always told you?"

She nodded but didn't say a word.

"You need to try at least one bite. You don't know if you'll like something if you don't try."

"Just like dancing?"

She giggled and nodded.

"Yes," Lucas looked at her then glanced at his daughter. "Just like dancing. How would you know if you liked to dance, if you hadn't done a few steps first?"

"Okay, Daddy. I'll try a bite."

"Good girl."

They ate their meal amidst banter of the weather, the goings on in town and the reopening of the studio.

"We expect Bree to start classes this week because one room is completed. Then she'll have use of the entire studio in a couple of weeks."

"Oh, speaking of classes," she wiped her mouth with the linen napkin. "I should tell you that I'm going to sign my students up to perform at the Founder's Day BBQ and Parade."

"That's great news." Theresa said.

She nodded, then glanced down at Dani, who looked up at her with big brown adoring eyes. "And, I have something I want to ask Lucas and Dani." She looked over at Lucas who's brow creased. "I have some ideas of the type of recital I want to put on and I wanted to know if Dani wouldn't mind having a solo part?"

"Really? Oh, Dani!"

"Wait. You want Dani to have a solo part in front of dozens of people?" Lucas asked, setting his fork down.

"I'm gonna have a solo, yay!"

"Why didn't you ask me before now?"

"I had just decided, Lucas. I have the perfect part which won't—"

"I don't want. . ." He stopped, lowered his head and exhaled.

"Lucas?" his mother asked, her gaze darting from her son to her granddaughter. "Why are you acting like this? We had this conversation, remember?"

"Daddy, can I dance a solo?"

She watched the emotions play across his face and could understand some of what he was feeling. But he had to trust her.

"Lucas, I told you I would watch out for Dani."

"Look, Son," his father started, steepling his fingers. "I think you should hear what Bree's saying. Do you honestly think she would put Dani in front of dozens of townsfolk to. . .well, you know what I mean."

Lucas nodded. He looked at his daughter who sat next to her, silent, her gaze sad. "Do you want to do a solo?"

Dani grinned and nodded. "Can I, Daddy?"

"I'm asking you, Dani. You need to practice extra hard if you want to do this."

"I will, Daddy. I promise."

"Okay then. I guess she's going to do a solo."

She grinned and rubbed Dani's back. "Thank you, Lucas. Dani's going to do great."

"I'm gonna dance and do a solo!"

"I can't wait to see you dance, Dani," Theresa said.

"Me too," her grandfather added.

As the tension eased and they went back to eating, a little

voice sounded next to her.

"What's a solo?"

She stifled a laugh so she wouldn't choke. After taking a sip of her water, she looked at Dani. "A solo is when a dancer performs a part by herself in front of the audience."

"I'll be alone?"

"Not really. You'll have your friends on stage with you, and I'll be right there too."

Dani's eyes rounded. "Will it be scary?"

She shook her head and smoothed her hand down Dani's curly hair. "It might be when you first go on stage, but after a minute you'll relax and do the dance."

"That's why you need to practice, Dani," Lucas encouraged, giving his daughter a big smile. "The more you practice, the better you'll know the dance and the more confident you'll become."

"Your father's right." She patted Dani's hand. "Tell you what. I'll help you practice as much as you like between classes. How does that sound?"

Dani grinned, bobbing her head up and down. "Will you come over here and help me?"

She glanced at Lucas, who smiled at her. "Yes, Dani. I'll come over as often as I can to help."

"Yay! I'm gonna dance just like Bree." Dani sang out.

"I hope you do, honey," she said, smiling down at the little girl who was slowly finding a place in her heart.

Thirteen

"Why don't you two take a walk. It's a beautiful night. No need to waste it," his mother said, as she walked out of the dining room with a handful of dishes.

"I don't mind helping," Bree said, standing and grabbing her plate and utensils along with her glass.

"You'll do no such thing. I've got this. Besides, I have George to help me."

"Me too, Gramma," Dani called out as she got up from her chair and picked up her plate as well.

"Yes, you too, Dani," his mom said, leaving the room.

He grabbed his plate, silverware and glass and followed Bree and Dani to the kitchen where they set their dishes in the sink. His mother wiped her hands on a dishtowel.

"Now, go on. We'll be fine. Right, Dani?

She bobbed her head. "Yup. I take good care of Gramma."

"See? Go on. Enjoy yourselves."

He chuckled, ruffling the top of Dani's head. "Okay."

He followed Bree out the back door. Daylight was fading away to darkness. The air was cool, which was typical for an April night in Maine and he was glad Bree had the foresight to bring a jacket despite the day having been warm. As they strolled down the drive to the sidewalk, he reached for her hand and clasped it within his own. Bree didn't pull away. As a matter of fact, she squeezed his hand. That was a good sign.

"You're growing on my family," he said, as they walked away from the house and down the quiet street.

"They're growing on me, too. You have a great family."

"I'm glad you think so." It made their relationship that much easier. "They're loved by the entire community." He chuckled. "When the Christmas season starts, my mother is a whirlwind of activity. She coordinates a fundraiser for needy children through the church."

"That's wonderful!" she answered. "My mother would be doing the same, if she were here." Bree glanced up at him. "I think my mother and your mother would've been good friends."

"Even though I was a 'bad boy' back in high school?"

Bree laughed. "She wouldn't have held that against you. And, I think it was all an act. You wanted everyone to believe you were this tough kid, but," She squeezed his hand and leaned into his shoulder. "You were really a nice guy under the leather and bad boy look."

He gave a shout of laughter, swinging their linked hands. "And what makes you think that?"

"Because I know my brother. Brett never would've hung out with a 'tough guy' who was looking to do bad things."

"Well, to be honest," he started, looking down at her. "I did get into a few scrapes. Dad always made me pay the price, literally and figuratively. Said I had to learn my lesson, no matter the cost."

"Smart guy."

"He was. I learned my lesson. After high school, I worked for his construction company along with Devon."

"Your father taught you well. You're great at what you do. So is Devon."

"Thanks. That means a lot coming from you." He stopped and turned to face her, their hands still clasped. He let her hand go and cupped her face, smoothing a thumb across her cheek. She trembled and leaned into his hand. He lowered his face closer to hers. He touched his lips to her soft pliant mouth. With a small gasp, Bree opened her mouth and allowed him to kiss her, thoroughly. He smiled against her lips, and he could feel her smile as well. He pulled back, lowering his hand to his side. "I love kissing you," he said, then wondered if he should've said it out loud.

Bree sighed, leaning her head on his shoulder as they continued walking. "I love kissing you, too."

He grinned. He couldn't think of any other woman who could make him this happy. He had tried with Daniella, but he had never been this happy with his wife. Why? He looked at Bree, her dark hair gleaming in the ebbing sunlight. Because you've always been in love with Bree. He gave a quick sigh. "Remember when you asked me about. . .Daniella?"

"Yeah. You were going to tell me when the time was right."

"I think the time is right. I should tell you about Dani's mother."

"Are you sure?" Bree stood straighter.

Another drawn out sigh. "I'm sure." He slowed his steps. "Daniella and I met six years ago. Through her friends. She seemed very nice. She was beautiful with long, dark curly hair. Dani inherited that from her. I don't know exactly what attracted me to her. Isn't that weird?"

Bree shrugged. "Depends, I guess."

He pulled his hand from hers and thrust them in his pockets. He suddenly felt uncomfortable talking about his wife, a woman he was supposed to have been in love with, to the woman he had always been in love with. He blew out a breath and looked up at the darkening sky. "It's not easy talking about her."

"You don't have to, Lucas. I'll understand."

He peered down at her. She appeared so innocent. Her tawny eyes bright in the fading light. "I want you to know I'm not trying to make you jealous."

Bree shook her head. "Of course not." She glanced away from him and looked down the road. "But, I'll admit I am. It's not because of you." She peered back at him. "Please tell me what happened."

He kicked a small stone in the sidewalk. "We had had a fight that morning before I headed out to work. She was tired she said. She needed a break from taking care of Dani. She told me she needed the day for herself and that I had to stay home from work."

Bree slipped her hand through his arm, and he tugged it against him.

"I was committed to a job that was time-sensitive. I had to be there. She got mad and told me she'd find a sitter. Oh, Bree. She was so angry. So spewed out some hateful words. I left, stunned. I figured she'd stay mad at me but get through the day. I never thought she'd actually bring Dani to a babysitter."

Bree stroked his forearm, a gesture to calm him or reassure him. He was thankful for that. He continued telling the nightmare of a story. "It was in March. The weather changed drastically that day. Actually, the Weather Channel had said there was a chance of snow squalls and bouts of freezing rain. According to the police, she had been driving too fast, slid on some black ice and hit a tree."

"With Dani in the car?" Terror floated on Bree's words. "Oh, my God, Lucas. I am so sorry."

He expelled a breath and squeezed the bridge of his nose. A habit he had developed when he was nervous or frustrated. "She was rushed to the hospital along with Dani, of course, and taken immediately into surgery. I got a call from my parents who had been contacted by the police. Evidently, they tried calling me, but I had my phone in the truck. Daniella had called me several times. Each call angrier than the previous one. The last one was sent only moments before the crash."

"Oh, Lucas!" Bree cried out as he shook with renewed guilt and despair.

"It was my fault." He sat down on the edge of a neighbor's lawn, pulling his legs up and leaning his forearms across them. "If I had only answered the phone earlier, maybe I could've talked her out of going anywhere. I should've stayed home like she had asked me too."

"How could you have known?" Bree stroked his back in slow rhythmic circles, lulling him into calmness. "But, even if you had stayed home, she would've still gone out and. . ."

He nodded. "But Dani wouldn't have been injured. Her mother had been reckless and selfish and nearly killed Dani!" He inhaled deeply and cradled his face in his hands. "Dani was in surgery when I finally arrived at the hospital." He heaved a sigh. "And you know what I did?" He didn't wait for an answer. He kept on talking. It felt good to talk to someone about it besides his parents. "I prayed for Dani, not my wife. What kind of husband does that?" He glanced at Bree. She looked at him with a glimmer of tears in her eyes. She bit her bottom lip.

"It wasn't your fault, Lucas." She brushed his arm then clasped it, bringing herself closer to him. "Dani was so young. Maybe you--"

"I went in there angry at Daniella and my heart breaking for Dani. At that moment, I hated my wife for nearly killing my child." His voice came out in a rush of hate-filled words. Tears blurred his vision. "I met with a priest who told me that what I was feeling was normal, but I should also pray for Daniella." He shook his head. "I couldn't, Bree." His voice cracked. "I couldn't." Tears slid down his cheeks. Was he actually crying for the loss of his wife two years after the fact? He hadn't shed a tear for her back then. All his tears had been for Dani and the horrible pain inflicted on her and the injury which would affect her for the rest of her life.

"Grief is different for everyone, Lucas."

He nodded and swiped at the tears. "Several hours later, the surgeon came out and told me Daniella didn't survive. She died during surgery. She had severe trauma to the brain as well as internal injuries. There had been severe hemorrhaging. If she had lived, she would've been in a vegetative state." He sighed. "It was a blessing." He tilted his head back and let out a low groan. "When I had heard that, I was relieved." He leaned forward again, resting his head on his arms. Bree continued to smooth his back. “Can you believe that? I was. . .thankful.” A small cry erupted. "She was at peace. I realized, at that moment, that she had never been at peace since Dani had been born. She had a hard time being a full-time mother."

"I don't know how you did it, Lucas. Grieving for your wife and dealing with Dani's injury." Bree shook her head. “I don’t think I could’ve gone through what you did.”

"I doubt that," he said. "People don't know how strong they are until they're faced with something that forces them to be, for the sake of loved ones.” He peered over at Bree. “I had to be strong for Dani.”

"How long was Dani in surgery?" Bree asked. She stopped stroking his back and nestled against his shoulder. He rested his head against hers.

"Dani's surgery took a few hours, but, thank God, she pulled through with flying colors except she had lost the use of her right arm." He heaved another sigh. "I was thankful she was alive. When she came out of surgery, I rushed into recovery, despite the doctors saying I couldn't. One surgeon took pity on me, knowing I had lost Daniella and allowed me in there with Dani. He knew I'd go in, regardless.

"Dani woke up and smiled at me, but her first words were 'where's mommy?' Hearing her ask for her mother with that sweet little voice put me over the edge but I refused to let her see me break down. I held it together until she fell asleep. Then I cried. Not for me, but because my little girl didn't have her mommy. A woman she loved and adored."

"I am so sorry, Lucas. I can't imagine the pain you went through."

He scrubbed a hand down his face. "Dani didn't handle her mother's passing very well. She was only three years old. How do you explain to a child their mother is never coming home?" He fell silent for a few minutes. They sat there in their own thoughts until he spoke.

"Dani had her moments of temper tantrums. She didn’t know how to handle her grief. It was tough for me and for my parents. Daniella's parents were grieving too. Dani wanted to spend time with them, and they wanted the same, but I couldn't bear not to have my daughter around me. I was so afraid she'd get hurt or. . .worse."

"Did Dani go through grief counseling?"

He nodded. "Yup, and through a lot of love and a lot of patience, she's doing really well. And I thank my parents for that. I don't know what I would've done without them."

"Your parents are amazing people. And you're amazing too."

He glanced down at her and kissed the top of her head. "Thank you." He reached for her hand. "Let's head back. I'm sure my parents are wondering what we've been up to."

As they walked back to the house, she said, "Thank you, Lucas, for telling me about Dani and Daniella. I know it was hard for you. I feel guilty now."

He spun to face her. "Don't you dare feel guilty, Bree. You deserved to know and besides, I feel a whole lot better now that I've poured my heart out to you." He clasped her hand. "I've been holding it all back, keeping it inside me for the past two years. Now that I've talked to you, I feel. . .free."

* * * *

Bree kept busy throughout Thursday and Friday with several errands and phone calls. She called several of Anna's friends and some people Aunt Merry suggested and ended up with several more students on her list. Her excitement grew, and she couldn't wait to get started. She created a list of students with their names, addresses and phone numbers along with ages on an Excel sheet. At the advice of her sister, she looked at Pinterest and discovered several ideas for a recital and how to teach children with disabilities. This was a whole new avenue she was going down.

With that thought in mind, she searched Google to see what she would discover. As she watched some of the videos, she was astonished at how many children with disabilities wanted to do some sort of dancing, even if it was only moving their arms or one leg or just their head. She nearly cried watching some of the videos. At the same time, it gave her a lot of ideas and questions she needed answers for, such as, would she need medically trained 'buddies' for her students with disabilities? Right now, she only had Dani, but what if more students, with limited use of their arms and legs, wanted to take dance lessons? She would definitely have to add that to her ever-growing To Do list.

She heard laughter coming from the kitchen. Aunt Merry had said Anna and Heather would be coming over. Needing a break, she headed to the kitchen and found Aunt Merry, Anna and Heather preparing batter for chocolate chip cookies. Feeling guilty she hadn't spent much time with them lately, she joined them to the delight of Heather. In the process of making chocolate chip cookies from scratch, they found themselves covered in flour and their laughter echoed throughout the house. For one quick moment, she imagined herself in her own kitchen with Dani by her side making a mess while baking goodies for Lucas. She smiled and Anna caught it.

"You look happy, Bree. What brings on that smile?"

"Oh, a lot of things, I guess."

"Would one of those *things* be Lucas?" Anna asked, a teasing lilt in her voice.

"Yes, and Dani." She scooped up some batter and placed it on the baking sheet. "We had a nice talk the other night and, although the story was tragic, he said I was the only one he had shared his thoughts with about losing his wife."

"Well, that sounds positive." Anna added a scoop to the sheet as well. "But, you haven't seen him since Wednesday, right?"

"Is everything okay?" Aunt Merry asked, wiping her hands with a paper towel.

"Yeah." She grinned. "I've been busy trying to get

everything organized for my classes."

"Oh my gosh. You're starting in less than a week!" Aunt Merry said. "I can't wait, to be honest." She nudged Heather. "You're excited too, right?"

"Yes!" Heather blurted out. "I can't wait to dance with my friends."

"And I can't wait to see you on the dance floor again, Sis," Anna said, before turning to place the cookie sheet in the oven. "It's been years since we danced together."

"Don't remind me. It makes me feel old." She turned back to her sister.

"You're only two years older than me. That's not old," Anna said, giving her a side hug.

A cold wave of awareness hit her. She was 'old' in the dance world of age. By the time most dancers reached thirty, they were close to retirement. Most couldn't keep up with the demands, considering all the stress they had put on their bodies since most had been children. And she was one of those statistics.

"Hey, why the frown?" Anna asked. She slid the spoon into the bowl.

"Oh, nothing."

"Mama says to turn your frown upside down," Heather said, as she lifted her lips into a big smile with her fingers, then she pushed her fingers downward, making her mouth frown.

"And your mother is correct." Aunt Merry said. "What happens, Heather, if I turn my frown upside down?"

Heather giggled and looked up at her with flour smeared over her face. "You're smiling!"

She laughed. How could she not smile, looking down at that cute little flour-smeared face?

"See, you're smiling, Aunt Bree."

"Yes, I am. Thanks to you." She touched her finger to Heather's nose.

Anna laughed with them. "What are your plans today?

Anything special?"

Shrugging, she said, "I need to go to the studio and do a routine—"

"Are you sure it's not to see a particular guy?" Anna teased.

"Actually, as much as I'd love to see Lucas, I do have to get some dance time in. I've been getting lazy and slacking off."

"Did you ever call about the Founders Day parade?" Aunt Merry asked, slipping a cookie sheet into the oven.

"I did." She smoothed her hands onto the make-shift apron—a towel tucked into her waistband. "And we're all set. Now I need to come up with a routine for the kids and figure out costumes and scenery." She paused. "Oh, and I asked Lucas and Devon if they could build a float. They agreed."

"Your father will help. He used to have a float, from years ago." Aunt Merry wiped her hands on a paper towel.

"Really?"

"Yup. And he's got the truck to pull it. You just need to spruce it up and add your own thing," Aunt Merry added, which thrilled Bree. It would save Lucas and Devon a lot of work.

"That doesn't give you much time—a month maybe," Anna said as she wiped down Heather's face. "Are you going to have all your students participate?"

"Sure thing. Most of my students are between the ages of five and seven. I'll come up with something." She tucked a thick band of hair behind her ear. "I've been looking at ideas on YouTube and have been choreographing a dance in my mind. I also have a few steps planned out to the music I want to use."

"Well, see? You've gone over one hurdle, so far," Aunt Merry said. She smiled her encouragement.

"Yeah, and a dozen more to go."

"It'll work out, Bree," Anna assured her. "It usually does."

"I know."

After baking the cookies and only eating two of them, she

called Lucas. It was nearing the end of his work day. She missed him and wanted to hear his voice.

"Hey!" Lucas said.

She heard a lot of noise in the background. "Sounds like you're really busy. I'm sorry I got you at a bad time."

"Bree, you never get me at a bad time," he said. "Well, not yet anyway." He chuckled and it made her smile. "What's up?"

"I finished making a few dozen chocolate chip cookies and now I'm thinking of going to the studio to dance." She squinted her eyes. What was all that noise in the background? "You having a party?"

He laughed. "No. I have the crew here now. That's why it sounds so noisy. And we're making great progress."

There was a pause and some muffled words.

"I have some good news for you."

"I love good news. What is it?" She smiled even though Lucas couldn't see it.

"We'll be done in a week."

"Really? Are you serious?" She couldn't contain her excitement. She spun in a circle. If she were there with Lucas, she'd be hugging him right now. And kissing him.

"I'm serious." He chuckled, warming her insides. "By this time next week, you'll have a newly renovated studio."

She grinned. "I can't wait to see it, Lucas."

"Speaking of that, I was wondering if you could hold back from coming here to dance so I can surprise you next week."

Her smile disappeared. "Oh. Well, I was going to swing by tonight to dance, but--"

"No, it's okay. I wanted to surprise you, that's all."

She felt bad for making him feel guilty. "Hey, no worries, Lucas. I can practice here. I promise I'll stay away from the studio until you bring me there, personally, to surprise me."

"Great!" Lucas paused. "I was wondering if you were busy tomorrow. I mean, I'm sure you are, but I was hoping you'd want to take a break and spend some time with me and

Dani."

"I'd love to, Lucas. What time?" Excitement tingled through her.

"We'll pick you up around eleven?"

"Works for me. What should I bring?"

"Yourself, Bree. Bring you and your wonderful self."

Heat crawled up her neck and into her face. Lucas could make her blush over the phone no less! "I should bring something. It's only right."

"Well, I wouldn't mind if you brought along some of those chocolate chip cookies."

She laughed. "No problem."

"See you tomorrow then," Lucas said.

"See you tomorrow, Lucas." Her voice sounded soft and. . .wanting. She hit End on her cell and grinned. She rushed to the kitchen where Anna was pouring a glass of water for herself and a juice for Heather. “I have great news!” she blurted out.

Anna spun around, nearly knocking over the glass of water. “Good gracious, Bree, you scared me half to death!”

“Oh, sorry. I’m so happy, and excited.” She looked around the kitchen. “Where’s Aunt Merry?”

“She brought some cookies out to Dad. So, why are you so excited?”

“Lucas has a crew over there to help him and Devon, and he said the studio should be finished in a week. Isn’t that wonderful news?” She hugged Anna tight, then pulled back. “I can’t wait to see it!”

“I bet. Tell you what,” Anna started, picking up her glass of water. “I’ll send emails with a tentative date to the parents. I’ll also post it to your Facebook page and Instagram. If the date changes, it would only be by a few days. At least your students will have a more definitive date now.”

“That’s a great idea, Anna. Thanks for helping me out with this. I really appreciate it.” She hugged Anna again.

“I know you do. But, I know there’s more to your

excitement than finding out about the studio."

She grinned. "I'm going on another date with Lucas. Tomorrow!" She grabbed a Tupperware container from the cupboard. "And I need to bring cookies."

Despite their talk on Wednesday night, Lucas was obviously in better spirits. They had talked several times in the last couple of days, on the phone, but he seemed even happier now. Every time she talked to him, something inside her bloomed. There was no doubt about it. She was developing some strong feelings for Lucas, but she wasn't sure if she could actually call it love.

Fourteen

Lucas sat on the couch with a cup of coffee and Dani by his side. The TV was turned on to her favorite cartoon while he read the newspaper. His mother and father had left earlier to get some groceries and do some errands. He was content and happy. If anyone had told him a couple of months ago he'd meet a wonderful woman who would mend his heart, he would've disagreed. But he had. And she was more than wonderful. She was beautiful, talented, funny, and she liked Dani. Having a woman in his life, who also liked his daughter, was a plus in his book. Of course, it would be so much better if Bree could truly love his daughter as her own. But, in order to do that, they would have to spend more time together. And that's why he had invited her to spend the day with them.

He glanced down at his daughter and smoothed his hand over the top of her head. She looked up at him and smiled. God, how he loved this girl. She was everything to him. God had answered his prayers when he begged Him to save his daughter. A small wave of guilt swept through him when he remembered he had never prayed for the well-being of his wife. He had been filled with too much anger. But, he had his little girl.

"Hey, Daddy," she said. "What're we doing today?"

"We're going on another picnic." He tapped her nose. "And Bree is coming with us."

Dani grinned. "Yay! Can she bring Buster?"

He didn't know what to say. He knew how much Dani loved being with Buster, but he wasn't as fond of the dog as she was.

"Please, Daddy? Can you ask Bree?"

He pulled her tight against him. "Remember, Buster

belongs to Bree's daddy. He's not really Bree's dog."

"Oh. I forgot." She pouted. "I know!"

Oh. Oh. Now what was Dani thinking?

"We can ask Bree's daddy."

He wasn't sure about this new idea at all. If the dog were with them, it'd be work for Bree. He wanted to have some quality time with Bree and Dani so they could get to know each other. Of course, Dani didn't understand that. She only wanted to have the dog around her. "Tell you what. I'll call Bree to see if Buster can come along. But, if he can't, we'll plan it for another time, okay?" He ruffled the top of her head.

"Okay, Daddy." She pulled away. "I hope Buster can come with us. It'll be so much fun." She leaned back, crossing her legs and went back to watching her program.

As much as he wanted Dani to be around children her own age, he also wanted to spend time with Bree and Dani, to watch how they interacted, how Bree would care for Dani. He needed to find out if Bree would fit into their lives, because he had to admit, he was falling in love with her and wanted her in his life.

He reached for his cell which had been on the coffee table and clicked on Bree's number. It rang five times before going to voice mail. He glanced at the time. It was ten o'clock. Maybe she was taking a shower. He said they'd pick her up around eleven. He left a message then clicked off and decided to try again in a few minutes.

"Well, kiddo, Bree isn't answering right now."

Dani pouted and crossed her arms over her chest. He wanted to chuckle, but he held back. This was Dani's way of wanting control of the situation and she thought if she pouted enough, he'd give in. Sometimes he did. "I'll call again in a few minutes." He tapped her leg. "C'mon. Let's get you dressed. We need to pick up Bree in a little while."

Dani scooted herself forward. She slid off the couch and, together they headed to her bedroom. It only took a few minutes to get his daughter dressed for the day. She was as excited for an adventure as he was. He had decided to bring Bree to the cabin. It was nearly finished, and he wanted to see her reaction.

Several minutes later, his phone rang. It was Bree. He grinned and answered. "Hey!"

"Hi, Lucas. We still on?"

"Of course, we are." He cleared his throat. "Dani wants to know if you can bring Buster."

He heard Bree sigh. Evidently, she felt the same as he did.

"Are you sure, Lucas? I mean, I don't mind, but I know you're not a fan of Buster."

He chuckled. She had that right. He caught a flash of pink from the corner of his eye. Dani stood next to him, bouncing on her feet.

"Is Buster coming? Is he?"

"I can hear Dani. She really wants to see Buster, doesn't she?"

"She does," he answered. He glanced down at Dani who stood there, her hands clasped together in prayer.

"Okay, I'll bring him."

"I'll tell her. See you soon."

"Can't wait," Bree answered and he smiled. He ended the call.

"Daddy? Is Buster coming with us?"

"He sure is."

"Yay!" she squealed, hopping around. "I get to play with Buster!"

"I'm going to pack us a nice lunch. Why don't you brush your teeth. I already set up your toothbrush."

"Okay, Daddy." Dani scooted off to the bathroom as he walked into the kitchen. He opened the refrigerator and pulled out some deli meat. He'd make some Italian subs. He wasn't sure if she liked them, but he'd take the chance. As he assembled the sandwiches, Dani came into the kitchen.

"I'm all ready. Can we go now?"

He laughed. "In a little while. I have to finish the sandwiches, munchkin."

"Can I help?"

Dani always wanted to help, but she was limited and sometimes when he or his parents allowed her to help, it often ended up in a bigger mess than usual. But she had to develop skills and he, as her father, had to be patient and understanding, even if the messes made him angry.

"You can put the bottles of water in the cooler," he twisted around and opened the fridge door. He pulled out several bottles of water. "Here. Put these in the cooler. Lay them flat."

She took a bottle and carefully placed it on its side. He smiled. "Great job, honey."

Dani continued until all the bottles were in the cooler. "Can we bring some fruit and some snacks?"

"Sure. Can you get the box of strawberries out? Remember how Gramma showed you."

Dani nodded. "I'll do a good job, Daddy. Watch me."

He watched as Dani reached for the quart size container of strawberries and pulled them closer to the edge of the tray. She lifted it up with her good hand then pressed the box tight against her. She walked over to him where he pulled the box away from her. He smiled. "You did a fantastic job!"

"Thanks Daddy."

A few minutes later, he had the cooler packed. He decided to grab their lightweight jackets, just in case. The weather could change at a moment's notice, and he wanted to be prepared.

"Okay, Dani. We're ready to head out. Got everything?" he asked as he picked up the cooler from the kitchen floor.

"I'm ready!" As she left the house and scurried down the short flight of steps to the truck, he realized he was as happy as Dani. He couldn't wait to see Bree. He set the cooler in the back of the truck and then buckled Dani into her car seat. Thank God, he had had the foresight to buy a truck with a back seat. He also hoped Buster would sit still in the car and mind Bree's commands. He'd deal with whatever came his way concerning the dog. He was happy that Dani was happy.

* * * *

Bree didn't know where they were going, but it didn't matter. She was thrilled to spend the day with him and Dani. She was surprised he had asked her to bring Buster, due to his fear of dogs, but then realized Dani wanted to see him. Buster sat behind the driver's seat, sitting up with his tongue hanging out of his mouth. Every once in a while, Dani would say something to him and he'd slump toward her so she could pet the top of his head. He'd close his eyes and let her rub his ears until something distracted him and he'd sit straight up, glancing out the window. She'd have to wash Lucas's windows though. They were smeared with snout-goo.

"I think you're going to love the house, Bree," Lucas said as they drove down the road. "It sits on the quieter part of the river and is quite beautiful. I specifically chose that spot because of it's. . .tranquility, I guess you could call it."

"Is it secluded?" she asked, wondering about the dangers of living in the woods on the edge of town, so far from safety.

"Yes and no," Lucas answered, turning his gaze to her. "You'll understand when we get there."

"Daddy, are we there yet?"

"Not yet, sweetheart. We'll be there shortly."

As they drove, she looked out the window at the passing scenery. Misty River really was a beautiful little town. Farmland stretched for several miles in both directions with the marshland off in the distance. The main part of the town had been settled on the widest part of the river, but as they drove further from town, the river wound through the forest. She would often hike through the woods as a teen, when she wasn't dancing her heart out, and she'd follow the winding river through the thick woods and would soon come out to either a farm or someone's backyard. That had been fifteen years ago. She wondered how much of it had been built up with new homes. For all she knew, Lucas's house could be sitting on a piece of land she had hiked through.

"We're almost there," Lucas said as he turned the truck onto a narrow, winding dirt road. Something about the road looked familiar. It was an old camp road she and her friends had occasionally hiked down to get to the river. Was he bringing her to the old camp house?

A moment later, the narrow road opened to a wider drive which led toward the river. To her right, a small rock wall stretched toward the end of the drive. This was the same road! As they neared the property, Lucas slowed then came to a stop at a huge cabin overlooking part of Misty River. No small camp house.

"Here we are!" Lucas announced, turning sideways, and settling his right arm over the top of the seat.

"We're here! Yay!" Dani unbuckled the belt but didn't move from her seat. She kicked her legs back and forth. "Come get me, Daddy."

He glanced back at Dani with a wide smile, then to her. His smile disappeared. "What's wrong?"

"You're not going to believe this, but I've been here before."

"You have? When?"

"Maybe fifteen years ago when my friends and I went hiking. We never knew where we'd come out after walking through the woods all day. One time, we came out here, at this spot."

"How do you know we're in the same place?"

"Because I remember standing over there," she pointed to where she believed would be a small sandy beach, "and looked across to that red house over there." She looked at the cabin. "A small house once sat here."

Lucas nodded. "I can't believe it. It's serendipity, for sure.

I bought it from an elderly man last year." He shook his head.

"So, this cabin is yours?"

Lucas grinned like the Cheshire cat. "It sure is."

She opened the truck door, looking at the river glistening in the sun, its surface as smooth as glass. The opposite shoreline, with the lone red house, was mirrored on the water. Birds sang in the trees high above them. A loon called out to its mate. It was so peaceful.

As Lucas got out of the truck, she peered at the gorgeous two-story cabin, its logs gleaming like melted maple syrup in the sunlight. Lucas definitely had talent when it came to building a cabin. She wondered what else he had built in his career. She'd have to ask him.

While Lucas attended to Dani in the car seat, she walked over to the door on Buster's side and opened it. He whined and pranced on the seat. "Buster, I'll let you out in a minute, but first, you need to know the rules." She stroked his ears and cupped his head in her hands. "No chasing squirrels. Stay near the cabin. And play nice with Dani. Got it?" It was as if the dog understood. He bobbed his head, then maneuvered himself out of her hands. He cried again. "Okay, then. Have fun." She stepped aside and the dog leaped from the truck. He bounded down the lane to the cabin.

She let out a shrill whistle which startled Dani and caught Lucas's attention. Buster stopped and sat on his haunches. "I'm sorry, Dani. I didn't mean to scare you."

Lucas peered over at her as he pulled Dani from her car seat. "You sure you have him under control?"

She bit her tongue. She was here to have a good time. Buster had better not ruin it for her. She whistled again and he scrambled over to her. "Sit." The dog obeyed. She looked down at him. "What did I just tell you? Behave or you'll be on the leash. Got it?"

Buster whined and looked down at the ground. He didn't move until she had walked away from the truck. He followed at her heels. She knew he wanted to run and explore, but he had to know that they were in a different territory.

"It's beautiful, Lucas." She swung her gaze from the cabin to him, grinning. "It's just stunning. And big."

He shrugged and stuck his thumbs in his pockets. "Well, after looking at a dozen or more designs, I kept coming back to this one. It spoke to me. Know what I mean?"

She did, because the cabin spoke to her as well. She immediately felt at home. As she followed Lucas and Dani down the small path toward the cabin, she wondered what it would be like to be a part of Lucas's family. Maybe they would have a child, or children, of their own and they would run down the path toward this cabin. She could see herself sitting on the porch, admiring the view, watching Lucas fish from the dock.

"Bree?"

Her thoughts scattered. "Yeah?"

"You seem to be miles away. You okay?"

She nodded. "Yeah. I'm great. I'm admiring the view."

"Would that be the view of the cabin or. . .something else?" He turned and angled his bottom toward her. A loud laugh tumbled from her mouth. She glanced at his butt and shook her head. "Nah. The view of the river is much better." Then she winked at him.

They walked up three steps on the side of the cabin, whose front looked out onto the river, and walked to the door. It was unusually large for a typical house, but it suited this log cabin. On either side of the door were standard windows.

He unlocked the door and held it open for them. "C'mon in. You're going to love it!"

"If it's as nice as the outside, then I'm sure I will."

Dani rushed in, obviously knowing where she was going, but she stepped in cautiously. Once inside the huge foyer, Lucas closed the door with a quiet click and stood behind her.

She couldn't believe it. It was big. And airy. And. . ."This is so beautiful, Lucas."

He wrapped his arms around her waist and rested his chin on the top of her head. She leaned back, nestling against his solid strength. He smelled of fresh air and a hint of his spicy cologne. She closed her eyes. He kissed the top of her head, and she suddenly felt like she belonged. Here. In this place. With Lucas and Dani. In the distance, she could hear Dani's footsteps hurrying along the smooth floor, her feet thumping in a steady rhythm.

"I could stand here for the rest of the day, holding you like this, but I'd like to show you the house," Lucas said, lifting his head but keeping his arms wrapped tight around her.

She didn't want to move either, but she did want to see the rest of the cabin and what he had built with his own hands. "Me too, but I think there's an excited little girl who wants to show me around."

"As well as an excited man," he chuckled. "C'mon." He pulled away, releasing his hold from around her waist and clasped her elbow, guiding her forward.

They stepped further into the massive living room with its stone chimney and beamed ceilings. And to her right were massive picture windows looking out to the river. There was a deck just beyond the windows where one could sit and dream away the hours while watching the river and admiring the view of the forest.

"Oh, it's absolutely beautiful, Lucas," she breathed as she stood by the window and stared at the beauty in front of her.

"I'm glad you like it," Lucas responded coming to stand beside her and wrapping an arm around her shoulders. "Before I built this cabin, I would sit right down there," he pointed to a small sandy nook along the river's edge, "and fish to my heart's content." He sighed. "Caught some decent fish too."

"See? I knew I recognized this place. There is a small beach down there."

He grinned. "There is."

"When did you decide it was the perfect spot for your

cabin? She asked, leaning into him.

"When I was kayaking and saw the small, dilapidated house up here on the hill. I loved everything about the spot."

"It is a beautiful spot." She flitted her gaze to her left. "Oh, look!" She darted from his side. "This kitchen is just . . .I don't have words to describe it. Big. Beautiful. Wow, is about all I can say."

He chuckled, walking toward her. "It's nearly finished. Just waiting for the gas range to come in. It'll have six burners and a huge oven."

"You plan on serving the entire town?" She smoothed the palm of her hand over the granite countertops.

"You never know."

She touched the wrought iron handles on the knotty pine cabinets. She couldn't believe the workmanship Lucas had put into his home. And, of course, his crew, she assumed. It totally amazed her. "Did you and Devon build this house by yourselves?"

"No, we had the crew help. The same guys who are working on the studio. Even my dad helped."

"You did a great job. It's just amazing!" She admired the simplicity of the room and how open and airy it was. The kitchen and the living room made up most of the downstairs. There was a good-sized full bathroom on the first floor right off the kitchen and a huge bedroom. The bedroom was unfurnished, and she wondered how he would decorate it.

"This is where I need your help," Lucas said as though reading her mind. "This is going to be the master bedroom and I want your opinion on how to furnish and decorate it."

She stepped in and walked to the center of the room. It had to be at least fifteen feet by twenty, give or take a foot. It was nearly the size of the main room in her studio. One 'wall' was sliding glass doors that led to a deck overlooking the woods. The river was to her right. It was a room for peaceful dreaming with the lapping of the river and the hoots of the owls, maybe the lone cry of a coyote off in the distance.

"Well?" Lucas coaxed as he leaned against the doorframe, smiling at her.

She smiled back. She wasn't sure what to say. After all, this room would be his and. . .his wife's. And if she wasn't going to be a part of his future, then she shouldn't be giving him her advice. It wouldn't be hers. But. . .if she were to live here. . .She put a finger to her chin and turned.

"Well, if I was going to be sleeping in this room, I would have a king-sized bed against that wall." She pointed to the wall opposite the window. "So, I could look out the window before I fell asleep and again when I woke up." She moved closer to Lucas. "I'd build the bed from logs. Or with curvy limbs to add a decorative touch to the headboard or footboard. It would be sturdy and would fit the feel of the rest of the house." She glanced at him. He looked at her as though looking into her soul.

His eyes darkened and he pushed away from the doorframe. He stepped toward her. Desire flooded his gaze as his lids drooped slightly over his coffee-colored eyes. A warmth spread through her as he came closer. She bit her lip. Awareness pooled low in her abdomen and a flutter of excitement drifted up her spine like hundreds of butterflies had taken flight. He stood inches from her, his gaze flicking over her face as though he was trying to read her thoughts. If he only knew. She wanted him to pull her close, slant those firm lips over hers and take everything she had. Her breath hitched as he dipped his head until he was a hairs breadth from her mouth.

"You can sleep here, Bree, don't you know that?"

Then he pressed his mouth against hers and she moaned, reaching her arms up and entwining them around his neck. He wouldn't be able to pull away if he wanted. She took from him everything he gave and then some. His muscled body pressed against hers as his arms wrapped around her, holding her tight. Neither one of them wanted to separate from the other. She sighed as he groaned. The kiss intensified as he moved his hands up and down her back, then down further, cupping her bottom. She needed him more than she needed air. Her fingers slid through his hair, pulling his head closer, pressing his mouth closer.

"Daddy?"

Then a loud bark.

She squealed as he snapped his head back, her hands coming loose and sliding down his arms. She had forgotten about Dani. How stupid and foolish. Heat rose to her cheeks, and she was suddenly angry with herself, and with Lucas. What if Dani had gone outside alone? No. Buster wouldn't have let her. "Oh my God, Lucas. I--We--"

Lucas shook his head. "It wasn't your fault." He rushed out of the room.

It had only been a couple of minutes at the most, she thought. She ran from the bedroom and stopped at his side in the kitchen.

"Dani, are you alright?"

She nodded.

"You remember Daddy's rule, right?"

"Yup."

"Can you tell me what it is?"

Dani looked from her father to her then back to her father. "I'm never, ever to leave the house unless you or someone in the family is with me."

"Good girl," Lucas said, running a hand down Dani's slender arm. "Sometimes Daddy gets busy and can't be with you all the time, so I need to know that you're safe. Right?"

Dani nodded again. "I looked out the window and watched the river, then I couldn't find you, but I heard you talking in here."

"Well, I'm glad you didn't leave the cabin," Lucas said as he hugged Dani. He looked at Buster. "Good job, Buster."

Fifteen

"Can we have our picnic now, Daddy?"

He ruffled his daughter's hair. "Sure, Pumpkin. In a few minutes. I want to show Bree the bedrooms upstairs and I want you to come upstairs too. C'mon." He encouraged, as he turned the corner and walked toward the staircase to the left of the front door.

Bree followed behind them as they climbed the stairs to the second floor. The landing overlooked the living room below and Bree peered over the edge. Buster tried to squeeze his head through the slats. "I can't believe how big this cabin is. It doesn't seem this big from the outside."

"It is deceiving," he agreed. "I love the open concept of the house. I didn't want a place where there were walls everywhere. Not that that's a bad thing, but out here in the woods, I wanted something that fit with the natural environment."

Bree turned. "Oh, this is cute." She walked toward the back wall. A little alcove sat beneath a dormer window looking out to the same woods they had looked out to from the master bedroom downstairs. It was a small open area where one could sit and read either on the window seat or in a cozy chair. He had been thinking of Dani when he designed the cabin, but now that he thought about it, it suited Bree as well. He could picture her sitting in the alcove reading alone or reading to Dani. His heart swelled at the thought. As though reading his mind, she said, "I could sit here all day and read." Mission accomplished. He gave himself a mental fist pump.

"Let me show you Dani's bedroom." He led her away from the loft and walked to the right. He opened the door and she stepped inside, followed by Dani and Buster, of course. The room was smaller than the master downstairs, but it was still a decent size, about a twelve-foot square room.

"This is gonna be my room," Dani announced, striding forward. "My bed's gonna go here," and she pointed to the wall. "It's gonna be pink with princesses."

Bree grinned as he chuckled. Dani had big dreams of what she wanted her room to look like, but it would be near impossible to have a lot of pink considering the walls were made of logs. And he was determined he wasn't going to paint the logs pink regardless of how much his daughter begged him.

Bree leaned into him. "Ah, how are you going to make this into a princess room?"

He tilted his head toward her. "No clue. No pink walls for sure, but we can have a pink rug and princess curtains."

"Hmm, that might work." Bree stepped further into the room. "Dani, how would you like to have a little reading corner right here by the window?" Bree looked out the window towards the woods. "You know what?" She leaned into the window. "I think I see a fairy floating out there."

"You do!" Dani rushed over and gazed out. "Where? I wanna see!"

"Oh! She flitted off somewhere," Bree said.

He stood there watching the exchange between the two girls who meant the most to him. Grinning, he moved over to them.

Dani turned toward the dog. "Buster, did you see a fairy?"

Buster barked once as though saying yes.

"Fairies don't hang around too long." Bree turned away from the window and flitted her gaze around the room. "I bet, if you made a fairy room, one of them may come to visit."

"Really?" Dani's eyes nearly bulged out of her head, and he chuckled.

Bree nodded. "Maybe. And we could build a fairy garden right at the edge of the woods down there," she added, pointing downward.

Dani pressed her face against the window. "Will you help me?"

He wondered what Bree would say, now that she had suggested the fairy garden. Would she accept the invitation? He hoped so. He'd love to bring her back here again. Actually, he'd like to bring her back to live here. To his delight, and Dani's, Bree agreed.

"Daddy?" Dani looked up at him, her eyes bright. "I think I'm gonna have a fairy room, okay?"

He stroked the top of her head. "Well, now that that's settled, why don't we head out and have some lunch?" His stomach growled at the suggestion.

"Definitely," Bree said as well, rubbing her tummy.

"And you can show me where we can build the fairy garden, okay?" Dani said, grabbing Bree's hand and swinging it between them.

"Sure."

They walked down the central stairway and he led them out to the back deck overlooking the river. "Do you want to eat up here, Dani, or have a picnic closer to the river?"

"Down at the river, Daddy!"

He shrugged and looked at Bree. "Do you mind?"

"No, not at all. Lead the way."

He lifted Dani into his arms and carried her down the stairs. Once they were at the bottom, he lowered her to the ground where she shot off like a bullet toward the water's edge. "Dani, stay where I can see you."

"I can watch her, Lucas."

"You don't mind?"

Bree placed a hand on her hip. "Seriously? Of course not. Now go. We'll wait here."

He smiled his thanks then headed back to the truck. As he grabbed the basket along with a blanket, he grinned. He could imagine Bree living here with them, being a mom to Dani and, maybe, if they were fortunate, they'd have children of their own, running around the place. He whistled a happy tune as he strode back toward the little spot by the river. He stood back and listened. It sounded like they were having a serious discussion.

"I like you, Bree."

"And I like you, Dani." Bree smoothed back Dani's curly hair. "You're so sweet."

"Can we do a sleep over here?"

He could hear Bree nearly choke, but she hid it with a laugh.

"Well, I'm not sure I can do a sleepover here, but you are more than welcome to come to my house."

"Really?"

"Really."

His heart swelled. It would be the perfect opportunity for Bree and Dani to bond.

"I'd love that." Dani grinned. "You're really nice."

And with that, he walked over to them. "What did I miss? Anything good?"

Bree looked up at him as he unfolded the blanket. "Oh, just girl talk."

"Well, I think we should sit on the blanket and eat some lunch." He flipped it open and settled it on a thick patch of grass. They had found a spot about ten feet from the water's edge. It was a cozy spot, and he imagined having a nighttime picnic with Bree, sharing a glass of wine, or beer while looking at the stars. They would lie next to each other, snuggled close and talk, or kiss and—"

"Daddy?"

"Ah, yeah." He didn't know how long he'd been daydreaming. Bree looked at him with a shadow of a smile as though she knew exactly what he had been thinking.

"What did you make for a sandwich?" Dani asked, as she knelt on the blanket and scooted closer to Bree.

"I made you peanut butter and jelly." He lifted the lid and pulled out her sandwich, then unwrapped it. "Here you go,

Peanut." He grabbed a juice box and put the straw through the hole then settled that on a flatter part of the blanket. "Remember, don't squeeze the box."

Dani nodded, taking a bite out of the sandwich. Like most kids, she started in the middle and when she pulled back, there was a smear of peanut butter and grape jelly on both cheeks. He and Bree laughed. She looked like the Joker from Batman, but a whole lot cuter. He shook his head, chuckling at his daughter's antics.

"I made us Italian subs." He looked at Bree as he lifted out the bag. "I also brought chips," and "Pickles," he sang out as he lifted out a small jar, "And,. . .water. Ta-dah!"

Bree laughed, reaching out to help him settle the items on the lopsided blanket. "I think you thought of everything."

"I hope so. Too late to go back now."

For the first few minutes, they ate in silence as the birds sang their birdsong from the seclusion of the woods and the river ambled by, slow and steady. A loon called to its mate far off in the distance.

"It's so beautiful here, Lucas," Bree said, lifting the water bottle to her lips.

He followed her lead. He drank half the bottle then leaned back on his elbows, stretching his long legs out in front of him. "I love this area. It's peaceful, yet close to town. It's one of the reasons, I chose to build my cabin here." He looked down the river, then back to Bree. She had been watching him while eating her sub. "Devon's place is just down the road, that way." He pointed in the direction they had come in from. "I don't think I shared with you, our plans."

"Your plans?" Bree echoed before taking a bite.

He reached down for his sub. "Devon and I are planning on building some cabins along the river. You've heard of glamping, right?"

Bree's forehead creased in confusion. "Can't say that I have."

"Well, glamping is short for glamorous camping."

Bree laughed, then covered her mouth.

"We're not going to build a huge glamping resort, but something small. Rustic, but fun. A place where families, or couples, can get away from it all and enjoy what we have to offer—fishing, kayaking, hiking or laying in a hammock all day, reading—"

"Or sleeping," Bree added. "I've never heard of glamping, but then again, my world was ballet and not hanging out in the woods, except when I was a teen and I hiked . . .sometimes. I was a city girl for ten years."

How could he forget she had been gone for ten years? She had left right out of high school. Although he had been married, there were moments when Bree would pop into his mind, and he'd wonder what she was doing or where she was performing. It wasn't until after Daniella passed away that he started watching YouTube videos of Bree. Did she still dream of being on stage in front of hundreds of people?

"Lucas?"

He shook his head, pushing the question away. "Oh. Sorry." He took another swig of his water. "Yeah, so Devon and I put our heads together one night, while at the tavern, and thought it wouldn't be a bad idea to build a small glamping resort along the river."

"Have you started building yet?"

"Only one. But we have the permits to build more. We had other jobs to finish and then renovating your studio and now, well, I think we'll be able to start on more cabins. If all goes well, we can have our first customers by the end of July."

"That fast? Wow!" Bree responded, changing her position so she was lying on her side.

His throat went dry despite having had a drink of his water. Her body was all subtle curves and strength. She was solid, yet soft. How he wanted to lie next to her and slide his hand over the curve of her hip and tug her closer to share a kiss. He cleared his throat and took another swig of his water.

"Well, maybe by mid-summer. I need to place ads first. What's wonderful about this resort is that I can rent the cabins all year."

"I can't imagine you and Devon building cabins like this," Bree pointed to his cabin, "And still having it done by early summer."

He chuckled. He had obviously led her to believe the cabins would be big. "Ah, no. The cabins will be much smaller. We're thinking A-frame style. Some will have one bedroom; others will have two. They'll be cozy, yet comfortable. Small, with an open floor plan to make the cabin look more spacious."

"Sounds like you put a lot of thought into this."

"We did." He nodded towards Dani. She was kneeling on the edge of the blanket, gathering small stones, twigs, and leaves, along with acorns and pieces of grass. Bree turned her gaze to where he indicated and smiled. After a moment of watching his daughter concentrating so hard on the task at hand, he had to ask what she was doing. "What's up, Dani?"

She turned to him and grinned. "I'm collecting things for my fairies."

"Ohhh," he nodded, then shot a glance to Bree. She was smiling too.

"Oh, that's right. I almost forgot," Bree said, sitting up. "We're supposed to make a fairy house, aren't we?"

"Uh-huh," Dani answered with a quick nod. "Can you help me?"

"I sure can." She scooted over to Dani. "What do you have there?"

"See?" Dani spread her arm out to show what she displayed haphazardly on the old quilt. "I don't have that much stuff, Bree. I need more."

"No need to worry. There'll be plenty of stuff to use by the tree where we'll build the house. The woods never run out of stuff for the fairies."

"Are you sure?"

"I'm positive." Bree brushed off the crumbs from her legs then stood. "Give me what you have, and I'll carry them over to the tree," she turned and pointed to a big pine tree on the edge of the woods whose base had a hollow in it. "And you'll be able to see it from your bedroom."

"I will? Yay!"

He picked up the remnants of their lunch as Dani and Bree headed away from the blanket toward the tree. Buster scampered along beside them. It didn't take long to clean up. He carried the basket and blanket to the truck and deposited them into the back. He grabbed the fishing rods along with his tackle box and turned toward the cabin. When he came around the corner, Bree and Dani were hunched over, looking down at the ground for 'fairy treasures'. He wondered if he should join in, but something told him to find a soft patch of grass and watch them. He set the rods down on the grass along with the tackle box. He crossed his legs and closed his eyes for a moment, soaking up the sun and listening to the chatter of Bree and Dani.

When he opened his eyes, he found Buster lying next to him. The dog's eyes were nearly closed as he lay in the patch of sunlight. Without really thinking about it, he found himself petting Buster, his hand sliding up and down the soft, red-gold coat. His hand wandered to the dog's head, and he massaged the dog's scalp and scratched behind his ears. Well, wouldn't you know! The dog wasn't as scary as he had thought. He was a big old puppy, just as Bree had said. He smiled. Maybe he would buy a dog. Someday.

For a half-hour, he watched his daughter and Bree build a fairy house that was quite impressive, considering they weren't using glue or nails to hold everything together. He was sure the whole house would be tumbled to the ground by the time he returned in a few days. A simple run up the tree from a squirrel would knock the fairy house down, but they were laughing and giggling and having a wonderful time. He wouldn't spoil it by telling them the house would be smashed by that evening.

He pulled out his cell phone and pressed the camera icon. He took several pictures, then leaned back, enjoying the sight before him. They were so good together, Dani and Bree. She was patient, kind and so helpful, and it filled his heart. Dani's own mother hadn't been that patient. Bree may not know it, but she was a natural at nurturing. He decided from this day forward, he would do what he had to do to convince Bree to stay here in Misty River and not pursue another job in some big city. Didn't she know she belonged here with him and Dani?

Bree turned and smiled at him. He waved back, grinning. Bree's eyes widened as she nudged her head toward the dog. Buster lying next to him while his forearm rested across the dog's back. He shrugged then gave her the okay sign.

"Bree, I think we're done," Dani said, wiping her hands down her shorts, smearing dirt on them. "Daddy, come look!"

"Be right there."

Bree twisted back to Dani and rubbed her back. "It's beautiful, Dani! The fairies are going to love it." She nuzzled Dani's cheek.

"I agree with Bree, Dani." He hunkered down by the one-foot-tall stick building. It appeared as though the house was made up of three rooms, each one with a roof made from moss and oak leaves. Strips of bark made up the walls.

"I made a fairy bed, too, Daddy!"

"I can see that." He peered into one of the side buildings where Dani had made a bed from moss and pine needles and a big oak leaf for a blanket. "It looks really comfortable." He stood and reached into his back pocket. He pulled out his cell. "Okay you two. I need a picture of the two of you with this beautiful fairy house."

Bree giggled and lifted Dani into her lap. She hunkered onto one knee next to the fairy house and wrapped her arms around Dani's waist. They grinned.

"One, two, three." He took the picture, then glanced at the phone. "It's beautiful."

"Can I see? Can I see?" Dani asked, pushing off Bree's lap and running to him. Bree stood as well and walked over to him, probably curious to see how it had come out.

He leaned down to show Dani the picture. Bree beamed in delight. She pushed strands of hair behind her ear and leaned in as well, her cheek brushing his. He kissed her cheek lightly and she blushed. It was adorable.

"I love it, Lucas." Bree's voice seemed thick. Did she mean the photo or the kiss?

"I'll send it your phone."

She nodded. "I'd love that. It'll be a treasured moment of a beautiful day."

* * * *

Bree was having such a great time. She had meant it when she said she'd treasure the moment. If nothing came of their relationship, she would at least have some photos to help her remember this.

"It's such a beautiful afternoon, I thought we'd get some fishing in." Lucas bent down to retrieve the rods and picked up the tackle box.

She must've made a weird face because his smile faded.

"You don't know how to fish, do you?" It was more of a statement of disbelief than a question.

She shook her head. "But I can learn." She wanted to make this a fun day, which meant giving in to doing something she may not like, but it would please Lucas.

"Can I fish too, Daddy?" Dani asked, reaching up for a rod.

"You sure can, but I need to help you, okay?" He ruffled her hair. "C'mon. Let's head down to the dock and I'll get the rods ready."

"Ahh, we're not using worms, are we?" She wouldn't be

fishing if she had to put a worm on a hook.

"No. I have lures. But maybe next time." He grinned, then laughed when she responded with a smirk and a shake of her head.

"I'll watch you fish next time. I don't do worms."

"Ewww, worms are yucky," Dani responded, agreeing with her sentiment.

"Yes, Dani, worms are yucky." She laughed as they strolled to the dock.

Lucas put the lures on the rods and once he had them set up, he cast the line for her then handed her the rod. She didn't have a clue as to what to do.

"Ahh, Lucas, what happens if I catch a fish?" She looked at her rod then back at him. He was sitting cross-legged with Dani in his lap, holding the fishing rod for her.

"See the bobber on the end of the line?"

"Yeah."

"When it bobs, hence the name, then you pull hard and reel it in."

"Reel it in?" Boy, she felt stupid right now.

"The reel is on the rod. Right where your hand is. Turn the handle and bring in the fish. But don't do it too fast."

"Sure. Okay, I've got this." She turned her gaze back to the river and sighed. Buster came over to her, nudged her thigh then sat back on his haunches, watching the line as well. Several minutes had gone by without a single bite.

"Daddy, this is boring," Dani commented, twisting around to look up at him. "We haven't caught any fish yet. I thought we were going to catch fish?"

"Me too," she said, looking at Lucas.

"See, that's the beauty of fishing." He looked at Dani, tweaking her nose, then looked over at her. "You just sit and wait. Relax. Think. Envision catching a fish."

"Right. Just relax." She closed her eyes, sighing. "Think. Envision catch—" There was a pull on her line. "What do I do?" She gave a nervous laugh. "I don't know what to do."

"Pull back to set the hook."

Set the hook? She pulled back. Was the fish still on?

"Now reel it in."

She turned the handle. She could feel a tightness on the line. She had a fish! Lucas must've stood because she suddenly felt his presence next to her, but she couldn't look at him.

"Keep going. Not too fast. Good."

All her focus was on reeling in her first fish. Ever. As she reeled the in the fish closer to the dock, Buster scampered around and barked which sent several birds in flight.

Dani squealed in delight too. "Bree caught a fish! Bree caught a fish, Daddy!"

Lucas reached out and put his hand over hers to help her. "I think you caught a good-sized fish, Bree."

"Really?"

Lucas nodded. She continued reeling in the fish.

"Lift the rod."

She followed his instructions and grinned.

"There it is!" Lucas said, beaming in delight, sounding like a doctor announcing the birth of a child to its mother. "A large-mouth bass." Lucas reached for the line and helped her with the fishing rod. She didn't know what to do and felt as though she had four thumbs.

"Here, you take the rod, Lucas, so I don't drop it and lose the fish."

"Okay, but you'll have to hold the fish."

"What?" Had she heard him right? Hold the fish? No. Absolutely not.

"I want to get a picture of you with your first fish. This is a celebration. A first!" he said, reaching into his pocket for his cell phone.

She couldn't help but smile. Her first fish. No one in the company would believe this. Not that she would be telling any of them. They were a part of her past. She was no longer in touch with any of them.

Lucas set the rod down on the dock, then showed her how to hold the fish for the best shot. He laughed as she grasped the slimy creature. The fish squirmed, wanting back in the water. She held him tight at the belly and tail. Ewww, this was gross! "Hurry up and take the picture, Lucas. This thing is gross."

He chuckled. "It's not a thing, and it's not gross." He aimed the cell phone at her. "Okay, smile, Bree. Pretend you really enjoyed yourself."

"Hold the fish, tight!" Dani said, bouncing on her toes. Buster pranced but didn't bark.

She was about to smile when the fish squirmed from lack of oxygen. She almost dropped it, but out of reflex, she squeezed it while shutting her eyes. Her lips twisted and curled. This was gross!

"Oh, this is too funny. I have to show this to my parents. Heck, I have to show it around town."

"Lucas, please take this fish. Now." A sense of relief flooded her when Lucas took the fish from her hands and removed the hook from the side of its mouth. She grimaced again.

"Okay, ready?"

She tossed him a glance. "Ready? For what?"

"The rule of fishing is that when you catch your first fish of the season you have to kiss it then release it back in the water."

"What?!" Was he crazy? She wasn't about to kiss a fish. Eat one, yes. Not kiss one.

Lucas held the fish by its mouth bringing it closer to her face. "C'mon, Bree. One quick kiss. If not, then you'll have bad luck for the rest of the season."

She closed her eyes and touched her lips to the skin of the fish's head. Ewww. The things she'd do now that she was with Lucas. Never in her wildest dreams did she think she'd be fishing and kissing a fish!

"Great picture, Bree," Lucas said as he lowered the fish

into the water. He then rinsed his hands on a damp rag. When he stood, he was beaming. And her heart swelled.

"I can't believe you caught a fish. I am so proud of you, Bree." He pulled her close. "You're my type of woman." He kissed her forehead then released her.

The statement caught her off guard. "Am I really?"

He touched his finger to her chin and tilted her face up. "You are. I love being around you and discovering something new about you every time we're together."

"Like finding out I'm not into kissing fish?"

He laughed. "Exactly. But I am glad that you're into kissing me."

She grinned as his lips met hers, then her smiled faded as she kissed him back. Yes, this was definitely better than kissing a fish.

Sixteen

Bree sat in the backyard with a book in her lap and an iced tea in hand. She loved this time of year when the trees were beginning to bud, and the flowers started to sprout. Several apple trees in the background had flowered along with the dogwoods. The grass grew green, and the birds sang among the trees. It was peaceful and she didn't have a care in the world. Lucas would be doing the finishing touches on the studio with Devon, and she hoped she'd be able to see him tonight. She didn't have any plans for the day. It would be low-key. She took a sip of her cold drink then closed her eyes and leaned back, letting the sun warm her.

The phone rang, startling her. She glanced at the screen but didn't recognize the number. "Hello?"

"Hello, is this Bree Thompson?"

"Yes it is." She set her tea down on the table.

"This is Margot Devereaux from the Artistique Ballet Company in Philadelphia."

Her eyes widened.

"Did I catch you at a bad time? I was hoping we could do the interview today instead of Thursday as originally planned," Margot stated.

"Ah, no, this isn't a bad time at all." Stay calm, Bree. You've done this before.

Margot asked about her experience although she was sure Margot had read up on her before even calling, after reviewing her resume'. She held her excitement at bay and answered all the questions professionally and honestly, including her injury. Margot paused a moment, then she was put on hold. Her heart plummeted to her feet. She had lost her chance. Her injury had ruined her career. When Margot started speaking again, she squeezed her eyes shut.

"Miss Thompson, we would like to request that you attend an audition on May twentieth. We'll be starting the auditions at nine a.m. I'll send you all the information via email."

She suddenly felt giddy and nauseous all at the same time. Her head bobbed up and down then she realized Margot couldn't see her. "I'll be there, Miss Devereaux. Thank you."

"It was a pleasure speaking with you, Miss Thompson."

"Thank you for calling, Miss Devereaux." She ended the call and heaved a sigh. She had an audition! She stood and danced in a circle, raising her arms high. "Yes!"

She was so excited she had to share it with someone. She'd call Lucas. No, wait. She had to tell him when the moment was right. She didn't want to share it over the phone. Besides, she had a feeling Lucas wouldn't take the news well. She needed to think of a way to tell him what her plans were and how she could approach the subject without upsetting him and Dani. She shook her head and decided to work on her plans for the recital as well as her plans for class which was two days away.

Two hours later she was startled by the sound of her aunt calling out for her. "I'm in the den, Aunt Merry." She heard the shuffle of her aunt walking down the hallway and a second later, she peeked her head in the doorway.

"Are you hungry? Your father and I brought home Chinese food."

She grinned. "Chinese food? What are we celebrating?" It couldn't be the fact she had an interview. She hadn't shared the news with anyone.

"We thought it would be. . .something different to do."

"Okay then, lead the way." She stood and followed her aunt down the hall to the kitchen. Her father stood at the table, opening the bags. He looked up at her and smiled. "Thought we'd have take-out tonight. It's been a long time."

Nodding, she headed to the table to sit when the back door swung open and a familiar figure strode in.

"Brett?" She rushed over to him as he held out his arms. "Oh my God, you're home!" She hugged him close, as he wrapped his arms around her, squeezing her tight in his usual bear hug. He let go of her, laughing. "When did you get in?" She spun her gaze to her father and her aunt. "Wait. You two didn't go shopping in Portland. You went to the airport!"

"Guilty," Aunt Merry said. "We wanted to surprise you." She reached into the cabinet and grabbed some plates.

"Well, I guess you did." She twisted her gaze from her father to her brother. "When did all this happen?"

"I needed a break. Decided to take some vacation time and called Dad." He walked to the table to his usual seat he had sat in since he was a child. "I made Dad promise not to tell you."

"Well, this is a surprise. How long are you home for?"

Brett shrugged. "A few weeks, give or take."

She couldn't believe it. Her brother was home. "So, this is the real reason for the Chinese food."

"Guilty, again," her father said as he grabbed a plate and sat. "It's been hard keeping this a secret." He opened a white carton. "Well, dig in. We don't need to be formal just because Brett's home."

"That's good to know," she answered as she reached for the box with the beef teriyaki. As she scooped food onto her plate, she smiled as Brett shared a funny incident that had happened on the plane. "I thought I was going to have to use my skills and help the woman give birth right there on the plane."

"But you didn't?" Aunt Merry asked, spooning rice onto her plate.

"No, thank God. She was having Braxton-Hicks contractions. Once we landed though, I advised her to go straight to the hospital." He skimmed his gaze to her. "So, Bree, I hear you have a man in your life now. Someone I know, too."

Oh-oh. What would he think of her dating Lucas? How did he know who she was dating? Despite their texting back and forth for the last few weeks, she hadn't shared her dating life with her brother. She flung her gaze to Aunt Merry who, at that moment, hung her head. It didn't matter whether Brett liked it or not. It was her life. "Yes, Brett. You heard right. I'm dating Lucas."

Brett winked at her then dove into his meal. Odd, she thought. She didn't think Brett would like the idea. After all, back in high school, he had practically threatened Lucas with bodily injury if Lucas had asked her out.

"What else have I missed in this little town?" Brett asked, glancing at her and her aunt.

"Well, Jamie's been asking about you," Aunt Merry said. "That girl still has a crush on you."

"Why, I'll never know," Bree answered with a laugh. "I try to tell her what a pain in the butt you are, but she won't listen. She adores you, Brett." She swore she saw his ears turn bright red, but it could've been the sunlight streaming in through the back door. "Have you been in touch with her?"

He shrugged, which meant he knew more than he was letting on and wasn't going to share. "We've texted once in a while. I can't believe she hasn't settled down yet."

"She's holding out for you, Brett."

"Really?" Brett looked at her as though she had sprouted horns.

"Yeah, really. Anyway, I have some good news to share."

"Oh?" her father asked.

"Yeah, I had a phone interview with Margot Devereaux."

"The woman from the dance company in Philadelphia?" her aunt asked, as she set her fork down.

"Yes. She interviewed me this afternoon and wants me to audition for them."

Her aunt squealed. Her father stared at her, his face unreadable. And Brett looked confused.

"Oh, Bree, this is wonderful news!" her aunt said as she reached out and squeezed her hand. "When are you auditioning?"

"The twentieth."

"Of June?"

"No. In May."

Aunt Merry's smile disappeared replaced with a frown. She glanced at her father who frowned as well.

"What?"

"That's Mother's Day weekend, Bree. It's the same weekend as the Founder's Day Festival. You know, the one you and your students will be performing at?"

"Oh, God. I can't believe I didn't realize that." She shook her head. "I was so excited at the prospect of an audition, I forgot it was the same weekend."

"Well, you could always call back and reschedule, couldn't you?" Brett asked. Obviously, he didn't understand how auditions worked in the ballet world.

She heard her cell phone ringing from the den. "Excuse me." She stood and hurried to the den. "Hello?"

"Hello, beautiful."

"Hi, Lucas."

"I have Dani here. She wants to say good night."

"Okay. Sure."

"Hi, Bree!"

"Hi, Dani. How are you?"

"I'm good. I had fun on Sunday. Did you?"

"I sure did," she answered, grinning. She did have fun. More than she thought she would. "Have you seen any fairies, lately?"

Dani giggled. "I think so. Gramma says that we have fairies in the backyard too!"

She laughed with Dani. "Maybe they followed you home."

"Can you come over and help me build another fairy house in the backyard?"

She laughed again. "Not tonight, sweetheart."

"Okay. Maybe tomorrow?"

She heard Lucas's voice in the background.

"Goodnight, Bree. Here's Daddy."

"Goodnight, Dani. Sweet dreams."

"Hey," Lucas said. "Sorry about that. She's excited to make another fairy house with you."

"I bet. We'll do it soon." Should she tell Lucas her news? How would he take it? She sighed.

"You okay?" Lucas asked, concern edging his words.

"Yeah. I'm fine." She was such a liar. She should tell him. "Oh, I almost forgot. Tell Dani I said thanks for giving me so many wonderful ideas for the recital." Guilt swept over her. How was she going to pull this off?

"I will. Bree, are you sure you're alright? You seem, distracted."

"I'm fine. Really." She flipped hair away from her face. "I was thinking about Sunday, that's all."

"Oh? And what were you thinking about?" Lucas let out a husky laugh. "I'm sure it wasn't about fairy houses."

"Actually, I was thinking about the kiss." Butterflies fluttered in her belly then gave way and tumbled lower in her abdomen, causing a stir and creating a heat that made her squirm.

"Ah," he responded. "Bree, do you feel what's happening between us?"

Her breath caught. How was she supposed to answer? She didn't know what to tell him, especially since she would be auditioning and could be leaving Misty River in the near future. Yes, she had feelings for him. Strong feelings. But she was afraid to tell him. Because, if she told him, it would mean—

"You still there?"

"Ah, yeah. Sorry." She blew out a breath and tugged back her long hair. "I. . .I don't know what's happening."

"If it helps, I know," Lucas said, soft and tender. Her heart twisted.

She bit her lip. He's going to say it.
"We're falling in love."

* * * *

Lucas sat on the sofa, thinking about the conversation he had with Bree earlier in the evening. He believed they were falling in love, and when he had declared the sentiment, Bree had been hesitant to agree. Had he been mistaken in thinking she was falling in love with him? He loved her and wanted her in his life, but she seemed to push it away. Was she having second thoughts about their relationship? What was holding her back from making a commitment? With every passing day and every moment, they spent together, he fell more in love with her. He knew she had feelings for him. He couldn't understand why she couldn't express them. He scrubbed his hair back. As much as he opened his heart to her, she kept hers closed. Maybe they needed some alone time. He had mentioned going kayaking with her, and she didn't object. So, maybe she would go. If it were just the two of them, sitting in a narrow kayak, she'd have to talk to him. She doubted she could sit for a couple of hours on the river without speaking.

He stood, deciding he needed to take a drive. He grabbed his jacket and keys, then walked over to where his father sat back in his easy chair, half asleep, with the nightly news softly sounding in the background. He leaned in, touching his father's shoulder. He didn't want to startle him.

"Dad." He nudged him again. "Dad." He nudged him a bit harder. Man, the guy could sleep. He was jealous.

His father blinked his eyes open. "Huh?"

"I'm going for a drive. Can you and mom keep an ear out for Dani?"

His father nodded. "Sure, Lucas. Anything wrong?"

"No. Just need some air. Call my cell if you need me."

His father nodded again. "I'll head up to bed and let your mom know too."

"Thanks, Dad." He headed for the door as his father stood from the chair, moaning. He closed the door behind him and walked to the truck. Not having any idea of where to go, he backed out of the driveway and headed down the road, letting the truck take the lead as he thought of Bree and the life they could have.

Twenty minutes later, he found himself in downtown Misty River. He drove slowly down Main Street, its quiet darkness surrounding him, relaxing him. It was Sunday, so everything had been closed up for the night, even the tavern. The vintage streetlamps cast a soft glow along the pavement and illuminated the quaint store fronts. It was a cute town and hadn't changed much in nearly two hundred years. The citizens over the decades had vowed to keep the town small and quaint. Along the way, the citizens came up with the town slogan: '*Where friends are family and visitors come to stay*'.

He had always loved Misty River and had always wanted to live here. Yeah, he would be a resident of this little town soon, but it would be on the outskirts, living in a cabin along the river in the woods, just him and Dani. Unless. . .

He stopped the truck and realized where he was. Bree's studio. And the lights were on in the back. His heart raced and he came full alert. He drove the truck to the side of the building. Then he pulled out his cell when he noticed a car closer to the back entrance. Bree's car. He scanned the area outside, and realized it was safe. No one lurked in the shadows, so he shut off the truck, got out then headed to the back door.

It was locked. Well, at least she was staying safe. He moved toward the windows and peeked in. Bree was dancing, moving her arms wide as her feet fluttered against the floor. She bent down as though picking up a flower, then stood on her toes. She leaned down again, this time with one of her legs reaching out to the back. She was beauty in motion. He was happy to see she was safe, but he was curious to know why she was here at such a late hour. It was close to ten o'clock. He couldn't call her. Her phone would most likely be with her things in the corner somewhere. He'd knock. See if she answered.

He walked over to the door and knocked lightly. After waiting about twenty seconds, he knocked again, this time louder. Still nothing. Maybe she had earbuds on and couldn't hear him. He'd try one more time. He lifted his hand, knocked louder, and called her name at the same time. "Bree! It's Lucas! Open up." A moment passed. He turned to leave when the door opened a crack.

"Lucas?"

"Yeah, Bree. It's me. Didn't mean to scare you."

The door opened wider. "I heard a knock but wasn't sure if I should answer."

"I wanted to call but figured you wouldn't have your cell phone on you." He looked her over. No way would there be a phone tucked away in her close-fitting leggings and cropped top. His throat grew thick and his heart quickened when he noticed her tight abs.

"Come on in. No need to stand in the cold air."

"Sure." He walked inside as she held open the door.

"What are you doing here?" She closed the door behind her then stepped to stand in front of him. "Is everything okay at home?"

"Yeah. Just decided to take a drive, that's all." He swiped a hand down his face.

"I went to bed early and couldn't sleep, so I decided to come here and dance." She smoothed a hand down his flannel clad arm. "What brought you here?"

He smiled at her. "I think you know." Bree's eyes hooded, and she stepped closer. They were as close as two couples could get. "What was keeping you awake?" He clasped her around her small waist.

"I couldn't stop thinking about us." She leaned into him. "I kept thinking about what you said on the phone."

"That we're falling in love?" She tensed against him, and

he tried to stay calm. Don't push her.

She nodded, then stepped away from him. She crossed her arms and turned away. "When I can't sleep, I often work out. In the city, I'd do some dancing wherever I could find room. My apartment was small, so it made it difficult to dance. But now that I have my own studio," She turned and flashed him a bright smile.

His heart fluttered and tumbled. God, she was more beautiful to him each day.

"So, I come here and dance. Sometimes, dancing energizes me, sometimes it relaxes me."

"I love watching you dance."

"You do?"

"Of course I do. It's beautiful. You make it look so easy. No wonder Dani wants to be like you."

"Dani wants to be like me?"

He grinned. "Yeah. You're her idol." She blushed, looking down at the floor. "Now that I've seen you in your element, I really want Dani to dance and see what she can accomplish."

"Really?" Her gaze shot to his. She grinned. "I'm so happy, Lucas. Dani's going to do great. As a matter of fact, I was practicing a routine I want the kids to do for the performance. It's fairly easy and uses the basic steps."

He chuckled. "Sure, if you say so." He stuck his hands in his pockets. He had to or else he'd scoop her up and place kisses everywhere. "Me. I'm two left feet."

"Ahh, no, you're not. We danced together, remember? Up close and personal. And you're a wonderful dancer. You said so yourself." She came closer to him.

He remained rooted to the spot. He couldn't move if he wanted to and he sure as hell didn't want to. Bree seemed all too aware of what she was doing. She leaned into him. She was a mixture of lilac and clean sweat, and it stirred his senses into overdrive. He swallowed, his throat thick with desire. She lifted her hands to frame his face. They were cool and soft. Damn!

He yanked his hands from his pockets and clasped hers within his own. He could play this game too. He clasped her hands where her fingers stroked his cheeks. He inched closer to her. Their mouths were a hairs breadth from each other. Her breath was minty and warm against his lips, and they tingled with the need to press against hers and devour her.

"Bree," he groaned then captured her mouth. She pulled her hands from his and moved them to the back of his head and nudged him closer. He took the invitation and kissed her with all the pent-up passion he felt for her. Couldn't she feel how much he loved her? She responded to his kiss, yet he knew she was holding back. She pulled away. He leaned his forehead against hers and expelled a frustrated breath. This woman could tear him apart! She got him all hot and bothered and then splashed the proverbial cold water on him. He nodded, then released her, lifting his hands to grasp her shoulders. She loosened her hold on the back of his neck and smiled at him.

"I forgot what I was going to tell you," she stated. Her eyes flitted back and forth as she took in his gaze which probably told her he was frustrated and confused. He inhaled, needing to get his emotions in check, to stomp down the desire raging in his blood. He would need a long, cold shower when he got home.

"You were telling me what a great dancer I am."

She nodded, then licked her lips. God, didn't she know what she was doing to him? He should let her go and leave. "You're a great dancer, and an even better kisser," she whispered.

This time, he grasped her wrists from behind his head and brought them to her sides. She continued staring at him, but a crease formed between her brows. She squinted.

"And I love kissing you, Bree. Really. But, I need to know," His voice sounded husky to his own ears. "Please tell me how you feel."

Bree lowered her gaze and stepped back, giving both of

them a little bit of space. He still clasped her hands as anxiety soured his stomach. Something in her eyes told him she wasn't going to admit it. Something was bothering her.

"You have no idea how much I want you, Bree. I want to say so many things to you, but don't know where to start."

Bree pulled her hands away from his and hugged herself. "I have some things I want to tell you, too, Lucas, but I—" She turned away from him and his heart stuttered.

"It sounds like you're avoiding saying something I don't want to hear."

Bree shook her head. He reached out and touched her shoulder. When she didn't flinch or move away, he turned her around to face him, then pulled her in for a hug. He held her close, stroking her hair and listened to her heart beating frantically against his own. What was bothering her so much she couldn't' tell him? Maybe she was trying to find a way to call their relationship off. No. She wouldn't have kissed him like she just had. Unless it was a good-bye kiss. No. He refused to believe she wanted nothing more to do with him. So, what was wrong?

"Bree, you can tell me anything. You know that, right?"

She nodded, then heaved a sigh. "I know."

"So, what's bothering you? It can't be that bad."

Bree nudged away from him and looked into his eyes. "Okay, I'm just going to spit it out and hope that what I'm about to say isn't going to—"

"Tell me, Bree."

"I. . .I couldn't sleep because I kept thinking about what you said over the phone earlier. Do you remember what you said?"

"Of course I do. I'm falling in love with you, and I hope you feel the same." He took a step closer.

"Well, I. . .Lucas, I'm scared. I'm confused." Bree stepped back and paced in front of him.

"Bree, if you have something to say, please tell me." Frustration, fear and anxiety curled low, and he suddenly felt nauseous. The look on her face told him he wouldn't like what she had to say.

She thrust her hands against her hair, pulling back her ponytail. "Okay then." She heaved a sigh. "I have an opportunity to audition for a principal role for a company in Philadelphia."

What? She was leaving? He put a hand in his pocket and scraped his other hand through his hair. This time, he turned away from her. "So, that was a good-bye kiss?"

"No. Not at all, Lucas."

"How long have you known about this?" He heard her frustrated sigh which matched his own.

"I had the interview on Monday. Yesterday."

He nodded. Well, at least she hadn't kept it from him for a week or more. He didn't know what to say or do.

"I don't know what to do because, you see—"

He twisted around, swallowing the tightness in his throat. It burned with the want to scream, but he held back. "Look, I get it Bree. No need to explain." He headed for the door.

"Lucas, you don't understand."

He opened the door and hurried out. Bree was a few steps behind him.

"I want you to know—"

He didn't want her to see the hurt and anger. He needed to get away before he said something he'd regret.

"Lucas!"

As he jumped into his truck and slammed the door, her heard her running down the gravel walk toward the truck. He turned on the ignition and pulled out of the lot, watching her from his rearview mirror. He knew tears streamed down her face. A mirror image of himself.

Seventeen

Tears streamed down her face. She thrust her pointe shoes into her bag and stepped into her crocs. She swiped the tears from her face as she tried to lock the door, but her hands shook so bad, she couldn't manage it. Whatever! She'd leave it unlocked. Someone can break in for all she cared.

She stumbled through a haze of tears to her car and opened the door. She tossed in her bag and slid into the seat. Suddenly, she was drained of all energy and slumped against the steering wheel, sobbing. Why didn't she just tell him how she really felt? She loved him. Why did she tell him about the opportunity to dance with an up and coming company? Why? She punched the steering wheel and cringed. She couldn't sit in the parking lot all night. And she knew she wouldn't get any sleep. She leaned back, started up the car and pulled out of the lot. Should she chase down Lucas and explain? But something told her he wouldn't listen right now. She'd give him his space and hoped they still had a chance.

When she stepped into the kitchen, hoping she wouldn't be seen, she found Aunt Merry making a cup of tea.

Her aunt looked at her with wide eyes. "Where did you come from? I thought you were in bed."

"I couldn't sleep," she mumbled, setting her bag on the floor by the shoe mat. "Got any more of that?"

"Sure do." Aunt Merry grabbed a mug from the dish rack. "Were you out with Lucas?"

She slipped off her jacket and tossed it on top of her bag. She'd deal with it later. "Not really."

Aunt Merry tossed her a quizzical look.

"I was at the studio. I thought if I danced, it'd relax me enough to finally go to sleep." She watched as her aunt set a teabag into the mug. "But I did have a surprise visitor." She clasped the mug her aunt handed her. She curled a leg under her as she sat at the table opposite her aunt.

"So, who was your surprise visitor? Someone I know?" Aunt Merry teased, wiggling her eyebrows.

"As if you didn't know." She tried to smile, but it probably looked more like a smirk. "It was Lucas. And I was thrilled to see him, but. . ."

"But?"

"He said something . . ." She inhaled and let it out slowly. "Well, it made me uncomfortable."

"Oh-oh. What'd he say?"

"He said he loved me."

"I knew it!" Aunt Merry grinned. "Did you tell him the same?"

She shook her head and wished she had. She regretted it now. "I said something that made him angry."

"What'd you say?"

"I told him I was scared and confused, and then I blurted out that I had the chance to audition for a company in Philadelphia. He took it as though I was breaking up with him."

"So why didn't you tell him otherwise?"

"Because he turned away and left."

"Did you try to stop him?"

"Of course, I tried." Frustration edged her voice.

"Why would Lucas walk out without letting you explain? He doesn't seem like that kind of guy." Aunt Merry waved a hand and shook her head. "Wait a minute. First of all, why did Lucas show up?"

"He told me he couldn't sleep and was out for a drive and ended up at the studio. When he saw the lights on, he thought there might've been an intruder. Instead, he found me there, dancing."

"Well, I'm glad he checked it out, just in case there had been an intruder,"

"Yeah, me too. And I'm glad he showed up, because I wanted to tell him what's been on my mind since his phone call earlier." She took a fortifying gulp of her tea and winced. She twisted her ponytail and let the loose strands weave through her fingers. "Instead of telling him how I felt, I decided to. . .show him."

Her aunt's brows rose as her eyes widened. "What did you show him, or maybe I shouldn't ask."

"I kissed him. Really kissed him, Aunt Merry." Heat rose to her neck and up the sides of her face. "I can't believe I'm sharing this with my aunt."

"Hey, I'm glad you're comfortable enough to talk to me about this. It's something a mother and daughter would do. . .right?" Her aunt reached out and touched her hand.

She laughed, despite her depression. She couldn't imagine talking to her mother like this, either. "Maybe." She took another sip.

"So, what are you going to do now?"

"I don't know." Tears blurred her vision and she swiped them away.

Aunt Merry patted her hand. "I can't see Lucas storming off without letting you explain yourself."

"Well, he did. And I'm angry. But not at him." She heaved a sigh. "I'm mad at myself."

"Then call him. Maybe he'll listen this time."

She shook her head. "I'll give him some space. Let him cool down."

"Are you sure it's the right thing to do? Maybe by not calling, he'll think you really are calling it quits."

She huffed, then took a sip of her tea to swallow down the tightness in her throat. She wanted to cry. She wanted her aunt to hold her as a mother would and tell her everything would be okay. Instead, she set the tea aside on the table, leaned back and let out a huge sigh, full of frustration and pent-up anger. She slumped forward and covered her face with her hands. "He's in love with me, Aunt Merry, and I can’t seem to tell him how I feel.” Her voice came out muffled from behind her hands.

“Are you in love with Lucas?“

"I don't know." She lifted her head and slid her hands down her face. "I care for him. I really do, but I don't know if it's love."

"Why do you say that?"

"Because when I thought I was totally and completely in love, I was betrayed. And got injured because of it, lost my job and here I am!" Wow, she sounded a tad cynical. "I don't want to be in love because I don’t want to get hurt." Again, she twisted her fingers through her ponytail, one of her habits when she was nervous or annoyed. She felt like an idiot. Of course she wanted someone to love her, and she wanted to love him. Desperately. But. . .but what?

"How do you feel when you're around Lucas?"

"What?"

"Answer the question, Bree. What do you feel?" Aunt Merry prodded.

Oh, God. Aunt Merry was making her look deep inside herself. To feel what she didn't want to feel because she was scared. "I feel wonderful, Aunt Merry. I feel cherished and beautiful and. . .loved." The last word came out as a whisper.

"See?" Aunt Merry set her mug down and came around the table to sit beside her. She set an arm around Bree's shoulders. "You're in love. You just don't want to admit it." She leaned her head on Bree's shoulder. "Why is that?"

Her aunt was good. She had to give her credit. Aunt Merry could get info out of her without even trying. Her aunt had been able to do that since she had been a teen. She blew out a breath and leaned her head against her aunt’s. "I don't want to hurt them, Aunt Merry, but if I get the job as principal dancer, I’ll be leaving Misty River. I’ll be hurting them, and I can't live with that." She let the tears fall. “I love dancing and being on stage. But I love being here, too." A sob escaped and her throat tightened. "What am I going to do?" She cried for the loss of her career and the potential loss of a relationship with Lucas. No one could give her the answer. She had to figure it out on her own.

* * * *

Lucas hammered the nails into the two by four with such ferocity, he thought he'd break the wood. Devon shot him a glare.

"Hey, bro. Cool it with the hammering."

He ignored his cousin. Hell, he wanted to ignore everyone. What he wanted to do was head to the cabin and work until he dropped. His mother and father could take care of Dani until he worked Bree out of his system. What the hell was he doing right now? Why were they working on this studio if Bree was going to leave? What the hell, man!

"What's bothering you, Lucas. You're angry and taking it out on the walls and whatever else is in your way."

"Don't want to talk about it. Just do your thing and pretend I'm not here," he responded, not even glancing at Devon.

"Sure. I can handle this if you need to take off."

He shrugged and lifted the hammer. He slammed it down again. What he wanted to do was go to Bree and ask her what the hell she was doing. Why was she giving up on him and Dani? Again, the hammer came down hard. It was bad enough she had hurt him, was still hurting him, but she didn't have any right to hurt Dani. His daughter didn't know anything, yet. He wasn't about to tell her until he knew for sure what was going on. To make matters worse, he had to bring Dani to her dance lesson tonight. Her first one. Maybe he'd ask his mother to do it.

"Hey, I'm heading to the diner. You comin'?" Devon asked, removing his tool belt and setting it on the floor.

"Nah. I'll keep working on this wall. Bring back some meatloaf though."

"Sure. No prob." Devon started to walk away. "Go easy on the hammering, Lucas. Take a break."

He nodded and bit his tongue. He wanted to tell Devon to mind his own business, but he held back. It wasn't Devon's problem, and he shouldn't be angry at his cousin. He was mad at himself. Mad at Bree. He wanted to punch out his frustration on something. Too bad this little town didn't have a gym where he could work out or punch a bag. Hell, the tavern was open. Maybe he'd head over there and grab a beer. He could drown his sorrows in a bottle.

He stood and slammed down the hammer, satisfied when it made a loud thunk on the floor. He removed his tool belt. Maybe he wouldn't come back. Let Devon handle the rest of the renovations.

He tore out of the lot and headed down Main Street toward the tavern. He hit the brake when an older man, crossing the street, yelled at him to slow it down. He slammed his hand against the steering wheel. As he passed the diner, he saw Devon sitting in a booth with Kris Galloway sitting opposite him. Don't do it, man. She wasn't worth it.

A moment later, he turned down Riverside Road and parked in the lot of the tavern. A few cars and some pickups littered the lot. He strolled in and took a seat at the bar.

"Hey, Lucas!" Ed said, as he poured a beer from the Heineken spout.

He nodded. "I'll take one of those."

"Sure thing." Ed handed the frosted glass to a man at the opposite end and then headed back to the beer dispenser and turned on the tap. Golden beer poured into the frosted glass. "Can I get you somethin' to eat?"

Lucas shook his head. "Just the beer, thanks. Oh, and keep a tab running."

The barkeeper's brows rose. "Aren't you supposed to be working? None of my business, but you usually don't drink during the day."

He shrugged. "Taking the afternoon off. I may stay here

all afternoon and maybe into the night."

"If you get too drunk, I'll be shuttin' you off. You know that, right? Can't have my patrons getting plastered and then driving. Drink all you want, but you're not driving home if I see you're hindered in any way. Got it?" Ed explained, his broad face serious. "Got it." He snickered. I'll call Bree to be my designated driver. Yeah, sure! He took a hefty swig and let the cold brew slide down his dry throat. He slid his fingers along the base of the glass as images of Bree dancing last night came to mind. How she sauntered over to him and acted so brazen until he kissed her senseless. She admitted she had wanted him, but she had stopped him. It was as though she pulled away when she was getting too close. What was she afraid of? Why couldn't she tell him?

He slugged back another gulp and sighed as he set the cold mug down. He set his hands on each side of his face and closed his eyes. He thought Bree was in love with him, just as he was with her. What had changed? Why did she want to leave? After all the work they'd done on the studio, why would she walk away from it all?

"Hey, man. What are you doing here?"

Lucas snapped his head up and turned to see Brett standing there, leaning sideways against the padded edge of the bar. "Hey!" He stood and clapped his best friend from high school on the back. "When did you get into town?" He sat back down on the bar stool.

"Got in yesterday." Brett sat on the stool next to him.

Ed sauntered over, grinning at Brett. "Well, look what the cat dragged in. What brings you into town? Chicago finally tired of you?"

Lucas noticed Brett wince, then he frowned. Something was going on with Brett.

His friend gave a short chuckle. "I'm on vacation and decided I needed to see the family."

Ed nodded. "What can I get you? It's on the house."

"Whatever you have on tap. I'm not fussy," Brett

answered, leaning forward on his elbows. Brett glanced at him. "You don't look so good. What happened?" He twisted his gaze around. "Bree here?"

He shook his head and lifted his glass. He swallowed another strong gulp. Maybe if he kept drinking, he wouldn't have to answer Brett's questions. But it wasn't in his makeup to drown his sorrows in booze. He always faced his problems and his fears head on. "Don't know where your sister is. I came in for a liquid lunch."

"Sounds like you're trying to drown a memory." He nodded to Ed then continued. "I've been there, man."

Still, he didn't talk. He didn't even look at his best friend from high school. The one friend he could always count on. The one friend who had left town ten years ago and stayed away just like Bree had. What was it with them that they couldn't or didn't want to stay in Misty River? Only Anna had stayed because she had married her high school sweetheart. She and Jacob loved the town and couldn't bear to be away from it. The two people he cared for had left him. Huh.

"Want to talk about it?" Brett asked as Ed set his beer in front of him.

"No."

"Mind if I talk?"

"Go right ahead."

"Just like back in school." Brett lifted the frost mug and took a swallow. "I remember when you were so angry, you'd speak in monotone syllables, like you're doing now, and you didn't care what anyone said or did. You just shrugged--"

Lucas shrugged. Let Brett keep talking. At least he could keep drinking and pretend he was listening.

"And I'd do all the talking. Hmm, just like I'm doing now. Which means it involves a girl. Well, a woman now. Back in high school, it was girls. And usually it stemmed around my sister."

He turned to Brett. "You done?"

"Nope." Brett lifted the glass to his lips and took another

swallow. "What did my sister do to turn you into someone who wants to get drunk at noon?"

He shrugged. "Nothing. Everything." He blew out his breath. "God, I don't know." He clasped his fingers together and looked straight ahead, looking at nothing although there was a wall of bottles in front of him.

"Ahhh. She's broken your heart. Again."

This time he smiled. After all these years, Brett still knew him. Probably better than anyone. Man, he had missed him. Brett had been the closest thing to a brother anyone could ask for.

"Hey, you can tell me. I'm not going to share it with Bree."

He glanced at Brett. He was ten years older than when he had left town at nineteen. He had had dreams as well. To be a firefighter in a big city. And he had accomplished that. He had found his place in a firehouse in Chicago. Where in the city, he didn't know. They had kept in touch for a few months, then as time went on, each one becoming busy with their own lives, they had lost touch. Neither one reached out to the other.

"Tell me, why is it so hard for Bree to commit?"

"Bree has never committed to another man because she's committed to her dancing. She's married to her career."

He nodded. Maybe that was the issue. "So, although she could have feelings, she won't act on them because she'd have to give up her career."

"Pretty much." Brett lifted his glass. "She never dated in high school, remember?"

He did. "But that was because you threatened any guy who made the attempt."

"Damn right," Brett answered then chuckled. "I didn't trust the idiots she liked. She was too innocent, and I didn't want to see her hurt."

"So, I must've been one of those idiots," he chimed in.

"You? Nah," Brett shook his head. "Why do you say that? You didn't have any interest in Bree back then." Brett twisted sideways on the barstool. "Or did you?"

"Guilty. I'm an idiot," he responded, lifting his beer glass toward Brett. "I was very interested in your sister, and I know she felt the same."

"She did not."

"Did. She told me."

Brett shook his head. "Wow. I must've been blind. You acted like a tough kid," he made quote marks in the air. "And, knowing Bree the way I do, I figured she would never date a guy who was a bad boy. And my father wouldn't have allowed it."

"I remember going over to your house and watching her dance. She was always dancing. I figured she was ignoring me, but then she shared the other day that she was checking me out every time I went over."

"I did not know that," Brett said. "So, my sister had a crush on you. And you had one on her." He leaned back. "Huh."

"I'm curious," he started. "What would you have done if I had asked Bree out?"

"I don't know. That would've been weird to have my best friend dating my sister."

"And what about now?"

"Doesn't matter now. We're adults. We can make our own decisions. I'm not going to stop Bree from dating anyone. She has a mind of her own. If you and she are dating, I say go for it," Brett explained as he smoothed his hand down his glass. "Hey, I heard about your wife. Sorry, man."

"Thanks." He shook his head. "I wish I had asked Bree out all those years ago. Maybe we would've fallen in love, gotten married, had children."

"And the house with the white picket fence."

"Yeah. I did have that."

"You did? Wow. You and Daniella. Married." Brett shook his head. "Goes to show you never know where your friends will end up with in life."

"Daniella and I got married six years ago. Had Dani a year later."

"Daniella was such a quiet girl in school," Brett said. "Never thought you'd date her, let alone marry her. Wow. It just blows my mind."

"You can never tell," Lucas answered, turning back to his beer. He nodded to Ed for another one. "Yeah, bad boy marries nerdy girl."

"I wonder where you and Bree would be today if she hadn't chased her dream and stayed in town and married you."

"Living on the river, in a cabin with at least three kids." He started to relax, even though they were talking about Bree. It should've made his heart break even more than it was, but it helped to know that Brett didn't mind them dating. Well, it was for naught now.

"So, what the hell happened between you two?" Brett inquired. "I thought you two were happy. In love--"

"I'm in love," Lucas interrupted. "She's not."

"Oh. And what makes you think that?"

"Because when she was confronted with it, she backed away. Pretty much told me that she was leaving town."

"Leaving?" Brett's eyes practically popped out of his head. "What the hell?"

"My feelings exactly. How long was she going to wait before she was going to tell me? She has an audition in New Hampshire and she's going to it. If she gets the job, she'll be leaving."

"Did she tell you that?"

He shrugged and pulled a long swallow from the glass, practically emptying it. Ed set a new frosty mug in front of him. "Not really. But it was the way she talked about it. To be honest, I didn't want to stand there and hear her excuses, so I left."

"So, you don't really know, do you?"

No, he didn't. He felt like an idiot. He was an idiot. She

had wanted to explain, but he hadn't let her finish. He had walked away, assuming she was going to leave and never come back.

"Can I give you some advice?" Brett asked. He continued without waiting for him to answer. "Talk to her. Listen to her." Brett sighed, clasping his glass and looking down at the bar top. "If I've learned anything, it's that you have to give the woman you're with, a chance to explain herself. If you don't, she'll just grow angrier with each passing day." Brett shrugged. "It's your call though."

"I don't think she'll answer if I call."

"Then show up. Unannounced." Brett grinned. "What's the worse she can do? Slam the door in your face?"

Eighteen

Despite her anxiety and the shedding of many tears, she was excited for tonight. She'd be teaching her first class and she wanted it to be fun and exciting for her students. She wouldn't allow her depression and confusion lay like a gray cloud over her first session.

She decided the students would practice outside, on the grass. It had been a beautiful day and was supposed to be a warm night. The first class wouldn't involve too much dancing. It was more or less a 'get to know you' type of class where they could share their ideas and thoughts and she'd teach them beginner steps. She knew from their applications; the girls were all beginners. Their ages ranged from four to seven, and she was fortunate she only had ten students. Anymore, and she'd have to split the class, which meant hiring another teacher and she couldn't afford it, right now.

"All set for tonight?" Anna asked, as she helped Heather dress into a pair of tights and a leotard.

"I am." She had her binder with all the info and the pamphlets she would hand out to the parents. "I have everything here, and here," she added, pointing to her cell phone.

"Nervous?" Aunt Merry asked as she wiped down the kitchen table.

She shrugged. "A little."

"Nervous in general or nervous you might see Lucas?"

"Both." She sat in the chair. "What am I going to do if he shows up?"

"Well, you're going to act professional and talk to him as you would to any parent. Unless, of course, you want to run to him and kiss him and apologize, although I suggest you do that out of sight of the parents and the kids."

"I don't think I'll be running into his arms, Anna."

"Maybe not but enjoy yourself. Have fun with the kids. And I'll help wrangle some of them in if they get out of control."

'Thank you, Anna. I appreciate all your help and all you've done for me to get me here tonight." She stood and hugged her sister.

"You're welcome."

She walked to the door and grabbed her bag. With her gear in hand, she waved to her aunt and headed to her car and tossed the items in. She wondered what she would do when Lucas showed up with Dani. Would he ignore her? Would he be civil? She'd soon find out, wouldn't she? She got in the car, turned on the ignition and headed for the studio.

Ten minutes later, she parked her car in the lot. She was a little early and had planned it that way. She needed time for herself to set her mind on her class and to ignore anything negative that might come her way.

Earlier, she had put out a chalkboard on the step by the front door, asking the parents to bring the children to the back of the building due to construction. She had locked the door as well just in case someone decided to ignore the sign and walk through the building. God forbid if someone fell and got injured. She couldn't deal with the liability, especially before the business had officially opened. And she wouldn't be able to deal with an injured child. It'd break her heart.

She got out of the car and headed for a picnic table beneath the flowering apple tree. She set her things down and wandered to the edge of the property where a low picket fence stood, separating the studio property from the river as well as to keep people safe. She stood there, admiring the view when she heard her name called.

"Bree, over here!" Jamie sat in a kayak, waving frantically.

"Hey, Jamie! You're kayaking?" she called back. She noticed another kayaker behind her. His face obscured by his ball cap.

"Yeah, with me. Hey, Sis."

"Brett?"

He nodded then waved. "Talk to you later. Good luck," he called back as the two of them swept past her. Maybe they were dating, after all. She shook her head and smiled. They would make a cute couple. Jamie had been in love with Brett since kindergarten.

She turned and headed back to the table. She needed to set up an area where the students could sit in a circle. She had hoped to have some sort of area where they could dance. Actually, where she was standing would make a great spot. It was clear of trees and other obstructions. The grass was still short and didn't need mowing yet. They could do the simple steps right there. She'd need a blanket though. She headed toward her car when she noticed a familiar truck pull in. Oh God. Now what was she going to do?

Pretending she didn't see the truck, where Lucas sat behind the wheel, she opened her trunk and pulled out the blanket. She always kept a blanket and bottles of water in the car. As she closed the trunk, she could see Lucas getting out and moving to the passenger side to help Dani. She knew he had seen her. Anxiety swelled in her stomach, and she hoped the nausea would go away soon. She didn't want to feel sick on her first night with the students. Why hadn't Theresa brought Dani? Why did it have to be Lucas? Maybe he wanted to taunt her? Maybe he wanted to see her squirm? She hadn't done anything wrong. He was the one who had stormed out on her and hadn't wanted to hear her out. She had nothing to apologize for and nothing to be anxious about. She squared her shoulders and heaved in a breath of pine-scented air. Closing her eyes, she lifted her face to the sun.

"Bree!"

She almost dropped the blanket and bottle of water when she heard Dani's squeal of delight. The little girl rushed toward her, her dark brown curls flying loose behind her. She had missed Dani. Normally, she would've gone to their house for the usual Wednesday night meal, but tonight she had stayed home and invited Anna and Heather over for supper at the farm.

"Hey, Dani."

Danica hugged her around her upper thighs. "I missed you, Bree. You weren't at supper tonight."

"I, ah, I had to get ready for tonight's class. I'm sorry."

Lucas strolled up to them but kept his distance. He nodded and she nodded back. Well, this was going well. She could feel the change in the air. It was thick with tension. Dani was chattering away, but all she could focus on was Lucas and how good he looked and how wonderful he smelled. The breeze carried over his unique scent mixed with his woodsy aftershave. She glanced at him. He wore a blue dress shirt with crisp khakis and suede brown shoes. He looked so handsome. Was he trying to look good for her?

"Have fun, Dani." Lucas hunkered down and gave Dani a kiss on the cheek.

"Okay, Daddy."

"Ahh, aren't you staying to watch?" she asked as Lucas turned away from her.

He shook his head. "No. Got somewhere else I need to be. My mom will pick her up."

"Oh, okay." She swallowed, forcing down the tears clogging her throat. She wouldn't cry. She wouldn't. A small hand tucked its way into hers. She looked down. Dani glanced up at her with a huge grin.

"Are we gonna dance tonight?"

She inhaled, breathing in the last mingling scent of Lucas as he walked back to the truck. "Yes. A little dancing." She gripped Dani's hand as though it was a lifeline to her battered heart. She watched Lucas get into his truck and shut the door. She wanted to run to him, but stayed put, letting the sun beat down on her as he backed out and pulled away, taking her heart with him. Where was he going? Was he meeting someone? Another woman, maybe? Don't cry, Bree. Not in front of Dani. Don't cry. It was her mantra as they walked hand in hand toward the table.

"Can I help?" Dani asked as she released Dani's hand and set the blanket on the table next to her binder and her phone. She stared at the phone, willing it to ring and hoping it would be Lucas.

"Miss Bree?"

She shook her head then glanced down at Dani. "Yes?"

"Do you need help with the blanket?"

"Ah, yes. Yes, that'd be great." She walked to a shady area by the tree and unfolded the blanket. "You take that end, Dani, and I'll take this end."

"Okay." Dani took hold of the end of the aged quilt and tugged it as she walked away.

"Pull it out so the blanket is nice and flat."

Dani tried, but it was awkward, considering she could only use one arm. "Here, let me help." She walked to the other end of the blanket and straightened out one corner while Dani did the same with the opposite corner. In the process, Dani tripped and fell sideways. Her heart slammed into her throat, and she dove toward Dani, catching her around her hips and sliding her gently down to the blanket.

"Goodness! You scared the heck out of me!"

"I'm sorry, Miss Bree. I sometimes turn my feet the wrong way and sometimes I fall."

If it was that easy for Dani to fall sideways, what would happen when she tried to dance? Was this such a good idea? Maybe she should rethink this and talk to Lucas.

"Miss Bree?"

Bree turned toward Dani. "Yes?"

"When's everyone else coming?"

"Soon." She glanced at her FitBit. "Very soon." She hoped. "Dani? Why do you call me, Miss Bree?"

"Cuz, Daddy said to. You're my teacher now and I should respect you and call you Miss Bree."

"Oh." So, it had come down to being professional. Parent and teacher. Student and teacher. No more just calling her Bree because she was a friend of the family or her daddy's girlfriend. She was now the professional. Gone was the familiarity. She wished she could just go home and have a good cry. But, being the professional, she had to stay, pretend all was good in her world and teach her students the fine art of ballet.

The crunch of gravel beneath several sets of tires alerted her that her other students had arrived. She stood and holding onto Dani's hand, she walked toward the parking lot to greet them and show them where they would have the class. Anna came up to her and hugged her close.

"Did Lucas show up?" she whispered.

She could only nod. She was afraid she'd start crying if she talked to Anna now. Her sister patted her shoulder. "You'll do fine, Bree. Smile."

She inhaled and plastered on a smile while Anna took Dani with her and Heather to sit on the blanket. She needed to keep Lucas out of her mind and not think about what he was doing right now or who he was with. If he was willing to snub her so soon after a little fight, then he wasn't worth shedding tears for. This was one reason why she didn't believe in falling in love. It hurt too much when love was taken away.

* * * *

Lucas stood by the window, watching Bree greet the students and parents. She looked so sad. He wanted to rush out and wrap his arms around her and tell her he was sorry. It had killed him to walk away from her earlier. He knew she was jealous, thinking he was heading out to meet someone. His plans had been to go to the tavern, hang out with a few friends, but by the time he drove a few doors down the road, he had turned around and parked by the bakery. He had walked across the street and unlocked the studio's front door and snuck in, hoping she wouldn't decide to go in and catch him there. It wouldn't matter if anyone in town had seen him enter. They'd think he was working.

He had smiled, watching Bree interact with Dani. At least she didn't take out her anger and frustration on his daughter. That was a good sign. He debated whether to keep Dani home or have his mother bring her, but Dani had begged him to bring her to class. On the way, he had told Dani to respect Bree and to call her Miss Bree because the other kids would do the same.

He opened the French door, looking out to the back of the property just enough where he could hear Bree and Dani but kept himself back enough where she wouldn't be able to see him. The angle of the sun would prevent anyone seeing him inside due to the glare.

His heart crashed to his throat when Dani started to fall, but when Bree had rushed forward, catching Dani around her hips, he blew out an audible sigh. How could he let this woman go? She was in his heart, always had been, always would be. But, if she didn't want to be with him, he would have to set her free, let her live the life she wanted, which didn't include him or Dani.

When Bree and Dani walked away from the table to greet the others, he took a moment to gather his thoughts and wipe the tears from his eyes.

Slowly, a small gathering of girls, along with their moms, stood in the clearing. He noticed Anna had said something to Bree but, from where they were standing, he couldn't hear them. Anna had hugged Bree. Even from this distance, he could feel her pain, her anguish and he had been the cause of it. God, he was an idiot. He should just man up and go to her. Tell her exactly how he felt and demand to know how she felt about him. None of this dancing around their feelings.

He brushed a hand down his face and stayed within the shadows in the corner of the room where he could see them and hear them but couldn't be seen. He hoped no one needed to use the rest room. They'd have to come through the back door just a few feet from where he stood, and he'd be seen. Caught. He'd have to run fast to get out of the room before he could be seen.

Bree started talking about her expectations of the students as they sat in a circle on the blanket. Dani was sitting next to her, smiling and nodding. She asked the students to go around and tell each other their names. Dani went first. As each girl stated their name, they whispered to one another and to his delight, another girl leaned into Dani and shook her hand. Dani was beaming.

Bree had the girls stand up and they walked to the small clearing. The parents sat back in their chairs under the shade of the apple tree.

"I'm going to show you a few simple steps to start off. I know you want to jump right in and start dancing, but we have to learn the basic poses first."

A red-headed girl, with long hair, raised her hand. "Is that how you learned, Miss Bree?"

Bree nodded. "Yes. I was about your age when I started. My aunt, who used to own this studio," and she turned, looking toward the massive window. He ducked into the corner, his heart jumping into his throat. "Taught me how to dance. And, I had to learn the basics first, just like I'm going to teach you."

To his amazement, he watched as Dani moved her feet from the first position, as Bree called it, to the second and then to the third. They practiced it several times with Bree stopping to assist some of the girls with the correct positioning of their arms and their feet. He watched as Bree came over to Dani. While the other girls had their arms in a circle in front of them, Dani had used her good arm and had her bad arm reach out as far as it could to mimic the position. Some of the other girls nodded and smiled at Dani and his daughter grinned back.

She had the girls take a quick break and his heart thundered as he heard footsteps coming up the wooden stairs. He dashed out of the room, and had just rounded the corner of the doorway, when Anna came in with a couple of the girls. He headed for the men's room a short distance down the hall and had managed to close the door when he heard Anna and the girls chattering away as they walked past. He let out a breath he didn't know he'd been holding. No one would come in here as they were all girls. He took a moment to gather himself together. He listened for Anna and the two girls to come out when he heard more girls heading down the hall. It seemed they were encouraged to take a bathroom break before resuming their lesson.

He checked his watch. Six-thirty. Class ended at seven. Five minutes passed and then it was quiet. The girls had done their business and had headed back outside. He waited another minute, just in case. When he was sure no one else was in the girl's room next door, he opened the door and listened. God, he felt like a spy. This was ridiculous! He was spying on his daughter and girlfriend. Was she still his girlfriend? Only he could make amends and have her back where she belonged. In his arms. In his life. He hurried to the room he had vacated ten minutes earlier and stood in the shadows.

Bree showed the girls the other basic positions and he marveled at her beauty and grace. The girls begged her to do a small dance for them and she obliged. Smiling, he watched as she performed a pirouette, then stood on her toes, lifting her left leg back and up as she lowered her upper body down, reaching her arms out to skim across the grass. The students oohed and ahhed and, as Bree came to a stop after another fast spinning pirouette, the crowd applauded. Bree grinned and curtsied.

He imagined her on stage, doing the same. This is what Bree wanted. This is why she was leaving them. To chase her dream of dancing for a crowd and receiving their applause and praise as reward. Was it an ego thing? Did she need her ego stroked so bad that she was willing to give up on him? On Dani who looked up to her? Again, anger surfaced. He couldn't believe Bree was that shallow. He turned and left the room. He wanted to slam the door, but realized the sound might carry to the back, and he didn't need Bree to know he had been there. He shut the door tight, locked it up and strolled across the street. He didn't need to worry about Chloe seeing him. She had been at the class with her daughter, Sophie.

Jumping into his truck, he started it up. He had five minutes before he was expected to pick up Dani. Wait. He had told Bree his mother would pick her up. But he had lied. He wanted Bree to think he was going out on a date. He wanted to make Bree angry. He wanted to hurt her. He pounded his fist against the steering wheel. Damn it! He headed down Main Street toward the tavern. Had it only been a few hours since he had left the place? He and Brett had talked like they had back in high school. They had become reacquainted, so to speak, and Brett had advised him to talk to his sister. Brett truly believed Bree had strong feelings for him. Lucas had shrugged it off.

As much as he wanted to drown his sorrows in another glass of beer, he had to turn around and pick up Dani. He wondered what Bree would think when he showed up instead of his mother. He smiled despite his anger. Well, it was now or never. He turned the truck around in the lot of the tavern and headed back toward the dance studio, wondering how Bree would react when she saw him, again.

As he pulled into the parking lot, the moms and their daughters were heading out to their cars, chattering away and laughing. Each one held a piece of paper in their hands. Probably a schedule. He knew Dani would be talking non-stop once he picked her up. That would be a good thing. He waited a full minute before he stepped out of the truck. He passed two of the dance moms and nodded as they said hi in passing. He could feel the tension building and his palms sweat. He came to the walkway when he heard Dani's voice.

"Daddy!" She rushed over to him, the paper dangling from her hand. He lifted her up.

"There's my girl!" He hugged her close, avoiding Bree's gaze. "How was class?"

"It was fun! I made two new friends and we're gonna dance together on Sataday." Dani spilled the words out so fast, she was breathless.

"That's wonderful." He bounced her on his forearm, and she giggled. "Wanna talk to Miss Bree?"

"I don't--"

"Lucas?" The sound of her voice halted him as he started to turn. Her smooth, melodic voice didn't sound angry or sad.

"Can we talk?" Bree stood inches away, her eyes begging him to hear her out.

God, how he wanted to hold her close. Inhale her sweet scent and kiss her senseless. Instead, he pushed down the temptation and set Dani on the ground. "It's getting late. I need to get Dani home and showered, get her ready for bed."

"Oh. Yeah. Okay." Bree stammered. "There's class on Saturday at nine-thirty. Will you be there?"

"I doubt it." He couldn't look at her. If he did, he wouldn't be able to look away. He'd have no choice but to crush her against him and not let go. "I'll be at the cabin." He hated lying to her. "I won't be home for the weekend."

He headed toward the truck holding onto Dani's hand. He wouldn't look back. He forged ahead, putting Dani in her car seat all the while, pretending he didn't care. He could feel her gaze on him, begging him to turn around. His heart thudded, echoing in his ears. As he snapped the seatbelt in place around Dani's waist, everything blurred. He twisted his face sideways and rubbed his face against his sleeve. I love you, Bree. I just can't have you. He got into the truck, closed the door, and pulled out of the lot, forcing himself not to look in the rearview mirror.

"Daddy?"

"Yeah, Pumpkin?"

"Are you mad at Bree?"

He shook his head. "Not really."

"Then why didn't you talk to her?"

"I'm just tired, that's all." He turned on the music CD she liked. *Frozen*. She had every song memorized. He found himself singing along softly as Dani belted out the words to "*Let it Go.*"

Maybe he should heed the advice of the song and just let it go.

Nineteen

When Bree arrived home, her face was puffy, and her eyes nearly swollen shut from crying for the last hour at the studio. She had sat in her office and cried, sobs wracking her body, and all the while she kept wondering what she had said that made Lucas despise her so much.

A knock sounded and she sniffled into her pillow. "Go away, Aunt Merry." Her request was ignored because, a few seconds later, she felt the mattress sag as her aunt sat on the edge. She twisted to her side, her arm tucked under her pillow. "I don't feel like talking."

"I know. I thought I'd just sit here and be available if you want to." Aunt Merry pushed back strands of damp hair from across her forehead. Her aunt's touch was soothing and soft and reminded her of her mother who would come to her room and do the same thing after she had had a nightmare.

She groaned into her pillow and curled herself tighter into the fetal position. "I want to be alone, Aunt Merry. I can't ugly cry if you're here with me."

"Don't hold back on my account. Ugly cry all you want."

When she thought back to those teen angst days, she realized her tears had been wasted on some crazy kid from school who she thought she had a major crush on and "really loved." Aack! But she also remembered crying over Lucas. She had met Lucas when she was fifteen and Brett was sixteen. Her brother had brought Lucas home to hang out and she had fallen in love with Lucas at first sight. Of course, Lucas had never given her a second thought. Or so she believed, until he had shared a couple of weeks ago how he had a crush on her in high school.

"Bree? What caused the fight?" her aunt asked, peering

down at her.

She shrugged, burying her face in her pillow as a fresh onslaught of tears rushed forth. Her body shook and Aunt Merry stroked her back.

"Lucas loves you. You know that, right? So, I'm sure you can talk this out."

"He hates me now."

"Oh, he does not." Her aunt sounded so much like her mom, and she cried all the harder because of it.

She twisted to lie on her back and Aunt Merry pulled her hand back. She tried to grab a tissue from her nightstand, but Aunt Merry had grabbed it first and handed it to her. She blew her nose and crumpled it in her hand. She reached for another, then in a huff, grabbed the entire box. She'd need them.

"Call him."

She shook her head as fresh tears flowed down her cheeks. Pulling another tissue from the box, she grumbled. "Damn box!" She picked it up and flung it as hard as she could across the room. It hit the dresser with a soft thunk and landed on the carpeted floor. Aunt Merry stood to retrieve it.

"I don't think it's the tissue box's fault, you know. Poor thing. Took quite the blow to the side. It's ripped open. Poor thing."

She tried not to smile, but she could feel her lips tilt upward and her aunt saw it.

"See, I knew I could get some kind of a smile from you."

"I'm not smiling," she mumbled into her tissue, swabbing at her nose again. Once her aunt handed her the mangled box, she took another tissue and wiped her eyes. They were gritty and burning. Her nose felt raw, and her throat was sore from sobbing so much.

"God, I feel like I swallowed the Sahara. Can you get me a cold glass of water?"

"Sure."

"And a cold cloth for my eyes?"

"On it."

After her aunt left the room, she grabbed her cellphone, which had been sitting on the nightstand, just in case Lucas called her. She glanced at the screen. Nothing. She scrunched her eyes tight, forbidding the hot tears from streaming down her face, but it was no use. The tears came anyway. He wanted no part of her. Pressing the contacts button, she scrolled down to his name. Her thumb hovered over the call button. She inhaled then tossed the phone onto her bed.

"Oh, Lucas. Please call me." She stared at her phone, willing it to ring or at least ping so she would know she had received a message.

There was a knock. "Bree?"

God, it was Brett. "Yeah." He opened the door wider and strode in. "I heard what happened." He stood there, tall and imposing, his arms crossed over his chest, stretching his gray tee tight. He was a formidable sight. And he was looking for a fight. Especially with Lucas.

"I warned him, you know."

She nodded. She bet he had. And Lucas probably scoffed at the threat.

"What did he say to make you look like a . . .a hot mess?"

She swiped at her eyes again and smirked. "Geez, Brett, thanks for the compliment."

He shrugged, unfolding his arms and came to her side of the bed. Instead of sitting on the edge, he hunkered down and looked at her. "I talked to him today, Bree. He feels terrible."

"You did? When?" She needed to know what they had talked about.

"At the tavern. Around lunch time." He stood then sat on the edge of her bed. "We talked for quite awhile. Got reacquainted, but talked about you most of the time."

She gave her brother a half-smile. "I bet he told you I had an audition and might be leaving, right?"

Brett nodded. "He's hurting, Bree. As much as you are."

"It didn't look that way tonight when he dropped off Dani."

"What do you mean?"

"He was all dressed up as though he were going out on a date."

Brett leaned back on his arms and chuckled. "If I know Lucas, he did it to make you jealous. He doesn't have anyone else in his life, Bree. He loves you."

When she glanced down at him, lying across her bed, she said, "Do you think he'll see me if I call him?"

"Well. . .maybe after you clean up a bit. You're all splotchy and red. And your eyes are almost swollen shut and..."

"And you'll stop making her feel worse than she already does," Aunt Merry said, as she came into the room holding onto a tall glass of ice water and a white face cloth.

"Hey, I tell it like it is."

"Yeah, we know. And it doesn't always help," her aunt added, nudging him aside as she sat next to Bree and handed her the glass of water.

She wrapped her hands around the tall glass and took a long gulp. She sighed and took another swallow, closing her eyes and letting the cold water soothe her raw throat.

"Here," her aunt said, handing her the cloth. "Lie down. This should help with the swelling."

She took the cloth from her aunt's hand. "Get off the bed, Brett."

Her brother scowled and stood. "Do you want me to talk to him for you?"

"Please don't, Brett. I mean it." Why wouldn't they leave her alone and let her drown in her own sorrows? Didn't they realize it was her fault and not Lucas's? Why did they want to blame him? She had done this.

"He needs to know how he's hurt you, Bree."

"I think he does," she answered, knowing in her heart that Lucas was probably hurting as well. He wasn't shedding bucket loads of tears though. Instead, he was probably drinking his fair share in beers at the tavern. “I’m sorry," she said, looking from her brother to her aunt. "I'm not in a good place right now, and I know you want to help, but. . ." Another sob burst out before she had a chance to stop it. "It's not his fault. Really. It's mine."

"And how is it your fault that he hurt you?" Brett asked, sticking his hands in his pockets and swaying back on his heels. "I don't get it."

She sighed and sat up, letting the cloth fall to her lap then back to Brett. "It just is. I. . .I don’t really want to talk about it.” She looked up at her brother. “Please let it be, Brett.”

"Alright. I'll leave him alone. This time. But if I find out he's hurt you again, I will go after him,” Brett promised.

"I don't need you to fight for me, Brett. I know you mean well, but getting into a fight with him, isn't going to change the result. It'll still be the same. Except one or both of you will be hurt." She blew out a long breath. "And I don't want either one of you hurt because of me."

Aunt Merry sidled over to her and wrapped an arm around her shoulder. She leaned into her aunt, the closest thing she had to a mother right now. She had a habit of hurting those she loved most because of her own selfishness, her own wants and needs. And what about theirs? Yet, despite those she had hurt, they still cared for her and loved her. Maybe Lucas could still love her.

* * * *

Lucas tipped back the bottle and chugged down the remains of the beer. He tossed it into the cooler and reached for another. It was going to be a long night. He sat back against the Adirondack chair and stretched out his legs as he gazed out to the river. He couldn't bear to be at his parents and have them question him to no end about what happened between him and Bree. He couldn't bear to tell Dani, yet, that Bree wouldn't be over for dinner or hanging out with them on the weekends. Damn you, Bree!

He twisted the cap off the Michelob and flung it into the fire pit. He really didn't need the fire to keep him warm, the anger inside him kept him burning. How could she do this to him? To them? He thought they wanted the same things, but she still wanted to dance with a big company, to see her name plastered in lights and her videos gathering thousands of views. Big deal. Was she that shallow? He hadn't thought so, but now he didn't know if he knew Bree at all.

He took a long swallow, letting the cold brew soothe the ache in his throat. Four beers later and it still hadn't soothed the ache in his heart. Nothing would. She was lodged in as tight as a pine beam to a rafter.

A spark shot up from the fire, startling him. He wasn't anxious, was he? He rubbed his eyes, feeling the dampness of tears against his palm. Tears slid down his face. Pain hit him hard in his chest. The last time he had felt this way was when Dani had been motionless in the hospital bed, and he had been incapable of helping her.

He was feeling the pain of loss. The pain of losing something you had taken for granted every day until it was gone. Forever.

He wanted to obliterate the memories of the last few weeks and live his life as he had before Bree had come back to town. But had he truly had a life then? Not really. He got up, went to work, did his daily grind, went back home, ate supper, played with Dani, read her a story, put her to bed and ended his night with a brew before collapsing into his own bed and repeating it all over again. Boring!

And then Bree had come home. The dull, grey aura of his life had brightened. She had brought light to his life, and Dani's. His daughter had never been happier. So, why was he giving up on Bree? Was he destroying the only happiness he had known in ten years? Was he willing to give up Dani's happiness because he was being selfish and most likely, stubborn?

He plucked his cell from his back pocket. No calls. He had hoped Bree would've called, crying, yelling, apologizing. It didn't matter. As long as he could hear her voice.

So call her, man! He shook his head. He'd look like a fool. You are a fool! He gulped more of the brew. He had her on speed dial, of course. All he had to do was hit the number. His thumb hovered, then he yanked his thumb back. He glared at it. Traitor!

God, he must be buzzed. He was arguing with himself and glaring at his thumb. You're a strange one, he thought, tipping the bottle back against his mouth once more. Good, maybe this time he'd get so drunk, he'd forget he had even tried to call Bree.

He inhaled, breathing in the crisp scent of pine as a soft, cool breeze rustled through the trees. A loon sounded far off in the distance. The water lapped on the small beach about fifty yards away where they had a picnic last weekend. How had his life changed in just a matter of days?

He slammed his fist against the arm of the Adirondack chair. The only way he'd get any sleep was to call Bree. He glanced down. It was already after eleven. Too late to call. She was probably asleep. He'd call in the morning to see if she was willing to give it another chance. Right now, he needed to get some shut eye. The beers he had guzzled now soured his stomach. Tomorrow might see him having a hangover.

Light filtered across his lids, waking him up. He groaned and smashed the soft pillow over his head to block the light. Pain thrummed in his head. He reached for his phone, but it wasn't next to him where he had collapsed on the living room floor. Where had he put it?

Flinging the pillow aside, he turned to his back and squinted against the sunlight streaming in through the living room window. He sat up and leaned his forearms on his bent knees. Despite the pain throbbing in his skull, he smiled. The sunrise over the river was gorgeous. Brilliant hues of orange and pink painted the horizon. How Bree would love this! As quick as the smile had come, it had disappeared. Bree would never see this view if she chose to leave Misty River. His heart constricted with physical pain. Now he knew what it meant to have a broken heart.

A thin veil of fog floated over the dark surface, hence the name of the town. Evidently, the early settlers who had lived on the river, named the town after the mist they had witnessed each morning. To think he was witnessing the same view, or close to it, that the early pioneers had seen two hundred years ago. He wished Bree was sitting beside him, or lying beside him, looking at the deep forest beyond the river as the world slowly woke around them. Birds started to sing and chatter and even though he was still aching for Bree, it did bring some sense of happiness to his soul. With a sigh, he kicked the sleeping bag away from his legs and stood. And immediately felt a spasm in his back. Sleeping on a hard floor didn't help his back. He must've passed out soon after getting in the sleeping bag because he didn't even remember his head hitting the pillow. He needed to find his phone.

He walked to the kitchen in desperate need of coffee. And there was his phone, sitting on the corner of the counter, balanced precariously on the edge. He grabbed it, realizing he didn't remember even putting it there. It was six-thirty. He'd have a cup of coffee, clean up his mess and head to his parents. He'd spend time with Dani and get Bree out of his system.

Thank goodness he remembered to bring along a small coffee maker from the house. And the cabin did have electricity and running water. He pulled out a bag of coffee from the meager supplies he kept on hand. He thought of Bree as he went through the motions of making his coffee and wondered if she was awake, making her own cup of brew and thinking of him. Should he just call her? Then again, there was no reason for him to apologize. She had decided to leave town. She had decided to give up on them.

He took a sip of this coffee and thought back to the

incident. He hadn't really allowed her to explain all the details to him. What a jerk he'd been. Hell, what a jerk he was now! She had said she had been called to audition. Okay, that didn't mean she'd get the job. It only meant they had an interest in her, but they may not hire her. He leaned his elbows on the counter and cupped his face in his hands. God! Maybe she didn't want to do this and was hoping he'd stop her. And he had walked out the door, pretty much telling her it was okay for her to leave. He had been an idiot! A damn fool!

He stood, thrusting a hand through his hair then scrubbing his hand down his face. What if he called and apologized for his behavior and asked her to tell him about it. He just wanted to see her face. Wanted to see her smile again. Wanted to hold her tight and kiss her. He wanted *her*.

He'd head to his parents, take a shower, spend time with Dani and then maybe he'd show up at the studio with some excuse and hopefully meet up with her. If she tried to walk away, he'd follow her, even if it meant walking right into her house. He knew Bree's aunt would take his side. With a plan in mind, if he could call it a plan, he emptied his mug.

He then went to his sleeping bag and rolled it up. He picked up his pillow and phone from the floor and set everything by the door. He then wondered where his shoes were. He hadn't slept in them which surprised him. As he walked through the living room, he found one shoe by the sliding door to the deck. He found the other one on the deck. He shook his head. He didn't have any recollection of even removing his shoes.

A few minutes later, after locking up the house and putting his gear in the back of the truck, he started the engine and headed down the dirt road. He flipped on the radio and slammed back against the seat, swearing as he did. Evidently, he had turned the volume up as high as it could go and forgotten to lower it before shutting off the truck yesterday. As if on cue, *Perfect* played. The song he and Bree had danced too at the tavern several weeks ago. It was the moment he knew he never wanted to let her go.

A half-hour later, he was pulling into the drive. He knew his parents would be awake and most likely Dani too. He plastered on a smile and, after gathering the gear from the back, he ambled up the steps then into the house.

He no sooner opened the door, when Dani flung herself at him, wrapping her left arm around his leg. He nearly tripped but, thankfully, had caught his balance. "Watch it, Dani," he said as he dropped his duffle bag at his feet. He lifted Dani high in the air. She laughed and it was the sweetest sound. Regardless of how low his spirits could go; Dani could always lift them up.

"Hey there, Son! We weren't expecting you for a few more hours." His father lumbered over to the coffee maker and poured the dark brew into a large mug. "Want one?"

"Sure do." He set Dani back on the floor and stroked her unruly hair. Dani took off to sit in the chair. He walked over to the counter then opened the cabinet, pulling out a mug. He handed it to his father who filled his cup then pushed it back to him. "How was Dani?"

"Good as always, right Peanut?" His father asked, looking down at Dani, who nodded her head vigorously. His father then looked back at him. "You don't look so good."

He swallowed the strong coffee. "I'm okay. Had a few beers too many last night."

"Did you get any work done on the cabin?" his father asked, heading over to the kitchen table. He let out a harrumph as he sat.

Lucas followed him and sat kitty corner to his father. "No. Too much on my mind." He lifted Dani into his lap. She snuggled into the crook of his left arm. "I didn't sleep well either."

"I bet." His father let out a small laugh. "Sleeping on a hard floor isn't good for anybody, no matter how young you are."

"It was more of what was on my mind, more than what I

was sleeping on."

"Oh. Anything you want to talk about?"

"Sure, but not now." He nodded down to Dani. "Maybe later."

His father nodded in understanding. "Your mother's worried about you too."

"Yeah. I know."

"So, what are you going to do?"

He looked down at Dani. "Hey, sweetheart, do you mind going into the living room or into your bedroom for a few minutes?"

"How come?" came her soft reply. She tended to be extra clingy when he was away for a night or two. Probably a fear he would never come back due to what had happened to her mother.

"I just need to talk to Grampa about something, that's all."

"Is it boring?"

He chuckled. "Yes. Very."

"Okay then." She sighed and pushed herself off his lap. "I'm gonna watch tv."

Once Dani was out of earshot, he turned his gaze back to his father. "Bree and I had a fight, and I haven't spoken to her." He picked up his mug and took another swallow.

"What started the fight?"

He sighed. "She told me she had an audition."

"So?"

"And if she does well, they'll hire her. And she'll leave."

"Who's leaving?" his mother asked, as she came upstairs from the basement, a laundry basket tucked at her hip.

"He thinks Bree might leave town if she gets hired at this audition," his father explained in a rush.

His mother's eyes rounded. "Bree wouldn't leave. Not now."

"Well, no, not now, but she'll eventually leave."

"And what makes you think that?"

"It's her dream, mom, to dance in front of millions of

people. To perform on stage."

"Did she tell you that?"

"Yeah. Well. . .kind of." He looked down at his mug. "And I don't want to take away her dream. It was my fault anyway."

"What was your fault?" his father asked.

"I wouldn't let her explain. Instead, I walked out the door of the studio the other night."

"You're too stubborn for your own good, Lucas," his mother scolded him, swatting his arm. "You've always done that. The minute you think you're going to hear something you don't want to hear; you leave."

He nodded. His mother was right. "I'm a fool." He took a swallow of the coffee and set his mug down. "I've been wanting to call her several times already, but each time I pull out the phone, I stop. I don't know what to say."

"How about 'I'm sorry.'" His father chuckled. "Sometimes we have to be the first to apologize even though we may not be wrong. But, in your mother's words—"

"Swallow your pride and apologize. She'll forgive you," his mother added.

"And what makes you so sure?" he said.

His mother walked to the coffeemaker and poured herself a cup of coffee. "Because if she loves you, and I believe she does, she will." She looked at him over the rim of her mug. "You know, I've been talking to her aunt."

"And?"

"Talk to her, Lucas."

He would. Once he was showered and dressed. Then he'd beg for her forgiveness and find a way to make it up to her.

Twenty

Bree decided she wasn't going to waste any more time shedding tears for a man who claimed he loved her but wouldn't call. She had cried herself to sleep the last three nights and had the bags under her eyes to prove it. Anna and her aunt did their best to cheer her up by talking about the recital and the costumes. As much as she wanted to crawl under the covers and stay there, she knew that keeping busy was the best way to keep her mind off Lucas.

She and Anna had perused Pinterest for costume ideas yesterday and she had to admit, she was excited for the recital. It would be a lot of fun. Anna took it upon herself to write down the online info to order the costumes. They needed to do it soon as the recital was a few weeks away.

Her phone pinged. She picked up her cell, clicked on the green button out of habit and then noticed the number. Lucas!

"Hello?" She tried to sound as cheery as possible.

"Hi, Bree." There was silence and she wondered if he had hung up.

"Lucas?"

"Yeah. I'm here." His voice, husky and low, made her toes curl. God, how she had missed talking to him. "I. . .Oh, hell. Bree, I'm sorry."

She hadn't expected him to sound so angry when he apologized. "Ah, you don't sound very apologetic." She could see him thrusting his hand through his hair, tilting his head back and letting out a deep sigh. And there it was. The sigh.

"I'm sorry. Really."

"Why didn't you let me explain things, Lucas? We could've avoided all this."

"Because I'm an idiot."

"I'm not going to disagree with that, Lucas." She needed him to know that he couldn't walk away every time they had a disagreement. "You really hurt me, you know."

"I know." Another sigh. "I can't begin to tell you how sorry I am."

"I had a relationship before you and. . .and he did the same thing to me. Always thought I'd come crawling back to him, begging for forgiveness, but I won't be a doormat, for you or—"

"Don't say it, Bree. I can't stand the thought of you being with anyone else. But, I do want to talk to you. Wait." He cleared his throat. "Let me rephrase that. I want you to tell me what you're thinking, what you're feeling. I want to make it up to you."

She smiled. She knew he meant it. She could hear it in his voice. "I'd like that."

"Does that mean you're accepting my apology?"

"Well," she dragged out, then laughed. God, it felt good. "Yes."

"Mom was right."

"What?"

"Mom said a woman would forgive a man if he apologized."

"Huh. I never heard that one before, but it sounds about right." She leaned back against the chair. She wasn't sure if she should be bold enough to ask, but she did anyway. "When do you want to get together?" She hoped it would be soon.

"In an hour? I miss you, Bree."

And she missed him, more than he would know. "An hour is perfect."

"Great! See you soon. Oh, dress casual."

"Alright. See you soon." She hung up and grinned. She tossed her phone on the table and stood. She did a quick little happy dance.

"Someone's happy all of a sudden," Aunt Merry quipped. "Lucas called?"

She nodded. "We're getting together in an hour."

"That's great!" Aunt Merry set the laundry basket down. "Any idea where you're going?"

"Not a clue. But it doesn't matter. I'm happy I get to see him!"

Aunt Merry smiled and sat down, reaching into the basket. "Don't do anything I wouldn't do," she said with a sly grin.

"We're going to talk. That's all."

"Suuuure."

"And the rest is none of your business." She was happy and excited. "I'm off to shower and get dressed." She rushed upstairs as her aunt's laughter followed her.

She jumped into the shower and let the steam wash over her. She thought of what she would say and explain it in such a way Lucas wouldn't feel as though she was casting him aside. She loved him. She wanted to be with him, yet she wanted the opportunity to audition. For what purpose, she wondered. Was it to be on stage again in front of hundreds of people or was it more than that? Was she trying to prove something? And then she had her answer. Yes. She needed to prove to herself that she could still dance. She could still be somebody. She wasn't a lackluster dancer who was close to retirement. She could dance as well as anyone ten years younger than her. And she would show them. But that's not what Lucas wanted to hear. He wanted to hear her tell him she would stay in Misty River. She would give up everything for him. But could she give up on herself?

She toweled off, the questions still swirling in her mind and the more they tumbled around, the more confused she became. She would explain to him the best she could and then they could spend the day together.

As she dressed, her gaze went to the drawings and photos she had printed off. All ideas for the performance at the Founders Day Festival. She'd have to remind Lucas about the props and scenery, and the float.

She sat at the vanity and applied her makeup, making sure she looked her best for him. Although she knew Lucas wouldn't mind if she wore a scrubby pair of jeans, a faded tee and her hair mussed up. He loved her just as she was. She heard the front door open and Aunt Merry greeting Lucas. Buster barked and she wondered how Lucas reacted. She jumped up, grabbed her purse and hurried downstairs.

When she reached the bottom, she expelled a breath and stopped short. Lucas was hunkered down, his hands on both sides of Buster's head, ruffling his ears. Wow! It didn't take long for his fear of dogs to evaporate. Buster licked Lucas's face. He looked up at her and grinned.

She rewarded him with a smile of her own. He looked gorgeous. She raked her gaze over him as he stood, taking in the sight of his blue tee stretched tight over his muscled chest. Her gaze roamed down to his flat stomach and his slim hips encased in khaki shorts. She realized he was ogling her as much as she was ogling him.

Aunt Merry cleared her throat. "Okay you two. You'd think you'd never seen each other before."

Bree lifted her gaze to Lucas's handsome face and felt the flushed heat along her neck Was he blushing? He appeared to be a bit more bronzed than usual. He scrutinized her as heat pooled low in her belly. This time she cleared her throat. "Ready?"

"Ready."

His voice was husky and she wondered if there was some sort of innuendo to his statement. Probably.

She smiled at Aunt Merry and walked to Lucas. He wrapped an arm around her waist and the butterflies that had lain dormant for two days, took flight and skittered up her spine. She nearly stumbled as she stepped down the stairs, but Lucas grasped her tighter around her waist. It had only been two days, but it seemed like a week. She had missed him.

He opened the door for her and she settled herself in the

seat, buckling herself in. He hurried to his side, got in and buckled up, then turned on the ignition. As he settled back in his seat, he glanced at her. She suddenly felt shy and awkward.

"Everything okay?" Lucas asked, turning onto the main road. "Bree, I really am sorry for how I acted the other night. . .and day."

She nodded, glancing his way. "I know you are." She clasped her hands in her lap. "I'm sorry, too." She huffed out a breath and tilted her head back. "I don't know what to do, Lucas."

"What is it you want to do?"

"Dance. It's as simple as that. But. . .I feel old some days."

"You're not old—"

"I know, but in the dance world, I'm getting pretty close to retirement age, believe it or not. Most dancers hit their prime in their early twenties and retire in their mid-thirties, or later."

He nodded as though he was trying to understand. "It seems that you still have several more years left to dance."

"Probably." She realized what he had said. Was he encouraging her to continue her career? But what about their relationship?

"What's going to happen to us, Lucas? If I go to this audition and get the job that means we won't see each other as often—"

He reached for her hand, pulling it from her lap and held it tight. His hand was warm and calloused, hard and tough, yet held hers tenderly. His thumb stroked the top of her hand. He looked at her, his eyes filled with hope, and love. "We'll find a way, Bree. I've been thinking about this for the last couple of days and, although it'll be hard, we can try to find a way to make it work."

She wished she had his confidence. He didn't know much about the ballet world and the hours of dedication it took. Hours of dance each day only to go home and collapse in bed and start again the next day, especially when it came close to doing a show. He didn't know about the tours from city to city, touring in other countries and being away for weeks at a time. She knew he would eventually walk away from her. The only relationship she had before Lucas was with Wyatt. Any guy she dated before Wyatt was short-term because they didn't want 'to wait around' until she 'had time for them.' She needed to let him know, with blunt honesty, then, if he still thought they could have a long-distance relationship, she'd agree to it.

She squeezed his hand. "Okay, but I really need to tell you what it will entail. You may change your mind."

* * * *

They arrived at the River's Edge Boat and Kayak Rental. He remembered Bree saying it had been a while since she had been kayaking. It was a surprise he had planned in hopes she still wanted to see him.

"We're kayaking?" Bree asked, her eyes alight. "Oh, I haven't done this in years! I think I was around sixteen or seventeen at the time."

"Is this okay with you?"

She twisted her gaze from the stand of bright colored kayaks to him. "Oh, yeah. Definitely!" She kissed him on the cheek. "Although I don't know how good I'll be at paddling."

He chuckled. "It'll be fine. I'll sit in the back and do most of the work." He reached into the back of the truck and took out a blanket and a cooler. "I even brought refreshments."

"Great idea. So, where are we going on this excursion?"

He winked at her. "You'll see."

Once the attendant got the kayak off the stand and into the water, Lucas assisted Bree into the small craft. It wobbled, but it didn't seem to bother Bree. Must be the dance experience. She would obviously have excellent balance control. She had removed her shoes and kept them off, tucking them into a cubby on the side of the kayak. He stepped in and while doing so, tilted the kayak a bit too much, startling Bree. She flung out her arms and grasped the sides of the kayak.

"Sorry. I'm not one for agility when it comes to these things." No, he was more like a large bear, jumping right in, causing the kayak to roll haphazardly.

"Warn me next time." Bree gave a short laugh.

"Will do." He sat on the small black seat behind her and was glad of that. He stretched out his legs as much as he could and grabbed the oar. He turned to the attendant. "All set. Can you give us a shove?"

"Sure thing," the guy said, and bent down, pushing the kayak further into the river.

"Thanks," he called back, then plunged the oar into the river. He angled the oar to turn the kayak toward the left.

They were silent for a few minutes as they glided down the river amidst the marshland. It was peaceful and a sense of contentment washed over him. They passed a huge house sitting up on a small knoll to his left. He didn't know much about the history of Misty River.

"Hey, that's Kris Galloway's house!" Bree said. Well then, she obviously knew some of the history. "Wow, although it needs a good paint job, it's beautiful."

"How old is it?" he asked, turning the kayak closer to land to get a better look.

"Oh, it's got to be a hundred years old. Kris's great-grandparents built it. It's one of the first homes in town. Did you know she's renovating it soon?"

He shook his head.

"Yeah, she's looking for contractors. It's been a bed and breakfast for fifty years now, but it's fallen into disrepair because her grandmother, who still lives there by the way, couldn't keep up with the demands. She had to shut down the business several years ago."

"So, what's Kris going to do with it?"

"Oh, she's looking for contractors and is hoping to re-open by spring or summer."

Huh, he'd have to talk to Devon about bidding on the job. "Did she put out an ad?"

"I think so." She glanced over her shoulder to him. "You should call her if you're interested. I bet she'd hire you, especially once I give her a great review about your work."

He grinned. "I'd appreciate that."

She laughed. "No problem. Although I'm sure your credentials are exemplary and you don't need my review."

"All reviews are needed, Bree."

She nodded. "I'll have to call Kris and ask about her grandmother. I haven't seen her in a couple of weeks. Her grandmother hasn't been well lately."

"She's a grand old lady."

Bree shot him a look.

"The house, Bree. I don't know the grandmother, although I'm sure she's grand as well."

Bree laughed and it warmed his heart. He turned the oar to move out of the marsh where the kayak had drifted and maneuvered the kayak to get them into the main river. A few kayaks glided past them. They waved to the passers-by.

"This was a good idea, Lucas."

He grinned and hoped she'd like his other ideas as well. He was surprised when Bree lifted the paddle and dipped it in the water. It took her a minute to get the hang of handling the paddle, but once she did, they fell into a rhythm, like dancing.

He had more work on his end with having to steer the kayak, but the sound of the paddles slapping at the water, the drip of water and the warm sunlight on his body lulled him into a sense of peacefulness he hadn't felt in a long time. He needed this. They moved at a leisurely pace, and he had lost track of time.

"Lucas, there's your cabin!"

He shot a look to his left. She was right. Had they travelled this far down river already? He grinned. It was a beautiful cabin. It sat on a knoll, the deck stretched across the back where he had stood side by side with Bree only a week ago.

And, hadn't it been last night, he had passed out drunk thinking of Bree? And here he was now, sitting in a kayak with her, when only yesterday, at this time, they hadn't even been talking. What a difference a day could make. In a few weeks, he hoped he and Dani would be settled in. And he hoped Bree would settle down with them as well, but he couldn't push her. Not yet.

"It's a gorgeous cabin, Lucas. You should be proud."

"I am." It had taken a lot of sweat and man hours, but it was nearly complete. Now, if only Bree could complete him, he'd be the happiest man on earth.

"I love your cabin. It's in a perfect location." She sighed and brushed her hair back from her eyes. "I'm glad you had invited me to take a look."

"I'd like to have you over again. . .soon."

She tossed a glance over her shoulder and grinned. "I'd love that."

His heart sang and if he wasn't in the kayak, he'd be holding her close and kissing her. They paddled in silence, each in their own thoughts when he realized they were close to the destination. He twisted the paddle in the water to steer the kayak to shore. Bree lifted her paddle out of the water.

"Why are we turning in here?"

"It's my surprise," he answered. "There's something I want to show you."

"Oh?"

He steered the kayak as close to shore as possible. When the kayak scraped the sandy bottom, he lifted himself from the seat. "Don't move. I'm going to get out and push the kayak onto the beach."

He stepped into the water, taking care not to tip the kayak and startle Bree again. He noticed she had grasped the sides, just in case. He waded in the water toward the front of the kayak, where Bree sat. She started to stand, but he stilled her with a hand to her shoulder. "Stay right there. I'll pull the kayak closer and get it up on shore."

She nodded and settled back. He strode to the front of the kayak then bent over, grasping the front of the kayak. He heaved the kayak several feet on to the small beach. Sweat beaded his forehead. It was going to be a hot one. "Okay, you can step out now." He walked back into the water and held out a hand.

"I feel guilty."

"Why?"

"Because you had to tug the kayak on shore by yourself with the added weight of me in it."

He scoffed. "It wasn't that bad." He chuckled. "I'll blame it on the case of beer I have tucked away in the cooler."

"Seriously?" She giggled then stepped into the ankle-deep water while holding onto his hand. She gasped as her feet sunk into the soft sand. "The water's cold, that's for sure." She stood beside him then leaned in and kissed him on the cheek. "Thanks for being so chivalrous."

Stunned, he could only stare at her. Then he smiled and bowed. "I'm at your service, madam."

They laughed, then stopped and looked at each other. He wanted to grab hold of her, tug her close and kiss her with all the pent-up feelings he had inside. But he held back. They still had some talking to do. "I'll grab the cooler and blanket then I'll show you why I brought you here."

He walked further into the water until he was at the back end of the kayak. He reached in and lifted out the cooler and the blanket. When he turned, he noticed Bree looking at the tiny A-frame house in the distance. He wondered what she was thinking as he sloshed out of the water and walked toward her. Nodding his head toward the tiny house, he said, "See that?"

"Yeah. I noticed it while you were getting the cooler. It's really cute."

"That's where we're going." He stepped ahead of her. "Follow me." They walked down a narrow pine laden path toward the A-frame house. The shade felt good on his heated skin, and he inhaled the tangy scent of pine in the air. Birdsong drifted in the air and the soft rustle of a breeze through the trees added to the ambience. With each step, he relaxed. A moment later, he stopped at the foot of the steps. Bree came to stand next to him. He looked at her then at the tiny house before them.

"It's so cute, Lucas. Who does it belong to?"

He turned to her. "Me."

"You?"

"Remember when I mentioned how I wanted to build a glamping resort?"

She nodded.

"Well, this is the model of what Devon and I plan to do." He strode up two steps to a small deck. After setting the cooler and blanket on the deck, he turned. "This is my dream, Bree."

Twenty-One

Bree waited beside Lucas as he unlocked the door and opened it. "Come on in and I'll show you." He held out his hand and she grasped it. He held it tight, and she squeezed his fingers. He looked at her and smiled.

As she stepped inside, she couldn't hold back the grin. It was . . .adorable! It was the only word she could find to describe the place. "Lucas, this is so cute!"

"Well, I wasn't actually going for cute, but I'll accept it. I was hoping for efficient, rustic, compact." He stepped further into the room and extended an arm turning in a circle. "It's small but has all the comforts of home."

She moved her gaze around the small area. The house was one large room, similar to a studio apartment, but on a much smaller scale. Stairs led to a loft above their heads. A king-sized bed stood over in one corner complete with a colorful quilt and pillows with curtains on the window. A pine chest of drawers sat opposite the bed against the other wall beneath the window which looked to the front of the A-Frame and out to the river. "It's beautiful, Lucas."

She moved to the kitchenette and stopped next to a hand-crafted knotty-pine table with four matching chairs. In a few short strides, she stood at the kitchen sink looking out to the woods through the window. An apartment-size fridge stood to her left and next to that was a small four burner stove with an oven. Lucas was right. It had all the comforts of home. Just, cozier.

"It really is amazing," she said, leaning over the sink to get a better view beyond. The woods were thick with pines. It was quiet, almost too quiet. "The people who rent this place better like the woods, and the quiet."

He came to stand beside her and put his hand to her lower back. "I hope so. There's cell phone service, but it's spotty. I didn't hook up a TV. I wanted to create a place where people could get away from the hustle and bustle of everyday life. To set down their phones, get away from social media and tv and enjoy each other's company. You know, play games, go fishing, kayaking, that sort of thing."

"I think you've thought of everything." She twisted sideways and his hand slid from her back. She grasped his forearms and looked into his warm gaze. "You are so talented. Do you know that?" She needed him to know his worth, although maybe he already did. But she needed him to know how much she valued him as a contractor, as a friend, as a man, and perhaps as a lover, someday. If things worked out between them. She knew they needed to talk, but she didn't know where to start.

"But it's nice to hear it from you. You're important to me, Bree, do you know that?"

Her heart skittered. "I do."

He chuckled. "Here we are, facing each other, and you said, 'I do'. What does it remind you of?"

She inhaled, almost coughing. Good gracious! Was he thinking about marriage? "It seems like that, doesn't it? But. . ."

"Oh, oh. What's brewing in that pretty head of yours?" He tilted his head to touch her forehead. It was cool. She closed her eyes. She wanted to feel, that's all. No thinking, just feeling. As she held onto his upper arms, he lifted his hands to her shoulders. "You do crazy things to me, Bree. Crazy, wonderful things."

"I could say the same for you, Lucas." She inhaled his scent. The familiar, woodsy aftershave he wore. What was it about him that stirred her soul and wanted to make her forget her dreams of dancing. What if she gave in to his sweet onslaught of seduction and took the plunge? Would it be so bad? She loved him. He loved her. So why was she fighting it?

"You are the best thing that has ever happened to me."

He leaned in and his warm breath caressed her lips. She licked her lips anticipating his kiss, but he didn't move. He cupped her face in his large hands as his thumbs caressed the hollows of her cheeks. "You're so beautiful. You're—"

"Just kiss me, Lucas." She sucked in a breath as he brought his mouth down on hers. He captured her mouth gently, dancing over her lips, creating a tingling sensation throughout her entire body. An ache far below swelled into need. She wrapped her hands around his neck, needing something to hold onto as she felt herself falling. Falling in love.

His tongue pressed against the seam of her lips, and she opened for him. Heat flushed her body and her heart thundered against her ribs. She sighed against his mouth when he pulled her tight against him.

He pulled back, his forehead pressed against her own. "I want you so much, Bree, but it has to be right. I want total and complete honesty between us. So, until we know where we're going with this relationship, we should hold back, just a little." He smiled down at her.

She turned her head sideways and nestled against his shoulder. Lucas held her there, smoothing his hand over her back in soft, slow circles. She sighed.

"Why don't we have some lunch and then we can talk."

She nodded, smiling up at him. "I think that's best." She kissed him on the cheek and stepped away, heading for the door. "Do you want to eat on the small deck here?"

"Sure, unless you want to sit closer to the water?"

She glanced from the river to the deck then to him. "Let's sit by the river. We might as well put the blanket to good use." She grinned and hurried out the door. She leaned over and picked up the blanket. She heard him groan behind her. She twisted around. "Race ya! First one to the kayak wins." She took off in a run down the pine laden path. She heard his running steps behind her which stoked her to run faster.

The kayak came into view. She'd beat him. Suddenly, his arms wrapped around her waist causing her to stumble, but he lifted her up. She squealed then laughed, squirming in his arms. "No fair!" She tried to wriggle free and reach the kayak, but he held her firmly. He lifted her into his arms and ran the short distance to the kayak.

"We both win," he said, holding her against his chest as he would a young child. She reveled in the feel of his muscled chest against hers. He gazed down at her, his eyes crinkling.

"Okay, you win. Now you can put me down."

"I kind of like where you are right now."

She giggled. "Seriously, Lucas. I can't eat lunch with you holding me like this."

"We'll skip lunch and—"

She swatted his arm. "No. Remember, it was your idea to talk."

"You're right." He helped her stand then took the blanket from her and spread it out onto a grassy area. He was about to sit when he snapped his fingers. "I left the cooler back at the house. Be right back."

She watched him run back to the cabin until he was a small figure in front of the A-frame structure. It was a nice place for a couple or even a small family. Lucas had put a lot of thought into this, and she couldn't wait to hear more about his resort plans. She watched as he strode back toward her, the cooler in hand. A moment later, he plopped down beside her.

"I brought roast beef sandwiches today along with some beer and fruit."

"Sounds delicious."

He pulled out two cold beers and uncapped one, handing it to her. He then did the same for himself. She took a long pull on the beer and sighed as cold liquid slid down her throat. She crossed her legs and glanced over at Lucas. He had taken a swallow as well and was now pulling out the sandwiches. After handing her one, he took one baggie for himself. They opened them at the same time and ironically bit into their sandwiches at the same time. She wanted to giggle. It was like a rehearsed dance. Each one doing the exact move without having to think about it. Her gut was telling her he wanted to say something but didn't know where to start. She didn't know either.

The sun dappled the grass and blanket around them as the warm breeze tousled her hair and caressed her skin. She lifted her face to the sun, feeling the heat settle over her although her body was heated enough by sitting so close to Lucas. She sighed then opened her eyes and went back to eating her sandwich.

"How's the sandwich?" Lucas asked. Evidently, he must've thought she didn't like it because she hadn't been eating.

"Oh, it's great! I'm just enjoying the sun on my face."

"It is a beautiful day. Couldn't wish for a better one."

"So, now that you've shown me the house, what are your plans for the resort?"

He grinned. "Devon and I plan on building six more of these cabins along the river here and hope to have them open by mid-summer. I doubt we'll rent them all out this summer." He brushed crumbs off his shorts. "We're trying to get the word out by social media and ads. We got a few bites."

"How much are you charging?" She bit into the sandwich. "This is good!"

"Thanks." After taking a swallow of his beer, he continued. "Probably two and a quarter a night during peak season and foliage season. It'll be half that cost during the winter months. We've researched other resorts and that's the going price."

She glanced back at the little house on the edge of the woods. "I think the resort will do well." She bit into a chip. She was sure visitors to this area of Maine would pay the price considering they were an hour's drive to the White Mountains, a fifteen-minute drive to a wonderful beach and a half-hour to Portland. And, although it felt as though they were miles away from town and secluded, it was only a fifteen-minute drive to downtown. "I'd spend that kind of money to stay here."

He leaned into her and whispered, "Why do that when you can stay at my cabin, for free?"

Her eyes widened, then she grinned. Lucas smiled at her--a heart-melting smile that made her heart tumble. For one split half-second, she wanted to accept his offer. But she couldn't. Lucas kissed her cheek and she leaned in closer to him. He tugged her closer and wrapped an arm around her as she leaned her head on his shoulder. Both of them looked out to the river, each lost momentarily in their own thoughts.

"Lucas?"

"Hmm-mm?"

"Why did you invite me to the cabin and ask me what I would do?" She thought she knew his answer, but she wanted to hear it.

"I value your opinion, Bree, and to be honest, I wanted to see your reaction." He touched a finger to her chin and turned her face toward him. "You do know how I feel about you, don't you?"

She nodded.

"I'm going to lay it on the line, Bree." Lucas looked at her with those beautiful brown eyes, and she couldn't look away if she tried. "I was hoping, if things work out like I hope they do, you will live there with me and Dani."

Whoa! She hadn't expected that. She lifted her head and pulled back. She glanced at their entwined hands. "Lucas, there's something we need to talk about, and I know that's why we're here." She inhaled. Her heart constricted. She prayed he wouldn't repeat what he had done the other night.

He squeezed her hand in reassurance. "Go on. I'll listen."

"I care for you, Lucas. A lot. And I care for Dani." She shrugged. "Maybe it's love to most people, but I'm not sure what love is." She heaved a sigh and looked down at the ground. Just say it. "I don't want to make any promises I can't keep." She turned to sit on her knees and faced him. She clasped his hand tight, willing him to understand where she was coming from.

He reached up and caressed the side of her face. "It's okay, Bree. You can tell me."

“You know I have an audition in Philadelphia." She picked at her sandwich. "Part of me wants to go, and the other part of me wants to stay." Bree grabbed her ponytail and ran her fingers through the strands. "I don’t know what to do.” She looked at him, her gaze begging him to give her the answer, but he couldn’t. Bree had to look deep within herself and make the decision on her own.

Lucas continued stroking her cheek. "Daniella regretted her decision to marry me." He sighed. "I couldn't bear it if you felt obligated to me in any way only to walk out on me and Dani later." He kissed her forehead. "You have to be sure, Bree, in your heart and soul." Lucas smoothed his hand along her jaw, and she leaned into it. "I can't tell you what to do. It has to be your decision. And yours alone. I'll support you in whatever you decide."

* * * *

She sat by the window of Sweet Cheeks Bakery, with a cup of coffee and a decadent chocolate mint cupcake sitting on her right. She glanced form the chocolate confection to her pad of paper, deciding if she should write down what was on her mind regarding the festival performance or just dive into the cupcake and wallow in its mouth-watering goodness. She really should get her work done and, as a reward, she would have the cupcake. She had been thinking about the sequence for her solo dancers, which was one of the reasons she was sitting in the bakery at this moment. She needed to talk to Chloe and get her opinion.

"Sorry about that, Bree," Chloe said, as she strode to the table carrying her own cup of coffee. "I had to take out the last batch of cupcakes."

"No problem. I wouldn't want you to burn your cupcakes on account of me," she said. "I'm sorry if I'm pulling you away from something important. We can do this another time."

Chloe shook her head, her blonde hair cascading over her shoulders. "No. I need a break and besides, we haven't really seen each other, except briefly during dance classes." She took a sip of her coffee. "I've missed you."

"I know. I've missed you, too. I've missed everybody. I didn't realize how much until I came back."

"Well, you know what they say, absence makes the heart grow fonder."

"There is some truth in that, for some people," she answered, thinking about her brother and wondering if he had missed the town as much as she had. She hadn't seen much of him since he had come home.

"You talking about your brother, or my ex," Chloe asked.

"Both. I didn't want to say it, but I know how hard it is for you to be reminded of Tyler." She lifted her cup and took a sip of the warm, rich coffee.

"It used to, but it doesn't bother me much now." Chloe swept back her hair. "It's been five years. Time to move on."

Sadness lingered in her friend's eyes. Chloe still loved Tyler despite the fact he walked out on her when she was pregnant with Sophie. "And yet, here you are, still single and raising your daughter on your own."

Chloe nodded. "She's the best thing that ever happened to me. Other than Tyler." She waved her hand in the air. "Enough of that. So, what brings you here to my little sugar shack?"

She smiled at her friend. Chloe always had a way of dismissing what was truly bothering her and moving on to another subject. "I've been watching the girls closely the last few classes and there are a few with a lot of potential. I'm thinking of giving them a solo part."

"That's a great idea. Who are the lucky girls?"

"Sophie, for one."

"Really?" Chloe's eyes lit up.

"I was hoping you'd approve if I offered her a solo part."

"Are you kidding me?" Chloe beamed. "Sophie will be ecstatic! She'll be dancing from now until the end of the recital."

"I'm also offering solos to two other students. I think they'll do well and they're perfect for the story I want to tell."

"Who are the other girls?"

"I'm going to keep that to myself until I talk to the parents. I hope you understand. I'm not telling you because I think you'll spoil the surprise, it's just that I want to tell the parents first."

"Not a problem. I totally get it." Chloe took a sip of her coffee.

"Good. I didn't want you to think I'd do anything to hurt your feelings." She felt like she was.

"I understand. It'll be exciting once the girls know who has solos. Will they be practicing separate from the other dancers?"

"Once I share the news with everyone, I'll use a portion of the class for them to practice with the other students watching. It's how everyone learns, by watching the other dancers."

Chloe nodded. "Makes sense."

She bit into her chocolate cupcakes and moaned. "Wow!"

"Good, huh?" Chloe said.

She swallowed. "I have to tell you, these cupcakes are to die for!"

Chloe smiled broadly. "It's a new recipe. I don't know what to call it though."

"Well, if I think of anything, I'll let you know."

"Not to change the subject, but I'm curious. How are things with you and Lucas?" Chloe asked, lifting the mug to her mouth.

"We're doing okay."

"Just okay?"

She shrugged. "Well, we had a talk yesterday, after not speaking for a couple of days—"

"Ah, so that was the tension I felt the first night of class. I can't imagine the two of you having an argument so soon into your relationship. You guys seem so happy."

"You knew what was going on?"

"I didn't know what was going on, but I knew something was off when I saw Lucas storm off after dropping Dani off to class. And, there was a peculiar look on your face."

"Do you think anyone else noticed?"

"Probably not. But, if they did, they probably chalked it up to anxiety."

"I hope so. Gossip spreads like wildfire in these small towns."

"Do you want to talk about it?" Chloe asked.

She shrugged. She didn't want to rehash the incident, but she did want to get it off her chest. "I needed to tell Lucas something important and instead of listening, he walked out on me." She moved a finger around the rim of her mug. "I still don't think everything is worked out."

"What did you need to tell him?" Chloe encouraged.

"I have an audition in Philadelphia in a couple of weeks and, if they offer me the job. . ."

Chloe nodded in understanding. "You'll be leaving. . .again." Her friend's gaze held sadness.

She sighed and thrust a hand through her hair, pulling it back over her shoulder. "And Lucas doesn't want me too, of course. I've grown close to Dani and I. . .care about Lucas and I don't want to see it all end, but. . ."

"But, you feel the need to go in search of your dream."

"I. . .I don't know what I want, Chloe." She peered down at her coffee. She was so torn between two loves in her life.

Chloe reached over and held her hand. "I think you do. You just won't admit it to yourself or anyone else. Why did you hesitate when telling me how you feel about Lucas?"

"What do you mean?" she asked. "I do. . . care for Lucas."

"You hesitated just before you said the word, care. I think you were going to say something else, and you don't want to say it."

"I can't admit to something if I don't know what it is, Chloe. I'm torn in two." She heaved a sigh and leaned back in the chair.

"I know. I wouldn't want to make the decision you have to make. But, I think you'll make the right decision when the time comes."

"I hope so." At this point, all she wanted to do was toss a coin and see how it landed. Heads she'd stay. Tails she'd leave.

"What else has been happening as far as planning the recital? Chloe asked, bringing her hand back to clasp her mug.

"Well, I'm hoping the guys, including my dad and Lucas's father have started working on the props and scenery. I had asked Lucas, last week, if he wouldn't mind helping and he said he'd love to." She took another bite of the cupcake and rolled her eyes. "Devon and the crew will probably help out, too, and help make the float."

"That's great news! One less thing for you to worry about."

"I have to make some sketches for him." She giggled. "You won't believe who gave me the idea for the theme."

"Lucas?"

"No. Dani!" After swallowing the last bite of cupcake, she continued. "Dani suggested doing a fairy theme and I thought it was a wonderful idea. Lucas and the guys will be making overgrown flowers and mushrooms. Those will be on the float and then, at the festival, the guys will take them off and put them on the stage."

"Sounds like a plan," Chloe stated. "I'm so happy, Bree, you're excited about this. The girls are so happy you're teaching, and the moms, too."

The feeling of belonging swept over her. Did she really

want to leave now when everything was working out so well for her here in Misty River?

"You only have a few weeks left before the performance," Chloe reminded her.

"I know, but I'm not worried. Anna's working on ordering costumes. The guys are making the scenery. Aunt Merry's helping Anna and I'm hoping the girls will have fun."

"Of course they will!" Chloe said. She glanced at her watch. "Well, I hate to end this, but I do have to get another batch in the oven." She stood and grabbed their mugs.

"Thanks for the cupcake and coffee." She leaned over and hugged her friend. "My turn to treat next time." She picked up her pad of paper and tucked it in her purse. She headed for the door then turned. "To die for."

"What?" Chloe's brow furrowed.

"Your cupcakes. Name them 'To die for."

Twenty-Two

Lucas stood back and looked at the pieces of painted scenery leaning against the fence of Mr. Thompson's yard. He was surrounded by six guys, including his dad and Bree's father. All of them looked from the wooden pieces to him.

"I think I'll get a better idea if I set them up by how they'll look on stage." He walked to one of the painted mushrooms. "Dad, why don't you move the giant mushroom closer to me by about eight feet." His father nodded and trotted off to the red painted mushroom and moved it until he shouted stop. "Devon, I'll have you and Bill move the stand of trees a few feet behind Dad and more to his right."

The guys moved forward, pulling the wooden stand of trees to where his father stood. He gave the guys the thumbs up. So far, he had two ten-foot-long pieces of wood painted to look like an enchanted forest with a castle high on a hill in the background. That would obviously stay in the back. To his right, he had his father with a large red mushroom with white polka-dots standing about five feet from the forest. Devon, Joe and Henry Thompson had moved a stand of trees to his father's right.

He turned to Brett and Blake. "You guys can move that tree," he pointed to a lone pine tree, "and the yellow mushroom next to my Dad." Once the pieces were in place, the crew moved back to stand next to him. "Looks great." So far, the scenery melded together nicely. All they needed were a few more flowers and mushrooms and they'd be done. Unless Bree had other ideas.

"Oh, my goodness! How beautiful!" he heard Bree say as she strode into the yard with his mother in tow and Dani following behind them. She had a hand over her mouth. She glanced from him to the scenery. "Wow. I can't believe this!"

"It's so pretty, Daddy!" Dani squealed, running in front of him and dancing around. "Can I keep them after the recital? I can play with them in the yard."

He looked from Dani to Bree and shrugged. "Well, I'm not sure about that, Dani. Let's see what Bree has mind."

"I'm not sure yet, Dani," Bree answered, her gaze still locked on the enchanted forest before her. "You guys did an amazing job." Bree moved to stand beside him. She wrapped an arm around his waist, and he smiled.

"Don't worry. We have a few more pieces and then we'll be done. We'll work on those tomorrow."

"I really appreciate the time you guys are putting into this. It's better than I imagined, and I'm so thankful." Bree let go of his waist and clasped her hands in front of her chest.

"Your father was gracious enough to let us create the scenery here." He nodded to Mr. Thompson.

"Thanks, Dad," Bree said.

"It was the best place," Henry answered. "I have the wood, the tools, and the barn for storage."

"And we brought the paint, the beer and the muscle," Brett piped in.

Bree laughed. He grinned in response. "We have a few other surprises up our sleeves, but we'll save that for the day of the performance."

Bree's forehead creased.

"No need to worry. You'll love it."

"I can't wait to see what you have planned." Bree turned to face him. "The dress rehearsal is the night before--Oh! What about the float?"

Her father gave Bree a lop-sided smile. "No worries. I have the float in the barn, ready to be spruced up with the scenery and props." He tapped Bree's shoulder. "Don't you worry. It'll look beautiful when it's done."

"Thanks, Dad. You're the best." Bree hugged her father and grinned. Lucas loved seeing her so happy. She turned to face him. "Lucas, I have an idea."

"Sure, what is it?"

"Can the guys show up the day of the festival to unload the scenery pieces from the float to the stage? I know it's a lot of work, but my whole dance is based on the scenery."

He almost laughed when he caught Bree's mouth dip in a pout and her eyes drooped low. She was trying the old puppy-dog look to get him to agree. And it worked. "Sure, no problem. I think everybody in town will there. I'll get help, one way or another." He slipped an arm across Bree's shoulders. "You worry about teaching the kids how to dance and we'll do the rest."

"Sounds good," Bree said, nodding. "I can't wait to see it all set up in the park. The kids are going to love it!"

The guys started to move the backdrop pieces when Bree halted them. "Wait. I have to get some pictures." They groaned but moved back to their places like dutiful students. "It'll only take a minute, guys."

"Bree, you know I hate to have my picture taken," Henry said, as he stood next to Brett.

"Dad, you look fine." Bree pulled out her cell. "Lucas, you need to get in there, too."

He hurried to the group and flung an arm over his father's shoulder and grinned. Bree clicked several pictures then held her hand up. She glanced down at her cell. He chuckled and shook his head.

"Okay. All set. Thanks." Bree tucked her phone in her back pocket.

With a collective sigh, the guys moved apart. Dani ran over to the wooden pieces and danced around them. Bree lifted her cell phone again and snapped a few pictures before Dani noticed.

"Dani, come over here," he called out to his daughter. "We have to put them away."

"Aww," Dani said, slumping her shoulders.

Like a well-oiled machine, the guys lifted the biggest pieces and headed for the barn. Bree's aunt came out and grinned at his mother. The two women hugged.

"Supper's ready," Merry Thompson said. "Lucas, I expect you and your family to stay." Miss Thompson glanced at his mother. "You've fed Bree enough times, now it's our turn."

Lucas looked at his mother who nodded. "Alright, then."

"I'll see you in a minute," he said to Bree. "I should help put the scenery away."

Bree nodded and smiled at him. He caressed her hand and moved away, smiling back at her as though it would be for the last time.

"Lucas, wait," Bree called out.

He stopped.

"What did you tell your Mom when I didn't show up last week?"

He watched the guys drag the mushrooms into the barn. "I told her you were busy with getting your classes ready."

"Good." Bree released a sigh.

"I didn't want her to worry needlessly," he said, then jogged over to the guys.

They covered the scenery with the tarps once they had the wooden pieces leaning against a wall in the barn. The guys said their goodbyes, while his father and Henry waved and thanked them.

"Head to the house with Grampa, Dani. We'll be along in a minute."

"Can't I stay?" Dani asked, but his father put a hand to her shoulder. "C'mon, Dani. They'll be in shortly."

"Actually, Dani should stay."

"Alright then," his father said, then walked out of the barn behind Henry.

He frowned. Dani skipped over to stand next to Bree. She looked up at Bree with adoring eyes. Please don't break her heart, Bree.

"Before we eat, I want to ask you something. It's about the dance and Dani," Bree said, looking down at his daughter.

His stomach clenched. She was going to tell him Dani wasn't a good fit for the class. He curled his fingers into his palms and waited for the inevitable. "What is it?"

"It's not what you think, Lucas." Bree placed her hand on Dani's shoulder. "Dani has made significant strides, just like I thought she would, but. . ." She stopped.

Here it comes. Dani will be devastated.

"I'm not sure what you'll think."

"Just say it, Bree."

"I want to offer her a solo in the recital."

"Yay!" Dani danced in a circle then stopped. "What's a solo?"

"She's that good?" he asked. He couldn't believe it. He figured Bree would give her a chance then stick her in the back where no one could see her with her limp arm and staggering steps. "Are you sure it's the right thing?" He still didn't want to put his daughter in front of everyone only to make her look like a fool.

"Lucas, I'm surprised you don't trust me in this. I'm. . .almost hurt," Bree scolded him. "Dani's been practicing and doing really well. She deserves to have a solo. And she won't be laughed at."

"What's a solo?" Dani piped in again.

"Oh." Bree glanced down at her and smoothed her hand on top of Dani's head. "A solo is when a person gets to do a dance by themselves in front of the audience," Bree explained. "Would you like that?"

Dani's face lit up and she grinned. "I'm gonna do a dance alone?"

Bree nodded. "Would you like that?"

Dani looked up at her father. "Can I, Daddy? Please?"

He couldn't break his daughter's heart. If Bree honestly thought Dani could this, he had to trust her. She knew more about dance and ballet than he ever would. He had to let Bree do what she thought best for Dani, especially if they were going to be a family. . .someday.

"If Bree thinks you can do it, then I think you should."

"Yay!" Dani spun around and laughed. He chuckled and scooped her up. He nuzzled her nose which made her giggle.

"I'm happy to see you're excited about the part, Dani," Bree said, then laughed along with her. "You'll have to practice extra hard, okay?"

Dani nodded vigorously. "Okay. I promise I'll work really hard."

"I'm sure you will," Bree answered. "Well, now that that's settled, we should go inside. We don't want them to think we're up to no good."

He chuckled. "Not with Dani here as our chaperone."

Bree laughed and then reached for Dani's hand. They took a few steps when he stopped her with his hand on her forearm. "Don't mention the audition quite yet to my parents."

"Okay." She reached over and touched his hand in reassurance. "At some point, though, they need to know."

* * * *

Bree sat back in her desk chair and smiled. She was so glad Lucas and his family decided to stay for supper. She had missed them and was glad her aunt invited them to stay. Although she missed Theresa's wonderful lasagna, Aunt Merry had made a fantastic meatloaf. When Lucas remarked how delicious it was and how similar it was, if not better than the meatloaf at the diner, Aunt Merry smiled and winked at her as though she was keeping some sort of secret. She would definitely have to ask Aunt Merry what that was all about. Her gaze landed on the small calendar sitting on the corner of the desk. The recital date was circled in red, and it fell on the same weekend as her audition. Two more weeks. Her happiness disappeared when she realized she had to make an important decision. She couldn't miss the audition and she didn't want to miss the recital. The kids were depending on her to be there. Maybe she could change the recital to the following weekend. No, the purpose was to perform at the Founders Day Festival. She swiped her hair back. Somehow, she'd have to work it out.

For now, she had to focus on her classes and the solos for Sophie, Heather, Dani and Angela. She wanted to make sure she gave the girls the time they needed to practice their routines. Each one had a specific dance to perform. The solos were short—about a minute, maybe less. She could have the girls come a half-hour early or stay a half-hour later. She'd have to ask Chloe, Anna and Lucas and Jenn, Angela's mother.

She smiled broadly when Lucas walked in with Dani in tow. He grinned and kissed her.

"Dani's so excited to show you how she's doing with her solo. She's been doing great practicing at home. I try to help, but I'm useless when it comes to ballet."

She had an image of Lucas doing a pirouette and a plie' and she nearly laughed out loud. Instead, she smiled. "Speaking of practice—"

"Oh?"

"I was wondering if you could keep Dani here a half hour later, so I can help her with her routine. Or I can help her back at your place. Whatever works for you."

"We don't mind staying, right Dani?"

"Right! I wanna learn all my steps."

"Okay, then. It's settled." She hunkered down and hugged Dani. "Sophia, Heather and Angela will be staying, too."

As each student came in with their parents, she asked them to wait in the bigger studio. Once all the students were settled in the room, she had them sit before doing their stretches. The parents stood along the walls of the room.

"As most of you know, we're getting closer to our recital—" An applause echoed in the room. "And all of us need to really put our best foot forward, no pun intended," she added when some of the parents laughed. "A lot of you will be nervous, and that's okay. It's normal. But, the more we practice, the less nervous we'll be because we'll know our routines by heart, right?"

The children nodded and agreed with her. "I have four students who have solos. Two of them I can work with at any time, for obvious reasons." She smiled at Heather and Dani. "But I need to ask the other two parents," she moved her gaze to Chloe and to Jenn. "Are you willing to come in a half-hour earlier or stay a half-hour later?"

They talked for a minute amongst themselves and, it was decided they would stay the half-hour later, so they could get through supper during the week and have more time to get the kids ready on Saturday mornings. Bree knew she wouldn't have any trouble getting the girls to know their dance routine, because they were motivated and dedicated.

"Okay, class, let's begin. Everyone stand in a line." The girls stood and took their places. "Let's show your parents how well we've been doing in class. Ready?" The little girls' heads bobbed in unison. "Let's start in first position." She watched as the girls placed their heels together and put their arms out with hands at their hips or a close equivalent to the position. She smiled, remembering when she had to learn the steps. It could be awkward, especially for the very young. "And let's bend. Does anyone know what this is called?"

Heather raised her hand. "A dem-ee-play."

She chuckled. "Close. It's pronounced dem-ee-plee-ay." She turned and walked over to where she kept her iPod and turned on the music. "Let's keep going."

The girls followed her lead as the parents watched with grins and smiles. Then she decided it was best if the parents went to the waiting room so they could have more room to practice their parts for the recital. She tried to imagine the set-up of the scenery to know where to place the children. She went through the simple steps over and over with the music she would use for the actual recital. There were a few mistakes and a few falls and some squabbling about who was doing it right and who was doing it wrong, but overall, she had a good feeling the recital would go off without a hitch. Once the class was over, the girls curtsied to her, then ran out to meet their parents. Dani and Heather stayed behind to continue working on their solos.

"Should I still wait out there?" Lucas asked, pointing to the reception area over his shoulder.

"If you don't mind. I want the parents to be surprised when they see the kids do their solos for the first time at the recital."

"You're not going to have them practice at home?"

"They can, but I don't think you'll know whether they're practicing their solo or practicing what they learned as a group. Dani told me she's going to keep it a secret, right?" She peered down at the little girl, who looked back up at her with big brown eyes.

"I want Daddy to be surprised."

Lucas smiled down at Dani and ruffled her hair. "Alright then. I can't wait to see you in your costume and dancing on stage." He looked at her and smiled with love shining in his gaze. He smoothed the side of her face. "You were right."

"I was?"

"Dani's in her element, Bree, and you've done everything right to make sure she can do this without feeling like she's. . .different."

She clasped his hand. "She's going to do great, Lucas. No one even notices she can only use one arm. And if they do, they don't care. There's been no mention of her disability from the kids, or the parents."

Lucas gave an audible sigh and released his hand from her grasp. "So, what are your plans for tonight?"

"Well, I was planning on meeting this handsome guy," she teased, grinning at Lucas.

"Oh?" Lucas asked, reaching out and tugging her against him. "And where are you meeting him?" His breath caressed her face.

"Hmmm. I'm not sure yet. He hasn't told me." She tilted her head closer. Their lips were barely touching. "But it doesn't matter. As long as I get to spend time with him."

Lucas swept his hands into her hair and nudged her close so their lips met. She kissed him like she never had before, showing him how much she had missed him, how much she had longed for his kisses and being close to him. After a moment, they broke apart, breathing hard. Lucas caressed the sides of her face, his gaze deep and dark. His pupils had dilated, making his eyes look almost black and his heartbeat frantically against her chest. Her breathing matched his and she wondered if her gaze was as warm and dark and filled with longing. She wanted him to know how much she loved him. She inhaled sharply.

"What?" He stepped back, looking surprised.

"Nothing." She smiled but wouldn't share what she realized at this moment. What she had finally admitted to herself. She would wait and tell him tonight. "So, where should we go?"

"Can I go too, Daddy?"

She had been so engrossed in Lucas, she had forgotten Dani was standing there. She flicked her gaze to Lucas, wondering what he'd say.

"Well, Dani, I know I said you could go with us the next time Bree and I went out, but," Lucas caressed her face again. "I think Bree and I need to be alone, to talk."

"Please, Daddy. I wanna have fun with you and Bree." Dani lowered her gaze to the floor, her lips formed in a pout.

"I know I said I would, but—"

She had an idea and hoped Lucas would go along with it. "What if you stay at the house with Heather tonight?" She squeezed Lucas's hand, hoping he'd agree.

"Can I, Daddy? Can I?"

Lucas grinned, squeezing her hand back. "Sure, pumpkin. Why not?"

"Yay!" Dani jumped up and down. "I get to sleep over

Bree's!"

"Are you sure it'll be okay with your father and your aunt?"

She waved a hand at him. "Not a problem. Aunt Merry will love it. Dad will be overjoyed at having his granddaughter and her friend playing together."

"Okay, then." He kissed her again. "I'll pick you up at six."

Reluctantly, she let go of his hand and waved good-bye as they headed out the door. Her heart fluttered. These two had become so important to her. How could she leave them? Somehow, she had to find a way to continue her dream and be a part of their lives.

Twenty-Three

Just before six o'clock, Lucas pulled into the driveway of the Thompson's farmhouse. He had to admit he was a little nervous letting Dani spend the night. She had never spent the night away from him and his parents before. When he had told his parents, they were as excited as Dani. He had been hesitant, but after talking to his mother and getting some sound advice, he decided Dani deserved to experience a sleepover. Anna would be there with Heather along with Bree's father and Aunt Merry. And, of course, Bree would be there once he brought her home later.

He twisted around in his seat to look back at Dani. "You ready?"

Dani bobbed her head. "Yup."

"Okay then. Let's head into the house for your first ever sleepover!" He beamed at her as he opened the door while she unbuckled her seat belt. Anxiety creeped over him, but he tried to look happy and excited for Dani's sake. He lifted her small suitcase from the floor and helped Dani out of her seat and onto the ground.

"C'mon, Daddy!" Dani said, as she hurried up the path. "I wanna see Heather."

He watched her and realized Dani was getting older and he had to eventually loosen the proverbial apron strings. Bree had been encouraging him to let Dani experience what other girls her age were doing and his mother agreed. Besides, his mother and father deserved a night off. The door of the farmhouse opened, and Bree stepped out and hurried to Dani. She lifted his daughter up in her arms and hugged her then kissed her on the cheek. He grinned and the anxiety he had felt a moment ago ebbed away. Why couldn't Bree see what he saw? That they were meant to be a family.

He met Bree partway down the gravel path. Her sweet scent mingled in the air, swirling around him. She kissed him lightly and he smiled. "Dani's been so excited. I couldn't seem to drive here fast enough." He chuckled.

Bree set Dani down and held her hand. "Well, Heather and the rest of the family is excited to see Dani."

"They are?" Dani's eyes widened and she grinned.

"Yes, they are." She tousled Dani's hair. "Come on in. Heather's picking out a movie for the two of you." She opened the screen door and stepped into the hallway.

He followed behind. His mouth watered as the scent of fresh-baked bread floated toward him. "Smells good in here."

"Thanks. Aunt Merry has home-made bread in the oven."

"Maybe I'll stay here instead."

Bree nudged his arm. "Don't worry. I'll save you some."

Buster barked and came running down the hall, barreling toward Dani. He sucked in a breath and instinctively reached out to grab Dani, but the dog came to a halt a few feet away and sat on his haunches, his tail wagging furiously against the polished floor. He expelled the breath. Dani rushed over to Buster and bent over to hug him around his big, furry neck.

"Guess what, Buster?"

The dog barked.

"I'm gonna sleep over and you can sleep with me."

He spun his gaze to Bree who was grinning down at Dani and Buster. Would she actually allow that?

"As much as Buster would like that, Dani, I think it'd be best if Buster sleeps in my Dad's room tonight."

"Awww."

Relief washed over him. He wouldn't have to worry about the dog crushing his little girl in her sleep or knocking her off the bed in his attempt to take it over. "Bree's right, Dani. Buster's. . .big and probably wouldn't leave any room in the bed for you." He looked at Bree for a sign he was on the right track.

She nodded. "Daddy's right, Dani. When Buster used to sleep in my bed, I used to have to sleep on the couch. He takes up a lot of room."

Good save. He reached out and wrapped an arm around Bree's waist. She leaned into him and rested her head on his shoulder. For a moment, they watched as Dani talked to Buster and told him about her day. He heard the squeak of the back screen door open and then Heather's laughter.

"We're in the hall, Heather," Bree called out and then stepped away from him. Heather rushed to Bree and hugged her around her thighs. Anna followed behind with Aunt Merry and her father in tow as well. The narrow hall was crowded.

"Let's head into the living room," Aunt Merry suggested as she walked through the entry and into the spacious room.

Voices erupted all at once and he had a hard time figuring out who was saying what and to whom. Was it like this all the time? His house was never this. . .loud.

"Lucas?"

"Yeah?" He looked around and realized Mr. Thompson was trying to get his attention.

"Sorry about the cacophony in here. The girls get together and it's like a bunch of magpies invaded the room."

He laughed and walked over to where Bree's father was settling into his chair. Bree sidled next to him.

"Have a seat," Mr. Thompson said.

"No, we can't, Dad. We're heading to the tavern for supper and as it is, we'll probably have to wait."

"Alright, then."

Lucas realized he still held Dani's suitcase. He looked behind him to see Dani sitting on the bright rag rug next to Heather as they perused the stack of Disney movies. He strode over to where she sat and hunkered down next to her. "Here's your suitcase, Pumpkin."

"Thanks, Daddy," she answered, but never looked up at him. Well, she wasn't going to be homesick. And the thought saddened him.

"She'll be okay, Lucas. I promise," Bree said as she settled a hand on his shoulder. "Anna and Aunt Merry will keep the girls so busy, they won't know we're gone."

He stood and smiled at her. "I believe you."

"We found a movie, Bree," Dani said, lifting the case up for her to see. "Are you gonna stay and watch it with us?"

Bree looked down at his daughter. "Not this time. Your Daddy and I are going out."

Anna came into the room with a tray of beverages and a bowl of popcorn. "I've got refreshments. Who's hungry?"

"I am!" both girls said in unison, then they giggled as little girls do when they're excited.

"You sure you want to go out?" he said to Bree in a low voice. "I mean, there are Disney movies, popcorn and home-made bread."

Bree's gaze sparkled with laughter. "No. We're going out to spend some time together. But, we can spend a night doing exactly this another time."

"Promise?" he winked at her.

She responded by kissing him on the nose. "Promise." She grinned and his heart tumbled. Just one look could turn him inside out.

"Okay, you two. The girls will be fine. Don't you worry," Aunt Merry said as she brushed her hands toward them, urging them to head out.

"Bye, Daddy!" Dani said as she bounded toward him. He scooped her up and kissed her soundly on her cheek.

"Be good, okay? I love you."

"You be good too, Daddy. I love you." She patted his cheeks and kissed him. He would never tire of his little girl giving him her special kisses as Dani called them.

Bree chuckled next to him. She leaned in and kissed Dani on the cheek and to his surprise, Dani patted Bree's cheeks and kissed her back. His heart swelled.

"We better get going," Bree said.

He set his daughter down and brushed the top of her curly head. He breathed a sigh of relief. Dani was going to be okay. Bree's family would make sure of it. Then he realized Bree's family had already embraced him and Dani into their fold as members of their family. Why couldn't Bree see this?

Bree reached for his hand as he turned back to face Anna. "Dani knows to brush her teeth before bed. Oh, and she may need help with getting dressed, although she does pretty good. Let her do as much as she can. She'll let you know when she needs help."

Anna laughed. "Lucas. I do have a daughter of my own. I think I know what to do." She grinned at Dani. "We'll be fine. Now go out and have fun."

He felt like an idiot or worse, like an over-protective father.

"It's okay, Lucas. I promise. Aunt Merry and Anna will take care of her as their own." She squeezed his hand. "And, it's not a bad thing to be over-protective of your daughter. My dad was." She glanced over at her father. "Right, Dad?"

"Still am, " he responded with a laugh.

As they walked out the door and down the steps toward the truck, he decided he wasn't going to worry about Dani. He'd focus all his attention on Bree, the woman he loved.

* * * *

Bree was stunned to see Brett walking toward their table. She wondered if he'd cause trouble for Lucas even though she had begged her brother to stay out of it. He had been scarce the last few days, so as far as she knew, Brett didn't know that she and Lucas were okay. Brett came to a stop next to her chair and tilted his head toward Lucas.

"Hey, Bree. How's everything? You okay?" Brett turned his gaze to Lucas. "Any trouble here?"

She rolled her eyes. "Subtle, Brett. Real subtle. Yes, I'm fine."

Lucas tipped his beer bottle. “Nice to see you again, Brett.”

“You treating Bree right?"

She cringed and if she wasn't in a public place, she'd be telling Brett off. Instead, she stood and faced him. "Brett. I appreciate you wanting to make sure I'm alright, but don't make a scene. I'm fine. Lucas and I are fine." Her nerves were on fire, and she hoped she sounded calm. She rarely, if ever, confronted her brother. She usually agreed with him. They had always been close. But, this time, Brett looked as if he wanted to start a fight. "Maybe you should go home. I think you've reached your limit." She gave him her 'hairy eye-ball' and he had the grace to look away from her.

"Sorry, man." Brett nodded toward Lucas. "Just taking care of my sister."

"I get it. Really. But you don't need to worry about Bree." Lucas glanced at her, smiling. "I won't make the same mistake twice."

Brett seemed to stare down Lucas and she wondered if her brother would create a scene. Instead, Brett offered his hand. "Better not. She's too good for you, you know."

Lucas stood, grinned and shook Brett's hand. "She is. You've reminded me of that many times in high school."

They shook hands, then both leaned in and gave each other a man-hug. Sighing, she sat down. As Brett started to walk away, he clapped Lucas on the shoulder. All was good.

"Hey, want to sit with us?" she called out, then realized she should've asked Lucas first.

Brett shook his head. “I have a table already, but thanks.” He nodded to Lucas. “Catch you guys later.”

"Well, that went better than I expected," she said, leaning her elbows on the table. "I think I need another drink." She flagged down the waitress and ordered her beer. She gazed at Lucas who looked at her as though he wanted to eat her right up. He wore a lazy grin and spirals of warmth curled low. She wanted to get close to Lucas. Real close, which meant getting him on the dance floor. The band started up a romantic ballad. Perfect timing.

"Let's dance," Lucas said, reaching for her hand. She smiled. He had read her mind. She clasped his hand in hers as they walked side by side to the dance floor. Once they found a space, they turned into each other's arms. "You look beautiful tonight, Bree."

A blush crept to her cheeks. "Thanks. You tell me that every time."

"Okay, then I won't say it anymore."

She slapped him playfully on his arm. "Don't you dare. I love your compliments. It's just that I could look like a hot mess—all sweaty with tousled hair after dancing and you'd still think I was beautiful."

"Well, you are. I can't help it. You're always beautiful in my eyes."

She reached up and pulled his face down to hers then kissed him. She was only going to give him a short, sweet kiss, but she held him close as he answered her kiss with a more passionate one of his own.

"Hey!" someone said, brushing against them.

Lucas snapped back and tossed a gaze to his right. It was Brett, holding onto Jamie who smiled broadly.

"If you're going to kiss my sister, do it where I don't have to look."

"You're just jealous because Jamie hasn't kissed you," Lucas said then chuckled.

Brett shrugged, then pulled Jamie closer.

"And how would you know?" Jamie answered, winking at her. She figured her brother had kissed Jamie many times since he'd been home, but when Jamie was ready, she'd tell her.

Lucas pulled her tight against him and kissed her, hard and passionate. She tilted off balance. It was a good thing he had a firm hold on her or she may have fallen to the floor. She clenched his upper arms. "Goodness. Your kiss nearly knocked me down."

Brett and Jamie were lost in the crowd, twirling to the ballad as Lucas held her close. She swayed with him, her head nestled on his shoulder. This was so right. He was so right for her. She was happy. Happier than she'd ever been. So why was she choosing to throw it all away? The music ended and she lifted her head, smiling at Lucas. They walked back to their table and sat down. She took a swig of her beer while Lucas did the same.

"So, do you think Brett's getting serious about Jamie?" Lucas asked.

"Looks like it," she answered. "Jamie has loved him from afar since grammar school."

"Did he ever tell you why he came back all of a sudden?"

She shook her head. "He's really vague about it. Anna and I have tried to get it out of him, but he's keeping it to himself."

Lucas glanced around. The music grew louder, and the crowd became rowdier.

"How much longer do you want to stay?" she asked. It had been a couple of hours since they had eaten, and they had had a few beers. "I know we were planning on taking a walk, if you still want to."

"Of course I do!" He reached for her hand and clasped it in his own. "We can leave whenever you're ready."

"Hey, you two," Jamie said as she strode over to them, her blonde hair shining bright under the lights. "We're starting a game of 8-Ball. Wanna play?"

She shook her head. As much as she enjoyed hanging out with Jamie, she wanted to spend time with Lucas, now more than ever. She had something she needed to tell him, and she needed to say it tonight while she still felt brave enough to do so. "Sorry, Jamie. We're heading out. I've got Dani at the house and Lucas wants to head back."

"Sure. No problem." Jamie waved, then turned, heading back to Brett.

As she stood, Brett waved to her, and she waved back. Lucas gave a quick wave himself then they walked out of the tavern.

"Sorry I threw you under the bus, but if I had said we were going for a walk, she would've invited herself along." She swept her hair back. "I love Jamie and have fun with her, but, tonight, I want to be with you." She leaned in and kissed him on his bearded cheek.

"Well, I'm glad you used me as an excuse." He blew out a breath. "I'll be honest. For a moment, I thought you would ask them to come along."

"Really?"

"I don't mean it in a bad way." He shrugged. "You're generous and kind and love being around people, so I thought you'd tell Jamie it was okay for her and Brett to join us."

"I knew you didn't want them tagging along. Heck, I don't want them tagging along either. I love Jamie and I love Brett, but I. . " she almost blurted it out.

"What were you going to say, Bree?" Lucas turned her around to face him.

They were on the walkway that wound along the river away from the tavern. The antique lights cast dim shadows around them. Stars lit the sky. Warm air caressed her face as though willing her to tell Lucas what was in her heart. The roll of the river lapped against the rocks. It was so peaceful, tranquil and a perfect setting for what she had to say.

"Bree?"

She wrapped her arms around his waist and looked up at his handsome face. His dark brown eyes glimmered, then crinkled in a smile. She leaned into him, resting her head against the soft fabric of his shirt. He smelled of clean cotton and spicy aftershave. His heart beat fast beneath her cheek. She smiled. She wanted to stay right here, her body against his, feeling his warmth permeate her. She hugged him closer, and he wrapped his arms around her, pulling her tighter against him. He rested his chin on her head. This was the feeling of contentment. This was how it felt to be needed. To be cherished and. . .to be loved.

"I almost made other plans for tonight," Lucas said, his chin bobbing on the top of her head.

"You did?" Her voice was muffled against his chest. She knew he nodded although she couldn't see it. "And what were your plans?"

"Well, I was going to pack a basket of gourmet food along with some wine. I'd bring you to a secluded area of the park." Lucas pulled back, bringing up a hand to cup her chin. He tilted her face up to look at him. He smiled.

"And then," she whispered.

"And then I was going to seduce you." He clasped his hands along both sides of her face and brought her closer. His lips grazed hers.

She sucked in a breath. Shivers of desire skittered low. She caught her breath as Lucas smoothed his thumbs along the sides of her face then traced her brows and her cheekbones. He cupped her face, his thumbs resting in the hollows of her cheeks. His breath was warm against her flushed face. And then his mouth touched her lips softly, just a whisper of a touch. He was teasing her. Seducing her. And she wanted more. When his mouth pressed more firmly, she grasped his shoulders and kissed him back with a passion she didn't know she possessed.

His mouth left hers to kiss her cheeks, her nose, her eyelids, then he drifted over to kiss the edge of her ear, down to her earlobe. She clutched his shoulders as he held her tight. She couldn't back away if she tried. And she didn't want to.

"Lucas," she breathed. She felt his lips curve into a smile as he lowered his mouth to kiss the hollow of her neck. Her sighs grew loud. Anyone walking by would know what they were doing. But she didn't care. She wanted to stay here and let him continue to seduce her. He broke away and rested his forehead on hers as they tried to catch their breath.

"God, Bree."

"That was. . .wonderful," she sighed. "Your seduction skills are. . .exceptional." Her heart hammered against her ribs.

He lifted his head. "So, you've never been seduced like this before?"

She shook her head. "Never."

"Ever?"

"Never. Ever." She kissed him again. "Not even with my ex." She slapped a hand over her mouth. "I'm so sorry, Lucas. I shouldn't have brought it up."

He hugged her close. "Don't worry about it. If we can't talk freely about our past relationships, then how we can really know each other?"

"True." She pushed a thick strand of hair from her face. "But, how much is too much?" Did she really want to know everything about his life with Daniella or any other girlfriend he'd had? She knew the green monster of jealousy would rear its ugly head.

Lucas shrugged. "I guess we'll know when it becomes too uncomfortable to talk about."

"And we'll deal with it then." She turned sideways, still holding his hand and they started walking down the trail along the river. "I don't like talking about my past with Wyatt." She heaved out a breath. "I feel like a failure when I talk about something that was a disaster, such as my relationship and my career."

"You're not a failure, Bree," Lucas said. "It wasn't your fault you were injured and then lost your job because of it." He stopped and faced her. "Personally, I think it's the company's loss to have fired you because of an injury. But, if you hadn't been injured, you wouldn't have come back, and we wouldn't be here, right now." He grinned. "I think it was fate. It was meant to be."

She tilted her head to lean on his shoulder. They started walking again. "You're good for me, Lucas."

He wrapped an arm across her shoulders. "I'm glad, because you're good for me, too, and Dani."

"Yes. Dani's good for me, too. I love being around her." Lucas was right. He and Dani were good for her. She thought she had had everything as principal dancer for the ballet company, but, as she learned, a dancer could be tossed out and replaced before the door closed behind you. With Lucas and Dani, though, she had something she didn't think she had needed. Commitment. Love.

Lucas swept her close and hugged her. "Aww, Bree, you're the best thing that happened to me." He kissed her, his lips curving into a smile as their lips touched.

She needed to tell him. Now. She twisted away and looked out over the river. The surface gleamed under the stars. "Lucas, I need to tell you something." She turned and realized what she'd done. Luca's eyes were wide, his eyebrows raised, his brow furrowed. His mouth was a tight line. He glanced away. It was as though the other night was happening all over again. Stupid move, Bree. She flung out her hand and grasped his so he wouldn't pull away. "It's not what you think, Lucas. Really." She stepped closer to him and when he didn't back away, she smiled at him. "Lucas. You are the only man I want to be with." Still, his face held hurt, but he didn't move. She brought her hands up to clasp his face and she leaned in and kissed him. As he tried to tug away, she whispered, "I love you, Lucas."

"What?" his voice was a whisper against her mouth.

She tilted her head up. "I love you Lucas." She suddenly felt a sense of belonging. The stress of whether or not she should tell him, lifted and she grinned.

"Oh, God, Bree, I've waited so long for you to tell me." Lucas kissed her, cupping the back of her head, holding her there, kissing her over and over, reminding her this was where she belonged. In his arms. In his life. "I love you, too."

Twenty-Four

The following morning, Bree awakened to the sound of laughter and giggles from two little girls. They were standing by the side of her bed, but she didn't open her eyes. She pretended to be asleep.

"Do you think she can hear us?" Dani asked in a loud whisper.

"Nah. She's sound asleep," Heather answered. "I think she snores sometimes."

She had to stifle a laugh.

"She snores? I'm gonna tell my daddy then." This coming from Dani.

"Why do you have to tell your dad?" Heather asked.

Smart girl. Why did Lucas need to know if she snored? Which she didn't.

"Because, silly, if they get married, Daddy won't be able to sleep if she snores."

Get married? Did Dani think they would get married? Huh. The better question was did Lucas think they should get married? Suddenly, she wanted to open her eyes and surprise them, but was more curious to know what else they would say.

"Shhhh. We should talk quiet so we don't wake her up."

She let out a soft snore. The girls giggled.

"See, she does snore!" Heather said, then laughed. She snored again, this time a little louder.

"Wow! She snores loud," Dani said in awe.

This time, she made a loud snoring sound then pretended to be startled awake. She snapped open her eyes and acted surprised to see the girls there. "Oh! Oh my goodness. What woke me up?"

"You were snoring, Auntie Bree!" Heather said, then giggled as she leaned into the bed. "You snore really loud."

"I do not snore," she answered defiantly.

"Yes, you do. I heard it," Dani said. "I didn't know ladies snored."

"And you, little lady," she started, reaching out and tickling Dani's side, "also snore."

Dani laughed and squirmed. "No, I don't."

"Yes, you do," She tickled Dani again until the little girl leaned over onto the bed, squealing in laughter. She lifted Dani onto the bed so she wouldn't fall onto the floor from squirming so much. Heather scrambled on the bed as well. The two girls sat cross-legged on her left and stared down at her.

"What in the world are you two girls doing?" Anna asked as she stepped into the room. She moved toward the bed and sat on the edge. "Did you come in here and wake up your aunt?"

Heather peered at her mother over her shoulder. "Uh-uh. She woke up all by herself."

It was true. She had been awake. She just didn't let on she was. She was too curious to know what the girls would do if they thought she had been sleeping.

"I'm sure she did. With a little help from the two of you." Anna reached over and hugged Heather, then she hugged Dani.

"Do you know, Momma, that Auntie Bree snores?" Heather said wide-eyed.

"She does?" Anna responded in mock shock.

"Yup. And she can snore really loud." Dani added, her eyes round. "I'm gonna have to tell my daddy."

She glanced at Anna, stifling a laugh.

"And why does your daddy need to know if Bree snores?"

"Cuz if he marries her, and she snores, he won't get any sleep and he'll be tired when he works."

She laughed out loud. She couldn't help it. Dani was too

darn cute and so darn serious.

"Did your daddy say he was going to marry Bree?"

Dani shook her head, but looked at Anna, her big brown eyes wide and her face serious. "But, I think he likes her. He told me."

"Ahhh," Anna said and winked at Bree. "That's nice he likes Bree, but it doesn't mean he's going to marry her."

"Well, I'm gonna ask Daddy to ask Bree to marry him."

She let out a laugh and had a sudden urge to use the bathroom. It had been too much, and her bladder was letting her know.

"While you girls are discussing my future, I'm going to use the bathroom." She flipped off the blanket and got out of bed. "And, let me know what I miss. I'll meet you in the kitchen."

"Are you still making waffles?" Anna asked as she moved around the foot of the bed toward the door.

"Sure am."

"I'll let you know what Heather and Dani have planned for your future, Bree, after you come out of the bathroom."

She waved back at Anna as she walked down the short expanse of hall to the bathroom. She shook her head and giggled. What in the world had Dani meant by all that? Was Dani that observant to see how she and her father interacted? Had she noticed how they felt about each other? And, more importantly, would Dani rally tell Lucas how bad she snored? Maybe she should talk to Lucas before he had a moment alone with his daughter. As she stood in front of the mirror, straightening out her unruly hair, she wondered if Dani would ask her father to marry her. Her heart thudded and a flutter rose up her spine like tiny butterflies scurrying up her back. If Lucas did ask her to marry him, would she?

When she went back to her room, Anna and the girls had already left. She grabbed her cell phone from her purse and checked to see if Lucas had sent her a text. Nothing so far. He was either enjoying the opportunity to sleep in late, although she couldn't imagine Lucas doing such a thing, or, he was allowing her time to get the girls settled in for breakfast before he called her. She sent a quick text letting him know how well Dani slept through the night and that he should be aware that Dani may tell him some things about her that were not true. She ended the text with *I do not snore!*

As she walked down the stairs, she heard the girls laughing. Her father's deep, rumbling laughter followed. For a quick second, she wondered if they were still talking about her 'snoring'. But, as she walked past the living room, she saw the girls seated in front of the television, watching a cartoon. Her father sat in his beloved chair, laughing at the foolish antics of the characters. A bowl of popcorn still sat on the coffee table along with empty juice boxes and two empty glasses of wine.

"I'll pick up the clutter in the living room, Bree. Don't worry about it," Aunt Merry called from the kitchen. "I know you don't like to see the mess when you wake up, but you don't have kids. . .yet."

"Are you starting breakfast?" She asked as she watched Anna set out the waffle mix on the counter.

"No. I didn't know how long you'd be, so I thought I'd get everything ready for you."

"Oh. Thanks."

"Did you text Lucas yet?"

She nodded and smiled. "I warned him of what he might hear from Dani when they're alone. And I reminded him that I don't snore."

Anna laughed as she left the kitchen.

She had just grabbed a large bowl when her phone rang. She glanced down to see Lucas's response.

Not sure what you mean by I don't snore. I wouldn't know, but I'd love to find out.

She grinned and texted back, Right. I'm sure. I'll tell you about it when you pick up Dani

OK. Now I'm curious. Have you had breakfast yet?

Cooking it now. Homemade waffles. Come on by if you want some.

Maybe I will. Love you!

He signed off with a heart emoji and a smiley face. That simple emoji sent her heart soaring. She clasped the phone to her heart quickly then pulled it away as Aunt Merry came back into the room, carrying the two wine glasses. Anna followed with the left-over popcorn and juice boxes in hand.

"Lucas may come over to have breakfast with us."

"Oh. Okay. That'd be nice." Aunt Merry set the wine glasses in the sink.

"Hey! How are my favorite sisters?" Brett called out.

Anna's hand slammed to her chest, the bowl of popcorn spilling to the floor. "Shoot!"

The back door opened, and Brett stepped in, grinning. Then he glanced at the mess on the floor. "Oh. Ah, did I do that?"

Anna glared at him as she walked toward him. She gave him a hug then slapped his upper arm. "Now that you made me drop the bowl, you can clean it up."

"Good morning, Brett." Aunt Merry said. "I see that you haven't changed in all these years. You always seem to show up when it's time to eat," She closed the space between them and hugged him. "You haven't been here in a couple of days. Where you been?"

"Here and there." Brett hunkered down and scooped the popcorn into the bowl.

"Ah, Jamie's," she stated, opening the box of waffle mix. Brett winked back at her. "I was just getting ready to make waffles."

"Great! My favorite."

"All food is your favorite," Anna remarked, bending down to help him pick up the scattered popcorn.

"You're right about that," Brett said then stood, holding the bowl.

She blew hair away from her face and nudged her brother. "It's a good thing I love you or I wouldn't be letting you stay for breakfast."

Brett slapped his hand over his heart. "You wound me, woman." He emptied the popcorn into the trash can. "You'd actually let me go hungry?"

Shaking her head, she watched her brother and sister banter back and forth. They could go on for hours if they wanted to. She poured batter into the waffle maker and closed the lid. "Anyone want coffee?"

"I do," they said in unison as they walked to the table.

"I'll take one," her father called from the living room.

"I'll make the coffee," Aunt Merry said as she grabbed the coffee canister and opened it.

As she went about making waffles and coffee, she smiled, enjoying having her brother and sister there. It reminded her of when they were growing up, although Brett and Anna wouldn't have been so civil as they were now. If Brett had done back then what he had done just now, scaring Anna half to death and causing her to spill popcorn everywhere, there would've been an all-out fight going on. She always felt closer to Brett than to Anna, probably because she and Brett were 'Irish twins', only eleven months apart in age, yet a grade apart in school. Anna always seemed to be the big sister who mothered them, scolded them, and made sure they got their homework done. She didn't do it to be obnoxious. It was her way of showing how much she cared.

The waffle maker dinged, and she lifted the lid. She cooked a few more while Aunt Merry made the coffee then poured the coffee into mugs. As she set the stack of waffles on a plate and brought them to the table, Aunt Merry carried the mugs. Anna settled the girls in chairs as Brett sat in her spot while reaching for a mug. Her father ambled into the room and sat in his usual seat, at the head of the table.

"Hey, son. Where've you been?"

"Jamie's," she, Anna and Aunt Merry said together.

"No. I crashed at Blake's, not that it's anyone's business," Brett said. "And who is this pretty little girl," Brett looked at Dani then to Heather.

"This is my friend, Dani, Uncle Brett. We had a slummer party last night," Heather said.

Bree giggled at the mispronunciation.

"Slumber, Heather, with a 'b' sound, but you were close," Anna corrected.

"Uncle Brett, you're sitting in Auntie Bree's chair."

Brett smiled. "Oh. I didn't know. I'll move over one more seat."

"You don't need to move," she told him as she brought over her plate and a mug of coffee.

There was a knock on the door and she grinned, winking at Dani who was sipping from her juice box. "I wonder who that could be?"

Brett glanced up from piling waffles onto his plate.

She walked to the door and opened it with a smile. Lucas grinned back. He stepped inside and kissed her softly.

"Is there room for one more?" He stepped in and Dani squealed.

"Daddy!"

"Hey, pumpkin," he strode to the table and leaned down, hugging his daughter close. "How's my girl?"

"I'm doing good, Daddy." She set her juice box down. "Are you gonna eat too?"

"Of course, your daddy's going to eat too," she answered, heading back to the counter and grabbing another plate. She knew he'd be coming along and had made extra waffles. But they were lacking a chair. "I'll be right back. Gotta get a chair." She headed to the den and lifted the chair. As she turned, she nearly collided with Lucas.

"Here, let me help," he said and reached for the chair. Their hands touched and a zing raced up her arm. Then with sudden awareness she realized what she must look like. She was still in her pajamas and her hair wasn't even combed! God, she must look awful.

"You look beautiful, Bree," he whispered, then kissed her. She probably looked like a hot mess, and he still thought she was beautiful. He winked at her. "And I mean it."

"Thank you," she murmured.

They headed back to the dining area where everyone was eating, and Dani and Heather were sharing the story of Bree snoring. She wanted to run back to her bedroom and crawl under the covers.

"What's this about Bree snoring?" Lucas asked as he set the chair down next to hers. Right now, she wanted to change the topic of conversation.

"Yeah," Heather started. "We was in Auntie Bree's room while she was sleeping, and we heard her snoring."

Lucas peered over at her as she moved to the coffeemaker. "Really. She snores?"

"Yeah, Daddy! And sometimes it's loud," Dani interjected. "You can't marry her if she snores."

Everyone ceased talking. She groaned, shutting her eyes tight. She was mortified. It wasn't Dani's fault. Children at that age didn't have any filters, and she was just telling the truth as she saw it. She inhaled and blew it out slowly, feeling Lucas's gaze on her. The heat of embarrassment flowed over her. She poured the coffee, hoping someone would start talking about anything other than her snoring.

"Ahh," Lucas started. "And why can't I marry her if she snores?"

She willed Lucas to stop asking Dani questions. He was only making it worse by egging his daughter on. Please start a new topic. Anyone. Brett? Anna? Aunt Merry? Anyone?

"Because, Daddy, if she snores, you can't sleep and then you'll be tired all time."

Lucas let out a bark of laughter, startling her. She winced. Brett and Anna, along with her father and her aunt, chuckled.

"Daddy, why are you laughing?" Dani asked, her brows furrowed, and her mouth puckered.

"You said I couldn't marry her because she snored and that I'd be tired all the time. Where in the world did you hear that?"

"In school. My friend said that her mommy and daddy can't be married anymore because she snores."

She groaned as she added creamer and sugar to her coffee. Her family laughed and giggled, at her expense as she headed to the table, her head lowered. She wanted to laugh and wondered if Dani had misunderstood. Then again, she was in kindergarten and perhaps something got mixed up in the translation.

Dani sighed. "She said that her daddy was tired of her mommy."

"Ahh," Lucas said. "Well, there's no need for you to worry about such things. Let the adults take care of them. You just worry about being a kid, okay?"

Lucas nudged her elbow. "You okay?"

She nodded. "I don't snore." Maybe she'd eat in the den. She could only imagine what their conversation would be once she and Lucas were alone.

* * * *

Lucas and Devon had finally finished the dance studio the previous night. He had asked Bree on Wednesday, when he called to say goodnight, not to show up at the studio during the week. He explained they were nearly done, and he wanted to surprise her.

This morning, he and Devon walked through all the rooms and made sure everything was as it should be. All equipment had been put away, trash picked up and removed, floors washed, carpets vacuumed, and everything wiped down to a shine. He grinned with satisfaction.

"Lucas, I can't wait to see Bree's reaction!" Aunt Merry said, walking over to him. She gave him a hug. "I am so glad I hired you. You've done an outstanding job."

"Thank you, Miss Thompson."

"Oh, Lucas. After all these years? Please start calling me Aunt Merry. You're practically part of the family now!"

Mr. Thompson grinned and shook his hand. "Great job, Lucas. Better than I expected."

"That's a compliment, Lucas," Aunt Merry said, nudging Henry's arm. "You could've said it nicer, Henry."

"And what's wrong with what I said? Didn't I say it was *better* than expected?" Mr. Thompson looked at him. "You knew what I meant, right?"

He nodded. "Yes, sir. I did. Thanks for coming."

"Wouldn't miss it," Mr. Thompson returned. "Bree will love it."

"She certainly will," Chloe said as she approached him from behind. "I was at the farm earlier. She doesn't have a clue you're going to surprise her today."

"Daddy, when's Bree gonna be here?" Dani asked.

"Soon, Pumpkin. I'm picking her up in a little bit." He glanced at his watch. "I should head out." He looked around the reception area. Everyone was here, and Jamie and Anna were setting up refreshments. It was time to show Bree her studio.

Ten minutes later he arrived at the farm. Bree's car was in the driveway. At least she had listened and hadn't shown up at the studio unannounced. He knocked on the door. No answer. He rang the doorbell. Still no answer. Where was she? He heard Buster barking and figured Bree was with him. A good thing too. At least he knew the dog would follow her commands. He didn't worry about Buster when Bree was around.

The dog bounded toward him, but Bree wasn't with him. Fear enveloped him and he couldn't move. He was frozen in place with the beast scrambling toward him. Suddenly, Buster stopped and sat. The dog bent his head down then whined. He took a tentative step toward Buster and when the dog didn't move, he took another. Buster looked up at him, his tongue lolling out of his mouth then nudged his hand. The dog wanted to be petted. He stroked the top of the Buster's head and when he knew Buster had no intention of hurting him, he hunkered down and rubbed his hands on both sides of Buster's face. He swore the dog smiled at him.

"Where's Bree, Buster?"

The dog barked, got up on all fours and ran to the back of the house. He followed and stopped dead in his tracks. Bree never failed to amaze him. Her graceful body moved over the grass in several pirouettes before she stopped and ended with her back toward him, her arms in the air.

He clapped. "Bravo! Bravo!"

Bree spun around, her hand to her chest. She was breathing heavy then she grinned and ran toward him. "Lucas!" She hugged him and gave him a quick kiss. "What are you doing here?"

"I thought I'd show you the studio."

"Really? It's all done?" She folded her hands and brought them to her smiling lips. "Oh, I can't wait to see it."

"It must've been hard for you to wait."

"It was. I'm used to showing up at the studio whenever I wanted. That's why I was dancing." Bree blew some flyaways from her face. "I was so antsy, I had to do something to keep me from driving into town."

"So, you danced in the grass."

"I did."

"I don't think I've ever seen or heard of that before."

"Oh, I've done it before. I've actually had promo shots done with me dancing in the streets of the city. . .without traffic of course."

"Of course." He grinned. "I'm impressed you can dance on other surfaces. Doesn't it hurt your feet?"

She shrugged. "Not really."

"Wow. You must have strong toes, girl." He swayed back on his heels. "So, you ready to see the studio?"

"Hmmm, let me think," Bree put a her finger to her chin.

He laughed and stroked her arm. "C'mon. I want to show you your updated and fantastic looking studio."

"Let me take a quick shower."

"Okay, but make it real quick." He hoped she wouldn't take too long.

She giggled. "I'll be down in a flash. Don't leave without me."

Ten minutes later, Bree stood at the door, locking it up. "Okay, I'm ready. Let's do this!" She walked to the stairs, and he followed.

"Geez, Bree, why don't you be a little bit more excited," he teased as they headed down the stairs. "Wait." Lucas stopped her.

"Lucas, c'mon, I want to see the studio," she said, practically whining.

"You will, but I want you to wear a blindfold." He pulled out a clean bandana from his pocket.

"Really?"

He nodded. He had to put the blindfold on her now because once they got on Main Street, she'd see the sign and he didn't want to spoil the surprise.

She huffed out a breath. "Okay. I'll do it if it gets me there faster."

He wrapped the bandana over her eyes and tied it in place. "I'll help you walk to the truck."

"I feel like an idiot, Lucas. Half the town's going to see me wearing this."

"Who cares. I want you to be surprised before you step inside."

"Okay. I'm ready." She held her hand out and he grasped it. She squeezed his hand and giggled. "I can't wait!"

He led her down the path and to the truck, then opened the door. She clamored in and he shut the door. Bree was grinning from ear to ear and it filled his heart. All this work was worth seeing her excitement. Ten minutes later, he pulled in front of the little studio instead of the side parking lot. He wanted to see her expression the moment she took off the bandana. He took out his cell.

"You ready?" he whispered in her ear.

She nodded.

"I'll help you out of the truck, but don't take off the blindfold until I say so."

"Okay." She squirmed in the seat. "Hurry up."

He chuckled and got out of the truck. After clicking on the camera icon, he opened the door. "You can get out now." He helped her down. "Step up. There's a curb here."

"Can I take off the bandana now?"

"Open your eyes." He clicked the camera button as she removed the bandana and her mouth gaped open. Her hands flew to her mouth as she gasped.

Twenty-Five

She couldn't believe her eyes. *Misty River Dance Academy* had been painted in white on the bay window with a silhouette pink ballerina dancing over the letters. The elegant lettering had a whimsical touch to it, and it suited her. She smiled and leaned into Lucas, resting her head on his shoulder. "I love it."

"C'mon inside. It gets even better." He held her hand and, together, they walked into the studio.

Applause and shouts of congratulations echoed around the room. She clasped a hand over her mouth as tears welled in her eyes. Her friends and family stood before her, smiling and offering their support on this new adventure. How did she get so lucky? She had been away for ten years, had rarely come home, and here they were, clapping for her and showing their overwhelming support. How she loved all of them.

"Speech! Speech!" Brett called out, pumping his hand in the air.

She grinned then cleared her throat. It had been thick with unshed tears. "Well, I'm not very good at speeches—"

"Just good at dancing," her aunt shouted out.

"Yes, there is that," she responded. "All I can say is, thank you, everyone, for supporting me on this new adventure." She glanced at her aunt. "And, I owe all this to Aunt Merry who kind of pushed me into this."

"Kind of pushed you?" her aunt stated. "I had to shove you!"

Laughter and chuckles sounded around the room, and she nodded. Her aunt was right. She had been shoved, with both hands, to get involved.

"But I'm glad she did. I needed something to motivate me

to get out of bed each day." She looked at Lucas. "Thank you, Lucas, for seeing my vision and making this happen, for me and the students." She kissed him lightly on the lips. He grinned back at her and squeezed his arm around her waist. "Well, that's my speech."

Everyone clapped, then one by one, they came over and hugged her. Her cheeks ached from grinning.

"We have refreshments on the table, donated by our wonderful friends, Jamie and Chloe," Anna said, walking over to her. Anna hugged her. "I'm so proud of you, Sis."

"Thank you." She wished she had a tissue. A few tears ran down her cheeks and her nose dripped.

"Here, take this." Lucas handed her the bandana that had been around her eyes moments ago.

"Thank you." She took it from him with a smile then wiped her eyes and nose. She inhaled deeply to stave off any more tears.

"Enjoy the food and each other's company," Lucas started, "And take a self-guided tour if you'd like."

"Lucas and I are quite proud of what we've done," Devon said. "If he's not going to say it, I will."

Lucas chuckled then clapped Devon on the shoulder. "I can always count on you to say it as it is, Dev."

As people gathered in small groups and sat on the chairs and sofas surrounding the reception area, she noticed a few things had changed. "When did you do this?" She pointed to a wall.

"Oh," Lucas started. "One of the guys has a girlfriend who creates these beautiful quotes for walls. I guess she's doing a great business on Etsy."

"It's perfect."

"I agree," Lucas answered, standing beside her. "Wendy showed me several quotes about dancing, and I picked this one." He looked down at her, love swimming in his gaze. "It suits you."

With the sun streaming in through the double bay

windows, the reception area shone bright and cheerful. She was glad she had changed her paint colors. Originally, she had chosen a lime green with bright pink, but once she had gone through some Pinterest boards, she had decided on a pale teal and gray with accents of pale pink. The colors popped more dramatically against the gorgeous dove gray of the furnishings. These colors were professional and elegant with just a hint of whimsy.

"It looks very professional, yet. . .fun," Theresa said, as she came over to stand in front of her. Lucas's mother leaned in and hugged her. "I am so happy for you."

"I'm happy for you, too," Mr. Tanner said. He gave her a quick peck on the cheek.

"Thank you so much," she responded. "I was fortunate Aunt Merry chose Lucas for the job." She glanced at him and smiled. "He's a wonderful contractor."

"I learned from the best," Lucas acknowledged, giving his father a side hug. "Well, I think I'm going to show Bree the rest of the studio."

They passed the reception desk to her right as they came to her office door. A small sign hung at eye level and read: *Prima Ballerina In Charge.* She nodded with a smile. "I like it." She opened the door.

Sunlight spilled into the room, cascading over her desk. She expelled a breath. It was beautiful! The translucent glass window allowed light but provided privacy. A chevron print valance, in shades of gray and teal, hung along the top of the window. She remembered when she and Anna had gone through fabric samples, and she had specifically chosen this for the chairs and window dressing. The walls had been painted in the soft salmon-pink color. The poster of her in the performance of *Giselle* had been reframed and took front and center on the wall behind her desk. It had been her aunt's favorite picture. Other than her desk and chair, there was another easy chair sitting in the corner. A soft gray file cabinet sat in the opposite corner with a large philodendron sitting in a teal pot.

"Thank you, Lucas, for the putting the office together for me. The last time I was in here, it had been a shambles." She looked around. Nothing was out of place. Now she wondered if she'd be able to find anything. She swung her gaze back to Lucas. "Ahhh, where did you put everything? I was going to organize the paperwork—"

"Anna asked if she could help, and I took her up on the offer." He stuck his hands in his pockets. "She also helped paint the quotes on the wall."

"When did she find time to do that?"

"While we were at the lake." He twisted around in a circle, stopping to face her. "She did a great job, don't you think?"

"She did. I should've figured Anna would do something like this. I have to admit, she's much better at organizing than I am."

"Sit in the chair," Lucas suggested, pulling out his cell phone. "I want to take an official photo of you sitting behind the desk on your first official day of reopening the studio."

She moved around the desk and sat in the newly reupholstered chair. She smiled and Lucas took the picture. "I can't believe this is the same room Aunt Merry sat in each day. Thinking back on what it used to look like, it was. . .quite depressing."

"Well, I didn't have the luxury of a great contractor," Aunt Merry said from the doorway and suddenly she felt terrible for making such a remark.

"I'm sorry, Aunt Merry. I didn't mean to offend you."

"None taken." Aunt Merry folded her hands in front of her and looked around the room. She beamed. "Beautiful. It suits you, Bree."

"C'mon, I want to show you the rest," Lucas encouraged.

She stood and followed him out of the office with Aunt Merry behind her.

"You know what the larger dance room looks like."

"I know, but I want to see it anyway." She kissed him

lightly on the lips. "Thank you, Lucas, for doing all of this."

He glanced down at her, flinging his arm across her shoulders. "You're welcome. As I worked on this studio and got to know you better, I discovered more about you that I hadn't known before, and well, I wanted to incorporate your style into these rooms. I want this place to reflect *you.*" He opened the door to the main dance area, the larger of both dance rooms.

She beamed. This room had been painted in muted teal and another quote had been painted on the wall to her left. A long set of portable barres stood against the wall. The opposite wall, covered in mirrors, reflected the quote. The wall, opposite the entrance, had a French door leading out to the back where dancers could take a break and get some fresh air or families could sit while waiting for the students to finish class. From where she stood, she could see the river glistening in the distance.

The new Marley flooring shone bright. She walked across it while Lucas stood off to the side by one of the barres. She wanted to run and leap into the air, she was so happy. And, heck, why shouldn't she? With a small giggle and a lightness in her heart she hadn't felt in a long, long time, she performed several pirouettes. She repeated the moves again and when she stopped, clapping resounded. She spun around to see her aunt, her father and Lucas's parents, standing by the doorway against the wall. She laughed although she was slightly out of breath. "It's hard to believe that a couple of weeks ago, this room was a mess with dug up flooring, no mirrors and dingy white walls."

Lucas stepped closer to her. "I remember painting this room with you. It was the most fun I ever had painting." He leaned in and kissed her gently.

"Ditto," she responded, giving him a quick kiss. They walked out of the room, followed by her family, and headed for the next one.

The set up was identical to the other room including the

door to the backyard and it's view of the river, except the room was a bit smaller. This room would be used for her smaller classes of children. They didn't need as much room to move around. From this room, they walked down the hallway and checked out the restrooms which had been thoroughly cleaned and painted. A plumber had come in and checked the toilets to make sure everything was working properly before giving the thumbs up. The dressing rooms had been painted the same colors as the two studio rooms with benches in the center and lockers along the one wall. On the opposite wall were vanities. More quotes pertaining to ballet and other forms of dance, had been painted on the walls to give the dancers inspiration and motivation before heading to the dance floor.

"I just realized I have to remind my dancers to bring locks for the lockers. And, I have to make a list of--"

He chuckled. "You're always thinking, Bree. Always on the go. Do you ever slow down?"

"Yeah, when I'm sleeping." And then she realized she was busy even during sleep. "Forget that. I'm busy in my dreams too." She laughed. "I'm so excited though. I can't wait to see this place filled with dancers and watch their eyes light up as they learn and grow." She looked at Lucas.

He brushed her hair away, his hands lingering on the sides of her face. He was about to kiss her when three little girls bounced into the room.

“Daddy, did you see the rooms? They’re sooooo pretty!” Dani said happily.

“I can’t wait to dance in them,” Sophie said. Heather nodded in agreement.

“I think I have, Dani, considering I did all the work.”

“Hey, you forgetting your partner?” Devon spoke up. “The one who came up with all the great ideas?”

She laughed. “Right, Devon. I think they were my ideas that I showed you guys.”

“Well, both of them, and the rest of the crew,” her father

started as he came to stand beside Lucas, "did an outstanding job." He looked from Lucas to her. "He's a keeper, Bree." He turned and slapped Lucas on the back. "Definitely a keeper."

"Thank you, Mr. Thompson," Lucas answered, beaming in delight.

She never thought she'd see the day her father and Lucas would be friends, but here it was. Then, with sudden clarity, she realized what all of this meant. Her family, her friends, and Lucas thought she would be staying in Misty River. All this hard work was for her. And what was she doing? Heading off to Philadelphia for an audition, which could lead to a principal dancer role in the company. Tears filled her eyes. The happiness had dissipated, leaving her forlorn and full of doubt. She looked at Lucas, at Dani and the rest of her friends and family. How can she leave when everything she held dear was standing right in front of her?

* * * *

"What's wrong?" Lucas couldn't believe Bree had suddenly gone from feeling thrilled and full of laughter to crying. He had a feeling her tears weren't from happiness. Her forehead creased and the corners of her mouth dipped. He reached out, hugging her close. "What happened?"

Bree shook her head and sniffled. "Nothing."

"Nothing wouldn't make you cry."

"Why's Auntie Bree crying, Mama?" Heather asked.

Dani peeked up at them and frowned. "Bree, how come you're crying?"

Anna stepped over to them and rubbed Bree's back. "Bree?"

When Bree didn't answer, he glanced back at Anna. He was at a loss. "I think it's because she's really happy, girls." He nodded at Anna. "I think we'll leave Anna and Bree alone to talk." He scooped up Dani. "Let's see what goodies Chloe brought for us."

"Cupcakes!" the girls hollered out, and he cringed.

He walked toward the door, looking back at Bree who was leaning against Anna. The rest of the family followed him, all of them looking concerned. What had happened? She seemed so happy a moment ago. Then anxiety clenched his stomach. She wasn't happy at all.

As he approached the table, laden with an assortment of goodies from the bakery as well as finger foods from the diner, he saw Chloe talking to her Aunt Maggie. They turned to him, grinning.

"Lucas, you did a fantastic job!" Chloe said and gave him a hug. "Bree loves it."

He shrugged. "I'm not so sure now."

"What do you mean?" Maggie asked, holding onto her Styrofoam cup of coffee. "She looked thrilled a little while ago."

"Exactly." He set Dani in a chair in the waiting area and handed her and Heather each a chocolate cupcake. "She's crying."

"What!?" Chloe's eyes widened. "What for?"

"Beats me." He glanced back at the room he had just stepped out of. "She's with Anna. I. . .I don't think she likes it." He slumped into a nearby chair and looked down at the multi-colored carpet.

"Oh, that's not true and you know it, Lucas," Chloe said. "She adores it. That's why she's crying. They're happy tears."

"No, they're not, Chloe. I know Bree well enough to know she's unhappy." He needed to find out what was wrong. While Dani and Heather chatted happily on the other side of the room, his heart ached. He wished he knew what Bree was thinking, what she was feeling. Chloe patted him on the shoulder.

"I'll see what's the matter."

He nodded his thanks as Chloe left him feeling lost, confused and miserable. He scrubbed his hands together. And then he realized what he had wanted to forget. Bree was still leaving. He thrust his hands through his hair and leaned back against the soft cushion. His parents came into the room, both of them looking just as confused as he felt. They sat on the sofa kitty-corner to him.

"What happened with Bree, Son?"

"She—I don't know, Dad."

"She seemed to love what you've done to the place, and now she's upset," his mother commented. "Why?"

He huffed out a breath. "I was hoping Bree would see this place and the potential it held for her, and her students and she'd decide to stay." He shook his head and glanced at Dani. "I think she's still planning on leaving."

"Really?" His mother looked from him to Dani and frowned. "Dani will be so upset."

"I know." He stood, needing to move around and expel some pent-up frustration. To his surprise, Bree came over to him, remnants of her tears still on her cheeks.

"Lucas, I am so sorry I'm reacting this way."

He emptied the space between them. "What's the matter, Bree. Tell me." He clasped the sides of her face and peered into her sad gaze. He smoothed his thumbs along her cheekbones. "You can tell me anything. You know that, right?"

She nodded and leaned into his shoulder. He smoothed her back. Her heart beat against his own. Her chest rose and fell softly against his chest. He could hold her like this forever. Dani rushed over along with Heather and tried to wrap her around Bree, but her disabled arm only went part way. But it was enough for Bree to know Dani felt her sorrow and wanted to make her feel better. He saw Bree lift a hand and smooth it down Dani's hair and then cup her cheek. And then Bree stepped back, smoothing the tears from her cheeks with her hands. His arms came down to his sides. She heaved a sigh, blowing wisps of hair over her forehead.

"I thought you were happy with how the studio turned out?"

She looked at him and smiled, although it didn't reach her eyes. "I'm sorry, Lucas. I love what you've done. Really." She leaned into him, pulled his head down and kissed him. Hard. She didn't stop. He kissed her back, tasting the salt of her tears. They dripped into the corners of his mouth. She pulled away and looked around. "I need some tissue." She giggled.

"Here you go," his mother said, handing her a small packet from her purse. His mother always had tissues ready, or band aids, or a host of other things, because she never knew what she'd need with Dani in her care. She was always prepared.

"Thank you." Bree wiped her eyes then blew her nose. "I love everything about this. I'm so. . .overwhelmed with happiness."

He knew she was thinking about the audition, and despite all the work he had put into the studio, he would support her decision. She loved him, but did she love him enough to stay?

Twenty-Six

The days passed quickly for Bree and, although she and Lucas were happy, there was an underlying sense of anxiety when they were together. She would be flying out on Wednesday after the last class before the performance on Saturday. She'd be gone for a few days. Ever since the studio unveiling, her friends and family continued to ask her what her future plans were, and she had nothing to say other than the generic, 'Oh, we'll see,' or 'I don't know yet.' The truth of the matter was, she knew what she wanted to do, but she couldn't' admit defeat by calling the company in Philadelphia and telling them she would not attend the audition. It would mean she had failed.

Instead of going over to the Tanners for her usual Wednesday night dinner, she had invited Lucas over for supper, just the two of them. When she shared her idea with Aunt Merry of what she wanted to make for dinner, Aunt Merry winked then made plans for her and Henry to go out to a movie. Aunt Merry wished her luck as Bree mashed the potatoes. She couldn't wait to see Lucas's expression.

As she pulled the Pyrex dish out of the oven, the doorbell rang, and Buster barked. She set the hot dish on a trivet then wiped her hands on her apron.

"Hi, Lucas!" She greeted him with a kiss then stepped back. Lucas carried a wrapped box.

"Well, you look quite domesticated," Lucas said, glancing down at her apron with ruffled edges as he stepped inside. "You look like you stepped out of a vintage magazine."

"Almost. I'd need to be wearing a dress and a pearl necklace."

"True."

She pointed to the box. "And is that present for me?"

Lucas grinned. "I wanted to get you a small gift. . .just because."

"Ohhh, I love presents!" She strode to the living room and Lucas followed. "Dinner is just about ready. Have a seat, Lucas and I'll get you a beer."

"Sure." His brow creased. "You okay? You're acting. . .different."

"Am I? Huh." She left the living room and grabbed a Michelob from the fridge then brought it back to him. "I'll be a minute. Stay right here."

"Alright. I'll keep Buster company."

She laughed as she headed back to the kitchen. This was nice. She could get used to cooking for Lucas, and Dani. The idea of being a wife and mother appealed to her. She pulled out two of Aunt Merry's best plates and set them on the counter. Then, she went about slicing up the meat, dishing a heaping spoonful of mashed potatoes on the plates followed by mixed veggies. She set them on the table and lit the candles. After making sure everything looked just right, she untied the apron and hung it on the hook in the pantry. With a smile and a spring in her step, she headed to the living room.

"Dinner's ready, Lucas."

"Great. I'm starving. And it smells delicious!"

She walked ahead of him and stood by the table; her hands folded in front of her. "I hope you like it. It's your favorite." She swung her arm out.

Lucas sat across from her, grinning. "You made meatloaf?"

She nodded, smiling. "I did." She motioned to his plate. "Take a bite." She waited, her heart thrumming fast. She hoped it was as good as the diner's. Lucas closed his eyes while savoring his bite. What was he thinking?

"Well, Bree, I have to say. . ." He licked the fork. "It's the best meatloaf I have ever eaten. Better than the diner."

"Really?" Was he just saying that, because she used the exact recipe from the diner which originally had come from her aunt? "Huh. Go figure."

"Why?" Lucas said. "It really is fantastic, Bree. I love it!"

"I'm going to let you in on a secret." She leaned in. "The recipe the diner uses, is my Aunt Merry's. I used her recipe."

"Seriously?" Lucas's eyes grew wide. "The meatloaf that I love so much is your aunt's recipe?"

She nodded again. "Yup. I just found out last week. I thought it would be a great surprise."

"It is at that, Bree." He took another bite then a swallow of his beer. "Didn't I say I'd marry the woman who could make meatloaf as good as the diner's?"

"I believe you did say that."

"So. . .is this a proposal of some kind?"

She laughed out loud. "I didn't think of it that way, but—"

Lucas sobered for a moment. "I know. It's not the right time. Audition and such."

She nodded. "So, should I open the box now or later?"

"After you eat."

She dove into her meal and had to admit the meatloaf was fantastic. Lucas was right. It was better than at the diner. Maybe Jamie's cook had changed it up a bit, but she wouldn't change anything. It was delicious.

Fifteen minutes later, after some small talk and avoiding the elephant in the room also known as the 'audition', she drank the last of her water then wiggled her fingers at Lucas.

"Okay, I'm ready to open my gift."

"You sure?"

"Very." She stood from the chair. "C'mon, I want to see what it is." She scampered to the living room with Buster on her heels. She sat on the sofa with her hands on her lap, waiting to be presented with the beautifully wrapped gift.

Lucas picked it up from where he had been sitting earlier and handed it to her. "I hope you like it." He sat next to her on the sofa.

"Is this a going away gift?"

"Not really."

She ripped the beautiful, flowered paper from a rectangular box. Smiling at Lucas, she lifted the lid and removed the tissue paper. "Oh, Lucas!" She lifted out a beautiful turquoise silk blouse. It was better quality than the one she had to toss out due to a chocolate stain. "Oh, it's beautiful!" She smoothed her hand over the soft fabric. "I love it."

"It's my way of apologizing and ruining your blouse."

She leaned in and kissed him. "Thank you." She kissed him again and this time it was full of passion.

"Well, we'd better head out to the studio. The kids will wonder where I am."

On the way over to the studio, she realized she now had to face the task of telling the parents she may not be back for the recital. She was sure she'd be asked a lot of questions. Maybe she should have made her excuses. She leaned back against the seat and closed her eyes.

"You feeling okay?" Lucas asked, as they turned down the road heading toward the park.

"I'm fine. Just a bit anxious, I guess."

"Look," he reached out and held her hand. "I'll be there to redirect questions if I have to. And your Aunt Merry, Anna, and Chloe, will be there to help you."

"I know." She looked at their clasped hands and squeezed. "I'm nervous about what the parents will say or accuse me of." She rubbed her forehead. "I still have this need to prove something to myself."

He clasped her hand tighter. "Regardless of your decision, Bree, I'm always here for you. Always." Lucas lifted their hands and kissed the top of hers before setting them back down on the seat.

A moment later, they pulled into the parking lot. It was hard to believe that in a couple of days, the lot would be full, and the park filled with vendors, crafters and performers celebrating the Founders Day Festival. And her students would be part of it. A sense of pride filled her.

When she stepped out of the car, Dani bounded over to them. "You're here!"

"Hi Dani." She scrunched down, giving Dani a big hug.

"Are we dancing here?" Dani asked, holding onto her father's hand as they walked toward the gazebo.

"Yes, we are!" She forced herself to put some enthusiasm in her voice. She needed to get out of her doldrums in order to teach her class tonight. It was the last class before their recital on Saturday. "We're going to do everything tonight as though we were performing in front of our parents."

"I can't wait!" Dani replied as she let go of her father's hand and twirled around. Dani gasped.

Lucas lunged as she ran forward. She grabbed Dani's arm before she fell to the ground. "Goodness, Dani!" she said, wrapping an arm around the little girl's waist.

"You okay?" Lucas clasped his daughter's shoulders.

Dani nodded, looking from her father to her. "What if I fall during the recital?"

"I don't think you will. We'll be dancing on the stage under the tent, right over there." She pointed to the large white tent that had been set up earlier in the day. Daddy will make sure everyone is safe."

Dani nodded, her lower lip pouting. "Okay."

"Everything will be fine. Just dance like we did at the studio," she encouraged, then stood. Lucas did the same. He held onto Dani's hand and strode toward the gazebo. She looked to the parking lot where she heard the sound of tires crunching on the gravel. Anna and Chloe had arrived. Her support team. She stood there, waiting for them as other cars pulled in. Good, everyone was on time.

Anna came over to her and hugged her. "You look nervous."

"I am. A little."

"Well, don't worry about a thing." Chloe smiled at her.

"We'll keep the masses at bay."

She laughed and some of the anxiety lifted. "I knew I could count on you."

"Are the parents staying to watch the rehearsal?" Anna asked, glancing back at the parking lot.

"Oh. Actually," she started and touched Chloe's arm. "Do you think you could have everyone go to the bakery while we rehearse? I wanted to surprise the parents on Saturday, so I didn't want them to see any of the routines tonight."

"Sure. No problem. I have plenty of coffee and goodies to go around. My treat."

"Thank you so much, Chloe." She hugged her friend. "Well, time to share the news."

Anna rubbed her back. "You've got this. Be confident. Be excited."

She nodded, hoping she could do as Anna advised. She met Lucas by the steps of the gazebo as the parents strolled over with their kids. Once everyone was there, she asked for their attention. "Before we get started, I need to say a few things." She cleared her throat, looked down at Lucas, who nodded his encouragement, and then she glanced at the myriad of faces. "I thought it would be nice if the students surprised their parents Saturday by not having you watch their rehearsal tonight." Here goes. Grumbles and mumbles.

"So, I'm inviting all of you over to the bakery for beverages and goodies. On the house," Chloe said before any parents could object. "I think it'll be best for the kids if they can concentrate on what they're doing without us being around."

Heads nodded. Voices approved. Smiling faces looked at her. Some gave her a thumbs up. It would be okay. She smiled, folding her hands in front of her. "Alright, kids. Let's get in a line over here," she pointed to her left. "Wave to your parents. They'll be back in an hour."

As the parents walked toward the bakery, with Chloe in the lead, she looked down at Lucas. "You too."

"Me?"

"Yes, you. I want you to be surprised as well."

"What if something happens to Dani?"

"Really, Lucas?" She put her hands to her hips. "I thought you trusted me."

"Okay, but let me check the ground first while the kids warm up, then I'll leave."

"Fine." She gave a quick peck on the cheek and smiled as he walked off to where the kids would be rehearsing. "Alright. Let's do our warmups."

The students followed her through the motions of warm-ups for about five minutes and then Lucas came over, slapping his hands together to remove the debris.

"You should be all set. "

"Thanks." When Lucas continued to stand there, she grinned. "You can go to the bakery now, Lucas."

"Oh. Right." Lucas flicked his gaze toward the bakery, then back to her. "You sure?"

"Yes, I'm sure. Now go."

"Daddy, go. Miss Chloe has a cupcake for you," Dani spoke up, shooing him away.

"Well, in that case, I'd better get over there." He waved, then headed for the bakery just down the street.

"Okay, kids. Remember, tonight is a rehearsal which means we have to do everything as though it were Saturday and your parents and friends are watching." Heads bobbed. "And do all of you have your costumes?"

"Yes, Miss Bree," most answered in unison.

"Miss Anna dropped mine off yesterday," a little girl with golden curls said.

"She brought mine over, too," Sophie said.

"It seems that Miss Anna did a good job dropping off the costumes." She scanned the faces in front of her. "Any questions before we start?"

"Are we gonna wear makeup?" Dani asked. "Cuz, I wanna wear makeup."

She laughed. Oh, she wished she could be here to see her students perform. "Yes. Miss Anna and Miss Chloe, and maybe some of the other moms, will help all of you put on your makeup according to what animal or fairy you are."

The kids clapped. Chattering ensued. She clapped her hands to get their attention. "I know you're excited, but we do need to practice. We have a lot to do in the next forty-five minutes. Are we ready?"

"Yes, Miss Bree!" they chorused.

"Well, then, let's start." She imagined where the props would be and had the kids assemble in their positions according to where they would stand at the beginning of the performance. She was amazed at how well the students paid attention and didn't grumble when she had them stop and repeat a step.

"Miss Bree?"

She nodded to Sophie, Chloe's daughter who had just finished her solo.

"Are you gonna help us if we make a mistake at the recital?"

She tried not to wince. "I'll do my best. Besides, Miss Anna and Miss Chloe know all the steps and they'll be here to help you."

"Won't you be here?" This came from another little girl who had been shy and awkward at the beginning of class and had since blossomed, just like Dani.

"Yes. I will, but I want you to know that there will be other people here to help you." She hated that she had pretty much promised she'd be there when in all actuality she would probably miss the recital. She heaved a sigh. "Let's finish, okay?

The girls pretended to dance through the enchanted forest with the woodland creatures waiting for a special fairy to come out of hiding. The special fairy had hurt her arm in a horrible fall when she was trying to fly away from a hungry troll. Because the fairy was sad and afraid to fly, she had hidden herself deep in a tree. The other fairies and animals danced in the enchanted forest under a starlit sky, hoping the little fairy would come out and join them.

She smiled when she saw Dani's head peek out from an imaginary tree. Dani creeped her way out, looking all around as the other fairies and woodland creatures urged her to come to the meadow and dance in the grass.

"We're your friends," Heather said in her fairy voice. "We won't let anything hurt you."

Heather performed her solo act and she couldn't have been prouder. Heather's performance had been perfect. Dani followed Heather's actions and as the fairies and animals sat down in a circle around Dani, she danced and grinned. She danced among the flowers. She hadn't faltered in a single step.

She clapped as the students stood in a line and bowed toward her. She beamed. "Bravo! Bravo! I am so proud of all of you!"

"I think you did a fantastic job, Bree," Chloe said as she stepped up to her. The parents were heading towards them from the sidewalk.

"I can't believe how well they did," she said and grinned as Lucas came to her side. "Did you peek?"

He wrapped an arm around her shoulder. "I saw a little bit, but not enough to give it away." He nudged her close. "Sorry."

She swatted his arm. "I believe they're ready for their first ever performance." She moved away from Lucas and got the parents' attention. "Before you leave, there are a few things I need to mention." Gathering her courage, she let the words come out. "I'm leaving tonight for Philadelphia—"

"What?"

"Why?"

"What for?"

A host of questions bombarded her. She held up her hands. "Let me explain." She heaved a sigh. "I've been invited to an audition, but I believe I'll be back in time for their performance on Saturday."

"But, Miss Bree, you said you'd be here to help us."

"I know I did. And, I'm going to do my best to get here in time."

"Who's going to help the kids?" a parent asked. His voice didn't sound too happy. It was gruff and sharp.

"My sister, Anna and Miss Chloe will be here. They know the routine and what needs to be done."

"I can assure you," Anna spoke up, "that the kids will be fine, whether or not Bree is here. Let's be positive and upbeat for the kids' sakes, okay?"

Some parents lowered their heads in guilt. Others nodded and agreed it was the best thing to do.

"Okay, kids. Get some rest and be here early so Miss Anna and Miss Chloe can help with makeup."

After saying their goodnights, the kids walked off with their parents. A sadness crept over her as she realized she may not be back in time to watch the performance they had worked so hard to make perfect. All that was left to do was to get through her audition and get back here to make sure everything went without a hitch.

* * * *

They were on the way back to his parents' house and he wondered what Bree was thinking. She was subdued, lost in her own thoughts.

"Daddy?"

"Yes, honey?"

"Is Bree gonna stay at our house?"

He hoped Bree would stay to help put Dani to bed and then they could take a walk, or a drive. He glanced at Bree. "We'd really like it if you came over, if just for a little while." He nudged his head to Dani, who was humming to herself. "I think it would help her. . .cope."

Bree must've gotten the hint. "Oh, sure. I can do that."

"Great!" he answered, a little too enthusiastically. "Dani, Bree's going to stay for a visit."

"Yay!"

"But, I can't stay late." Bree looked from Dani to him then shook her head. "I need to go to the airport. I have a big day tomorrow."

"You do?" Dani asked, her eyes wide. "How come?"

"I'm meeting with some people and dancing for them, just like you'll be dancing on Saturday."

"Oh. Are you doing a recital tomorrow?"

He chuckled although his heart was nearly breaking. Bree laughed as well.

"Kind of."

"I hope you do a really good job," Dani said.

"Me too," Bree answered.

They arrived home several minutes later. His parents were sitting in the living room and greeted them with smiles. Dani shared how well she did at the rehearsal. He listened to her version of the actual events, but his mind was on Bree.

"She did an amazing job," Bree said. "She didn't miss a single beat of her solo."

"We can't wait to see her dance on Saturday," Theresa said, kissing the top of Dani's head. "I—We," she corrected, looking over at her husband, "are so happy you took the chance on Dani and gave her lessons."

He guided Bree to a club chair while he sat on the sofa kitty-corner to her chair. He knew what his mother was thinking. Dani wouldn't be performing if he had stuck to his guns by not allowing his daughter to take dancing lessons. Thanks to Bree's encouragement, Dani's confidence had grown in the last few weeks.

"Well, I'm glad you decided to take the chance as well." Bree glanced at him and smiled. "It was a wonderful experience for the two us."

"Did you teach before?" This came from Lucas's father.

Bree shook her head. "No. This is my first time. I've always been the student, never the teacher."

"Well, I must say, you've done a wonderful job."

"Thank you," Bree responded then tossed him a glance. "I'm glad Lucas took a chance on Dani as well. She's shown a lot of promise."

"It's time for you, little lady, to go to bed." He stood and walked over to where his mother sat and lifted Dani into his arms. She was half-asleep already. He held her tight.

"Can Bree put me to bed, Daddy?"

That took him by surprise. He looked to Bree. She nodded and stood.

"I don't mind." She followed him up the stairs and into Dani's bedroom.

While he picked out pajamas for Dani, Bree looked for a book to read to her.

"Here, Dani, I'll help you," Bree said as she sat cross-legged on the floor and picked up the pajama bottoms.

He watched and grinned as Bree helped Dani with her pajamas. He could imagine them doing this as a nightly routine in their own place. Perhaps with other children of their own. Dani laughed when Bree patted her bottom.

"Okay, time to brush your teeth and then I'll read you a story," Bree said, holding onto the book. "I think you'll like the book I picked out."

When Bree looked at him and gave him a dazzling smile, he couldn't help but feel his heart tumble in his chest. God, he loved her. He walked Dani to the bathroom and waited while she used the toilet. When she was done, he stepped inside and helped her brush her teeth. Once the task was done, he scooped her up and strode back to her bedroom where Bree waited on the side of the bed. He plopped Dani down where she squirmed and giggled. She scampered under the covers while Bree sat on the edge. He chose to lie on his side on the floor and listen, and watch. He was happy with how they interacted. He remembered back to the day when he wondered how they would get along. How far they had come along.

"Your feet are still dancing," Bree said. "Hopefully, this book will give you sweet dreams of dancing."

"What book are you reading?" Dani asked, tucking her hand under her head.

"It's the perfect book. Angelina Ballerina, Center Stage," Bree read, then turned the book so Dani could see the cover.

"You bought me that book, Daddy!" Dani said. "We haven't read it yet, have we, Daddy?"

He shook his head. He remembered Dani's excitement when he had brought it home to show her shortly after he had decided she could take dance lessons. They had tucked it away and forgotten about it until now.

"Was I center stage tonight, Bree?" Dani asked, sitting up, intrigued by the title.

"Yes, you were," Bree answered. She opened to the first page and started reading how Angelina had been practicing for their spring recital in Chipping Cheddar and how excited she was.

Dani grinned. "Just like me!"

Lucas chuckled. As Bree read the story, he could see the change in her expression as though the words had struck a chord somewhere inside her. Even her voice inflection changed.

"What does coree, that word mean?" Dani asked.

"It means to compose a dance," Bree answered.

"What does compose mean?"

He sat up. "Dani, Bree can't read the story if you keep asking questions, right?"

"Lucas, I don't mind, really. I mean, that's the point of storytelling, right? Kids should learn and be curious and ask questions when they're reading or being read to."

"Huh. I never thought of it that way."

"Anyway, compose means to put together something. Like composing music. A person puts musical notes together to make music. A writer puts words together to make a story. So, a choreographer puts together steps for a dance for the dancer to perform."

"Ohhhhh," Dani said. "That's what you did, right?"

Bree nodded. "Yes, exactly." Dani settled back down against her pillow as Bree continued reading. Lucas noticed Dani's eyes closing as Bree neared the end of the story.

"Miss Bree?"

"Yes, sweetheart."

"Can you read to me tomorrow night?"

Both he and Bree shot each other a look. "Well, peanut, Bree won't be here tomorrow night. She has to go out of town."

"Will you be back for the recital?"

"Yes, I will, Dani. Don't you worry. I wouldn't miss it for anything."

"Okay." Dani yawned. "Bree?"

"Yes?"

"If you don't dance anymore, you can make up dances, like Angelina the ballerina!"

Lucas looked at Bree whose mouth had dropped open.

"Ahhh, you're right."

"Good night Bree. Goodnight, Daddy."

He hunkered down and kissed her on the forehead. To his surprise, Bree did the same. She smoothed her hand along Dani's face, lingering for a moment. He wondered what she was thinking. "Sweet dreams, peanut."

Three hours later, Lucas drove back home after dropping Bree off at the Jetport in Portland. Bree cried and hugged him, and he thought she was about to change her mind and tell him to bring her home. Instead, she kissed him, tears streaking down her face. He had swiped them away telling her he would wait for her. He'd be in Misty River whenever she decided she needed to come home.

"I love you, Lucas. Always," Bree had said as she walked away, possibly to a new life.

Oh, how he wanted to hold her close and never let her go. Why couldn't she see that she needed to be here, with them, in this little town they loved so much. Why was she so insistent on leaving?

Twenty-Seven

Bree stood at the barre, surrounded by an array of other dancers, some in their teens, but most were in their early twenties. She felt old and out of place. It had been months since she had been in a studio as large as this, with leotard-clad bodies all around her, warming up and hoping for a chance to get accepted in the company or for a part in their upcoming performance of *A Midsummer Night's Dream*. She ignored the chatter around her.

As she watched them warm up and go through their practiced routines, she felt weary. What was she trying to prove? Why was she here? She was working on adrenaline right now. By the time she had landed, she was exhausted. And, she hadn't slept well.

The choreographer entered the room followed by the art director. Mr. Gleason stood by the window in front of her and the other dancers and demanded everyone's attention. She knew the routine. Everyone did. They moved in step to his commands. They broke up into groups and danced three or four at a time. The more she danced, the more focused and determined she became.

A young ballerina came up to her during their break, ecstatic that she finally got to meet her idol. She was stunned at first. She hadn't expected anyone to know who she was. Then as the young girl walked to her friend, she overheard her say, "I hope I can still dance when I'm old like her!"

What the— She wasn't old! She could still dance. She was one of the best.

The choreographer, Mr. Gleason, called her up front and asked her to perform a routine they had done earlier as a group. This time he wanted the dancers to perform solo. She could do this. It was her chance to show them she could be a principal dancer. But she had to earn it. And it involved doing routines the choreographer and art director envisioned for the performance.

"Miss Thompson, are you ready?"

She nodded from the corner of the room. The musical director started playing and she moved to the rhythm of the music, completing pirouettes with ease, then performing several fouettes before moving into a tour jete', then moved into several pirouettes, ending with a grand jete'. She grinned inwardly. It had been that particular move during rehearsal in which she had injured her ACL. She had performed it with grace and ease.

"No. No, no, no!" Mr. Gleason tapped his cane and walked over to her.

What had she done wrong? She looked at the faces around her. Some smirked. Some grimaced. Some outright giggled.

"You're landing was wrong."

What? She couldn't believe it. It had been perfect.

"Why are you here, Miss Thompson?" Mr. Gleason asked, his gaze piercing. "Why have you come here to audition?"

"Because I was invited to—"

"Yes, yes, yes, but why?" His mustache twitched and she wanted to rip it off his face.

"I want to perform. I want to be a part of the company. I'm good, no, I'm one of the best at what I do and. . ." She couldn't answer. Lucas's smiling face merged over Mr. Gleason's. Why was she here?

"And?" The choreographer turned to the class. "Just because you *were* a principal dancer in one of the best companies in the world, doesn't mean you belong *here*."

She expected tears to come, but instead, ire shot through her. She straightened up. "Mr. Gleason. I have performed all over the world. I'm one of the best. I—" Someone giggled in the back, and it reminded her of Dani. "You know what?

You're right. I don't belong here."

"If not here, then where, Miss Thompson?"

"Someplace where I'm wanted. Where I'm needed." She paused. "And where I'm loved." Now the tears welled in her eyes, and she turned her back to Mr. Gleason and strode toward the door, her head held high. She pulled open the door.

"If you walk out now, Miss Thompson—"

The heavy door slammed behind her. She grinned then ran. She had a plane to catch.

* * * *

Bree had to hurry. She couldn't be late. As she quickly changed, she looked at the clock on the wall. She only had a few minutes. Adrenaline coursed through her. Happiness filled her heart. Her fingers twisted in her hair as she tried to put the long strands into a bun. She spun around and looked at herself in the mirror. And she grinned. Perfect!

She ran out the door of her studio and hurried down the sidewalk. Some passersby looked at her in wide-eyed shock. It was no wonder. She was dressed in an iridescent blue tutu with glimmering wings the size of a small child. She had made sure her fairy makeup covered most of her face so she would look unrecognizable. When the park came into view, her excitement swelled. The students would be ecstatic. And she couldn't wait to see Lucas's reaction.

The park echoed with the sounds of a carnival. Vendors cried out their wares, children squealed on the rides, and a short, stout man, dressed as a clown and carrying balloons, strode by calling out: "Get your balloon—a dollar each."

"Sir?"

"Yes?" He squinted at her then looked her up and down. "Can I help you?"

"Yes. I'd like to buy what you have in your hand. How much?"

"Ahh, are you sure?"

"Yes, I'm sure. Please, I'm in a hurry. How much?"

"Fifteen, ma'am."

"Look, I don't have any money on me," she pointed out her dance outfit, "but I'm the owner of the dance studio, down the street." She twisted around and pointed to her building about a block away.

"You're Bree?"

"Yes," she nodded, hoping her bun wouldn't come apart. "I'm on my way to—"

"Oh, Bree, it's Mr. Wilson. "Here, you take the bunch and don't worry about paying me. I'm happy to do it."

She grinned, as he placed the strings in her hand. "Are you sure?"

"Very sure." He patted her hand. "Now, hold onto these tight and have fun!" He winked and walked away.

Laughing, she hurried to the tent and tried to hide herself behind the massive balloons. She saw her students, dressed in their costumes, standing, or sitting in their spots by the beautiful array of props. Even more had been added since she had seen the props the day her father and guys had painted them. Several pots of flowers and ferns had been placed within the wooden props. She would bet a hundred dollars the flower shop loaned them for this occasion. How she loved this town! She hadn't realized how much she belonged here until she had left, the second time around.

An easel stood at the corner of the stage with a large poster announcing their performance. It read: *Students of the Misty River Dance Academy performing 'Dancing in the Grass'.* Below the title, it listed the soloists. And beneath their names were the rest of her students. Anna must've done this. She grinned and her heart swelled. She was home.

As she scanned the crowd, she wondered where Lucas was. And then she saw him. He sat in front, smiling at Dani. Thank God everyone's attention was on the kids. She would go backstage, without being seen, she hoped, and hide there until the time came for her to make a surprise entrance. She kept herself to the back, keeping the balloons close to her body and avoiding Anna and Chloe. To her surprise, someone had set up a changing screen.

"Bree?"

She stopped, frozen in place. Oh-Oh.

"Bree? Is that you?"

Sh-shh. She didn't want to be seen. She twisted around, her finger to her lips. Anna stood there, beaming. Busted. Anna walked up to her, her arms outstretched. Hopefully, no one had seen Anna and decided to follow her. Then her secret would be out. She had hoped to surprise everyone.

"Bree!" Her sister tried to hug her but the large wings were in the way. "What are you doing here?" Anna whispered. "What happened?"

"I'll explain later." She moved her hands urging Anna to leave her alone. "Don't give me away. Wait! What'd I miss?"

"Not much. Dani's already had her run-in with the troll, so now she's hiding from him. The woodland creatures did a dance and now Heather's up. Gotta go!" Anna hurried back to her seat.

Her heart hammered as excitement coursed through her body. It was the same feeling she had always experienced before going on stage. Her feet moved to the music. Realizing she still held the balloons, she looked for someone to hold them for her. A man walked past her, then stopped and stared.

"Bree?"

It was Blake. Good God, he'd ruin everything now. He could be loud and obnoxious. She immediately thrust her finger against her lips. He nodded.

"What's going on?" he whispered, coming closer to her.

"Here, take these and hold onto them. And don't say my name. I'm due on stage in a minute." She handed him the balloons. "I mean it, Blake.

"Sure. No problem." Blake held onto the balloons. "Break

a leg."

She grinned. "Thanks."

Blake moved away from her and around the side of the stage, presumably to find a chair.

Heather's solo was about to end. "We're your friends," Heather said, encouraging the little fairy to come out of hiding.

And then the surge of music, which was Dani's cue to dance in the circle in the meadow while the other fairies and woodland animals watched. She moved to the side. Any minute now. She glanced at the temporary wall behind the dancers, which had been painted with a mural of a castle high on a hill. She didn't remember asking for that. That must've been one of the surprises Lucas had mentioned he had in mind. Strings of fairy lights hung over the makeshift trees. It truly looked like a fairy-land.

When Dani turned to do a pirouette, she glided onto the stage, behind one of the make-shift trees. As Dani came closer to where she stood, she came out from behind the tree and grasped Dani around her waist. Dani squealed, then grinned as Bree lifted her high in the air, turning in circles, holding Dani high. "You can fly, little one. You can fly!"

Dani held her arms out and by God, if she hadn't seen it herself she never would've believed it. Dani's arm was straightening! Not fully, but more than it ever had before. She set Dani down, lifting her right leg high in the air behind her as leaned down, her hands smoothing over the artificial grass.

Applause and cheers resounded. As the music continued, the students rushed over to her as she knelt on the grass with Dani in her arms. The woodland animals cried out her name. She laughed. "Remember, you're still performing."

They rushed back to their places and finished the last of the dance steps to the continued applause of the crowd. The kids stood in a line and bowed. They turned to her and signaled her to come forward. How could she resist? She stood in the center with Dani in front of her, her hands on

Dani's shoulders as her family and friends clapped for her and the students. Their applause and cheers were better than any she had ever heard on any stage.

"Speech. Speech!" She looked to the back and sure enough, there was Blake, fist-pumping the air, grinning at her while his other hand grasped the balloon strings. His words echoed in the crowd.

As the applause dimmed and the crowd grew silent, she looked at Lucas for the first time since she had arrived home early this morning. She hadn't had time to call him, and besides, she wanted to surprise him and Dani. And, by the look on his face, she had. Chloe and Anna stood on either side of him, beaming. Jamie was standing next to Brett, behind Lucas, grinning.

"We're proud of you, Bree," Jamie called out.

"Thanks." She swallowed. She didn't know what to say, except what was in her heart. "I guess some of you hadn't expected me to show up today, but—"

"You said you would, Miss Bree!" Sophie hollered from where she sat a few feet away. Chloe laughed.

"Yeah!" the rest of the kids said. Giggles ensued.

"Yes, you're right, Sophie." She squeezed Dani's shoulders as she looked down at her. Dani peered back up and grinned. "I almost didn't make it though. You see, I had an audition in Philadelphia for a company, I thought was to be my new home. A place where I could continue to dance and be the person I always dreamed of being." She glanced to her left where her aunt stood next to her father. Her aunt wiped away her tears. Even her father brushed at his eyes. "When I first came back to Misty River, I couldn't wait to leave."

A round of shocked surprise swirled through the crowd which seemed to have grown suddenly.

She walked off the stage, towards the man she loved. "But, the longer I stayed in town, the more I realized how much it meant to me, and," she glanced at Lucas. Her heart swelled. "How much I've fallen in love with it and with the man who encouraged me to find my dream." She walked toward Lucas, holding on to Dani's hand. "I found where I belong." She held his hand. "I belong in Misty River with the man I love."

Dani looked up at her. "And me too?" The crowd laughed.

"And, with the little girl I love."

Lucas grinned, his eyes crinkling. He tugged her close and kissed her. "I love you, Bree."

"And I love you, Lucas."

"Dance with me."

"Always," she answered. The music started and they grinned. It was their song. She held Lucas close as they danced in the grass with the cheers of the townspeople surrounding them.

The End

About the Author:

Lori DiAnni writes small town sweet contemporary romance novels. Her Misty River Romance series feature four friends who find love in the small fictional town of Misty River, Maine. Lori is inspired by the small town she grew up in ---Essex, Massachusetts, as well as the small towns surrounding her current hometown of Sanford, Maine. Her stories contain themes of friendship; family; a strong sense of community and of course, forever love.

She enjoys going for long rides with her husband along the beaches of Maine and NH; going for walks; photography; scrapbooking; and spending time with her two daughters and two grandchildren. You can also find her watching her favorite channel--Hallmark.

* * * *

Check out her website at **https://loridianni.com** for freebies when you sign up for her newsletter, *Coffee and Romance.*

Acknowledgements:

This book couldn't have come together without the encouragement of my wonderful online friends on Facebook and Instagram. So many of you were there to pick me up and offer words of kindness along with motivation when I wanted to give up. There are so many of you and not enough room to name each one who has meant so much to me on my journey to publication. I think, and hope, you know who you are. I am forever grateful to all of you!

I also want to say thanks to Jade Webb of MeetCuteCreative for her beautiful work on my series covers. I will definitely pass your name along to future indie authors!

* * * *

NOTE: If you enjoyed reading **Dancing in the Grass**, please consider leaving a review wherever you purchased this book. Reviews are so necessary for authors, and I hope you will leave one. Thank you!

Thank you for reading **Dancing in the Grass.** I hope you enjoyed it! I had so much fun writing Bree and Lucas's story and it was hard to say good-bye to them, but they'll make appearances in my upcoming books in the series.

Other characters from this book will have their own stories as well.

The continuing **Misty River Romance Series:**

Wishing on the Stars, Book 2-- due out in November 2021
Kissing in the Moonlight, Book 3-- due out in Spring 2022
Falling Inn Love, Book 4--due out in the Fall 2022

Books 5 and 6 to be released in 2023

I love to hear from my readers. You can contact me at loridianni15@gmail.com

* * * *

Please feel free to visit my website at www.loridianni.com.

If you become a member of my monthly newsletter, you'll have access to aesthetics of my characters and the town of Misty River, access to character charts; Early Previews of future books and discounts!

Made in the USA
Las Vegas, NV
21 July 2021

26788619R00194